Books by Elizabeth Engstrom

When Darkness Loves Us
Black Ambrosia
Nightmare Flower
Lizzie Borden
Lizard Wine
Suspicions
The Alchemy of Love (with Alan M. Clark)
Word by Word (with John Tullius)
Imagination Fully Dilated (co-editor)
Imagination Fully Dilated vol. II (editor)
Dead on Demand (editor)

Suspicions

Suspicions

Elizabeth Engstrom

Triple Tree Publishing
Eugene, Oregon

© 2002 by Elizabeth Engstrom

ISBN: 0-9 6 6 6 2 7 2-9-6

SUSPICIONS

Library of Congress Catalog Card Number: 2001090499

Triple Tree Publishing
PO Box 5 6 8 4, Eugene, OR 9 7 4O5
(5 4 1) 3 3 8-3 1 8 4 — www.Triple TreePub.com

Cover and book design by Alan M. Clark
Printed in the United States of America
1 2 3 4 5 6 7 8 9

Dedicated to Al Cratty, of course

Acknowledgments:

No author can spend twenty years honing the craft of fiction without amassing a tremendous load of indebtedness. I owe thanks to each member of my small, deeply disturbed following, each teacher, student, and influential writer. My debt extends to friends and family members who have contributed mightily to my disquiet, which leads to this type of fiction. To name specific names here would be to exclude the majority. So if you're reading this and wondering if I'm including you, I am.

Table of Contents

Foreword — 10

Suspicions About the Unknown
    Introduction — 11
    Rivering — 12
    Renewing the Option — 21
    The Pan Man — 35
    Elixir — 45
    Ramona — 59
    Fogarty and Fogarty — 87

Suspicions About Death
    Introduction — 127
    Music Ascending — 128
    Undercurrents — 136
    One Fine Day Upon the River Styx — 145
    The Cloak — 156

Suspicions About Sex
    Introduction — 196
    Hot Cheeks, Cold Feet — 197
    In a Darkened Compartment — 204
    The Goldberg — 210
    Crosley — 216
    Fates Entwined — 236
    One Afternoon in Hana — 243

Suspicions About Friends, Family, Love, Work, Technology,
the Government, and Everything Else

Introduction — 249
Mothballed — 250
Reggie — 261
Gemphalon — 267
The Shyanne Letters — 288
Empty Walls — 302
Harvest Home — 307
Riding the Black Horse — 321
Genetically Predisposed — 326
Purple Shards — 337

Afterword - 345
About the Author — 346
About the Stories — 347

Foreword

I can't help having suspicions. I try to draw the line at being cynical, but in assembling this collection of short fiction that I have written over the years, I can't help but see a theme that runs through my work.

Apparently, I'm suspicious.

I'm certain that I first learned that things aren't always as they appear when I learned that my parents were just people instead of omnipotent gods. Psychologists say this is a milestone moment in the lives of most children. Perhaps I have never recovered. Certainly I continue to be suspicious about everything. Or maybe *suspicious* is too harsh a word. Perhaps I'm merely inquisitive. Perhaps skeptical.

Nope, I'm afraid that suspicious is the proper word.

I'm suspicious about pretty much everything, but mostly I have suspicions about other people's motives. Why are they nice to each other? Why are they nice to me? Why do they do the things they do, at the time and place that they do them? I want to know.

I want to know about The Great Unknown and why some people say they know more about it than I do. How did they get a special pass? I want to know about death, and why some people say they know more about *that* than I do. Ditto sex, a very interesting, sometimes funny, always intriguing topic. I want to know why some people have friends and some don't. I want to know why some families are close and others aren't. I want to know about love. And our government! I have been inside the Office of Disinformation in the Pentagon. Don't tell me I don't have a right to be suspicious.

For this collection, I have selected stories from the past twenty years of my writing career. In it, you'll read about my suspicions, as they are cloaked in fiction, and perhaps you'll recognize some of them as kin to some of your own.

If you have any of the answers to my questions—most not yet asked—please don't tell me. I've become fond of my suspicions, and they fuel me.

Suspicions About the Unknown

Life holds some pretty odd experiences—the unexplained Twilight Zone stuff that occasionally happens to all of us. Serendipity, divine intervention, ESP, telekinesis, magic, hypnotism, mind over matter, chanelling, past life regression...one gets the feeling that there's a master mind out there somewhere, and we're trying to get a grasp on the part we're playing while making up our lines as we go. But behind the scenes surely lurks a vast retinue of scene builders, lighting technicians, directors, makeup artists, special effects specialists and writers that are coaxing us forward hint by hint.

Will any of us ever be privy to a sweeping overview? Or is puzzling it out, piece by piece, a part of the script? Aren't you a little suspicious about the motives of those behind the scenes?

Rivering

Deborah pulled the old van to a rolling stop on the pebbled beach right at the inside of the river's elbow. She looked through the bug-spattered windshield and felt the weariness creep up the back of her neck. "Let's get out and see what she looks like, Moose." She unbuckled her seat belt, let it drop to the floor with a clank, then stepped over the dog and slid open the side of the van. The beach crunched underfoot as she stretched.

Moose, an ancient collie, slowly got out of the van after her. He too, stretched, then put his nose to the ground and began to wander.

"Don't go too far, boy," she said. "Dinner in a half hour. We'll start work in the morning."

Deborah limbered up after the long drive with ten minutes of calming yoga stretches. Then, before the daylight faded away, she walked down to the river's edge, took off her tennis shoes, and waded in up to her ankles. It was a perfect location. It looked just like the type of place the slivers would congregate.

Well, she'd find out in the morning.

She went back to the van, brought out the little cook stove, dipped water from the river and cooked up some dehydrated stew. It wasn't great, but it was easy and it was protein. She opened a can of food for Moose, and they set to their dinner.

Afterward, she didn't even wash the dishes. She set them outside the van, spread her sleeping bag out on the van floor, and fell instantly asleep.

All night long she dreamed of catching slivers. All night long she dreamed of catching the right slivers. Her slivers.

She got up before dawn, excitement brewing in her belly as the coffee brewed on the stove. In the early hours, she'd had an important dream, and she knew that this was the place. This was where she would find and catch the slivers she'd been rivering for all year. She wouldn't have to scout river after river, state after state, any more. It was such a peaceful idea, she hoped it wasn't just wishful thinking. But she'd never felt this way before. She'd never had a dream like that before, either.

She let Moose sleep in while she did her morning exercises, facing the color of the sky. Then she breakfasted on a peanut butter and honey sandwich, drank two cups of coffee, did all the dishes and roused the dog. "C'mon, Moose," she said. "It's time to find Dad."

She twirled the combination lock on the little safe she had installed under the driver's seat, opened it and took out the seven little leather bags, each with a long tether wrapped around it. She unwound the tether from her two and put the other five in her pocket. Then she got the net from the front seat and the little cooler with its chunk of dry ice.

Moose walked with her down to the river. She looked at the water, black in the early light. She squinted her eyes and looked downstream.

There! She saw one. The starlight caught a little flash of silver. An untrained eye might think it a minnow. Tingles ran up her spine. She took the cooler and the net upstream. She took off her sneakers and rolled up her pant legs.

She waded into the icy water slowly, quietly. The river undercut the bank the tiniest bit, and that's where they would be. She tied the tethers to the rings she'd sewn to the legs in her jeans, then dropped the pouches into the water and watched as they flowed downstream, moving in the gentle current.

Then she stood absolutely still.

Moose, seeming to sense the urgency, also remained motionless.

A little silver glinted in the water. She waited. It seemed to sniff the pouches, and then was off. Not the right one.

She waited until the sun came full up, until her feet were so numb from the cold that her back ached, and nothing had come for the bait. Moose had wandered away in hopes of finding a rabbit.

She brought in her two lines and set the other five out in the same way. No luck.

At noon, she brought them in, and stiffly walked up to the van. It was still a good place, and there were slivers here. It was just that *her* slivers didn't seem to be here.

She heated up some soup and lay down on her sleeping bag. Her bones ached from motionlessness, cold and disappointment. She'd try again after a rest. If she didn't get something soon, she'd be out of money.

She opened the pouches so they could dry. In the first one was the tip of Roger's forefinger, the crucifix he always wore, and a dried bud of his favorite rosebush. She lay these things out on a tray to dry. She couldn't let them rot. In the second pouch were her father's little toe, his wedding ring and the waterlogged and no-longer-recognizable picture of her mother he always carried in his wallet. The other pouches held similar pieces of the anatomy and significant memorabilia of the deceased. She didn't know these other people, and had nothing to do with them. She was rivering for hire. Paid to find dead people's souls, slivering about in the elbows of the rivers. And if she didn't have some luck soon, there would be no more customers.

Deborah would never forget how she first heard about rivering.

She had been eavesdropping on her parents' conversation when they had guests over. One of them had just hired a riverer to find his mother, so he could finally, once and for all, have control over her. The discussion heated, and while the adults went into the moral issues, Deborah went deep into her own world, thinking about the life of a riverer. And the concept stayed with her, as if she had heard her calling when she heard that conversation, and she waited patiently for her time to arrive. A year ago, it had.

When everything was laid out and drying in the back window of the van, Deborah had her soup. Rivering was a lonely business. It took a lot of energy to keep her doubts from taking over. She knew from talking to other riverers that success was infrequent, but she'd feel better if she could catch just one. Discouragement was heavy, sometimes. She'd been on the rivers, just her and Moose for almost a year. With no luck.

When Roger died, leaving so much unfinished business behind him, she knew she would go rivering for him. When he was laid out at the funeral home, she asked for a moment alone with him, and with her penknife, sliced the tip off his forefinger. She put it in her food dehydrator, and saved the little grey, curled slip of leather in her jewelry box.

When her dad died, she paid the mortician's assistant twenty bucks to cut off his little toe. And when Joey started college on a scholarship up at Colorado State, Deborah began rivering.

It wasn't long before she was out of money. But along the way, she'd talked with others who rivered and it seemed like there were no end to people who wanted to recover other people's souls. So she took out a little ad, and from the hundreds of replies, she selected five at a thousand dollars apiece, and now that money was almost gone, too.

That discouragement mixed with the loneliness of a riverer, and Deborah hugged the big, salty-smelling dog who lay next to her and fought back the tears. "You stink," she said to Moose. "Tomorrow I'll give you a bath."

After a short nap, Deborah repacked the tiny pouches and went back to that same spot in the river. The old timers always told her to listen to the messages in her dreams. She pushed her doubts back and let the truth come over her. She knew she would have success here.

She stood in the shallows with pieces of her father and her husband until she was almost blind from staring at the shining water. Then she changed, tied on the other five, and immediately there was a boiling stir.

One by one, she pulled in the pouches, very carefully, very gently. She had to know for sure which one had attracted the sliver. When only one pouch was left trailing in the current, and the sliver was still there, swimming wildly around it, she swiped with her net.

And she had it. She'd caught it!

"Look, Moose!" The dog backed away, slowly wagging his tail.

Very carefully, Deborah took the net to the shore, opened the little cooler and turned the net over onto the dry ice.

The ice sizzled and smoked as the sliver and the water from the net touched it, and for a moment, Deborah worried that she'd lost it. She blew down, and she could see it, a little silver sliver, lying still as death on the block of ice. She put the cover back on. "I got one, Moose," she said gently, her heart pounding. She opened the pouch and emptied its contents onto the cover of the cooler. There was an unidentifiable piece of flesh—an earlobe perhaps—a swatch of black hair, and a foreign coin. Inside the leather was written the name and phone number of the person searching. Seiji Okano. Deborah put the artifacts back into the pouch, opened the cooler, picked up the sliver and studied it. She expected it to look like a fish, but it didn't. It just looked like a little silver slip of something, about three inches long, maybe half an inch in diameter. No eyes, no mouth, no tail, just a little slip of silver. It was hard to believe that this was the soul of Seiji Okano's wife. She put the sliver into the pouch with the other things and put the pouch on top of the ice.

"We're on a roll now, Moose, buddy," she said, and stepped back into the water.

By dinner time, she hadn't caught anything else, but she believed wholeheartedly in her dream. This was her spot.

Probably every one of the remaining six slivers to be caught were here somewhere. And she would catch them.

That night Roger came to her in another dream.

"Deborah, I'm sorry," he said, over and over again. Her heart ached. He'd come closer, puppy-dog look on his face, hands out, and her heart would pound with fear and she'd back away. Then he would look hurt and turn away, and she would approach him again, *please don't go, don't leave me again*, but as soon as he moved toward her, "Deborah, I'm sorry," she would back away, fear pounding in her chest.

She woke up sweating. She hugged the dog and cried.

In the morning, she remembered what the old timers had told her. "They get frightened when they know somebody is rivering for them. They seem to have no control over themselves. They're irresistibly drawn to those things of the flesh, but they don't want to be. They'll fool with your mind. Pay no attention. It's just trickery, is all it is, it's just trickery. Stay calm and keep rivering."

In the early morning, she caught another one, and she noticed that her little block of dry ice would last two more days at the most. Then she would have to go to town, make her phone calls, ship the slivers to their owners and buy another block of ice.

At noon, she caught Roger.

When his sliver was safely frozen, tied inside the leather pouch, and resting with the other two on the ice inside the cooler, Deborah sat down on the beach, elbows on her knees, face in her hands. She didn't know what to do with him now that she had him.

And who said these things were their souls, anyway?

She knew what the old timers said. They said the souls were waiting for Release, a periodic occurrence when all the souls went on to their next assignment—whatever that was—all at the same time. Meanwhile, they were stored inconspicuously and economically as little pieces of solid light in the rivers.

So if Roger was in the cooler, would he go on to his next assignment from wherever he was, or would he miss out?

She picked up the cooler and ran to the van. She threw all her camping gear in, called the dog, slammed the door shut and went in to town.

At the first pay phone, she stopped, got out her address book, and made her calls. First was to Seiji Okano.

"Mr. Okano?"

"Yes?"

"This is Deborah Whittington. The Riverer. I have your sliver."

"You do?"

"Yes."

A long sigh on the other end. "That's wonderful."

"I'll ship it to you today. It will be packed in dry ice."

"That's fine."

She verified the address. "Um, Mr. Okano?"

"Yes?"

"What will you do with it?"

"Stir fry."

"Eat it?"

"Yes."

"Tell me, will that keep her from going on, I mean to the next…"

Mr. Okano hung up without answering.

She called the next person. A woman. "I have your sliver."

"Oh." She did not seem pleased.

"Don't you want it?"

"Oh, yes…I guess I do."

"I can release it."

"No! Please don't."

"I'll send it to you today, packed in dry ice."

"Fine."

"Do you mind my asking… What will you do with it?"

"I don't know yet. Keep it. Somehow."

"I see. Thank you."

Deborah hung up, then tended to the business of shipping the two and re-icing Roger.

She stopped in the local diner for a hamburger and a beer, but the waitress wouldn't serve her. "You're that riverer come to town, ain'tcha?"

"Yes."

"Take your business somewhere else, missy," she said, then turned her back.

"That's not exactly neighborly, Ginnie," a grey-haired police officer scolded her.

"Ain't Christian," Ginnie said in rebuttal, and as Deborah had noted the name Ginnie's Diner on the menu, she figured that Ginnie could refuse service to whoever she wanted.

Deborah felt everyone's eyes on her as she left, and tried to keep her back straight when all she wanted to do was argue with the woman. Either that, or cry.

Rivering for people's souls, it seemed, was a profession not kindly taken to in these mountain communities.

She got her lunch at a grocery deli in the next town, some dog cookies for Moose, and a six pack of Bud, then headed back to the river. She had four more to catch, and then she would retire.

That evening, she caught another one, but as she tipped the net to put it onto the ice, it fell onto the beach, and before she could think, Moose grabbed it and bit it right in half.

She screamed at him, he dropped it and slinked away, and there, flopping on the ground, were two half-slivers.

She picked them up, panic welling wordlessly within her, and she watched, her horror subsiding, as the the two parts grew together again in her hand. Healed. Instantly. Seamlessly.

She quickly froze it, then stowed it in the pouch. She took a deep breath and put the cooler out of harm's way.

That night, her father approached her in a dream. She sat by his side, felt his warm hands on hers, she saw the familiar wrinkles on his face. Her heart was filled with love for this man, but when she awoke, she knew it was more trickery.

Before noon, she caught him. She set his pouch next to Roger's, and then with hard-bitten determination, went back for the others. She had to finish. This was her spot; this was her job.

And she did finish. It took two more days to catch them all and get them shipped off, and then she was left with her two pouches on a shrinking block of dry ice. She sat in her van, hands gripping the steering wheel. Her job wasn't finished until they were taken care of.

What on earth was she going to do with them?

She could donate them to research. She'd heard about some robotics research being done on slivers.

She could eat them.

She could let them go.

She could pickle them and store them on her mantle.

A zillion ideas came up, but none of them were right. They had to be totally appropriate to Roger. And her dad.

She drove back from the post office to the same elbow of the river, took her beach chair out and sat in it to watch the sunset,

Moose on one side of her, the cooler on the other side. She brewed a cup of coffee and reflected on her life.

The pounding, driving force that kept her rivering was gone. Her future spread before her like an open field, and she felt she could build anything there she wished. She needed only step into the picture, but to do that, she had to step over the cooler.

Something must be done with the slivers.

Roger. Roger had been a jerk. He drank, he ran around with other women, he gambled and lost money they didn't have, and he paid little attention to Joey when Joey needed it the most.

Through it all, Deborah never stopped loving him. She knew that deep within him, he was a good man, and the things he did were somehow beyond his control. When he was straight, he was fabulous. They had such loving times, the three of them. He loved her, he loved Joey, he just had things he needed to do. Those things caused her endless heartache, and when he died... When he died of a cocaine stroke—his body dumped at the emergency entrance of a hospital by a car that sped into the night—he left her in far greater debt than she could ever imagine.

Her father bailed her out.

Her father. Lewis had been exactly the opposite of Roger. Lewis was the attentive father, good provider, model of perfection, a true-life Father Knows Best. From the outside. The truth was, he was cold. He kissed her cheek, but there was no warmth. He bailed her out, but when he wrote the check, there was no sympathy, empathy or anything, and her words of gratitude fell on ears of granite. He sent checks to Joey every Christmas and birthday, but when Deborah spoke with Lewis on the phone, he somehow never asked about Joey.

Lewis hurt Deborah far more deeply than Roger ever could.

And now she had control of their immortal souls, if those slivers were indeed their souls.

And if anything she did had any effect on them, but she believed it did.

She believed that those who rivered altered the course of destiny. That's why it was so hard. That's why hardly anybody did it. And those who did do it were driven. And everybody else hated them.

So what should she do with the slivers?

She opened the chest, took out the pouches. She dumped the frozen little slip from Roger's pouch and looked at it. She lay it on the ice, and took her father's sliver from his pouch. It was smooth and cold and solid.

Roger, so warm and so stupid. Daddy, so smart, but so cold. She knew what to do.

She went into the van and came out with a hammer and her cutting board.

First she smashed Roger's. With just a light tap, it shattered into hundreds of small, crystalline pieces. She dusted them off into a Ziplock bag and set them back on the ice. Then she smashed her father's sliver, and mixed the pieces together with Roger's in the bag.

She divided the pieces as evenly as she could and put half in the palm of each hand. She watched as they defrosted and grew together into two seamless wholes.

"C'mon, Moose," she said, and the dog walked by her side to the edge of the river.

"Maybe they'll average each other out," she said, and watched as the little silver slips darted out of sight.

❋

Renewing the Option

"I see you as a gambling man," she said with a sly grin. "Are you a gambling man?"

The question caught him a bit off guard, and he didn't know whether to match her directness or back down a little. "Doesn't every man fancy himself a bit of a gambler?"

Her grin faded, she stared straight into his eyes. They were dark blue, navy blue, Stefan noticed, not like any other eyes he'd ever seen. "I'm not talking fancy here," she said, suddenly serious. "I'm talking about high stakes."

He sat back in the seat, wiped his mouth with the cloth napkin and set it next to his plate. "Stakes?"

"The future," she said with an arch of the eyebrow. "Are you willing to gamble on your future?"

"What do you mean gamble? Don't we do a little bit of that every day? Isn't that what gambling is all about? Isn't that what life is all about?"

"Then you're not afraid?"

"We're all afraid."

"I don't mean 'we all.' I mean you. Are you afraid?"

He pushed his plate to the side, eager to be rid of it. "Of course," he finally said. "Terrified. Every day. Aren't you?"

"Not any more," she said, leaned back and lit up a cigarette.

He looked around nervously. "I think there's a special car at the back of the train for smoking."

"I know. I hate going back there. All I need are a couple of good hits, and I can get those before the waiter tells me to put it out." She never took her eyes from his. He was mesmerized by those dark blue shiny eyes.

She took a second pull from the cigarette just as the waiter came hustling down the aisle. Stefan admired the way the conductors, porters, and waiters just took the rocking of the train in stride. They never tripped or fell or stumbled or had to hold on to anything, even with a tray of food in their hands.

"Excuse me, miss," the waiter said, but she was stubbing out the butt even as he approached.

"I'm sorry," she said to him, unlocking her eyes from Stefan's for a moment. "I forgot."

"Thank you for your cooperation," he said, then took their dirty dishes and walked away.

Those blue eyes again. There was a storm behind them.

"Come with me," she said, picked up her purse, slid her cigarettes into it, then slid out of the booth. She wore a black sheath dress with black stockings and high heels. She didn't need to hold on to anything either, as she walked down the aisle, through the car couplings and back to her private room. She walked as if she'd been on the train a while.

Most people wore sweatshirts and jeans on the train nowadays. He felt as though she was from a different era, a time when train travel was civilized instead of cheap, social instead of low-class, a place to meet the creme de la creme instead of those whose fears of flying ruled their traveling lives.

And his linen slacks and silk knit polo were irresistible to her game, whatever it may be.

She had a private compartment, as did he. But whereas his had his business suit hanging in the slim closet, his suitcase in the overhead rack, and his briefcase open on the opposite seat with the latest issue of *Field and Stream* on top, her compartment was highly personalized.

She had framed photos on the windowsill. Silk scarves were wrapped around the light shades. A calendar with photographs of celestial bodies taken by the Hubble telescope hung on the wall. She had piles of books and magazines. She had dirty dishes, and laundry drying on the doorknobs.

"Come in," she said, and cleared off the reclining seat opposite hers. "Sit down."

Stefan looked around in amazement. "How far are you travelling?" he asked.

Those blue eyes again. "All the way."

They sat down opposite each other, the muted reddish-orange light echoing the last blast of sunset out the big window.

"If that window didn't take up the whole wall," he said with a smile, "I'd say you'd wallpaper it and put up curtains."

She didn't find that amusing. Instead, she pulled up the little retractable desk top and pulled a deck of oversized cards out of a plain cardboard box.

She leaned closer to him. Her eyes were bright with eagerness. "Mix the cards in a clockwise direction," she said.

"Just smoosh them up?"

"Whatever. Take your time."

He was humoring her, but he was beginning to feel a little cautionary, too. This woman could be off balance in some way that could spell trouble. He mixed the cards and indicated the photographs, jiggling on the window sill. "Your kids?"

"Concentrate on the cards."

He smooshed them, then fiddled them back into a deck.

"Now cut them three times."

He did as he was told and handed them to her. She took them with both hands.

"I'm going to draw one card. Only one. It will be your destiny card."

Stefan smiled at her. Those dark blue eyes had long, black lashes to go with them. And dark eyebrows. And dark hair, and white skin. He wished she wasn't quite so intense.

"Okay," he said.

She looked up at him, her eyes locked onto his, and she flipped a card over and lay it face up on the table. Neither one of them looked at it; they were looking into each other's eyes. Finally, Stefan looked down.

Death.

He smiled up at her. She was still looking at him. She picked up the card and put it back into the pack. "It was the death card," he said.

"I know," she said, but she hadn't looked at it. "It always is."

"Let me see," Stefan said, and took the cards from her. He'd seen Tarot decks before, but didn't know much about them. He quickly shuffled through. They were beautiful, with intricate art work and many strange symbols, but there was only one death card, and it was not to be mistaken. The hooded reaper with his scythe.

He put the deck back onto the table and smooshed them around again. This time he concentrated. He did it very well, mixing them up, mixing, mixing, mixing. Then he assembled it back into a deck, cut it three times and handed the deck back to her.

She flipped over a card and didn't even look at it.

Death.

Stefan sat back as she calmly put the card back into the deck.

"What do you mean, it always is?"

"I mean we're going to die on this train."

He stared at her. She looked calmly back at him, the intensity in her eyes replaced by a resigned, peaceful acceptance. "One more time," he said, and took the cards from her.

Death.

He took the death card, ripped it in half and threw it on the floor. He reshuffled the cards, cut them, handed them to her and she turned one over.

Death.

He slumped. "How can that be?"

"The cards are bigger than that," she said, indicating the torn card on the floor. "You can't expect a puny act like that to change destiny."

Stefan thought for a moment. "Everybody on this train?"

She shrugged. "You and me. That's all I know so far."

He took the Death card and stood it up on the window sill, next to a picture of two teenagers. Then he reshuffled the deck and turned over a card.

Death.

With calm, deep blue eyes, she lit a cigarette.

"This isn't funny," he said.

"You're right."

"It's a good trick. But I don't like it." He stood up, she stubbed out the cigarette. He looked at her, but he had nothing to say. She frightened him, and he didn't know what to do about that. He had no experience with women like her.

He left, and tried to walk down the hall without holding on to anything. He stumbled when the train lurched, and slammed his shoulder into the wall.

Inside his own compartment, the porter had made up the bed, so there was no real place to sit. He undressed, turned on the reading light, got into bed and picked up his magazine. But he was in no mood to read about fly fishing.

He clicked off his light and watched the lights pass by the big dark window. He thought of Jane, his wife, a talented violinist, and Stefanie, his daughter, just starting out as a freshman at Julliard, herself a gifted musician. He thought about his parents, and his job, and his friends.

How would it happen, this death? Train wreck, certainly. If it was to kill them both, then it would surely be a wreck. Would he wake up to the jolt, hear the scream of wrenching metal before it wrapped around his body and ripped it in half?

Or was a bomber aboard? Would a fire bomb vaporize him so swiftly that he would not even have time to awaken?

Or would a crazed gunman open fire in the dining car at breakfast, spraying his brains all over the people sitting across from him? Would his last thought be of his wife, his daughter?

He looked wistfully at the window ledge and wished he had their pictures in a little frame.

Or would his last thought be of that woman, that other woman, that scary woman, and her death's head Tarot card?

Stefan got out of bed, pulled on a pair of jeans and a sweatshirt and walked, barefoot, back through the car to her compartment door. He turned the knob and pushed the door open.

She sat, just as he left her, in the chair with the Tarot deck on the table in front of her.

"How?" he asked.

She shrugged.

"I'm getting off at the next stop. Get off with me. We'll rent a car or something."

A slow pitying smile tweaked up the corner of her mouth. "This train doesn't stop for us any more," she said.

And with a shudder, he tried to remember the last time the train had stopped, and he couldn't. He sat down in the chair opposite her. "Where did you get on?"

She shrugged again, and he couldn't remember the name of the city he lived in. Absurd. It was on the tip of his tongue. His address was. was… His wife's name… His daughter's…

He closed his eyes and felt perspiration bulge out of his pores. He took a deep breath, then indicated the photographs in the frames on her window sill. "Your family? Your children? What are their names?"

She looked passively at the photographs, then looked back at him, slowly shook her head and shrugged.

Stefan jumped up, his nerves on fire. "I was fine until I ran into you," he said. "Everything was going along just fine until you and your…" he pointed at the Tarot deck. He looked at her for a moment in frustration, then spun around and left the compartment.

In the hallway, he took a deep breath of train-recirculated air and tried to think, but there was some sort of a Saran wrap feeling about his brain. He leaned his head against the wall and felt the rhythmic motion of the wheels on the rails. He loved that rhythm. He loved riding trains. He'd always loved it.

If he couldn't die in the arms of his wife, he guessed he'd just as soon die on a train.

He looked back at the woman's compartment door. He could probably die in her arms, if he wanted to.

And he wanted to. Never had he met a woman more baffling or more appealing.

He went back to her compartment, opened the door, stepped in and took her hand. Wordlessly, and with complete understanding, she stood and let him lead her down the aisle to his compartment, where the bed was made and waiting.

In the terrifying urgency with which a dying animal breeds, they clasped lips, tore clothes and merged before falling onto the moving bed. And there, in a wrestling match more aggressive than loving, fighting the movement of the train rather than letting it soothe them, they kicked away restrictive clothing, then clawed and screamed their way to violent orgasms.

She sat up afterward, huddled naked in the corner, one bare shoulder against the cold glass. Stefan lay on his back and looked at her, watched her watch the passing scenery. Now the movement of the train lulled him. The fear and fury of his impotence in the train situation had spurted out along with his bodily fluids, and he felt relaxed and able to deal with whatever was coming. For the moment at least.

She looked at him just before his eyes closed. Those navy blue eyes of hers, against that milk white skin. How long had she been on the train, he wondered. How long? He'd have to remember to ask…

Stefan startled awake.

She was still sitting at the end of his bed, so he couldn't have been sleeping for long.

"Did you feel it?" he asked. "The train. It stopped."

She looked at him with sadness. "Maybe it did. There's a thing that the train does, perhaps it's just exactly that. Stopping. But I only catch it… like out of the corner of my eye." She smiled. "The corner of my id."

She touched his foot. "But the train doesn't stop for us."

"This is fucked," Stefan said, and got up. He pulled on his jeans and a t-shirt, opened the door and stepped out into the hallway.

He walked through car after car, seeing no one, finally arriving in the dining car. People were having breakfast. He stopped a waiter. "Excuse me?"

"Sir?" The waiter looked at Stefan's bare feet and frowned.

"What is the next stop?"

The waiter consulted his watch. Then he spoke, and it seemed to Stefan that he spoke in a foreign language.

"Pardon?"

The waiter repeated himself, but Stefan still didn't understand. His fear was turning into anger, and its potency had increased.

Stefan stepped closer to the waiter. "I still didn't understand you. Please speak slowly and distinctly."

The waiter spoke again, slowly and distinctly as asked, but it was a word and then a phrase that made no sense to Stefan at all. He looked around, at the woman and her two children sitting at the table next to where he stood.

She spoke, reaffirming what the waiter had said. Then the children said it, as if he was stupid or something, but it was no stop that he had ever heard of before, and chances were, he'd never know it when they did stop.

"Where are you getting off?" he asked the lady.

"There," she said, "at the next stop."

"And what is that?" he asked patiently.

"We just told you," she said, and turned to her menu, frowning at the children to do the same.

But the young girl, she looked up at him with a question mark in her eyes, and he knew that she didn't understand either.

He crouched down and looked at her at eye level. She was about twelve, and had beautiful blonde hair, light blue eyes and pink pouty lips. "Do you know the name of the next stop?" he asked her gently.

Wide-eyed, she shook her head no.

"I just told you," her mother said.

"Dummy," her brother said.

"Tell me again," she said, and the mother and the brother and the waiter all said it, but it sounded like noise from the throats of other-worldly beings. It sounded like a recording that had been electronically elongated. The girl looked up at Stefan with what appeared to be growing terror. Stefan knew the feeling.

"You're one of us," he said.

The girl clutched her brother's arm.

"Car forty-eight, compartment C."

"Call a cop," the mother said to the waiter.

Stefan stood up with weak knees and reassured her. "That won't be necessary. I mean no harm." He looked again at the girl.

"Car forty-eight, compartment C."

The girl nodded, and without a backward glance, he walked away from them, boldly returning the stares of the other diners.

The Navy-blue-eyed woman had dressed, and the porter had made up the bed.

"I don't know your name," Stefan said.

"The drivers license in my purse says my name is Mary, but I call myself the Mother of Wands."

Stefan had no response for that remark. Finally, he said, "You don't look like a Mary."

She shrugged, a gesture which was becoming an irritating part of her whole demeanor. Stefan sat down opposite her. "There's another," he said.

"Well," she said. "The event must be getting close. For a long time there was only me. Then you, the Father of Cups, and now, so soon, another."

"How long? How long was there only you? How long have you been on this train?" But he couldn't look at her answer, at the shrug. "It's a little girl."

And with that, a timid knock on the door.

Stefan opened it and she stood there, her hands clasped nervously in front of her. "I'm afraid," she began, "I'm afraid... I think they got off the train without me," she said, then began to cry. "I can't find them anywhere." He put his arms around her, then brought her in and set her in his seat.

"The daughter of Stones," Mary said. She pulled out her Tarot deck, pulled up the little table, and coached the girl on how to shuffle the deck.

Mary flipped over the card and Stefan didn't even have to look at it. The sharp intake of breath from the girl told him everything.

Death.

He rang for the porter, who brought a ginger ale for the girl and a bottle of brandy and a bucket of ice for the adults.

"Okay," Stefan said as he poured two stiff brandies, then gulped half of his, "enlighten me."

Mary shuffled through the deck of cards and handed one to him. It was long and smooth, heavy and felt authoritative. On the back was a painting—why hadn't he noticed it before?—of a train. A train at night, the track weaving through a skyscape of stars.

He turned the card over and there was the Father of Cups. It looked like him.

"Let me see the others," he said.

She handed him the Mother of Wands and the Daughter of Stones. There was no doubt. Pictures of Mary and the little girl.

"How many cards in the deck?" he asked.

"Seventy-eight."

He sat down on the arm of the girl's chair. Do you think this train is collecting an entire deck?"

She shrugged.

"Do you think we'll die when the deck is assembled, or do you think we'll be set free?"

"Some group karma to be settled, I imagine," she said.

"Why me? Why you? Why *us*?" Stefan asked. "Is there something else we have in common?"

"I saw a flying saucer once," the girl said, and Stefan remembered a dream he had a long time ago, a dream that terrified him with its implication of the magnitude of his responsibility in the greater scheme of things. The dream made so much sense he sat straight up in bed saying, "Of course!" and then, with consciousness, the dream vaporized. He couldn't even remember the gist of it. But it was a dream, the likes of which he'd never had before or since. It was an extraordinary experience, the residue of which still dusted his psyche.

When the girl said, in her twelve-year-old way, "I saw a flying saucer once," Stefan knew exactly what she meant. She could have said, "We all like the train." or "We all have blue eyes." or "We're all Americans." Instead, she said, instinctively, "I saw a flying saucer once." So had he, after a fashion.

He looked at Mary. She looked back at him, her expression no longer blank and vague. No telling what Mary had experienced, but she resonated with the girl's statement just as he did. Another weirdness to add to the pot.

He finished his brandy and poured himself another, then picked up the cards, turning them over and over in his hands. They felt like a living thing, squirming, almost, in his grip. "Where'd you get these?"

Mary shrugged.

"Don't do that any more," he said. "Don't just shrug. Help me out here. I think there's a way out of this predicament, but we have to work together like a team, like a... a deck, and shrugging doesn't get it."

"I can't remember," she said. "I think they were in my room when I got on the train."

Stefan lay the Daughter of Stones card on the table.

The girl regarded the card with what seemed like adult composure, then turned her pretty eyes up to his. "Looks like me."

"It *is* you," he said.

Stefan turned the cards up one at a time on the table. Some of the faces were familiar. One man he'd seen in the dining car, another was the porter.

"It's happening," Mary said. "Finally."

"Do we go along with it?" Stefan asked.

She shrugged, and caught herself, mid-shrug. She smiled up at him. "What else?"

"Change things."

"One of us could leave," the girl said. "Jump off the train. Then there'd never be a full deck."

"Then the rest of us might just travel on this train for eternity," Mary said, "never fulfilling our destiny."

"But the cards are here for a purpose. To tell us. To alert us," Stefan said. "Group karma, you say? Don't you think that happens all the time? People who go to war in the same unit, people who work in the same office, people in the same families. But what about us? We've been *gathered.*"

Another knock on the door. Stefan opened it to find a young woman holding an ice bucket. "Hi, excuse me, but the porter said you had ice," she giggled.

"Seven of swords," Mary said.

Stefan looked at her. She held up the card, and the woman came in, took it and looked at it wonderingly. "All four families are represented," Mary said. "Cups, Swords, Wands and Stones."

"Maybe we should have a meeting," he said.

"I have a feeling we don't have time," Mary said. "As soon as the deck is assembled..."

"What's going on in here?" the woman with the ice bucket asked.

Stefan looked at her, smiled and shrugged the way Mary did, then emptied half the ice bucket into hers. "Party it up," he said, then turned to the little girl. "I want you to take these cards, and match them up with the people on the train. I want to know how close we are to completing the deck."

She nodded, took the Tarot deck and solemnly left, instinctively knowing the gravity of the mission.

"And then what?" Mary asked.

Stefan shrugged. They smiled at each other. "Something to do while we wait," he said. "Although... Come on." He grabbed her hand, pulled her up and out the door.

They went down the stairs to the loading platform. The sense of the train's speed was more evident, louder, scarier.

Outside the window, the wide open countryside passed. If he jumped here, assuming he didn't break something in the process, he'd have a long walk to civilization.

Stefan looked for a conductor, but seeing none, he opened the heavy door and pulled it aside.

What passed outside the door was like nothing he had seen before. It certainly wasn't the outdoors scene that showed outside the windows.

The windows looked out on countryside, with trees and fields, fences, livestock, blue sky, clouds, country roads.

Outside the open door was what appeared to be a continuous sheet of brown paper. Cardboard. There was no horizon, there was nothing beyond the tracks. Stefan thought if he had a long stick or something, he could reach out and touch the paper, perhaps he could tear it and see what lay beyond.

He stuck his head out and looked up. Seamless, dark blue ceiling. The train seemed to be going through a tunnel of cardboard that melded into a dark blue at the top. Stars? Were there stars up there? The train was going too fast to tell. It made his stomach queasy.

He turned and looked out the window in the door on the opposite side. They were passing a pond. Brown ducks floated lazily and white, long-legged birds fished in the shallows. In the distance, dust trailed a tractor.

Stefan looked at Mary, who looked at the floor. Wordlessly, she turned and walked back up the stairs.

Stefan closed the door. Out the window, he saw the outskirts of a small town with a big balloon flying over something—a new shopping mall probably. Never had he felt so hopelessly out of control.

He followed Mary back up to his room, where the little girl waited, breathlessly. "They're all here," she said, "except for these ones."

"Major arcane cards," Mary said. "Sun, Moon, Wheel of Fortune, Fool, Hanged Man... These don't have people on them. This is it, then. We're all assembled."

Stefan's mouth dried, and he sat down in the chair, and pulled Mary into his lap. She struggled for a moment, it was such an odd thing for him to do, and yet it also felt like the perfect thing to do.

He flashed for a moment on seeing a Tarot layout. Two cards were crossed. He and Mary were crossed.

The compartment door opened and the girl with the ice bucket came in again, and with her came another boy.

"Two of Swords," Mary whispered. "I think we've been shuffled, laid out, and now we're being read."

The idea could not have been more absurd nor more appropriate. Everyone held still, almost holding their breath. Stefan had an eerie, goosebump feeling that he was being examined, that the lid on his life—whatever it contained—was being pried open and the contents poked around in and stirred up.

Eventually, the feeling passed, but then he felt Mary stiffen in his arms, and he knew the same examination was passing through her.

And the train zoomed past towns and cities, through stock yards and switching stations and on toward twilight.

Several times during the long, strange night, people changed places. Stefan found himself walking through the corridor, passing people whose faces were blank, only to sit, compulsively, next to someone he had never met. They would sit side by side, or facing each other for the duration of that horribly intimate examination, then he would stand again, and walk through the train, zombie-like, until the next chair in the next car beckoned irresistibly, and he sat.

While he waited, he looked around and saw a perfect cross-section of humanity. A beautiful teenage girl; a retarded little boy. An old man with years of wisdom on his face, an old woman ravaged by disease and reeking of alcohol. Stefan couldn't remember the details of his life before boarding the train, but he had a feeling about it, kind of a spirit shadow image that felt okay, but not great. A fair amount of satisfaction resided in his habits, but there was a time, he could tell, when he hadn't lived up to anywhere near his potential, and spent time embarrassing himself and those who loved him.

He wondered if those who were reading his life saw all of that. Was it true that they read his intentions and not necessarily the results of his actions? Or were the results all that mattered?

The train lurched, and everyone in the club car looked around at each other. The train slowed, the wheels grinding, and a new landscape began to show itself out the windows.

Dachau, and the ovens are smoking.

Dresden, and people on fire run screaming through the ruins.

My Lai, and machine guns cut a row of people in half before they fall into the ditch.

Iraq, and burnt corpses sit at the wheels of a hundred miles of military jeeps.

Turkey, and bloated, gassed peasants feed flies in the sun.

Los Angeles, and a man is dragged from his truck to be beaten almost to death.

New York, and a jogger is gang raped, beaten and left to die.

Cincinnati, and a woman slaps her child and calls him stupid.

Are we the temperature of society? Stefan wondered. Are we the periodic cross-section that is examined to see whether or not there is hope, whether or not this experiment called "humanity" should continue?

Whose experiment are we, anyway?

He looked around at his training companions and knew that though his past may have been murky, for the most part, as an adult, he felt he had done the best he could with what he had to work with at the time. At least he hoped he had. He searched his soul and found it wanting, but not by much. He hoped to God that the others found peace in their souls, too.

The grip on him eased as the view out the window returned to normal. It appeared as though they were entering a large metropolitan area. People outside waved to the train as they had always done, all across America.

Stefan felt almost normal. He looked around and saw the others stretching and standing, as if awakening.

We've passed, he thought. We must be making progress.

Mary.

He rushed back to her compartment, and she was there, sitting in the seat, her bags packed, the Tarot deck on the table before her.

"It's over," he said. "We didn't die."

"Shuffle the cards," she said, her gaze as steady and as intense as ever.

He sat down opposite her and did as he was told. She took the deck from him with both hands. "I'm going to draw one card. Only one." He nodded. She turned up the card.

Judgment.

His eyes locked onto her infinitely-deep Navy blue eyes.

Heavy footsteps came down the corridor. "St. Louis," the conductor said. "Next stop, St. Louis."

"That's my stop," she said, grabbed her bags and stood up.

"Will I see you again?" he asked, and even as he did, he knew the answer.

She shrugged.

He helped her with her luggage, and stood on the platform as she disembarked, but aside from a vaguely uncomfortable, uncertain smile, and a cursory wave, he was pretty sure that she didn't remember him.

But it didn't matter, because he'd be home in the arms of his lovely wife in—he tapped his watch—less than an hour, if the train was on time.

✳

The Pan Man

When Constance awoke to the crowing of the rooster, the sun was already flooding through the windows. She stretched luxuriously, feeling guilty for sleeping so late, especially since it looked to be a wonderfully unseasonable spring-like day.

She got up, wrapped her robe around her, slid her feet into the lambskin slippers and padded into the kitchen. She stoked the fire and set the kettle on, then made her morning trek to the outhouse.

It was a beautiful day, she noticed. A glorious day.

The three sheep looked up, expecting their due of hay, the chickens scurried around, and the cat walked with her. It was so different with Jim gone.

When Jim was home, which was all the time except when he went hunting twice a year, he did most of the chores. He got up well before dawn, fed the livestock, started the fire, and usually had breakfast cooking by the time she got out of bed.

It was a luxury, really, to sleep in so late and feed the animals at a leisurely pace.

There was much to do yet. While Jim dealt with the firewood, Constance was in charge of splitting kindling. And she had the week's bread to bake, and it was a perfect day to do laundry and hang it out in the sun.

But the beauty of the day after a cold and stormy winter made her a little dreamy, and a little lazy, and by the time she had finished in the outhouse and was making her way back to the cabin, she had decided to set aside at least an hour to sit in the sun and spin.

Spinning the fleeces from the sheep was the winter job. All winter long, she dealt with those fleeces, washing, dyeing, carding and then spinning and knitting. This winter she'd made each of them bulky sweaters and long johns, and that was necessary work, but the spinning was such a wonderful pastime, she would relish a little sunshine and a little spinning, where the contented dreams of her imagination could wind on and on, just like the yarn she made. She'd never be able to afford such a luxury when Jim was home, and even though getting in the meat was a lot of work for him, she knew he enjoyed his three day trips away with his friends.

Having decided to spend a little time in solitary pleasure with her spinning wheel, Constance went about her chores with a purpose in mind. She opened all the windows to let the fresh air in, fed the animals, mixed the bread, then swept the cabin and beat the rugs as it raised. She washed clothes while it raised for the second time, and chopped wood to heat up the oven.

Then, when it was in finally in for the baking, she took her spinning wheel and a kitchen chair out onto the old wooden porch.

The sun was warm, and even though the air up in the Cascade mountains was always cold, and chilly now in February, she took off her sweater, leaving only a thin cotton dress, so her pale white arms could see the sun. Jim would never approve. He would want her dressed in woolens anyway, just because the calendar still read February. But Jim wasn't home.

She chose wool she'd dyed with Queen Anne's lace, a weed, really, that was abundant around the cabin. The wool was a lovely yellow-green, and she set to treadling the wheel and spinning the yarn. This would be knit into a little coat for their baby, she thought, whenever the good Lord found fit to bless them with one.

The spinning wheel ran smoothly, and the sun beat down warmly, and Constance thought back to their first arrival in the woods. They lived in a tent while Jim cleared the land, loving every moment of it. And in the two years they'd been here, many things had changed, but her love of her husband and their love of this land hadn't. And probably never would.

Birds twittered and darted in front of the cabin, picking up little pieces of straw to build nests, and Constance spun on.

She saw the grass turn green in front of her, and little wildflowers and the bulbs she'd planted in the fall grew. She felt the wool slide through her fingers in an even, fine thread and she dreamed of the family they would someday have.

And then she heard the bells.

Her father was a minister down in California, and some proud rich man who'd come to love the Lord had given him a set of three beautiful bells to ring of a Sunday morning. And the reverend rang them with glee, summoning everyone within earshot to the House of worship for Sunday services. They were huge bells, each hanging from its own tripod of lodgepole pine. They weren't only beautiful, they were glorious sounding bells, with a rich, deep tone. Her papa's ministry increased about sevenfold after that, and he grew wealthy off the goodness of the Lord and their congregation.

Constance heard the bells as she sat on her front porch and spun.

Papa was a good man, she thought, and she remembered her daily Bible lessons, and she remembered her mama before she died. Her mama was a soft, loving woman who was always putting the coffee pot on in the middle of the night to help some neighbor in distress. There were always neighbors in distress, it seemed.

Too bad Constance and Jim didn't have any neighbors. She'd like to help them the way her mama had.

Constance heard the bells, they seemed to be getting louder. The bells. The glorious bells.

Daddy would ring those bells early on Sunday morning, while he was still in his nightshirt. Mama would open the window and say, "Hush that, now, it isn't proper. You'll wake the dead." And Daddy would say, "Good. Then maybe they'll come to church, too."

So once awake, the townspeople had nothing better to do than to come to church. Mama stopped complaining after a couple of weeks of heavy collection trays.

And all of Constance's friends came. They had their ribbons and bows and lace and new shoes. They sat in the third pew and since she was the minister's daughter, she always had to wear her gloves, but she took them off as soon as the service got underway. The girls giggled and looked around at the boys while the sound of her father's powerful voice went on and on.

One by one, those girls found boyfriends and got married, but Constance didn't find anyone she liked for a long, long time. And then, of course, her mama died and she had to help her daddy and she had to play the piano in church and wash his clothes and bake his bread, wondering day by day if spinsterhood was to be her lot in life.

And then Big Jim O'Connor came to church one day. Constance took one look and lost her heart. And she married him the next Sunday after church and he moved her to this land he'd staked in the Cascade mountains high in the Oregon Territory.

Her girlfriends rang those bells for her as she and Jim rode off on horseback to their new home that Sunday afternoon. They rang those bells and rang those bells and Constance cried because it might be the last time she'd ever hear those bells... Until now, that is. Constance could hear those bells now as she sat and spun the yarn for her mama's grandchild, in fact the bells kept getting louder and louder. Tears she never had time for began to pour out of her heart. Tears for her mama, tears for her papa, alone down in California, just him and his Bible and his bells.

Tears for the womb that had remained empty for two years, tears for love of the land, love of her man, yet with the sadness that her wonderful childhood of giggles and play had gone forever. In its place was the work of a woman, the load of responsibility.

Constance cried and spun and listened to the bells. They were nearer now, yet softer. She cried and heard the bees and felt the hot sun and watched the wheel spin around and around, and the grass was green and the wind whooshed in the pines, and she laughed and she cried and she spun and those bells, those bells, those glorious bells.

She looked up and a man stood in front of her.

"Daddy?" Her hand whipped out and stopped her wheel.

But it wasn't her daddy, it was a stranger, come up the path and she was so busy with laughing and crying and spinning that she'd let danger enter her world.

"No, ma'am," he said with a soft voice and Constance turned her chair over in a scramble to get up and get away from him.

Jim had left his loaded shotgun next to the door in the kitchen. Constance backed toward it, wiping the tears from her vision.

The man certainly seemed to be no threat, and yet...

"Pardon me for giving you a start. Usually people hear me coming from a mile or so away."

The man was wearing a leather harness fitted with hooks, and hanging from those hooks were cast iron pots. He was covered with cast iron pots and pans and lids. He lifted his arms and they touched, bonging softly. He turned around and Constance heard the bells of her father's church.

"Name's C. Crickett Wilson, ma'am. I make the finest cookware in the territory."

Constance knew she should continue to back toward the kitchen door, reach inside, grab that gun and run this peddler off their land. How dare he come sneaking around!

Yet he didn't exactly sneak up on her, he couldn't really, not with all those cast iron pots hanging on him. He looked gentle, he was certainly soft spoken. She leaned against the house.

"Is your husband at home?"

"He's out cutting wood. He should be back any time," Constance said, hoping he couldn't read the lie in her face.

"Well, then, may I take a moment of your time to show you my fine wares?" C. Crickett Wilson was perspiring. "And may I have a drink from your well, please?"

"You stay right there," Constance said. It sounded like a half hearted attempt at a threat, and somehow she was ashamed.

She went inside, leaving the door open. She looked at that shotgun and touched it, and decided she didn't need it. She dipped a cup of water, slipped into her sweater, and returned to the front porch. Mr. Wilson stayed put, just as she told him.

"Much obliged," he said as he drank the water down. He smacked his lips and handed back the cup with a smile. Then he took off his hat and wiped his forehead with his handkerchief. The pots rang. He cleared his voice. "Now, then." He removed a Dutch oven from its hook on his right shoulder. "A right stewpot. Ain't she a beauty?" He held it out to her.

Constance knew she shouldn't be talking to this Mister Wilson while Jim was away, but he was such a nice gent, and he had walked all the way up here just to see her, she couldn't just turn him away without giving his wares a complete looking over, now, could she? She stepped forward.

"Maybe you better have a seat, ma'am."

Constance looked at him, but she sensed that he knew what he was saying, so she righted her chair, and sat down. She was still looking down on him from the porch as he stood in the dirt. She still felt like she had the advantage. C. Crickett Wilson handed the pot up to her. She held out her hands.

When she touched it, the world turned dark, discordant, threatening. The pot fell from her hands as Constance gasped and recoiled.

The pan man's eyes were green, she noticed. Green and deep set. They were squinting at her. "No good, huh? Well, not everybody matches up with every pan."

Constance looked at the Dutch oven that had landed upside down on her porch. She moved her foot away from it as if it would bite.

Mr. Wilson began removing his pans one at a time, polishing them with a chamois he pulled from his pocket, and then stacking them on the porch. Each time he took a pan from its hook, he squinted up at Constance.

"We don't want anything too heavy now, do we?" He kept up a comforting banter as he went through these practiced motions, but Constance had missed most of his words. Her heart was still pounding from the very strange experience she'd just had. She wondered if she was sick. She felt her forehead. Perspiring, but not feverish. What on earth could have made her feel that odd way? She ought to tell this peddler to be on his way. They weren't in the market for cookware; they had no money.

Constance felt that her shaky knees would support her and started to stand, holding to the back of her chair. She should lie down, just in case it was something serious.

"Please, please, just a moment more," he said. "I know I've got something here for you."

Constance sat down again, knowing she would be rid of him in a moment. If she ever felt that dizzy again, experienced that horrible nose-dive into swirling black poisonousness...

"This." Mr. Wilson held up a small, flat pan. "My omelette pan. Do you have chickens?" He squinted up at her.

Constance nodded.

"Make your husband an omelette he'll never forget with this one." He gave it a final wipe with his cloth, then handed it up to her, squinting.

The pan had an energy of its own; Constance could feel it before she touched it. Then she took the round griddle from him and began to giggle. It tickled. She looked at the pan and wondered how in the world someone could make an omelette on such a silly pan and giggled and giggled, and then the pan man tried to take it away from her, and his face was so serious that she just had to laugh. He had these absurd little eyebrows that kind of tented up over his eyes and he'd missed a place when he'd shaved this morning and she held her sides and laughed, the pan banging on her chair, and she felt weak all over again from the giggles.

He wrested the pan from her grasp, though, and she was left to wipe her eyes and her nose and wonder at the mirth that came and went so fast.

Such an odd morning, Constance thought.

"...pride myself on suiting the pan to the customer," Wilson was saying, "but not even a lid would tone down that terrible giddiness... Here." And he thrust a little long-handled cup at her.

It felt warm and comfortable. "It's lovely," Constance said. She wanted to just sit and hold it. The cup was finely crafted, it gave her such a sense of peace...

Mr. Wilson peered at her. "You like it?"

"Oh, yes. It has..." she felt a loss of words.

"Balance."

"Yes. Balance." Constance looked around. It seemed as if they day just became a little bit nicer, the colors a little brighter, hope a little higher.

"Do you like it?"

Mr. Wilson's question brought her back to earth. She held it out to him. "Yes, of course, I'd love to have such a ladle, but I'm afraid I have no money."

"I don't trade in money, my dear. If you like the cup and it suits you, then it is yours. Let me just look it over..."

He took the ladle from her, produced a flannel cloth from somewhere under all his pans and began to rub it.

I could never take this from a strange man, she thought. What on earth would Jim have to say about that? He never even wanted her speaking to strangers.

"Uh-oh," Mr. Wilson said. "This cup has a crack in it." He smiled at her. "Can't have flawed merchandise, no sir. It's unpredictable, that's the problem. Can't never tell..." He set it on the step and began bonging around his wares, looking for something.

"That's fine, Mr. Wilson," Constance said, as she stood up slowly and backed toward the door. "We're not interested in any cookware now, really we're not."

"Oh? Did I tell you? It's not a matter of money?"

"Yes you did, and I thank you for coming all the way up here, but I really must insist you go now. My husband will be home at any moment."

"Aha." Mr. Wilson unhooked a loaf pan and held it out to her. "Here's a beauty," he said.

Constance looked at the little man. He certainly seemed harmless. And her loaf pans were almost beyond salvage. She had planned to get a new one the next time Jim took her to town. This one was cast iron; it would last forever. How she missed her mother's cast iron cookware! In spite of herself, she stepped closer again to Mr. Wilson and held out her hands.

The loaf pan, when she looked at it, was ordinary. Black, loaf-shaped, with a lip at one end where it could be hung on a nail. But it was anything but ordinary in her hands. It felt fluid. It felt strong and utilitarian. She thought she could bake the best bread in the world with this pan. She thought she could provide hearty nutrition for Jim and their family-to-be with no other tool, no other implement, nothing else, nothing else but this loaf pan. This marvelous, marvelous loaf pan.

"I must have it," she said.

"Good. Good. Well then, for another drink of water from your well, it is yours. And I'll be on my way."

"I must pay you."

"The pleasure on your face is pay enough for me."

"We don't take charity in this house."

"My dear, my dear, what I am offering you is not charity, not at all. It's a gift. It would please me if you took this pan as gift from me. I make these pans myself. Each one is personal. Each one is individual, just like my customers. And I seek out the people who need them, and I match them up with one of my creations."

Constance just stared at him.

"Don't you see? This is what I do."

"Then I must give you something in return," she said, but he halted her with an upraised palm.

"The pan will exact its own price, Missy," he said. "The better the pan, the higher the price. This one here," he pointed to the loaf pan she held, "is a fine pan, but it won't be too expensive. You'll lose a lamb, perhaps, or maybe your husband won't get that deer he's hunting. I have some that are more expensive, but that one you've got there... it's a good choice."

Constance looked over at the sheep, peacefully grazing, and she felt a chill. She pulled the sweater tighter around her shoulders. She wasn't sure she understood the man at all. What an odd little man.

She dipped him another cup of water and watched while he drank it.

"Good luck to you, Missy," he said, and started off down the way he'd come up, his pans bonging in a musical rhythm that was very pleasant to the ear.

She took the pan into the house, feeling its energy, feeling the wonderful, comforting weight of it, and she wanted to bake more bread. Immediately.

But she hung the pan on the wall, and vowed that she wouldn't touch it again until it was paid for. She wasn't sure she quite believed the odd little vendor, but then again... She wasn't so sure she should have taken the pan without knowing its exact price, either. She'd keep the whole thing from Jim, that's for sure.

The sky clouded over, and a cold wind blew through the cracks of the cabin. Constance donned a heavy sweater and went outside to bring in her wool and spinning wheel, and that's when she saw it, the ladle. The cracked ladle. The pan man had left it on the step. She grabbed it on her way into the house, and after storing the wool and stashing the wheel, she lit a lantern in the sudden dusk and inspected it.

It still made her feel wonderful when she held it. It was like holding something precious, yet invincible. She felt safe with it in the house. The fears of being alone fled.

And there was a crack. A little tiny, hairline crack from the handle down the cup.

Constance dipped it into the water. It held. It dripped a little bit, maybe, but it was a serviceable utensil.

And the price could not be high at all. Something very, very small. A stubbed toe, perhaps, if there even was a price.

Maybe he had thrown it away, and there would be no price.

At any rate, she was happy to have it, and hung it on the wall next to the loaf pan.

She stood back. She had begun a collection of cast iron cookware. Somehow, the cabin finally felt like home.

Jim came home without a deer. Constance tried to be glum about it in front of him, but baked a loaf of nutty wheat bread in her new pan to celebrate. The bread was cooked to perfection, evenly browned and wonderful. Constance thought it tasted better than her other bread, and even Jim commented on it.

And being a busy man, he never asked her about the new loaf pan or the ladle.

But the ladle bothered Constance. It just hung on the wall. She swore she would not use it until it had been paid for. She tried to believe that it was free, but her father had always taught her that nothing in life was free; everything must be paid for, so on its nail it hung, until she was certain that it was hers to keep.

A thousand times she looked at it, and a thousand times she resisted the impulse to touch it, to hold it, to run her hands over it. It was so gentle, it was somehow comforting. She wanted to ladle a hearty stew with it, stew made with her own garden vegetables, and the meat they either raised or hunted themselves. But she left it hanging on the nail.

Spring brought its own set of chores, and with summer came other problems. But the nights were mild and romantic, and as summer waned, Constance knew a growing in her belly.

The cabin felt different after that. Jim was as excited and as thoughtful of her well-being as she was. He began to whittle toys of a long summer evening. He talked to her tummy as if it was already a person, and the way it wiggled around inside, she guessed it really was a real person. How odd for Jim to know it before she did.

They went to town and stayed over until Sunday to go to church, and met two ladies who said they'd be pleased to come attend the birth. When her time came, Jim wouldn't have to ride far to fetch some help. They went to that church every Sunday as long as Constance was able, and when she felt she shouldn't ride any more, those women came up to visit with her and make sure everything was progressing right. Sometimes they would bring her a special tea, sometimes a jar of preserves.

But as the winter set in and the snow began to drift, Constance worried.

"I can do it, Constance," Jim kept reassuring her, and as her ninth month waned, the strange February warmth spread again across the Cascades, the snow melted, and one spring-like afternoon, Constance had Jim mount up and ride for the midwives.

She swept the cabin and put on a pot of stew. These things take time, she'd heard, and she sat down every time the baby pulled on her.

By the time Jim returned with the ladies, the stew was bubbling happily and the baby was close.

"Heat some water," someone told Jim, and it kept him busy, while the other hung a sheet from the ceiling to make a little private room for Constance and the baby.

Little Jimmy came into the world with a sploosh and a cry, and Constance reached down and picked up her beautiful, beautiful son. She opened her dress and let him nurse, while the ladies fussed over her bedding and the swaddling. Holding him gave her such a calm feeling, it was like holding something precious and invincible.

When everything had settled down, and the baby had fallen asleep, Constance was starving. She had Jim take down the curtain partition. "Offer the ladies some stew, Jim," she said.

He got the bowls down from the shelf.

She looked down at her son, at the hairline crack that ran through the side of his nose to his lip, parting it all the way through his tender little gums.

"You can use that ladle," Constance said. "It's paid for."

✳

Elixir

Having been born with defective cones in the retinas of his eyes, Simon could not tell what color the prostitute's garter belt was, only that it was one of those tear-away kinds. It gave a satisfying amount of resistance before the Velcro ripped apart and he held the bit of cloth in his hands. He unhooked her hose then pushed her breasts out of the top of her bra and suckled them.

She felt so good to him.

Her skin was young and tight, smooth and flawless.

He flipped her over onto her belly and brought her hips up to him and rubbed against her. He liked the way her loose breasts filled his hands.

"What's this?" he asked as his fingers found a lump on her ribcage, inches under her right breast.

"Nothing," she said, and she jerked from under his touch.

The last thing Simon needed was a lumpy prostitute. He felt his magnificent erection deflate. He turned her over and held her down with one hand. It was a definite lump.

"It's nothing," she whined, but he held her still to feel it. He'd gone to medical school for two years before they found out he was sub-normal, could only see black and white, and invited him to take up some other profession. The veterinary school had no problem with his disability, but he had never been able to quench his thirst for human anatomy and human medicine.

God, he wished he could have a normal life, normal sex with a normal girlfriend. No. Not him. He had to pay for his sex. Always had, always would. And what did it get him? Lumps.

He touched it and it hardened.

She bucked under him, trying to throw him off. "Leave it alone," she said.

He took a tighter grip on her, noticing with wry humor that his erection was coming back. He didn't know if it was the anomaly or the wrestling that did it. He held her still and palpated the lump. It grew and became hard.

"It's a nipple," he whispered, and his erection thrummed. He slid inside her, gratified by the little sigh that escaped her. Then he moved slowly, one hand fingering one fine, firm young breast, and one hand toying with the odd little nipple. Life was indeed grand.

He pushed her away and looked down on her in the dim light of his bedroom. Beads of sweat stood out on her upper lip. Strands of hair stuck to her forehead and temple. He didn't think he'd ever really aroused a woman before. Her nipples were hard—he turned her and looked—all three of them. He touched the one, the strange one, gave it a gentle squeeze and a drop of liquid appeared.

His erection grew to what felt twice its normal size.

He rubbed his penis on her leg and took the little nipple in his mouth. He sucked and drew in a tangy little taste. It tasted like… tasted like something fresh, something from his childhood. An experimental taste… He couldn't quite recall…

He sat up, savoring the flavor, trying to remember, trying to remember.

She touched his arm. He looked at her, at her young face, at her shimmering eyes. He looked at the geometric pattern in the sheets, and it looked different. He didn't recognize it. Everything was different. Everything seemed to be more sharply defined, as if he had suddenly discovered a new depth of perception.

Colors! He was seeing colors! He closed his eyes and rubbed them, thinking as he did so, that it was the logical cartoon thing for him to do, but when he opened his eyes again, the colors were still there.

Colors everywhere!

His erection gone, his lust forgotten, he leaped out of bed and turned on the light. He grabbed his bathrobe. It was absolutely beautiful. "What color is this?" he asked.

"Kind of a teal," she said.

"Teal," he repeated. He picked up a book. "And this?"

"Red," she began to smile.

"And this?"

"Brown."

"This?"

"Green."

"Is this green, too?"

She nodded.

"And this?"

"That has more yellow in it."

"Yellow?"

She looked around, saw a shirt hanging on the hook in his open closet. "Yellow," she said and pointed.

"Yellow," he said with reverence, and he went over and took the shirt out of the closet. It was the most beautiful thing he had ever seen. He put it on and then went into the bathroom. He turned on the light. "Ha!" he shouted. "My eyes are green. My bathroom is blue. My towels are..." he brought them into the room.

"Orange," she said.

"Orange! Ha!" He went around the room, touching things he'd seen thousands of time before, but always in black and white. He'd never known color before, never. He was overwhelmed with the profusion of colors, with the subtleties. He looked at the oiled wood in an oak barstool for a full five minutes. He opened all the cabinets and was shocked with the colors on the packages. The pictures, the paintings on his walls...

Eventually, he remembered the girl in the other room. He went back to her. She was sitting up, smoking a cigarette. Her bra and the discarded garter belt were both red. She smiled at him. "I can't believe this," he said. "I've never seen color before. Never. It's uncanny. Suddenly, I can see! I can see!"

She smiled, a slow, amazed smile. "So," she said, taking a long pull on her smoke. "You're the one."

"The one?"

"The one my mama told me about." She shook her head, stubbed out the cigarette. "Amazing. Fucking amazing."

Simon looked at her, but he had no patience for her. "I don't know what you're talking about," he said.

"Doesn't matter." She put on her garter belt, pulled her flagging stockings back up and fastened them. "I'll leave you to your colors." She slipped into her dress, then held out her hand. "Twenty."

He fumbled for his pants, then fumbled some more in his pockets. He pulled out two bills and looked at them. "They're beautiful," he said.

"Yeah," she said, then took them from him. She opened her purse, stuffed the money inside, then took her lipstick out. "Do ya like red?"

"Yes," he said.

"Good." She wrote her phone number on his mirror.

Simon couldn't believe the diversity of nature. He almost wrecked his car (white with tan interior) driving to work. The world was so green. He marveled at his receptionist (redhead with dark green eyeshadow and pink lipstick), at his waiting room (green walls, green floor, green plants, green draperies, brown chairs), at the colors of the drugs and their labels that he'd seen every day for years upon years. But most of all, he was stunned by the colors of the animals that came through his door.

The first patient was a yellow and black and white cat with the deepest yellowish-green eyes he'd ever seen. He couldn't stop gushing about how beautiful the cat was. At first the owner was pleased, but as Simon kept petting the cat, staring into its eyes, the owner began to shield her pet from him. Finally she picked up the cat and held her protectively. Simon looked up and the woman regarded him with suspicion.

Simon realized he better be careful.

The next was a Weimaraner. He couldn't figure out what color it was. When the owner left with her dog, he called the receptionist in and asked her what color that dog had been. "Sort of liver colored, I guess," she said, and suddenly Simon couldn't wait to do surgery to see what colors lay inside the critters.

Oddly enough, the rich red color of the blood at the first pressure of the scalpel made his stomach turn. He had never been squeamish before, but then he had never seen the color of blood before.

He was astonished at the colors inside the dog he was spaying. He loved it. He wanted to poke about in there all day, he wanted to open her up wide and look at the lungs, at the heart, at the brain.

Self-restraint came hard. But he made his way through the day.

What a marvelous day.

It wasn't until almost a week later that he took the time to wonder why he could suddenly see colors. It took him almost a week to begin to take the new sight for granted, to have the time to wonder about such things.

It took a week. About as long as his new sight lasted.

At first he noticed that the blood had turned gray.

And then he noticed that all the cats were gray.

And then he noticed that his yellow shirt was gray.

He began to hyperventilate, and had to go for a walk. By the time he got back, the whole world was gray again.

He bought a bottle of wine on the way home to keep him company. Black and white company. It was all that he deserved.

He poured a glass of the gray liquid and sat in his gray chair in his gray living room and drank. He could see the bedroom mirror through the door. He could see her phone number, written in black, on his mirror.

He drank until he couldn't stomach any more, then lay down on his bed and fell into a restless sleep.

He dreamed in color. Fabulous technicolor images swept through his psyche for hours. He saw himself in his dream, gaping at the kaleidoscopic images.

When he awoke, he tasted it. Her elixir. He needed more.

Agitated, he called his receptionist and had her cancel his appointments for the day. He needed to think. He needed to plan.

He paced the room, the hooker's phone number burned into his deformed retinas. He needed to call her. He needed her.

He hated needing her. He felt like a junkie.

She could use him. She had something he wanted, something he needed, and she could blackmail him, she could use that against him. There was no telling what price an unscrupulous prostitute would put on such a personal, rare drug.

He would pay it, whatever it was.

Or would he? Was there a limit? After all, he had lived for almost forty years without seeing colors, and now, after one week, he was ready to sell his soul to have color sight?

It didn't make sense.

Of course it made sense. He wanted it simply because it was glorious to have, and because for the first time he felt equal with everybody else. He felt normal. He knew that nobody could tell by looking at him that he was different, but he *felt* different. He knew. He could tell. And when he had proper sight, he didn't feel inferior any more. He'd always lived feeling lower, slimier, less worthy. It took nothing for Simon to tell himself over and over what a worm he was, and believe it.

But that was stupid. He might *feel* inferior, but he *wasn't* inferior.

He had to have his color sight back. It was the one thing, the *one* thing that made him normal. Absolutely normal. Above ground and on a par with everybody else.

He picked up the phone. And then put it back. He had to have a plan first. He had to know exactly how much he would pay.

He paced into the night, growing ever more agitated.

He called the office and left a message on the service for the receptionist to cancel his appointments for the next day, too.

Then he sat down and let reality flow over him. The idea that he'd had in the back of his mind, that one idea, that bad idea he hadn't let come forth. It now cloaked his mind like a mildewed blanket.

He wouldn't pay anything for her. He would have her, hold her, keep her. He would be in control of this situation. He was tired of being on the ends of everybody else's strings. First his parents, and then the idiots at the medical school. Then his veterinary professors. Then his clients. It was as if he had no guts.

But now *he* would be in control. For once.

His penis pushed against his pants as it began to swell. He went to the clinic to gather up a few things he needed.

Then he called her.

No sooner had she walked in the door, then he had her on the floor, ripping at her clothes. As he was doing it, he wondered at his behavior, this was so unlike him, but he was so eager, so anxious, so desperate...

And she liked it. She liked it a lot.

Ahhh. The fluid coated his tongue like oil, and when he finished revelling in its odd flavor, he opened his eyes to spectacular color.

He grabbed her hand and pulled her along to the bedroom.When he was finished, they lay together, she smoking a cigarette, he trying to memorize the nuance of every color, shade, hue and tone within eyeshot.

"What's your name?" he asked.

"Alexandria."

"Will you marry me?"

She snorted and got up off the bed, gathering her clothes.

He lay calmly, watching her dress. She frowned at him, and showed him the torn seam in her blouse. He'd ripped the button off her skirt, too, and broken its zipper.

She walked over to his side of the bed and stood looking down at him, her long, smooth legs within reach. He reached. She backed away. "Twenty," she said, "plus another twenty for the clothes."

"Marry me, Alexandria."

"No way."

"Please?"

"Why?"

"I have to have you."

"You know my number."

"That's not good enough," he said.

"Tough. Give me my money."

"I'm begging you."

"Simon," she said, her eyes earnest. "Your color sight doesn't come from me."

He opened the headboard and withdrew a syringe. Before she could react, he grabbed her and shoved the needle deep into her butt. He pushed the plunger and a full dose of animal tranquilizer entered her bloodstream. She stumbled from him, and made it through the living room to the door.

He caught her before she fell, and carried her back to the bedroom.

He spent an hour removing her clothes. He looked at all the colors in her faded denim mini-skirt, inside and out. He investigated all the details of her panties, her blouse, her underwire bra. He inspected her from pink-polished toenails, up through bronzed legs, to reddish-blonde pubic hair, across tan lines to her lovely breasts, the freckles across her chest that matched the ones on her nose, the remnants of red lipstick, and her hair, reddish blonde, like down below. She was long and lean, and he liked her lines.

He touched a nipple and it shrank like the sea anenomes he'd seen at the aquarium. He touched the other one. It did the same. Then he touched the little strange one, and it too, acted like the others.

He squeezed it, but no fluid came out. He suckled it, but got nothing. He covered her with a blanket and waited for her to waken.

She slept for two days.

He monitored her vital signs with growing dread. After the first day he was certain he had killed her—induced an irreversible coma. You jerk, he said to himself. You low life. You *worm*.

Eventually, she moaned, and turned over, and her eyelids fluttered.

He was so grateful, he cried.

He dressed her in his bathrobe and made her some soup. After she had eaten, and her headache had subsided somewhat, he got her up and walked her around the apartment until she felt better. He apologized over and over, but she seemed to have no memory of why she was still there.

He seized upon the opportunity and convinced her that she had merely fallen ill, and he had nursed her back to health.

"How long have I been here?"

"Two days."

"Two days! I have to call my mother."

He handed her the phone. She dialed with pale fingers.

"Hi, Mom, it's Alexandria. I'll call back later." She hung up. "Machine," she said.

She's reasonable, Simon thought. Surely I can reason with her. "Alexandria," he said. "We need to talk."

"About what?" She was looking better by the moment.

"I need you. I want to have you with me. All the time."

"You mean like live together?"

"Yes."

"I don't think so."

"Why not?"

"I don't even know you."

He got off the bed, onto his knees and took her hands in his. "Listen. It's through you that I've found life. I've become whole. Without you, I'm nothing. I *need* you. I've got to have you."

She pulled his bathrobe tighter around her. "You're scaring me," she said. "I think I better go home."

"No. Please don't. Please stay with me. I beg you."

She got up to leave and he hit her with the needle again. This time, the dosage was right.

When she became unconscious enough, he rigged up an IV, dripping an ever-so-slight mixture, just enough to keep her subdued. He strapped her to the bed, and when she was secure, he showered, shaved and went to work.

When he returned home, she was in much the same state. He stood looking at her half-lidded eyes, and the pulsing began again in his loins. His dreams of being a doctor flew through his mind. With her, he could be a doctor. He could go back to medical school. Then he would be more than equal. Then, maybe, he would even be a little bit superior for a change.

He walked over to her, and saw the dark circles under her eyes. He saw the gumminess at the corners of her mouth. The nipple stayed dry.

Over the next few days, he kept her in a catatonic state, but the reality was this: Alexandria's elixir was a product of her arousal, and as long as she was sedated, she would secrete no milk of the gods for him.

Defeated, watching the colors slide into shaded halftones, he took the IV out of her arm, put a bandage over the bruise. He felt even lower now that his last-chance experiment had failed. How long would he have kept her there? Weeks? Months? Years? What had he been thinking? His actions were criminal, monstrous. He was a slimeball. He should be shot. At the very least, he didn't deserve her. Didn't deserve her youth, her body, her devotion, her... her elixir.

He untied her and lay down next to her. She put an arm around him, a heavy, unwieldy arm, and he held her close, crying into her hair, ashamed to the very roots of his soul at what he'd done, at the way he'd behaved.

But his self-recriminations hadn't diminished his excitement, and as soon as she began to respond, he was out of his pants and into her, his hand toying with that odd little nipple. With her half-conscious arousal, it oozed and oozed, and Simon lapped it up like a puppy.

Once a week. That's all she would agree to.

Every Monday night at eight o'clock. Every Monday night he waited for her, fear keeping his bowels in a clutch. What if she'd been killed during the previous week? Found somebody to love and moved to Memphis or something?

But every Monday night at eight o'clock, she showed up.

She squealed as he grabbed her in a bear hug and whirled her to the bedroom, where he would tease her until that sweet little gland began to overflow, and then he'd make love to her. He would beg her to marry him and she would laugh him off.

One Monday night he begged her to have his child, and that got a different kind of a laugh. She dressed and left, and Simon lay on his new, wildly colorful bedspread, and thought about that. She could be convinced to have his child, he realized. Then they would be bonded together forever. He went to work on it.

The following week, they lay together on his bed after having some of the best sex of Simon's life. She was smoking, staring at the ceiling; he was toying with her delicate ear.

"Make you a deal," she said.

"Hmmm?"

"I'll have this baby for you on one condition."

He waited.

"If it has the gift, you must give it up and let my mother and me raise it."

"The gift?"

"You know," she said, and he knew what she meant. She meant the nipple. The elixir. The breast from heaven.

This was something he hadn't considered. What if the baby did have it? Wouldn't that be a perfect, loyal, lifetime source?

You pervert, he thought. You snake. You would suck your own child's breast? He was disgusted with himself, especially since he knew he could.

"You would live with me throughout your pregnancy?"

"I could."

"And after?"

"We'd have to see."

"And if the baby didn't have the gift?"

"We'd have to see."

"Okay," he said simply, and the deal was struck.

She moved in the next day. Simon came home from work and found her waiting for him in his bedroom. She grabbed him by the tie and pulled him to the bed. Her hungry mouth moved over his while her hands deftly unbuckled his belt, unzipped his pants and pulled them to his knees.

With a ferocity he'd never seen in her, she threw him onto the bed and straddled him, lowering herself slowly, carefully, hotly, deliciously down onto him.

He closed his eyes. This was too good.

He looked up at her, and her eyes were closed. She was concentrating. A drop of clear fluid sparkled on the tip of her third nipple, beckoning him, tantalizing him. He touched it, then licked his finger. Oh, God, this was good.

She began to move, her inner muscles fluttering, and then it felt as if her womb extended its lips and sucked the semen from him as through a straw. He came so hard, so fast, there was no time to relish the feeling. In one long agonizing spurt, he was finished.

She put both hands on her belly and smiled a quiet, secretive smile. She nodded. "Done," she whispered, and rolled off him, falling into a deep sleep with one leg still thrown over his wrinkling pants.

The next day, the supernumerary nipple dried up and became little more than a little discolored lump on her rib cage.

Alexandria was pregnant.

He went to work and when he came home there was usually a homecooked meal waiting for him. She seemed to enjoy playing house as much as he did, until his color sight faded back to black and white. Then he grew irritable and grumpy.

She blossomed and grew round and plump, rosy and giggly.

He glared at her.

She laughed at him.

He counted the days. They proceeded with infuriating slowness. Nine months of black and white. After having color sight for so long he felt seriously handicapped. And bitter. Totally and absolutely inferior. Useless. Worthless.

She used that. She spent all his money on baby things. She seemed to favor pink, referred to the baby as "she," and when he questioned her about it, she said that her mother had pronounced the child "the one."

"The one?"

"Perfection," she said.

A girl. That news was the only encouraging thing in his life, since he had no intention of giving any girl child of his to this prostitute and her weird mother.

Early one morning, after a restless night, when Alexandria's belly was hard, swollen and veined, a knock came on the apartment door. Simon wrapped his bathrobe around himself and opened the door.

A hawkish little woman brushed past him, throwing her damp coat and wet umbrella onto his new red and yellow sofa that had been gray to him since the day it was delivered.

"Excuse me," he said.

"Make tea," she said to him, and walked directly into the bedroom.

He followed her in.

"Mama," Alexandria said, then frowned as a contraction worked its way through her.

"Your mother?" Simon said. It was inconceivable that this lovely, soft creature could be the product of this hardened, wrinkled, gray thing with rodent teeth and glittering eyes.

"Tea," she said again, then crossed her arms until Simon left the room.

He brought back three cups of herbal tea on a tray as another, harder contraction pulled on Alexandria.

"Want me to call the doctor? Should we be getting to a hospital?"

"No doctor," the woman said. "No hospital. We'll take care of this right here." She looked at her watch. "And soon." She pulled a bottle from her bag and poured some thick black liquid into Alexandria's tea. "Drink up, Alexandria." She turned back to Simon. "Leave."

"Leave? No way. This is my child, and I'll be here for her birth."

"This is not your child, you ninny. This is *our* child. Get out of here."

Alexandria gasped and clutched with pain.

Simon's stomach seized. He hated to see anyone in pain, especially Alexandria.

"I have pain medication," he said. "Alexandria, do you want something for the pain?"

"Nothing," the woman said.

"I'm asking *Alexandria*," Simon said, feeling a test of wills boiling up, and feeling equal to the task. He'd throw this old woman right through the window if he had to, and he'd take Alexandria to the hospital.

The woman stood up and faced Simon. "I'm telling you that we know better than you do how to handle this. She can have nothing for pain. Now leave this room."

"And *I'm* telling *you* that this is *my* house and *my* child and if you aren't a little more reasonable and considerate, *I* will ask *you* to leave."

She stared at him.

"I'll call the authorities," he said.

"You don't know what you do," she said. "You don't know what you do."

"I've had medical training."

"You see yourself as unworthy," the woman said. "Therefore you are. You endanger this child."

Alexandria wailed.

The woman whipped up the sheets and Simon saw the baby's head crown between Alexandria's legs.

"Get towels," the old woman hissed. "Lots of towels."

"Mama…"

"It's coming," her mother said, and pushed Simon toward the door.

He came back just as the baby's head came out. Its little cheeks were fat and full, but dark colored. Very dark.

"One more," the old woman said, and with a heartwrenching grunt from Alexandria, her mother pulled the baby out by the arm. "A girl," she said.

Simon dropped the towels on the floor. "Does she have it?" he asked.

"She's not breathing," the mother said, then held the baby up by one foot.

"Make her breathe, Mama," Alexandria begged.

"Does she have it?" Simon asked. "Let me see."

"*Get out of here*," the mother said, as she put two fingers in the baby's mouth and wiped out something thick. She whacked the child on the butt, but there was no response.

"Let me see," Simon said, he was too eager, too anxious, he couldn't stand it.

The mother put her mouth over the child's and sucked, then blew in little puffs. She listened to the chest, but there was sadness in her eyes. "There is no life," she said, and straightened up, looking far older than she had when she walked in.

Alexandria sat up, wailing, reaching for the dead baby that was still connected to her by its umbilical.

Simon picked up the warm, slippery little thing. Under its right nipple was another nipple, tiny but erect, and what looked like a tiny breast beneath it. He pushed on it gently with his thumb. Liquid.

He kissed the child on the forehead, on one fat little cheek, and then he put his lips to the nipple and sucked.

"No!" the mother yelled.

"No!" Alexandria screamed.

But with a little pop, it opened, and a bitter liquid gushed into his mouth and down his throat. He swallowed before he could react. It must have looked like black pus, he thought, as he winced and spit and thrust the cooling child at its mother.

Both Alexandria and the woman watched him.

He wiped his tongue on one of the towels, but the taste was oily and wouldn't go away.

The mother slapped her moist, smelly palm against his eyes. "*As thou seeist thyself*," she hissed at him.

"Worm," Alexandria whispered.

Simon knew he was beneath contempt, and his sight faded, faded, faded.

The next time Simon awoke, he didn't know if it was day or night. His house was absolutely silent.

He felt his eyelids. His eyes were open, but he saw nothing. He stared into nothing and wondered what had happened. He must have passed out.

Then he noticed a flickering movement out of the corner of his right eye. He sat up in bed and turned his head to the right. Something slipped past his vision. Something white?

Something in the house?

Heart pounding, he lay awake, unseeing eyes open wide, afraid, wondering.

And then he saw something right directly in front of him. It wasn't completely dark. He wasn't totally blind. He tried to focus on it, but it was too close, it was too close. He waved his hands in front of his face; nothing there, *he was still in his bed, but what was he seeing?*

He buried the back of his head in his pillow, then threw the pillow on the floor, but that didn't seem to help. He was still too close. It wouldn't focus.

Then, with a force of will, he kind of moved backwards in his mind, and the object retreated.

Black shiny tunnel wall. Moist. Damp. Close. Earth. He could smell it. He could taste it.

What the—?

And then, as a white grub dragged a bit of a green leaf past him and the root he was hiding behind, he knew. He knew that his life had been colorless before Alexandria, and that he deserved this new sight. He had acted abysmally, sinfully, beyond all respectable behavior, but he wished she had just blinded him instead.

"As thou seeist thyself," the old woman had said. He was a worm, always had been, always would be, and he knew exactly what that leaf tasted like. Tangy. Fresh. Like Alexandria's elixir.

✴

Ramona

"So, there you have it," Ramona Wilson said as she scooped the Tarot cards up and carefully molded them back into a deck. Bonnie sipped her coffee and tapped her nails on the Formica table.

"More coffee, ladies?" the waitress asked.

Ramona checked her watch. "Thanks, no, I've got to be going."

"Wait," Bonnie said. "You can't go now. You haven't told me whether to move to New Mexico or not."

Ramona laughed. "I'm not going to tell you anything of the sort. Anyway, it's our fourth anniversary, and I'm making lasagna for Daniel."

"But what about the cards? Aren't they going to tell me whether to move?"

"I'm not a psychic, Bonnie," Ramona said, wrapping the cards in a purple silk scarf. She slipped them into her purse. "I bought a deck of Tarot cards and a book and learned how to read them. My advice is worth exactly what you are paying for it." She looked at the ticket the waitress had set on the table. "A dollar twenty." She laughed. "If it were me, I'd use something else to base my decision on."

"But you must have *some* kind of faith in the cards."

Bonnie was looking desperate. Ramona had seen that look before. She wouldn't pull the cards out of her purse for Bonnie again. Reading the cards was a fun thing to do, and surprisingly accurate, but some people took it too seriously.

"They're just cards, Bonnie. Your life is *your* life. Don't give it over to some pieces of colored cardboard. Make your own decisions."

"But—"

"The cards said some change is on its way. The cards said that your stability was about to be shaken a little bit. But that's pretty general. What you do with that information is up to you. Your *life* is up to you."

"Could I ask just one more—"

Ramona put her hand over her friend's hand. "I've got to go, sweetie. Another time, okay?"

"Yeah, okay." Bonnie fished in her wallet for money, and when she looked up, Ramona saw tears in her eyes. "I just don't know what to do," she said, and a fat tear fell off her eyelid and landed on the table.

Ramona had no words for her.

Bonnie put three bills on the table and slid out of the booth, slinging her purse over her shoulder.

"You'll do the right thing," Ramona said.

"Yeah, sure," Bonnie snapped. "I've made one bad move after another and am about to make another. My whole life is a mess, but suddenly, I'm about to do the right thing. Maybe I'll throw myself off a cliff. That might be the first right thing I've done my whole life."

Outside the coffee shop, Ramona gave her friend a hug, but Bonnie wasn't returning it.

They parted with vague promises to meet again, and Ramona got into her Volvo. She sat for a minute with the air conditioner on and the windows open and adjusted her sunglasses in the hot California sun. She thought she better be very careful, or this Tarot business would start costing friendships.

Then the sun darkened and all sound went away. Ramona peered into the windshield, but what she saw was the interior of the nuclear lab control room.

She saw Daniel, his lab coat. She could even read his name tag, DR. WILSON.

Daniel saw something alarming on the control board. He double checked it, then worry wrinkling his brow, he slapped a red button. Someone wearing a yellow lab coat came over to him, and they spoke. Daniel's face turned red. He shouted something. His coffee cup, the cup Ramona had given him for Valentine's Day, began to tremble and slide across the table. Then the room started to shake. Technicians ran around, then they stopped, stunning realization stamped on their faces. One man crossed himself. Daniel looked straight ahead, said something softly. Then the control room wall blasted inward with fire and glass and silent fury.

Sounds, the loud, noisy sounds of a normal day in the mall parking lot returned to Ramona as if plugs had been pulled abruptly from her ears. Her grip on the steering wheel almost crippled her hands. Cords and tendons stood out on her forearms. She jumped out of the car, perspiration running down the side of her face, and she looked in the direction of the nuclear lab, afraid of what she might see—a mushroom cloud or something. Smoke. Anything.

The sky was clear and peaceful.

She looked around. People inside the restaurant were eating and talking, people were getting into and out of their cars as if nothing had happened. Ramona's legs turned rubbery, and she held on to the open car door to keep from falling.

She had wished for psychic powers since she had been a little girl. She had watched psychics on talk shows, had read everything she could about their abilities, had practiced fruitlessly, and had envied those who had premonitions or visions or anything that smacked of a sixth sense. But she, herself, had never had a true psychic experience.

Until now, if that was what it had been. There was no other explanation for what she had seen. If the lab hadn't exploded as she watched it, then it soon would, she knew it.

She looked again toward the north, but there was no smoke. No explosion.

With trembling hands, she pulled her cell phone from her purse and dialed the lab.

"Mission Laboratories," the receptionist answered.

"Dr. Daniel Wilson, please."

"One moment."

"Hello?" He sounded normal.

"Hi, honey," she said, still gulping air, still breathless.

"Hi."

Ramona felt awkward, and wasn't sure exactly what to say. "What time are you coming home?"

"The usual time," he said. "Why?"

Ramona was afraid she would cry. She didn't want to cry on the telephone. "I don't know," she said, "I just wanted to hear your voice."

"I'm busy, Ramona," he said evenly. She knew he was irritated. He didn't like her calling him at work.

"I know, I'm sorry. I'll see you at home. I'll have dinner ready."

"Okay. Bye."

"Love you," she said.

"Me too."

Ramona hung up the phone and wiped the tears from her cheeks with the palm of her hand. "Get a grip," she told herself, and started the car. It appeared to be a normal day.

She felt anything but normal. But she turned on some music, and she drove herself home, trying desperately to put out of her mind the look in Daniel's eyes just before the wall exploded.

The service had cleaned the house while Ramona shopped and then had coffee with Bonnie, so the house smelled good, the kitchen was spotless and there were fresh flowers in the dining room. Ramona changed clothes and then started making lasagna, Daniel's favorite. She worked in a frenzied heat, cutting off a fingernail with the paring knife and not even realizing it. It could have been the end of her finger. She slowed down, but her insides were jittery and her hands unsteady. When the pan was finally in the oven, she began to wrap the engraved money clip she had bought for an anniversary present, but as she pulled the wrapping paper from the drawer, she had a better idea.

She'd take him away. A vacation.

If there was going to be an accident at the lab, she wanted Daniel to be as far away from there as possible.

She checked the oven, then jumped into the car, ran to the mall and bought him a blue Patagonia jacket. It was perfect. The blue would match his eyes and he would look Nordic and handsome with his graying blonde hair. He'd love it. They'd go away—hiking in the mountains. Maybe there was still enough snow that they could go skiing. He *couldn't* object; it had been way too long since he had taken any vacation time, and they hadn't gone away together for more than an overnight since their honeymoon four years ago. It was time. Now. She had been warned for a good purpose. She had to act. She couldn't just let it happen.

On the way back to the car, she popped into the travel agency and scanned the rack of brochures. She picked up a half dozen—two from Colorado, two from Canada and two from Hawaii, just in case the way to his heart might be tropical instead of alpine.

She rushed back to the house, wrapped the jacket, put away the money clip for another time, checked the lasagna, then set the table, including candles, opened the wine and changed into a new dress. She spritzed on some perfume, touched up her makeup and piled her long, black hair on top of her head. The seduction of her life was about to take place. She had to convince him to go away with her, and she had to convince him to go away *now*.

She sat heavily on the end of the bed.

His life depended upon it.

Her chest felt heavy and tears welled up in her eyes. She pushed them down, checked her watch. He was late. She got up and went to the nightstand phone. She dialed the switchboard of the lab.

"Mission laboratories," the receptionist answered.

Ramona hung up. It hadn't happened yet.

Somehow she had known that. She knew that she had been given time. She didn't know how much time, but she knew she was given the opportunity to get Daniel out of there alive.

He must be very important. He must have important work ahead of him. And he did. They hadn't even started their family yet. That might even be the reason he was being spared. Perhaps their son would grow up to be some kind of pivotal personality in the fate of the planet.

Relax, she said to herself, went down to the kitchen, poured herself a glass of wine from the corked bottle in the fridge and sat on the edge of the couch, nervously waiting. She shuffled through the travel brochures, but didn't find them as interesting as she would when he came home. She tapped her feet, she picked at the cuticles on her manicured fingernails, rehearsed her plea. She drank the wine and went back for more.

With the second glass, she did calm down, and began to make a case for each of the brochure locations she had chosen so haphazardly. When she heard the electric garage door open, she closed her eyes, breathed a "thank you" prayer and poured him a glass of wine.

He came in looking gray and tired. He kissed her cheek almost absent-mindedly, accepted the glass of wine, put a professionally-wrapped package on the kitchen counter and went upstairs.

He'd stopped on the way home to get her a gift. That's why he was late. She put his gift with hers on the table, lit the candles and dressed the salad.

A few minutes later, he came down looking refreshed after a shower and a change into a sport shirt and jeans. This time he grabbed her and pulled her close for a long, enthusiastic hug, kiss and little dance around the kitchen.

"Mmmm, smells good," he said. "Feels good, too."

She laughed and pushed him away. He leaned against the counter and watched her move around the kitchen.

Her family and friends warned her not to marry an older man, but they had no idea. Daniel was the best of the breed, and she thanked God every day that he had chosen her. He was smart, funny, spiritual, emotionally and physically fit, and she would walk through fire for him any day of the week. He was fifty and she was thirty, so they were both verging on the far edge of starting a family, but they were still going to do it. They were going to start late this summer, she had decided, so they'd have an Aries baby.

If Ramona could help divert the disaster at the lab.

"How was your day?" she asked.

"Hard. Long. Having some personnel problems. And I'm under a deadline to complete a project. It's way behind, and I'm doing quite a dance to keep the bigwigs off my neck. They're saying that funding is on the line, and this guy, the maintenance head is such a flake—" He interrupted himself to help her bring the heavy lasagna pan out of the oven. "Damn, that looks good."

She put it on top of the stove, turned off the oven, shed the mitts and brought the salad bowl to the table. "Come," she said, and he followed her to the table, said grace, and they began to eat.

Ramona found she had little appetite. She ate most of her salad, then dished up the lasagna, but she wasn't much for either conversation or food. She was eager to get to the point, and it was difficult for her to wait.

Finally, it was time. Dishes done, wine glasses replenished, they sat on the sofa and Daniel handed her his little package. She kissed him, and opened an exquisite pair of diamond earrings. She immediately put them on, felt their delicate dangle on her lobes. She'd always dreamed of a man who bought her diamonds.

"Mine next," she said, then handed him the package and moved to the other side of the sofa. This was too important to be nuzzled into insignificance. This was life or death.

He opened it, exclaimed pleasure, and pulled it on over his shirt. It looked to Ramona exactly as she had imagined. It made the blue in his eyes sparkle, the blonde in his hair look even blonder. He looked like a ski god. "I love it," he said, brushing his hands over his chest.

"It comes with these," she said, then pulled the brochures out from under the throw pillow. She fanned them out and handed them to him. "Or anywhere else you want to go."

"Really?" he seemed pleased.

"But we have to go soon," she said. "Right away. Tomorrow."

He smiled indulgently at her, and she was ready for that. That's why she'd moved to the other end of the sofa. "I mean it, Daniel."

"What's up?" His smile turned to one of concern.

"You haven't taken a vacation since our honeymoon. And it's time. We need to go away together. You need to get out of here."

"You're right," he said, hands open in surrender. "Okay, we'll go."

"Really?"

"Sure. Soon as this project is finished. Maybe a month. I can put in for the time off tomorrow."

"No," she said firmly. "That's too long. I want us to go away now. Right now." Her carefully constructed composure began to melt, and she felt her lips pull back in that awful crying grimace.

He threw boxes and wrappings on the floor, slid to her end of the sofa and brought her to him. He hugged her and held her as she sobbed her heart out. "What is it, darling?" he asked, pulling the pins out of her hair and stroking it as it fell around her shoulders. "Tell me." He rocked her and she sobbed into his fuzzy new jacket until the emotional storm passed, but her fear had not. He settled her, but she clung to him, and he took her upstairs, undressed her gently, kissed away her tears and made love to her while wearing his new blue jacket, and she wore only her diamond earrings.

The next morning, Ramona felt emotionally hungover, and a little foolish as well. She got up with Daniel and fixed him breakfast, but as soon as he left the house, she began to worry again.

By mid-morning, the worry had turned into panic. She began dialing the lab's switchboard and hanging up as soon as the operator answered. She began to time herself so she would do that only every half hour. Between calls, she paced while chewing on her newly manicured nails. She listened to the radio for news reports of an accident at the lab. Her stomach churned.

Just before noon, Ramona realized she was going to drive herself insane if she didn't do something else. Instead of sitting around and waiting for it to happen, she decided to take another pro-active approach.

She showered, dressed and went to the travel agency. After perusing the brochure stand and then talking nervously with the travel agent, she settled on tickets to Colorado. They'd leave in the morning and take a two-week trip into the Rockies. She fumbled out her American Express card, the agent ran the tickets, gave her some phone numbers for hiking guides and outfitters in the area, and Ramona walked back into the surrealistically bright sunshine.

Then she went back home and fretted. It was the longest day of her life. She prayed, she cried, and listened to the radio, she shuffled brochures. She threw away her Tarot cards, retrieved them from the garbage under the sink, cut them up into little pieces and threw the mess into the garbage can outside. She resisted calling the lab, she tried to lie down and sleep, but images of that vision or premonition or whatever she'd had kept haunting her.

When Daniel came home, she realized she hadn't given a single thought to dinner, but that was only a passing thought, because before he had put his briefcase down, she was next to him, begging him, pleading with him.

"I'm afraid for our marriage," she heard herself say.

He looked at her in surprise, and in desperation, she tried everything she knew. "I feel like I'm about to have a breakdown. I need us to go away together, Daniel. Look." She showed him the tickets on the kitchen counter. "Hiking in the Rockies. We leave tomorrow. Please, Daniel. Please." She started to cry again, and clung to him.

He gripped her arms gently but firmly and sat her down on the couch. She tried to lean into him, but he wouldn't have it. He straightened her up and instead of comforting her, he confronted her.

"What's this all about?" he asked. "The first I heard of this idea of going away was yesterday and now you're a wreck over it. What's behind this, Ramona?"

She didn't want to tell him. "It's been four years," she said unevenly.

"I know that. And I said that I'd schedule some time. In about six weeks. In four, maybe six weeks, the project will be finished, and I'll be free to take some time off."

"I can't wait that long. We have to go now."

"You're being unreasonable."

"We have to go now," she had nothing else to say.

"Then you go."

"No! You have to come with me." Ramona felt her eyes fill up with tears again. She didn't want to cry and be hysterical with him, she wanted to be rational. He's a scientist. He responds to reason. But at the moment, rational thought was beyond her. Way beyond her.

He stood up and took off his suit coat, then sat back down and pulled her to him. "I think *you* need a vacation, Ramona," he said. "You go to the mountains and I'll join you if I can."

She sat up and wiped at the moisture on her cheeks. "You never take me seriously," she said.

"How can I when you act so impulsively? I have a job. I have responsibilities."

"I don't, and that's the problem as you see it."

Daniel didn't respond, and Ramona knew she was right. He looked at her as being young, as being emotional, irrational and irresponsible. And, she had to admit, that was precisely how she was acting. But it was the same old argument. There was a problem with marrying a man twenty years older, she realized. She'd seen glimmers of it off and on, and they'd had the same old argument in different clothes now for the entire four years of their marriage. *He* was the important one; in his eyes, she just lay around reading magazines all day.

Ramona was tired. Daniel was immovable.

And maybe he was right. Maybe she *did* need a vacation. Maybe she *was* out of control. Maybe that vision thing *was* all in her mind.

In the morning, she packed a suitcase for each of them, got their backpacking gear from the basement, and put everything into the trunk of Daniel's BMW. Feeling refreshed and sure again that this was the only way to go, she lay his airline ticket over the top of his coffee cup. "Daniel," she said. "Be spontaneous. Come with me."

He smiled indulgently at her, and she hated that attitude of his. "You'll feel better after getting out of town for a while," he said.

They drove to the airport in silence, then left his suitcase and backpack in the trunk while they checked hers through. At the gate, she held up both tickets and smiled invitingly.

He plucked one and said, "I'll turn this in for credit on the Amex card."

That did it. She grabbed the front of his coat and pulled him off to the side. It was time to get serious. Everything was on the line, now, everything. She was surprised it took getting to the airport gate to motivate her to be honest and direct. She backed him into a corner by the telephones. "Listen," she said, "I know you don't believe in psychic phenomena, and I'm not sure I believe in it either. But I've got to tell you, Daniel, I've had a psychic experience. A premonition. A real one, Daniel, and it's about an accident at the lab."

That tiny indulgent smile threatened the corner of his mouth again and she slammed her hands against his chest.

"Don't scoff at me," she said. "You wanted to know what's behind this sudden panic attack to get you out of town? I've seen the lab blow up, Daniel, and you were there."

"You know how I feel about that kind of psychic stuff."

"That's why I haven't told you before now. Listen to me." She pulled up close to him, those damned tears about to turn her womanish and foolish again. *"There's going to be an accident.* Please come with me." She knew she had lost him as soon as she began to cry.

"Our safety security is the best, Ramona. There isn't going to be any accident. But I understand. Listen, this is a common thing among the wives of nuclear scientists. It's called stress. Come on, they're boarding your flight. You go to the mountains, and I'll try to join you for the weekend or something, okay? We'll have a second honeymoon up in some cabin."

"Our marriage depends upon this, Daniel. Your *life* depends on this…"

"Go have a good rest. Have some fun." He kissed her on the forehead, making her feel even more like a little girl, then he walked her out to the gate. The attendant took her ticket and she looked back with one last pleading look, but Daniel, looking gorgeous and professional, just blew her a kiss and waved.

On the airplane, she ordered a cocktail, and when she opened her wallet, Daniel's photograph was the first thing she saw. She looked at it, and remembered his face as it was in her vision—angry, afraid, then peaceful, and she saw his mouth move and realized that he was saying, "Ramona."

She jerked back with the memory, her knee upsetting the tray table, and the little cup of ice went flying into the aisle.

"I'm sorry," Ramona said to the flight attendant. She tried to talk, but the sob was stuck in her throat. "I just need a rest."

"Me, too," the attendant said, and set a small bottle of scotch next to a fresh glass of ice.

Ramona looked at the photograph of Daniel once more. That had been a real psychic experience. Any doubts she'd had about herself were gone. She'd done all she could to pull Daniel out of the way, but what was to be was to be, she thought, opened the bottle of scotch and began her bittersweet, lonely vacation. She felt as though she'd never see him again. Hardest to take was knowing that his last thought would be of her.

* * *

The lodge the travel agent had booked was rustic and beautiful, with stone and rough hewn beams. Her room overlooked forested hills, and as soon as she had tipped the bellboy, she picked up the phone and called the lab.

"Dr. Wilson."

"Daniel, hi," she said, feeling sheepish and a little shy.

"Hi," he said, taking on the tone of interest and undivided attention. "How is it?"

"The lodge is beautiful. I love it here." She stood up and looked out the window. "I can see the mountains. They're right outside. I'm going to go for a walk before dinner."

"Watch out for bears." He laughed.

"Come be with me? Please?" Now she was beginning to whine and she hated herself for it.

"You needed to get out of town, Ramona. Please do. Rest. Relax. Have some fun."

"It will be hard without you."

"Try. Don't call me for a week."

"A week?"

"A week. Take a real break."

Maybe he'll miss me if I'm out of his life for a week, she thought. Maybe then he'll join me.

"Okay," she said.

"Good. Now go and enjoy yourself. But don't forget to come home to me, and don't forget how much I love you."

"I love you too," she said, then hung the phone up with trembling hands. A tear dripped onto her wrist.

"Stop it!" she yelled at herself, then jumped up, went into the bathroom, washed her face, reapplied makeup, and headed downstairs for a real drink.

The lounge was homey and comfortable, with deep green carpeting, intimate leather chairs, high ceilings and low lights. A circular fireplace dominated the center of the room, and people were relaxing with cocktails, their feet up on the rim of the stonework.

Ramona sat at the bar, ordered a scotch and looked around. It was early; not too many people were there. She sipped her drink slowly and firmed up her resolve. If she did not run home to Daniel, he would come here after her. He would. She knew he would. He'd miss her.

But she had doubts about that, too. Daniel had lived alone a long time before she came into his life.

A nice looking guy in an expensive sweater and corduroy jeans came up to the bar and ordered three beers. She felt his eyes on her, and turned away, but she couldn't ignore him for long. Eventually she looked up and he was still looking at her. She should have been annoyed, but she was ready for a little flattery.

"Hi," he said.

"Hi."

"Just get in today?"

She nodded, looked at the bartender, but like a good one, he pretended to see and hear nothing.

"Why don't you join us?"

She looked up at him. He picked up the three beers and nodded toward the corner of the room, where Ramona could see a couple sitting.

"C'mon," he encouraged her. "Don't sit here alone. Are you waiting for someone?"

"Not really."

"Well then," he said, teasing her with mock exasperation, "come *on*." He walked toward them, looking over his shoulder as if encouraging a puppy to follow him.

She did.

Carl introduced Susan and Jake. Carl and Jake were lifelong buddies, and Susan was with Jake. They'd taken a two-day warm up hike earlier in the week and in the morning they were headed out on a three-day trek.

Ramona sat back and drank her scotch and basked in the warmth of their easy friendship. They talked and joked and laughed, telling stories about the last hike, poking fun at each other, all in slightly inebriated good humor.

Carl was in his late thirties, Ramona assumed, his dark hair beginning to thin a little bit on top. He wore dark rimmed glasses and had fun-filled brown eyes and full, sensuous lips. His teeth were small, even and straight. He was clean and presented himself well. Jake hadn't taken such good care of himself. He was leaner and paler. He had that gray look of a long-time smoker, although he didn't smoke anything at the table. Ramona doubted a smoker could hike in this altitude. Perhaps he had been sick. His hair was blond, his voice husky, his teeth stained.

Susan was younger, probably in her early twenties. She adored Jake, and he ate that up. She wore bangs and a ponytail and skin tight leggings over young legs. She looked like a cover girl, with classic model's looks. They were always touching each other, clearly in lust.

Carl fetched another round of beers, with one scotch, and when those were gone, Susan and Jake excused themselves and went to bed. Carl moved his chair closer to Ramona's.

"They're great," she said, indicating his departing friends.

"They are. They're a lot of fun."

"Wait right here," he said, putting a hand on her shoulder, and then he disappeared. When he returned, he had fresh drinks and a huge plate of nachos.

Ramona was starved, but she hadn't realized it. Someone threw a fresh log into the fire pit and sparks flew in a beautiful blaze. The warmth of the scotch, the food, Carl's attention and being so readily welcomed into their circle of friends eased Ramona's spirits. She ate and drank with enthusiasm, engaged completely by Carl and his refreshing youth. She had never considered Daniel to be old, but Carl was certainly younger, and there was something to be said for the flexibility and enthusiasm of a younger man.

She sat back in her chair and listened to him tell a story about last year's snow camping adventure with Jake and Susan, and realized that this trip was exactly what she needed. Some space to herself. Some fun. Some fresh faces.

When she finally wiped nachos off her fingers and hungered for a cup of coffee, she was feeling right at home in the lodge and with Carl. He fetched coffee, and they turned their chairs around and put their feet up on the lip of the fire pit like the others. The bar, Ramona noticed, had filled up.

They took off their shoes and let the fire warm their socks. Carl touched her toe with the tip of his. "It's always a struggle to escape work and life and get up here to the mountains," he said. "But once I do, I can't imagine that it was so hard to get here. God lives in these mountains, and somehow in daily life I forget that. Every time I get up into the silence of the forest, I remember what I'm about. Every time I swear that I won't forget again, but two weeks back at work and it's as if I had never come."

"But the experience stays with you."

"It does, but not the way I would like it to. Sometimes I feel that coming up here is futile."

"I think these times when you commune with nature are cumulative. The more you do it the more you're able to hang on to it."

He agreed. "I guess it's it's working down there that's really futile."

She shook her head. "There's something to be said for keeping your business and personal lives clean and tidy and together. I think it was Somerset Maugham who said something about it being easy to be a holy man when you live on top of a mountain."

"Razor's Edge."

Ramona nodded, sipped her scotch. She was feeling warmer and more attracted to this guy than she should.

"You're right," he said. "We work down there and just when it's about to beat us into the ground, we have to come up here, breathe free, hug trees and meet beautiful women. Then, recharged, we can lift our swords high over our heads and jump back into the pit."

She laughed. The "beautiful women" reference made her face glow. "I don't consider where I live or what I do a pit, but it's sure good to get away."

"I do. Where I work is a pit. Politics. Backstabbing. Ick."

"Let's not talk about that. I came up here to get away from professions and labels and titles and histories." She surprised herself by saying that, but she realized it was true.

Carl was silent, watching the sparks fly out of the fire. Ramona watched him watch the fire, the glow reflecting in his beer, in his glasses, in his eyes. "Yeah," he finally said. "I don't want to bring that place up here. I don't want to bring any of my history up here at all. Let's start out fresh, you and me, right here, right now. I don't want to know about your job or your family or where you grew up or anything. I think we should stay in the present. Just talk about who we are and what we're thinking and feeling right now."

Ramona finished her coffee and set the mug on the wide stone of the fire pit. "Okay," she said, caught up in his boyish enthusiasm, "but that has to extend to Susan and Jake, too."

Carl drained his cup and set it next to hers. "They'll get behind that." He took her hand in both of his and said, "Come with us tomorrow."

"A three-day hike?"

"Yeah. It'll be great."

"What would Jake and Susan say?"

"I don't care. I want you with me."

Ramona sat quietly, thinking. It would be poor judgment to go away for three days with people she had just met in a bar. "I don't think so."

"You're going to sit in this lodge by yourself for the next three days? What fun will that be?"

Ramona thought about it. She could see herself pacing, stewing over Daniel. She'd have to fight the impulse to call him every minute of every day. The hike would only be for three days—and she wasn't supposed to call him for a week. Three days away from a phone might be a good idea. "I'm not sure I've got the gear for a three day hike."

"We do. We have everything. All you need is a sleeping bag and hiking clothes. You have that, right?"

She nodded. "I don't know, Carl. I don't know you guys."

He spread his arms out and that boyish charm came oozing out. "Here I am," he said. "What you see is what you get. I'm a nice guy. Susan and Jake are great. And look. We're fresh, we come with no histories."

She laughed.

He leaned back down in his chair and moved it over closer to hers. "We're going to hike up a fairly easy trail. Jake's had some medical problems, and he keeps up pretty well because he does this all the time, but he has his limitations, so it'll be a pretty easy hike. There's a pristine little lake up there where nobody goes. I brought a little fishing pole and you can worm my hook for me."

Ramona smiled. This man was adorable. And intriguing. And his attentions most flattering. She found her face a little bit too close to his and was afraid that the scotch had distorted her judgment. She felt like kissing him. She wanted nothing more than to just move the last couple of inches and press her lips up to his in a sweet, chaste, soft-lipped kiss. He would smell like Old Spice and taste like coffee…

"Please?" he whispered.

"Ask me in the morning," she said, rousing herself. She stood up.

"We're going to meet for breakfast at seven," he said.

"Call me at six. Room 158."

Carl stood up. "I'll walk you to your room."

The bar was emptying as all the hikers were headed to bed for an early morning start. Carl walked behind her up the mighty split-ing staircase and down the hall. He took the room key from her hand and unlocked her door, then handed the key back to her. She let his fingers linger on hers.

"Please come with us tomorrow."

She smiled shyly like a teenager. "I'll think about it."

"I'll call you at six."

"Okay." Ramona was afraid he was going to kiss her. She was afraid he wasn't.

He didn't. "Good night," he said, smiling that same kind of shy smile.

She went inside, locked the door and put both hands over her mouth. What the hell was she doing?

Hey, she chastised herself. There's no harm in a little flirting.

But it wasn't right somehow, and she knew it. Especially since Carl was so damned attractive. He had that little boy enthusiasm that she hadn't seen in a long time.

And she couldn't help but compare him to Daniel. Daniel loved her and he was sweet and wonderful, but he didn't have that glow, that adventuresome quality. Had he ever? She couldn't remember. The scotch was making her dizzy.

She washed her face, got into her jammies and slid between cool sheets. She looked at the pillow next to her and wished somebody's head was there, but right at that moment, she didn't know whose. The only thing she was absolutely sure of was that she was going to go hiking with Carl and his friends. Limited though it may be, she wanted more of that kind of attention. It was harmless, and it made her feel good about herself.

Her last thought before sleep was that Daniel was right; she needed this vacation. But it probably wasn't exactly what he had in mind for her.

The next morning, she was up, showered and had her back-pack ready to go before Carl called. They met in the lodge restaurant for a hearty breakfast, and then distributed the provisions among the four. Everyone was happier for a lighter load, especially Susan. Jake's was the lightest of all.

They had final cups of coffee in the early morning mountain sunlight and looked at the map provided by the lodge. There were hundreds of trails, but the one they were taking led straight to the little lake. They helped each other into their packs and headed out, Jake taking the lead and setting the pace.

It was easy going. The trail was well maintained with bark chips and gravel in the swampy areas. Jake became winded easily, though the grade was relatively insignificant, so they stopped often. Ramona kept silent for the most part, listening to the friendly banter among the three old friends, chiming in when appropriate, and continually calling attention to the beauty of the forest.

Carl took the role of keeping history out of the conversation, which Susan and Jake goodheartedly agreed to, but which they all found surprisingly difficult. Ninety percent of their conversation, it seemed, wanted to revolve around past experiences.

Ramona knew that it wouldn't last, but it was an unusual and fun experiment, if but for a day. Besides that, she was becoming curious about her fellow hikers, and had to bite her tongue many times when tempted to ask Susan about herself. She discovered that if there were no past, there was relatively little to talk about.

They stopped for lunch at a point that looked out over a forested mountain and a river below. They ate in silence, listening to the birds and the wind in the pines. The air was cool, but the sun was warm, and after eating, Ramona took off her jacket, rolled up her sleeves and lay out on a little patch of grass.

Within a minute, Carl was by her side.

Ramona smiled. It was nice to be pursued. It seemed to her that she spent much of her time with Daniel trying to sell herself to him. Show him what a good wife she was—a good cook, a thrifty shopper, an enthusiastic lover. She not only showed him, but then told him in order to underscore the point. He appreciated her, she knew he did, but he always seemed preoccupied.

But this. Carl. It was nice to be pursued. It was nice to be cherished.

"Isn't this great?" he said as he spread out on the cold grass in the warm sun.

"The best," she said.

An eagle glided down the canyon and as one, they both sat up to watch it.

"Daniel would never take a long hike like this," Ramona said. "He'd be afraid he'd miss something."

"Your husband?"

"Yeah. We've been married for four years, but I don't know. He's always so preoccupied, and...I don't know, I guess I just thought marriage would be different."

"What happened to the no history policy?" Carl said, putting a hand on her arm.

Ramona picked a piece of grass and began to shred it.

"I mean if you need to talk, that's fine, you should talk with Susan, but the truth is, I really don't want to hear about your husband. Or your marital problems. It would make me crazy. I think you're the finest thing that's ever walked into my life, Ramona, and if all we have is this three day trip, then let's make it perfect and magic. I don't even want to know what's real in your life. My real life is stupid. This trip makes my real life look disgusting. I don't want you to know about it and I don't want to know about yours."

"Okay," she said. "You're right." His hand was still on her arm and she liked it. She lay back and closed her eyes, feeling the sun warm her face. "We're taking a step out of reality and it is very good."

She felt him lie down beside her. "Very good," he echoed.

They made camp in a spot that had seen many tents before theirs. Susan and Jake set their tent up while Ramona and Carl gathered firewood and started a small fire. Then, clumsy and tentative around each other, they put up their own tent. "Don't worry," Carl whispered to her. "Your virtue will be honored."

Ramona smiled with a slight blush. She was getting used to this flattery and she liked it. She liked it a lot. She was surprised to discover that she wasn't all that concerned with her virtue any more. If this was a step outside of reality, perhaps she could make love with Carl and erase it when she went home.

She shook out her sleeping bag and hoped that would shake out that thought. She didn't want to cheat on Daniel. No way would she cheat on Daniel. She would hate it if Daniel cheated on her. She wouldn't stand for it. And to jeopardize all that she had for one night with Carl—it was inconceivable. She'd have a hard enough time explaining that the two of them slept in one tent.

She didn't have to explain. She was doing nothing wrong.

Then why was she feeling so guilty?

Because she was feeling distant from Daniel and close to Carl, that's why. And that was both good and not so good.

Susan began rehydrating the stew while Jake whittled on his walking stick. Carl made coffee and set the dented pot close to the fire. Ramona bundled up in an extra layer of clothes, and sat on a log. The sunset turned the whole scene orange with a turquoise sky, then it was dark and there were more stars twinkling in the crisp cold sky than Ramona had ever seen before.

There was enough stew and French bread for seconds all around, then they sat back in contentment. Susan had packed in a big bottle of wine, and they passed the bottle around. "We have to finish that," she said. "I'm not going to pack it another day."

"Sonofabitch!" Carl said, and jumped to his feet. He slapped his forehead. "Idiot!" he said. He stomped around the fire, then stepped over the log and stomped around behind the tents.

"Hey, Carl," Jake said. "Settle down."

"Yeah," Susan said, sounding a little bit drunk on the exercise, the wine and the altitude. "What the hell's the matter with you?"

Carl stopped pacing. He was silent for a moment, then he stepped back over the log and rejoined the group. He sat next to Ramona, his arms crossed in a defensive posture. "I was supposed to call the office this morning. I was going to do that before we left.

There was a detail I was supposed to take care of, and the only way I could feel right about taking off was that I could call in and take care of that detail this morning." He hung his head. "I screwed up," he said. "I screwed up bad." He thumped his forehead with his knuckles.

"We could go back," Ramona said.

"Not until morning," Carl said, "and by the time we got to the lodge, it would be too late. I might as well forget it."

"Good idea," Jake said. "Forget it. They're all a bunch of assholes down there anyway. Let them deal with it themselves. Know what, Carl? You ought to quit that job. It'll kill you."

The group was silent. Ramona ignored Jake's assessment of the situation. Instead, she was impressed with Carl's attention to detail, with his dedication to his job. She felt responsible. She had distracted him. She leaned into him. "I'm sorry," she said.

He put his arm around her. "It's not your fault. My crew will either fill in for me or they won't. It's out of my hands."

"Fate," Susan said.

"Fate can be changed," Ramona said.

"How?" Susan said. "Fate, by the very definition of the word, can't be changed."

"Free will," Jake said. "Free will is a universal priority. Fate must be subservient to free will."

"Universal," Carl scoffed. "You have some kind of an information conduit to universal politics?"

"Just personal experience. Doctors gave me two months to live. Three years ago."

"So who's to say which was fated? That you die three years ago or that you live until now?" Susan asked.

"I don't know," Jake said. "I feel like I looked at death and knew that I could die when the doctors said. That felt like fate to me at the time. And I decided against it. I decided—I don't know—not to fight it, but to kind of slide under it instead. I just kind of circumvented it. And...so far, so good."

"I think fate is just a probability factor," Ramona said.

Carl squeezed her. "Well, whatever it is, it's out of my hands. I'm tired, and am going to bed. Coming, darling?"

Ramona smiled. "Yes."

"We'll make the lake by midmorning," Jake said. "Spend the night there, then it'll only take us one day to go down."

"I'm having a great time," Ramona said.

"We're glad you came along," Susan said.

Ramona crawled into the tent, shucked her outer layer of clothes and climbed into her sleeping bag, using her rolled up jeans as a pillow. It was nice being so close to Carl. His breathing sounded different from Daniel's, and he smelled different. He just had a completely different aura about him, and that was pleasant and a little bit exciting. Ramona stretched, tucked her down bag around her neck, and with her body exercised and feeling fit, her conscience clean and her mind free to roam the galaxies, she fell immediately asleep.

In the morning, they packed up, ate a quick breakfast and were on the trail before the sun burned off the dew.

Ramona's spirits were flying. She hadn't felt so free in years. She felt high. She felt like holding her arms out and twirling until she fell down. She felt like jumping into Carl's arms and kissing him long and hard, just from joy for life. It was the mountain air, it was the stimulating company, it was the difference a vacation can make.

Only once did she think about Daniel, and that was with a little pang of remorse that she had to get so goofy, had to make him banish her before she realized how much she needed a break. Well, she was taking it now, and it was glorious.

The others seemed to share her exuberance. The hike was filled with silly jokes and much laughter about nothing at all, except the love of life. Susan and Jake held hands much of the time, and when they stopped for breaks, they touched and kissed more than they had the day before.

The beauty of the small mountain lake literally took Ramona's breath away. She stood reverently in the chill late-morning air and tears of awe came to her eyes. The small lake was rimmed by ever-green trees. A couple of snags grew out of the south end. A hawk circled overhead, the sky was pale blue and the sun warm on her face. It was easy to imagine that she was the first person to have ever arrived at this spot. She didn't want to make a fire here, or even leave a footprint.

She heard a sigh next to her, and Susan put her arm around Ramona's shoulders. Jake put his arm around Susan, Carl snuggled up to Ramona's other side and the four of them drank it in like the smog-encrusted suburbanites they were.

Then they set up camp. When the small fire was going, Susan and Jake sneaked off into the woods, leaving Ramona and Carl alone. Ramona felt uncomfortable being alone with him, with their mutual attraction growing ever stronger. She was afraid she would do something foolish, and just as she thought of that, Carl came up to her and taking her face in his hands, he kissed her.

She let him, but she didn't kiss him back.

"I won't apologize for that," he said.

She had nothing to say. She wanted to cry. Not being able to look him in the eye, she stared at the buttons on his shirt. His hands slipped from her face to her shoulders, down her arms. His fingers touched hers, then he reluctantly dropped his hands.

"Why me?" he asked quietly, then put his head down and walked away from her.

She had to fight the impulse to grab at his sleeve, to bring him back for a real kiss. But she did fight it, and he pulled his fishing pole from his backpack and began to assemble it.

Ramona stood watching him. He threaded the line through the eyes, tied a hook to the end, attached a sinker, then stood up.

"I'm sorry," he said to her.

"I'm married," she said.

"I know. Story of my life. C'mon. Worm my hook."

Ramona smiled. They were back on even footing again, after a very close call.

Within an hour, Carl and Ramona had each landed two nice trout. The small lake was a fishing paradise. Just as Carl finished cleaning them, Susan and Jake came out of the woods, flush faced and laughing. There were threads of moss and bits of forest floor in Susan's hair.

Carl beefed up the fire and fried the fish right out of the lake, making for an early dinner. There was little conversation as they chowed down the fish along with some buttered rice, then again, they sat back, stomachs full, and that familiar warm camaraderie surrounded them as the sun lowered in the sky.

"We'll catch breakfast," Susan said, throwing her paper plate on the fire and watching it burn.

"Yeah, sure," Carl said. "You guys will be off in the woods, leaving Ramona and me to do all the heavy work."

"We can catch fish," Susan said, sliding around until she was sitting in Jake's lap. "Can't we, honey?"

"No," Jake said. "We have a date in the woods in the morning."

"Ooooh," Susan said. "Okay." She kissed him. "Never mind, you guys. Breakfast is on you, too."

"When's our turn?" Carl asked, and an embarrassed silence fell over them. "Sorry," he said, touching Ramona's shoulder. "God, every time I turn around, I put my foot in it, don't I?"

"It's okay," Ramona said, and looked up to see Susan and Jake watching.

"Back to real life tomorrow night," Susan said. "I hope there's an envelope waiting for me that says I got the new job."

"New job?" Ramona asked, grateful to her for changing the subject and releasing the tension.

"Major changes in my life," Susan said. "From A to Z. That's why I'm here. I needed a break before I went insane. I don't know how half my plans are going to work out and that not knowing drives me nuts."

"We could do a Tarot reading," Ramona said, then remembered she didn't have her cards. She'd thrown her cards away. Cut them up and thrown them away.

"You do that?"

"Yeah, but I didn't bring my cards."

"Well, you could read my palm or something instead, right? I mean if a person can do one thing, they can do another, right?"

"I don't know. I've never tried. I'm not psychic. All I know I learned from books."

Susan got up from Jake and came around. She held out her hand. "Try," she said. "See if I got that job."

Ramona looked over at Carl who looked back at her with expectation. Jake crossed his arms over his chest and relaxed. Ramona looked into Susan's light blue eyes and felt the budding of affection. She realized that she didn't want to lose touch with these people after this trip was over.

She took Susan's warm, small hand and opened the fingers.

All sound went away.

Susan stood confidently in front of the assembled professionals in the conference room. Her hair was pulled back, she wore a conservative pinstripe suit, and she spoke with conviction and passion about a chart that was on an easel next to her.

The sound of the forest and campfire burst back upon Ramona. She gasped.

"What?" Susan asked.

Ramona looked around her, cleared her throat. Everything was normal, everything was fine. She took a deep breath and tried to act as normal as everybody else. "Well, you got the job," she said.

"Really?" Susan folded up her hand and held it next to her chest. "That's great!" She hugged the still-dazed Ramona, then went back to sit next to Jake. He held her hand.

"A woman of many talents," Carl said, and when she looked at him, she saw that admiration light in his eyes again. Carl was smitten with her, and she wasn't helping his case any. "My turn," he said.

"No, I don't think so," Ramona said, not quite sure what had happened or how she should feel about it. She folded her arms across her chest and looked out over the sunset.

"Come on, Ramona," Susan said. "Do it."

"Come on, Ramona," Carl said.

"I'd rather not."

"Oh, be a sport," Jake said.

Ramona looked at Susan and Jake and realized that there was no reason for her to refuse Carl. She took a deep breath and smiled at him. "Okay."

He gave her his hand. It was soft and carefully tended, a manicured hand that had seen no manual labor. It had wiry black hairs growing out of the back of it. A nice hand.

She turned it over and smoothed out his palm with her finger. Sound disappeared.

Daniel saw something alarming on the control board. He double checked it, then, worry wrinkling his brow, he slapped a red button. Someone wearing a yellow lab coat came over to him, and they spoke. Daniel's face turned red. He shouted something. His coffee cup, the cup Ramona had given him for Valentine's Day, began to tremble and slide across the table. Then the room started to shake. Technicians ran around, then they stopped, a stunning realization stamped on their faces. One man crossed himself. Daniel looked straight ahead, said her name softly. Then the control room wall blasted inward with fire and glass and silent fury.

Ramona shrieked, dropped Carl's hand and scrambled to her feet, backing away from him, away, away, until she stepped right into the fire. Shrieking again, she jumped out, embers scattering, Jake and Susan scrabbling to get out of the way.

"Whoa," Carl said, then grabbed her in a hug, and she began to cry. She sobbed, weak-kneed, but Carl held her up and she clung to him as to a life raft. Daniel. She'd almost erased that experience from her mind, but it was real. That vision hadn't been an isolated incident. It was a premonition, she knew it. Daniel was going to die if she didn't help him.

"I think we better turn in," Carl said to the others, then he led her to the tent, took off her shoes and helped her to lie down. She continued to cling to him; she couldn't bear to be without touch, without warmth, without assurance and reassurance that she was real, whole, flesh and blood.

Carl wrapped his arms around her. She cried into his shoulder, and whenever she felt the urge to speak, he soothed her with soft shush-ing sounds and smoothed her hair.

Then he kissed her forehead, her temple, her cheek, her neck, her chin, and finally her mouth. His warm hands came up underneath her sweatshirt and massaged her back, and the passion that only moments ago had been tremendous fear, ignited into desperate lust.

Within moments, they had shucked their pants and he lifted Ramona over, where she lowered herself gently, then urgently, onto him. It was so new. She hadn't made love to anyone but Daniel for so many years, she felt like a virgin.

But their passion was at its peak and they danced wildly for barely a minute before they both came in a burst of energy, then Ramona fell over onto her side and wept quietly. Carl kissed away her tears, but they continued to leak unabated, even as Carl spoke soft words of comfort and affection.

Ramona felt drained. Physically, emotionally, mentally and now sexually. She was deflated. She wanted to feel horrible about herself for cheating on Daniel, but she hadn't even the strength for that. She barely remembered Carl covering them with his sleeping bag before she succumbed to a restless sleep.

In the morning, Ramona's swollen eyes popped open in a moment of disorientation. Carl breathed quietly next to her, and his hand was under her sweatshirt, cupping her breast.

Then she remembered the night before, she remembered the vision, she remembered having sex with Carl and she was horrified. It was as if that had been a different person. It was as if she had been drunk. But she hadn't been—

She didn't even have that as an excuse.

No, she had just cheated on Daniel. She had a premonition of his death and then had sex with a stranger.

She pulled away from Carl, pulled on her sweatpants, grabbed a towel from her backpack, unzipped the tent with shaking hands and stepped into the early morning mist. The other tent was silent. The world was silent, except for the calls of a few birds and tiny blips in the lake as fish fed.

She felt dirty, she felt used, she felt violated. She felt unfaithful and despicable.

She took her clothes off in the freezing mountain air and then stepped into the cold lake. Her feet ached the minute she stepped in. This wasn't a good idea, she knew, but she had to bathe. She had to bathe. She had to get rid of Carl. She had to clean herself.

Up to her thighs and she felt her heart begin to pound.

"Ramona?" She heard Carl call her, but she didn't turn around. "Ramona, that water's too cold."

She dipped down up to her chin and her breath literally froze in her lungs. She couldn't breathe. The water was so frigid it sucked the heat out of her bones.

"Ramona, come out."

She didn't want to die in this mountain lake, she had only wanted to bathe, but she couldn't move. She couldn't talk. She just stared out over the frigid mist-covered water and felt her life seep away.

Then there was splashing behind her and Carl lifted her up. Somehow, she got her legs to begin to work and she tried to help him as he half dragged her back to the shore. Carl dried his legs, wrapped his towel around her, put on his jeans, then rubbed her skin briskly as he dried her, helped her dress, then sat her by the campfire as he kindled it and got it going. They didn't speak.

Ramona felt like a fool, but she didn't care how she appeared before this man, or in front of these people. All she cared about was getting home. Getting back to the hotel, getting her stuff and getting back to Daniel. In time, oh God please, in time.

"I want to go," she finally said when the fire was roaring and she had stopped shivering.

Carl sat next to her. "Ramona," he said, "settle down."

"Don't tell me to settle down," she said. "I just want to get out of here."

"I'm sorry you're upset," he said, "but last night for me was…"

"I don't want to hear about it," she said, hearing her voice grow louder and out of control. "I don't want to *hear* about it, I don't want to *think* about it, I don't want to *remember* it. It never happened. It *couldn't* have happened." She stood up, unsteadily, then went to the tent. "I'm a married woman."

She threw her things into her backpack and stuffed her sleeping bag into its sack with a wild desperation. When she crawled out of the tent, she noticed that Susan and Jake were up and tousled, sitting by the fire, watching.

Carl held her by the arms. "Please."

She shook him off. "I've got to get out of here."

"Ramona, wait."

She shrugged into her backpack.

"Give me five minutes and I'll go down with you."

"I'm leaving now. You can catch up."

"Ramona, *wait*."

She stopped and looked at him expectantly.

"Five minutes." He offered her a granola bar.

She waved away the bar. "I'll walk slow," she said. She waved at Susan and Jake. "Bye," she said. They waved back. She started down the trail toward the lodge.

In less than five minutes she heard pounding footsteps behind her. Carl had hastily packed and he carried the tent. "What's the matter with you?" he asked.

"I must have been insane," she said. "There's a disaster about to happen and I'm the only one who knows about it. I'm the only one who can prevent it. I'm the only one who can do anything about it, and instead of taking care of this…this…this *massive* responsibility, I'm off on some goddamned three day hike, fucking in the woods like some…" She picked up the pace.

"Ramona, wait, slow down." He reached out and caught her sleeve, pulling her back, finally stopping her. "You're the one for me," he said. "You're what I've been searching for all my life."

She looked deeply into his eyes and wondered what in the hell she ever saw there. She pulled away from his grasp and started off down the hill again.

"Ramona, please," he ran to catch up to her again. "I'm serious. I want to get to know you. I want to know all about you."

Ramona picked up the pace again until she was fairly running down the trail. She heard him slow down to a walk, and she was glad, she was glad, she didn't want to see him, didn't want to look at him, didn't want to be reminded—

A root caught her foot and she tumbled, landing on her shoulder, then the world whirled as she rolled over and off the edge of the path, down into the trees. She banged her head, she was afraid she'd broken her wrist, and she began to cry again.

Within a minute, Carl was at her side, holding her head, stroking her hair, wiping away her tears.

He held her and rocked her and held her and rocked her and spoke tender words of love into her ear, and she just cried and cried and listened to him as her soul felt as though it were withering into a limp, black mass.

Shadows were lengthening into late afternoon when they got back to the lodge. Carl walked her to the door of her room and kissed her on the cheek. "Get some rest," he said. "I'll call you later for dinner." She nodded numbly and went inside.

She threw her backpack on the floor and took a long, needle-stinging hot shower, scrubbing her skin until it hurt. Then, wrapped in a terry robe with a towel on her hair, she sat on the edge of the bed and stared at the telephone.

Had it already happened? Did it happen while she was having sex in the mountains?

She picked it up and dialed, her fingers crossed.

"Mission Laboratories," the receptionist said.

Ramona hung up, then chewed on a fingernail.

It hadn't happened yet. But it would, she was certain of that. It would.

Mind eased for the moment, she decided to put off calling Daniel. He didn't want her to call for a week, but she would call him anyway, as soon as she calmed herself down a little bit. She'd rest a while, then make reservations to get home, then she'd call him. And when she got home, she'd grab Daniel by the hair, if she had to, and get him out of there.

She swung her feet up onto the bed, exhaustion finally taking its toll. She pulled the bedspread over her and fell asleep.

A knocking on her door brought Ramona up through the murky depths of sleep. She sat up, feeling disoriented. The room was dark, the towel had come off her head and her hair had dried in a swirl. "Yes?" she croaked out.

The knocking turned to pounding. "Ramona. Open the door." It was Carl.

She stood up, turned on a light, fastened her robe and shook her hair out. She opened the door.

He stood there with a bottle of champagne and two glasses. "Hi," he said.

"Hi." She was furry-brained and confused.

He kissed her on the cheek before she could dodge and brushed past her into the room.

Ramona wanted to brush her teeth, she wanted a glass of water. She wanted to brush her hair, she wanted to make reservations to get home. She wanted to phone Daniel. She didn't want to deal with Carl.

"It's celebration time," he said.

She closed the door and stood next to it, arms crossed over her chest. "Celebration?"

"Yep. I quit my job."

Was he drunk? This seemed to be a little bit irrational. "Just like that?"

He lifted the champagne. "Yep. Retired that damned lab coat. Just like that." He popped the cork, poured two glasses and brought one over to her.

She took it.

He put one hand on the wall over her head and leaned into her. His breath smelled warm and minty. "I just called them up," he whispered, then kissed her forehead, "and told them that I was in the mountains in love with a raven haired beauty named Ramona." He took her free hand and led her to the bed. He sat down on the edge. "Now it's time you knew all about me," he said. "Enough with this history gag order. My name is Carl Cannon. I'm—or I was until a minute ago—head maintenance supervisor at Mission Nuclear Laboratories. I was born in Detroit..."

Ramona never felt the glass slip from her fingers as the vision came back to her full force, this time complete, with horrifying sound.

Daniel stood in the control room. He saw something wrong, confirmed it, slapped the alert button which set off a shrieking alarm. A safety tech in a yellow lab coat ran into the room.

Daniel began to question him, his voice drowned out by the alarm.

"Cannon didn't specify," the technician said.

"Where the hell is Cannon?" Daniel said, his voice rising in fear.

"He quit."

"Quit?"

"He called in and said he was in the mountains, in love with someone named Ramona."

"Damn him!" Daniel yelled.

The building began to shake, his Valentine's Day cup trembled and jiggled along the table. Chaos broke out in the room as people began to run around in a panic. A moment later, everybody began to realize that events weren't to be stopped, and a horrible peace ensued. Someone turned off the alarm. One man crossed himself.

Ramona looked at Daniel and in that last instant of his life, he turned and looked directly into her eyes. She knew he saw her, in her lodge hotel room with Carl Cannon.

He whispered, "Ramona."

❋

Fogarty & Fogarty

Fogarty first met his bride in a culvert under the highway one night during a full moon. He was cold and tired, and a little anxious about being caught too far from home when the cold snap bit. He wasn't happy about taking refuge out in the open, either, where who-knows-what might come along and get frisky with an old man so casually dressed.

He found some old papers and leaves piled up in the corner where the wind had swept them, and he wound his way through the culvert, shuffling his feet, scooping up more and more to add to the pile. When he'd built himself a fair little heap where it was dry and out of the wind, he stepped gently across it to the concrete corner and sat down, then fluffed the leaves up around him.

The old autumn smell of the leaves was a pleasant change from the scent of his normal home, and he breathed in their acrid mustiness. He knew they would make him sneeze, but he couldn't help himself, he was suddenly very pleased that events had taken such a turn as this. He'd forgotten about autumn leaves.

When finally the sneeze did come, it came from deep down inside him, and his eyes opened wide as he felt it coming up, and he smiled in anticipation. Then his vision was blurred by a rush of tears, his eyes squinted up, and a blast shot through him that felt so good that he laughed out loud.

Fogarty wiped his nose on his shirt sleeve and saw that he'd sneezed almost all of the leaves off himself, so he began to gather them close again, chuckling to himself, feeling cozy in his new home.

In the midst of chuckling and gathering old crispy leaves and remembering that sneeze, he had the creepy feeling that someone was watching him. Fear jumped into his stomach and he stopped. He held perfectly still. The night was so silent, he could hear one leaf on his neck rub another in perfect rhythm with his racing pulse.

Then he heard leaves crunch. A step. And another, and finally a woman came into view, an old, frail woman, with a man's gray overcoat on, and some leather boots with good miles still in them, and socks and socks and more socks all up and down her legs. She wore a knit cap over a scarf, and she stepped gently on the leaves, warily walking around him, giving him lots of room.

Fogarty was stunned. There were indeed blessings on this night. First, autumn leaves. Then a sneeze to top all sneezes. And now, company. In the form of a lady, yet.

Look at ya, Fogarty, he thought. A lady. Where's yer manners? He jumped up. Leaves flew from him as if he'd exploded. The woman's face reacted with horror. He realized what a sight he must make, and immediately dropped to one knee.

"My dear," he said, and stopped her, mid-bolt. "I dint mean to startle ya. I was just lookin' fer my manners here." Her face softened, though she took a step back. "It's a cold night, and I been caught too far from my home, might I guess you is in the same?"

She said nothing.

"The night's full of blessings, it is," he said. "First, these leaves, ain't they glorious? And I think they're gonna be warm, too, and then a sneeze, and now some company."

She looked at him with an expression of interest, but still said nothing.

"Would you join me?" He stood up and shook out his aching knee, but held the palms of his hands out to her, so she wouldn't be afraid. "I'm Fogarty."

"Fogarty," she said.

"That's right!" He smiled, and wished he'd found a bath before now. "Fogarty. What's your name?"

She was silent.

"I bet it's a name as beautiful as yerself," he said, beginning to shiver, "but it's mighty cold here, and I'm going to get back down inside this blanket of leaves for some warmth. I would courteously invite you to join me. I can see as you're cold, too." He sat back down and began piling leaves up on his legs and his chest, moving slowly so as not to spook her.

"I don't normally live around here," he said, feeling her interest. She wanted to join him, he could tell. "I normally live way down south. Out of town. You live around here?"

She kept her silence, but took a step closer to him.

"Here," he said, and swept some leaves from the concrete. Then he sprinkled a soft bedding down. "Sit down here and I'll cover you up nice and warm."

She came over timidly, sideways, ready to run at his first false move. He held his breath—he wanted to have some company on this cold and lonely night—and gently smiled at her and encouraged her. Eventually, she sat in the spot he cleared, but as he moved to put leaves on her legs, she scooted over farther away from him.

He held up his hands. "Okay," he said. "You do it."

She picked up a handful of leaves and put them on her lap, then looked back at him. He nodded in encouragement, and scooped armfuls up around his own legs, then nodded at her. She copied his motions, and soon she was grinning and up to her chin in leaves.

They sat together in silence for a while, listening to the traffic on the highway overhead, the occasional rumblings, mostly, of the sixteen-wheelers. Then Fogarty saw a lightening of the sky, and he shook his arm free of leaves and pointed at it.

"Moon's about to come up," he said. "Another blessing." And she smiled at him and they waited for it together.

When finally the moon, gigantic and orange, arose over the skyline, it cast a bright, colorless light on the culvert, deepening sharp-edged shadows. Fogarty smiled and sighed, and turned to the woman to speak, but the moonlight on her soft face and bright eyes caught him off guard, and the breath caught in his chest. A lady, he thought. A real lady.

Leaves crinkled as she reached up and pulled off her knit cap, and then untied the scarf from under her chin. Her hair wasn't as gray as he thought it would be; it was fairly dark, and curly. She ran her fingers through it, fluffing it up a little bit, and the moon caught the highlights, and she smiled at Fogarty, and the little wrinkles around her eyes threw nets around his heart and he fell in love.

He gazed at her and gazed at her, until the moon arose above the highway. The dark shadow sliced across the culvert and left them again in the dark.

Fogarty felt her presence as rich as if it were liquid. He was mindful of his heart pounding, his breath rasping through dry lips, and he was mindful of his clothes and his beard and he reached up a hand through the leaves and smoothed down his own thinning hair.

The feeling was vaguely familiar, this feeling of warmth and excitement that jittered his stomach and spread until he could hardly sit still. Fogarty searched his fragmented memory, but found only the unsettling feeling that there had been a woman in his life once, a woman and a child—a son—but those thoughts were uncomfortable somehow, and he didn't dwell on them. It was just this first flush of love that dredged stuff up, he thought, and he ran his hand over his face and finger-brushed his front teeth real quick and then snaked his hand back under the leaves and began to pick at a hangnail.

"Where do you mostly live?" he asked.

No answer.

He turned to look at her, and there was a sparkle in her eye that must have captured all the starlight, and the streetlights, and headlights from passing sixteen wheelers as well as the blue neon from the diner two blocks down, and focused it into two little tiny pinpoints that beamed right into Fogarty.

He was mesmerized by those eyes—eyes he couldn't really see in the dark, he could only see the little pinpoints of light—they seemed to be looking right through him, right into his soul.

He looked for a minute into his own soul, and found it to be a good one. A worthy one. A clean one. Cleaner, at least, than the outside of him.

"I would please to know your name," Fogarty whispered, and just then the moon peeked down from between the two highway overpasses, and a swath of light fell on the concrete over her head and began sliding down. Their eyes locked and then the moon began with her hair, showing every detail, and then her eyebrows, and her eyes, those glorious eyes, were they brown? and then her nose, nice and straight, and full cheeks, then mouth with wide smile and deep laugh lines. Up to her neck in leaves, it looked to Fogarty as if a heavenly sculptor had been interrupted just as he finished the face of an angel.

The moonlight moved across the space between them, and up Fogarty's mound of leaves, and he could almost feel the light as she followed it with her eyes, up over his collar, to his loose neck, the beard stubble from his two day trek from home, his small lips and hooked nose, deep, recessed eyes that sometimes looked green, sometimes brown, and big, bushy eyebrows that looked like they ought to be on a man with a little more meat on him. He had a shock of hair right in the front, but then it thinned out to be a pretty poor crop, but had some good growth in the back. He kept it fairly trimmed; usually he kept a pretty good toilet. It was just because he'd been caught away from home two nights in a row, now... .

"Fogarty," she said, in a whisper as soft as a spider moving across a web.

"Fogarty," he whispered back, aching to hear his name again on her lips. No one had ever said it like that before. "Fogarty. That's me. What's yours?"

"Fogarty," she said again, and smiled, and her teeth were good and straight, and then the leaves rattled and her hand emerged from the pile, clean and as white as a lily.

"I been a good man, Lord," Fogarty said to the moon, and he reached his spotted hand out and touched hers. Her hand was warm and soft, and he said to her, "Yes, the moon has seen to bless us tonight."

"Bless us," she whispered. "Fogarty and Fogarty."

Fogarty's mouth dropped open, and he looked deeply into her eyes, and knew that his dream had come true. A dream he hadn't even known he'd had.

He saw the shadow begin to take the moonlight from the top of the culvert over her head, moving down toward her, and he knew this was his chance. He must rise to the occasion.

"You, Moon!" he said. "You and the Lord bless us, okay? Fogarty and Fogarty." Then he laughed and she laughed and they squeezed each other's hands, and then the moon, on track to its zenith, slid right on past, leaving them in the shadows of the overpass, listening to sixteen wheelers and the music in their own hearts.

The next morning, long before the sun could warm their leaves, Fogarty and his bride awakened to the sound of rush hour traffic over their heads. They smiled at each other with a tug of embarrassment that the rational light of day often brings, and Fogarty let go of the soft hand that had held his all night long.

"Oh, such a blessing to be up before the sun," he said, and stood up, gave a mighty stretch, then shook all the leaves out of his clothes. Suddenly, he found himself shy. When the sun came up, he and his new wife would have their first real look at each other. No, he said to himself, that's not true. The moon showed our souls last night and that's enough.

"Come, Fogarty," he said, and held out his hand for her, then pulled her up. She, too, stretched and grinned, then dusted off her clothes, pulling pieces of dried leaves out of her multi-layered socks. He took her hand and they climbed out of the culvert and walked into the city.

"Do you have clothes?"

She looked down at what she was wearing.

"Or belongings? Something to fetch?"

She lifted his hand to her cheek.

"Well then," Fogarty said, with a blush and a feeling of manly protectiveness. "Let's go home."

Hand in hand, they walked through the center of the city as if it belonged to them, Fogarty and Fogarty, and for once, no one hassled them. They walked through the center of the business district, and as the secretaries and executives sped by them with their clackety high heels and brisk swinging of briefcases, Fogarty held on to his bride a little tighter, and they both walked a little taller, and when they reached the area of used car lots and giant discount stores, both breathed a little easier.

The sun cast long afternoon shadows when they reached the far side of town. Fogarty tugged his wife's arm, guiding her down an alley. The wonderful scent of freshly cooked vegetables almost made him weak in the knees. "Come, Fogarty," he said. "Meet a friend."

Fogarty stopped at a green back door where at least a dozen cats were blinking their sleepy eyes in the dusk and waiting for a handout. He smoothed his hair back, brushed at his clothes, ran his hand over his face and finger-brushed his front teeth. Then he straightened his bride's hat and touched her cheek and knocked on the door.

After a minute, the door opened, and a little Chinese man stood with the bright light behind him.

"Fogarty!" he said, and his eyes squinted up with pleasure. "Long time. Come in, come in. You hungry?"

Fogarty looked at his wife and smiled, and she looked back at him with adoration.

"Who's this?" The man in the white coat looked the missus up and down, suspicion narrowing his face. "Fogarty, I thought…"

"Fogarty," she whispered, and Fogarty put his arm around her.

"Fogarty and Fogarty," he said to the Chinaman. "The moon has married us."

"Married?" The cook's expression opened up. "Married?" Delight opened his arms wide, and the door opened wide, and he hugged and kissed them both. "Come in, come in," he said. "Marriage feast."

Fogarty led the way to the little wooden table and chairs set in the middle of the Chinese kitchen. He pulled one out, but his bride's eyes looked around wildly. "Would you like to freshen yerself?" he asked. She looked at him without understanding, so he guided her to the restroom. She went in and closed the door.

Lee returned with his wife, whose name Fogarty could never pronounce, so he called her Donna, which always made her laugh gently behind her hand. Donna was big with child, and Lee big with pride.

Fogarty stood up when his missus returned, and she picked at her hat shyly as he introduced her, and Donna touched both her shoulders and made her sit down and Donna and her husband served them more than they could eat in a week.

"I work here sometimes," Fogarty explained. "I stop here coming home, and eat and sleep, and then I clean."

"He does a good job. He's a good man," Lee said.

"Yes," Donna said. "We like Fogarty. Good man."

Fogarty blushed.

"Sleep here tonight and in the morning we'll pack up your honeymoon food and you'll go on home. You're going to live at Fogarty's?"

All eyes went to Fogarty's bride, who looked at her plate. "I must work..." Fogarty said.

Lee shook his head. "Wedding present," he said, and Fogarty and Fogarty spent their second night together on futons in the store room while a busy restaurant went on around them.

In the morning, there were two white paper sacks on the counter, each filled with little white cartons of food, and Fogarty and Fogarty each took one and started home.

Fogarty was feeling more and more comfortable in her presence, and was glad the good Lord found him fit to receive a good woman. He didn't know what he'd do if he'd gotten a bad one. This one was pretty as a picture and modest and shy, nice and gentle. She needed a bath, though, and some fresh clothes. There would be time for all of that when they got home.

Outskirt buildings fell behind them as they walked the asphalt in the early morning. A few shacks came and went and they were beginning to see a few silos in the distance when Fogarty steered his bride down a rutted, packed dirt road to the right. They followed along, crossed the railroad tracks, and kept going.

"It'll be a blessing to get home early," he said.

She smiled up at him then looked back down at the road, shifting her bundle of Chinese food.

"It's not far now."

The road curved off to the left, but Fogarty led her down a footpath in the knee-high yellow weeds. Then he held the wires of a fence apart for her, and followed her through. They went to the right and followed the fence for twenty-seven fence posts, and the trail turned left again.

"Landfill," he said. "Been my home now for eight, coming on nine winters. You'll like it." He smiled, but she failed to look up at him, and suddenly he was overcome with uncertainty. He walked a few more steps through the litter-strewn weeds on the uneven ground. His stomach was jumping around inside of his belly and it felt a lot like shame. "Hey, Fogarty," he said, and touched her arm. She stopped and looked at him, and he saw that soft face and those fabulous brown—they were brown, they were wonderfully brown—eyes. "Hey, I'm pleased to be taking you to my home." A smile flitted across her face, and she looked down again. She's nervous too, he thought.

He pointed out landmarks to her, for when she went foraging, or if she ever needed to go to town. "My house is hard to find, you see, that's why it's been here eight, going on nine winters. Just keep seein' old Mr. Boiler's pipe sticking up over there, and the three cars piled on top of each other over there. The front door's right in the middle."

They went up over hills and slid down into the valleys as the terrain of the dump became more difficult. "They dump the fresh stuff more'n a mile off," he said. "Sometimes it smells, and sometimes there's a fire. Then I really smell it. This part of the landfill's done, though, so they leave it alone. Ha. Eight, almost nine winters, now."

The sight of Fogarty's front yard made him happy enough to want to hoot, but he didn't want to scare the lady, so he just said, "Home we are," and walked right up to the front door that used to belong to an old blue Pontiac, and opened it.

She looked inside, which was dark, and she took a step back and shook her head. Fogarty looked inside, down the dark stairs and said, "You're right, I forget. You stay here, and I'll put in the light."

He walked away from her, around toward the old boiler, and shifted some pieces of wallboard and siding. Light shone up the stairs. Then he walked around in a big circle, moving sheets of warped plywood and roofing paper, and more and more light came up from below.

He was sweating in the late morning heat when he came back. "Skylights," he said. "I cover 'em when I go away. Come, Fogarty," and he ducked down inside the door and went down to the bottom of the stairs, where he waited for her.

She followed, hesitantly, and when she got down, Fogarty took her hand, put his arm around her and looked into those deep, trusting brown eyes and said, "This is our home." He delighted in seeing the astonishment on her face as she looked around. "Aren't we blessed?"

Fogarty had spent eight, going on nine winters carving out a very personal space amid the debris. The ceilings were made of a patchwork of woods and old windows, propped up in crucial points by timbers that had seen better days, but never a prouder use. The walls and the floors were as colorful and kaleidoscopic as the rest of the place, a swirling interconnecting of color and form and texture. Each individual piece had been foraged from the dump, but there was no garbage, there was no junk. Everything had been used and no longer wanted by its original owner, but Fogarty had seen through stains and holes and rusts and found the nuggets of usefulness in another's trash.

The kitchen had a tiny woodburning stove, a Formica counter, and cabinets.

"Lee give me those," he said, and walked around her to touch the row of white dishtowels that hung on a rod over the sink. He felt a need to break the silence, put some animation into his home. He set down his white sack of Chinese food and took hers from her. Then he took off his coat and emptied the big pockets he'd sewn into the lining. He brought out a tall bottle of lamp oil, a dozen books of matches, two handfuls of warped candles and some dented cans of meat and fruit.

He looked around at his home and was pleased that he had tidied up before leaving on this last trip. He hadn't known he would be bringing home a wife.

"Come, Fogarty," he said, and took her hand. They moved past the kitchen, past the little plastic-topped dining table with two chairs, into the living room that had a sofa, a rocking chair with footstool, a scarred coffee table with a game of solitaire laid out and ready to play, and a whole corner filled with stacks of puzzles and games. A magazine rack held some old issues of National Geographic, and next to it was a big kerosene lantern on an end table.

Fogarty looked at his bride's face, but her expression of astonishment hadn't changed. His pride swelled into a smile.

"Come," he said again, and led her through a yellow gingham curtain into his bedroom. Both pillows were neatly plumped on a high double bed, an old quilt that looked handmade, was folded neatly at the foot; a plain wooden dresser stood in the corner, and

95

over it hung a mirror. A chunk of galvanized pipe hung from the ceiling, and clothes, neatly arranged on hangers, hung from it. "My apologies for that," he said. "A proper closet is next." The missus looked at him with wide eyes and a cocked head, and finally she began to smile.

"The bathroom's over here," he said, and took her gently out of the bedroom, past a blue and white striped curtain, where a plastic shower stall stood over a drain in the floor, and a step-ladder was propped up next to it.

"The water heats up on the woodstove," he said, and it goes up in that there bucket. Then," he opened the shower curtain, "I can stop and start the water here with this hose, so's I can wet down and soap up and then rinse off." A plastic sack of little hotel-sized bars of soap hung in the corner. A sparkling clean blue antique chamber pot had been set under a straightbacked chair that had the cane seating removed. "I use that," he said, "and empty it every day, but we can do something else, if you want."

Her eyes softened.

"There's a faucet just on the other side of that old boiler outside," Fogarty said. "It's such a blessing, it is. A picnic table used to live there too—I guess the workers used to eat there, and they put in a faucet and left it when they moved on to the north side. I been meaning to run a hose, but I don't want anybody to be finding the house, so I just go up and get water when I need it."

He got another noseful of her in his close quarters and realized that they needed some shower water right now. "I'll go get some now," he said, "and put on some tea and make us both a shower."

She just looked at him, and that jittery feeling returned to his belly. He didn't know if she understood anything he said or not.

"I only light the stove at night, usually, when nobody can see the smoke, but a hot shower and cup of tea is such a blessing when I first come home. I'll just do a little fire, just enough for baths."

He paused, anxious to get his chores done, but hardly able to move away from her. "There's clothes in that box over there, they're men's clothes, but they'll do until we can find you some fresh ones and get yours laundered."

He ran out of words and they stood together in the hallway, close, and Fogarty saw again what pretty hair she had peeking out from under that brown knitted hat, and what a soft face she had, and for some reason it didn't seem odd at all that she was here. After eight, going on nine winters living in this place all by himself, suddenly it was almost like he'd had her in mind all along as he worked every day on his little house, making it just right for her. And now here she was, and it felt normal and natural.

"So why don't you just…sit, and I'll get the water on and…so why don't you just sit…there?"

She smiled and he smiled back, and then he worked over the stove until he got a little fire going, put the pot on it, and went out with his biggest bucket. It would take at least two trips, he thought, but when he came back with the first bucketful, he found her asleep on his bed, her hat and coat still on, a warm flush on her cheeks.

"Such a blessing you are, Fogarty," he said to her, and went to take himself a shower.

Fogarty snapped awake, his body rigid with fear. Then he heard her soft breathing in the silent night and he relaxed. So strange to have someone else with him. In his bed. He looked at his bedside clock. Five-thirty. He looked over at her, a lump under the quilt, barely visible in the starlit darkness, and he could see shine on the little bit of curly hair that rested on the pillow.

Married you are, Fogarty, and he smiled up at the skylight. Married.

A vision of mounds and mounds of festively-wrapped gifts swam up before his watery eyes.

His heart thudded. A gift! I must be giving my bride a wedding gift! He slipped out of bed and put on clothes that were clean as of the day before. He left her sleeping and walked quietly up the stairs and out into the early morning chill.

He gave a mighty stretch and a yawn, then rubbed his arms in the cold. The morning stars winked down on him as he saw the first faint glow of false dawn in the east. East. That's where he would find a present for his wife. In the east.

He walked past the old rusted boiler, and gave it a little pat, hearing the hollow sound of its deep interior. Again, as always, his mind played on it for a few moments. That big old boiler was big as a house almost. It had a big use in it, just waiting to be discovered, he knew that. Maybe he needed to spend a few hours with it, just the two of them alone, and he could feel what the old thing was about, feel what it wanted to do with the time it had left as an old boiler before the rust turned it into something else. It was real big, and good, and mostly dry inside. He would spend some time with Mr. Boiler soon.

Fogarty walked on past the boiler, toward the lightening sky. He walked up and down the hills of trash, through the areas he knew by heart. He'd picked over all this place long, long ago, and while the landscape always shifted, changing with the winds above and the decay below, the substance never really altered.

Dawn grew brighter, and the orange glow spread horizontally. Fogarty stopped for a moment to just watch as the clouds in the sky caught fire, and then he caught his breath as the surface of the debris of the dump turned yellowish-orange for miles in front of him. He wheeled around and sure enough, the stars still held their ground in the west, waiting until the last minute before fading out.

Fogarty found an old, dented suitcase half buried under some plastic bags full of some rotted something, old weeds, probably, and he pulled it free and sat down on it to watch the sun make her appearance. He sat and watched, seeing the patterns in the clouds, luxuriating in the richness of the colors spread before him. Dawn was his favorite time. It meant newness to Fogarty, freshness. Dawn always tugged on something deep within him, making him think about his life, and how good it was. He always had enough of whatever he needed. He picked up cans and old bottles whenever he went foraging, and when he ran out of oil for the lantern, he went into town to the place that gave him money for his pickings. He grew his own vegetables, year after year, using seed from the previous year's harvest. He found lots of burnable things for his stove, so he was warm in the winter, and there were plenty of clothes, and he had the company of the birds and the boiler, and the sun, and now and then a meal and some work with Lee and Donna.

And now he had Fogarty, his wife. What a blessing she was.

The sky began to turn blue and shadows formed on the hills and debris in front of him, making strange patterns of light, all still with a reddish glow. He laughed aloud at the idea that he could make animals out of these shadows as easily as he made animals out of the clouds. And these changed as fast as the clouds too, turning into something different every few seconds.

Ah yes, Fogarty, he thought, plenty of blessings right here. He had everything. He had his mornings, and his quiet time, and his sunrise, and this old suitcase to sit upon as he thought about things, and he had a long life, and good teeth, and…he looked around. He would like to have an orange tree. He would like to grow fresh oranges.

He watched the sunrise turn to yellow and he thought of ripping deep into a rich, juicy orange, and the ache began behind his ears and his mouth began to water. Maybe I can grow an orange tree inside that boiler, he thought, and then I can just go up there and say 'hello, Mr. Boiler, I've come to thank you and your orange tree by having myself a little orange breakfast, yes, I did, thank you very much,' and I'd peel myself a big, fat orange and let the juice run down my hands. Yes, he thought, that's just what I need.

He bounced up and down a little on the old dented suitcase as the sun sent glory to surround the eastern sky, and Fogarty tasted orange juice in his mind. The suitcase made a funny noise as it dented in and out, and he laughed out loud and did it some more. Then he stood up and took a look at it.

"Hey, Mr. Suitcase," he said. "You're a good old chair. You're a good old sunrise chair." And he laughed until he saw a piece of fabric sticking out the side, caught when the suitcase had been closed. It was dirty and faded, but it had flowers on it, and intrigued, Fogarty stood up and picked up the suitcase and looked closer at the fabric.

Maybe Fogarty would like that, he thought, and he snapped up the suitcase clasps. He opened the lid, and neatly folded inside was a dress, lying there pretty as you please, with a piece of its hem creased, faded and dirty where it had been out in the weather for years. Fogarty lifted the dress as if it were made of spun dreams, and held it up high to the sunrise. "Oh, you is a beauty, you is," he said, and tried to imagine the missus in it. He couldn't quite remember what she looked like, except that she had those soft brown eyes. She'd look just wonderful in this dress, he was sure.

Under the dress were little zippered bags with stockings and ladies personal things, some makeup and bottles of soaps and lotions. There was a bright yellow sweater that smelled a little musty, but that could be washed out all right.

Oh, Fogarty, he thought. This is a wedding present fit for your bride.

He looked at the sunrise, and though the sun hadn't peeked over the horizon yet, it was full daylight out, and the shadows had softened. Fogarty would be waking up soon, he thought, so he refolded the sweater and the dress, put them back in the suitcase and began a proud walk home.

She stood in the middle of the living room as he brought the old suitcase down the stairs. She wore his old plaid bathrobe, and her hair was squished down on one side where she'd slept on it wet and fresh from a washing.

"Hey, Fogarty," he said. "Morning to ya."

She looked at the ground and picked at her fingernails. She looked small, and frail, and afraid.

"Look what I gotcha," he said, and he hefted the suitcase, then brought it over and set it on the coffee table.

Curiosity brightened her eyes and she looked at him with a question.

"It's my weddin' present to ya," he said. "Go on, open it. I think you'll like it. It was a blessing from the east."

She just looked at it, a little expression of pleasure around her mouth.

He reached over and snapped open the locks. "Go on," he said. "Open it."

She looked up at him with those doe eyes and he felt silly.

"Don'tcha like it, Fogarty? Don'tcha want to see what's inside?"

She blinked once, and his face flushed. He didn't know what she wanted. He reached down in exasperation and turned the suitcase around to face him and flipped up the clasps.

She put a hand on his arm and bent down, over the back hinges. "What? What is it?"

She reached over, tugged on something, and Fogarty heard paper tear. Then she stood up, and in her hand she held a little, tiny piece of yellowed paper. She looked at it, and her eyes opened wide with wonder, and she handed it to him, excitement putting a flush into her cheeks.

It was a piece of a page torn out of what looked like a paperback novel, only it was so faded and water stained that hardly anything was legible at all. Fogarty looked at it, front and back, and started to set it down, but the missus held his hand and urged it again toward him.

He took a long look at her, and she nodded in encouragement, and he looked at the scrap again, impatient for her to be done with this silliness and see his wedding present. He examined the paper again, and just where it was torn were two words, faded almost into obscurity. Almost, but not quite. The words were: Mary languished.

"Mary la lan lang ished Mary lang-ished. Mary languished," Fogarty read, and the missus nodded her head.

"Mary languished," she said. "Me," and she thumped her chest with her fingertips for emphasis.

"You?" Fogarty was astonished, surprised and delighted. He hadn't seen her with this much enthusiasm. "Mary languished?"

She took the paper and licked it, then stuck it to her cheek. Her posture took on a whole new angle.

"Well, Mary Languished," Fogarty said. "Well," he said with a big grin, "well, Mary Languished Fogarty, this suitcase must be for you. It has your name on it. And when you're done opening it, we can use it for a sunrise chair outside."

Mary Languished touched the piece of paper, smiled at him with stars in her eyes, and got on with opening her wedding present.

Fogarty leaned over the fender of the old red Corvair and picked little weeds out of his vegetable garden. He had vegetables growing in every engine compartment of every car in this side of the dump. His fingers touched the hairy leaves of the squash vines and stroked the smooth skins of the zucchinis and he hummed softly to them. "Beauties, you is. Beauties." He kept an ear cocked for Mary Languished, expecting to hear her footsteps. She'd taken to exploring the landfill, spending her days foraging, just as he'd done. She'd brought home some little things, some nice little things, Fogarty thought, like a pottery jar to hold the cookstove matches. It was rough on the outside and swirly blue on the inside. Very nice.

He told her about the dangers: big rats that came out at night, and about the kids, teenagers, mostly, that came to shoot their guns. He showed her some hiding places he'd made, and how to find them, and she seemed happy and competent in the landfill. He tried not to worry when she went out, but he did anyway.

He left the zucchinis and went to the yellow Volkswagen, where tomatoes sprawled about. He looked out across the horizon, but could see nothing—nothing but the same landscape he'd seen every morning. No movement, no sign of life, no Mary Languished.

He spoke softly to the tomatoes, thanking them as he used his penknife to cut the ripest—four had to be cut today, that meant tomatoes for lunch and dinner and breakfast again tomorrow, but maybe he could dry some too, so they could have some hot tomato soup when the snow began to fly.

With gentle fingers, he put the four red fruits in the cut-off plastic jug he'd tied to his waist, and looked up again to see if he could see Mary Languished. She'd been gone quite a while.

The potatoes were in the bed of the old pickup truck, and he took his time going over to them. Providing food for two people was a lot more work than for just one, but mosttimes he found it a joyful chore.

Mary Languished had turned out to be a startling and pleasant addition to Fogarty's life. He had to keep reminding her to change clothes, and he had to make sure she bathed regularly, but life took on a whole new depth with another person in the house. There was a person to talk to, instead of the clock, or the chair, even if she never answered. She was quick with certain games and puzzles, and others didn't interest her, or she didn't understand them. She kept quiet most times; she hardly ever spoke, but now and then she'd get involved in a project and begin to whistling, a sound so beautiful to Fogarty's ears that he would go all soft and wilty, listening. He'd learned to not let on, though, or she'd stop and blush and not do it again until it just came out of her automatically.

He wanted to ask her about her music, wanted to ask her about her life, her background, how she came to be in the culvert under the freeway that night, but he knew that the way to ask people things was to share with them about yourself, and Fogarty just plain couldn't remember those things about himself. Now and then, little scraps of memory, like bits of ash floating on the wind, would flutter through his mind—a child's face, a refrigerator door, an office phone number—but then they would be gone, and he would be left with just a lingering feeling of things left undone. There wasn't anything he could do about those things—he had to just let it all be.

Fogarty lifted up the black plastic that covered the heavy bunches of potatoes and cut off two nice ones for the day's eating. Then he looked off in the direction Mary Languished had gone, and worried anew. He hoped she wasn't out there in trouble. He hoped she hadn't hurt herself trying to bring something back that was too big for her to handle. He hoped nobody had seen her and given her a hard time.

He hoped she wasn't out there whistling into nobody's ears and wasting the music.

He went on to the general vegetable garden in the topless bus and checked on the seats filled with late summer meals. Between the carrots and the broccoli, he stood up and looked out the broken bus window, and saw her coming over the hill. Sure enough, she was carrying something, and she was hurrying.

His heart flew when he saw her coming toward him, and he knew he was growing to love Mary Languished, with a deep, permanent kind of love. That, too, brought a tickle from the feather of a memory, but nothing substantial enough to even stop him for a moment. He picked a sprig of parsley and pulled up one fat carrot, grabbed a handful of snap beans that were growing up over the back emergency door, put them all into his side carrier, and went down the bus stairs to meet her.

"Fogarty!" she yelled as soon as she saw him, and she began to hurry faster. He looked around quickly to make sure nobody was lurking within shouting distance, for she surely was shouting. "Fogarty!" she said again, and made straight for him. He'd never seen her so excited. Her hair was flying out from under her knitted hat, and she had on that pretty summer dress he'd found in her wedding present suitcase that fit her slender frame and made her look pretty and fresh as springtime, even though the weather was closing in on autumn and she was closing in on middle age. She wore it with her old leather boots for tramping through the trash, and a half dozen pairs of mismatched socks, and now those unlaced old leather boots were stomping along, making a terrible racket. The dress was flying out from behind her and her eyes were as wide open as they could be, and she carried a blue bundle in front of her.

"Fogarty!" she yelled again and this time she sounded so urgent he began to run toward her.

She stopped, and bent over at the waist, he could see her taking deep breaths, trying to catch her wind, as he ran up toward her, and when he reached her, she looked at him with wild eyes and thrust the bundle into his hands.

The bundle moved, and Fogarty jumped and would have thrown it down, except for the expression on Mary Languished's face. He held it out away from him until she pulled back the blanket top and there it was. A baby. A baby looking back at him with clear blue eyes.

Fogarty just stared at the infant, astonished beyond words, beyond thoughts, even. A baby, who'd have thought a baby would be out here? Who brought it here? Nobody came out here, how'd it get here? And it was healthy—at least it looked plump and well fed—and happy—at least it wasn't crying. *What was a baby doing here?*

He looked at Mary Languished, whose face was still red and wet with perspiration, and she was still breathing hard from the run home with her find. She looked back at him, expressionless. "It's Moses," she finally said, and touched the baby's forehead.

Fogarty carried the baby into the house, and for the rest of the day, he and Mary Languished took turns looking at him.

Fogarty could feel his shoulders relax every time he looked at Moses. The pudgy little baby with the penetrating blue eyes had the same effect on Mary Languished, Fogarty had seen it. When the baby looked up at him, he felt something move deep inside him, something big, something gentle. And all the tension went out of his neck and his shoulders, and his back, and he stood taller and felt his face get looser, and his big hands hung slack and comfortable at his sides. He could gaze into the child's remarkable eyes and let the world pass him by.

Fogarty had Mary Languished mash up some zucchini and corn and feed it to Moses, who seemed to like it all right, but Fogarty knew that the child needed milk...milk and other things. That night they put him down in a dresser drawer at the foot of their bed, and he stayed quiet all night.

The next morning when Fogarty got up, he found the drawer empty. Mary Languished had the baby, waltzing him around the little living room, singing.

Fogarty looked at the two of them, and he began to remember the nightmares that had flitted through his dreams. Nightmares of responsibility. How would he find milk for the child? Moses needed milk, and a crib and a high chair. And diapers, oh Lord! It was enough trying to keep Mary Languished clean. How could he keep the baby in clean diapers? What would he do if the water faucet were taken away? Or if something happened to him? What if the baby got sick? And whose baby is it, anyway?

Then Mary Languished laughed and twirled and handed Moses to him, and he took the child and gazed into those clear, blue eyes and the nightmares fled and his shoulders relaxed and the only thing that mattered was his son.

After breakfast, Fogarty fashioned a sling so Mary Languished could carry their boy, and they went up and out into the sunlight.

"Blue place," was all Mary Languished could say to describe to Fogarty where she'd found the baby. Fogarty had never seen a "blue place" in the dump, and couldn't imagine what she was talking about. He wanted to find this "blue place." He thought if there was a baby in the blue place, then there might be baby supplies there, too. Mary Languished gave him a queer look, then shrugged and led the way, Moses snugly tucked into the sling across her front.

They started off north, silently trudging, listening to the crunch of their footsteps, the gurgle of the baby. They watched for people, cribs, high chairs and anything blue, and they smelled autumn on the breeze.

Fogarty hiked on, surveying his kingdom, pleased that everything seemed to be right with the dump. There was no evidence of vandals or vermin; no major disturbance around his home. The only clues that things weren't as they seemed, were the baby and Mary Languished's mention of a blue place.

Suddenly, Mary Languished hugged the baby to her and began running, her unlaced boots flopping around her feet. She reached a plastic sack with handles, and lifted it high.

Fogarty caught up with her and took the bag. Inside was a nice sweater, slate-blue, Fogarty's size. He liked it. There was also a new toothbrush, still sealed in its package. "Good, Mary Languished. Good work. Thanks to you." He smiled and bowed.

"Blue here."

"Blue what?"

"Blue air."

"Blue air?"

"Blue air, blue," she gestured widely, "trash, blue...Blue!"

"Where?"

"Here," she said, indicating the whole area with a sweep of her arm. "All this. Blue."

Fogarty couldn't make any sense of what she was saying. "What do you mean, blue, Mary Languished?"

"Fogarty," she said, matching the seriousness of his expression. "Blue. Everything blue."

"Where was the baby?"

She walked a little way and stopped. She stared at the ground, and then pointed. Fogarty followed her and looked where she pointed. In a little sheltered area was a wooden cradle with an odd little symbol carved in the headboard.

Fogarty squatted down and ran his finger over the symbol. It was black, as if burned into the old wood. There were three round dots like three points of a triangle inside an oval. He straightened up. "Where's the blue?"

Mary Languished looked around. She shrugged.

They looked at each other for a long moment. Fogarty felt some deep, familiar emotion come welling up within him; he felt like running away, he felt like crying. Then Moses began to squirm inside the sling and Mary Languished pulled him free of the restrictive cloth and held him up to the early morning sunshine. She smiled at the boy and turned him so Fogarty could see his face.

The baby looked wise, somehow, and Fogarty gazed into the little face until he felt that smile come out from the inside of him, and soon they were all laughing.

Mary Languished set the baby into his cradle. "Such a blessing," he found himself saying to her. He put his arm around her and they both looked at their son, and in a few moments she picked up the baby and he picked up the cradle and they made their way back home.

Fogarty found it hard to go up the stairs. He was ready to go to town; he had his coat on, his lining pockets empty and ready to be filled with supplies, a few extra bags tucked away. He thought of the long walk out of the landfill, along the road and into town. He thought of finding bedding for the two days it would take for him to finish foraging in the city for the things that he and Mary Languished and Moses needed. He thought of those things, being out there in the cold, alone, while they were warm and comfortable in their little dwelling, and he was very reluctant indeed to climb up the stairs.

But Moses needed milk and meat and diapers, and Mary Languished needed some female things and Fogarty had to provide those things for his family. And he had a twenty dollar bill that felt warm and pleasant in his pocket.

Mary Languished had gotten up to see him off, and she stood in the kitchen, wearing his bathrobe and holding Moses. Fogarty resisted the temptation to go to her, take the baby and just hold him and rock him.

He looked at her sweet face, still sleep-puffed, and wondered if she'd change his diaper even once in the two days he'd be gone. He'd already reminded her three times that he'd be gone two nights, and how she had to bathe herself and the baby each night. She never talked, so he never knew if she understood.

He wanted to leave feeling confident about her, he wanted to see a little row of white dishtowels in the kitchen, too, but instead, he gave her a last smile and a wave, and went up the stairs, opened the old blue Pontiac door and his breath steamed out into the starry, dewy, early morning.

He felt naked without his customary bags of bottles and cans and selected little items he'd scrounged to sell. He felt incomplete without them, but he didn't miss them; those things never brought him more than three or four dollars anyway. He had a whole twenty-dollar bill this time, and he could buy just about anything he wanted with that.

He patted his pocket one more time, felt the money, and set off down the trail toward the fence. He wanted to be well away from the landfill by daybreak.

"Such a blessing," he said to himself, as he walked over familiar territory under familiar stars. "Such a blessing to be free and rich." He stopped for a moment and scratched his head. "And to have a family waiting at home," he said, and smiled.

Dawn began as he reached the fence; the stars had faded into blue sky by the time he reached the main road, and the full adven ture of the trip before him filled his soul with excitement and his feet became lighter. He ran through the list of purchases again in his mind, and wondered if he'd have money left over to put a little wager in on one of the ponies running.

No, Fogarty, he said to himself. No more ponies. Have you forgotten the sickness? He hadn't forgotten. No more ponies, he promised himself, and he walked along the road into town as traffic picked up, and he thought of the place where he'd found the money—the same place he'd found the cradle for Moses. The Blue Place, Mary Languished still called it.

The Blue Place.

Fogarty had gone back there a few days after finding the cradle, and he found a high chair, right in the same place. It was a wooden high chair that looked just like the cradle; it even had the same carved symbol on the back of the seat: three dots, like the points of a triangle, inside an oval.

Mary Languished loved it. She set Moses in it, and he sat up as pretty as you please and grinned at his parents.

The few days after that kept Fogarty busy with putting down the last of the vegetables before the frost, and then he knew he was going to have to hustle to scavenge enough bottles and cans for all the things they needed to get them through the next couple of months. Usually, harvesting and laying in the last of the vegetables was a joyful chore, but this time as he worked, he worried.

He kept one eye on the sky, and the other on the last tin of meat in the cabinet, and he worked hard, and fast. The baby needed milk.

Scavenging had become harder. Fogarty wasn't as strong as he once was, and the landfill was growing. The trash shifted and changed like the ocean, with the winds constantly rearranging the top, and the rot, rust and decay rearranging below. But for eight, going on nine winters, Fogarty had scavenged the whole area, and bottles and cans and saleable goods became harder to find. The richest deposits of bankable items were closer to the fresher land- fill, and that was far, far from his home and risky.

And now, the Blue Place.

The Blue Place pulled on Fogarty—pulled on him the same way that clear-eyed gaze of Moses did. Fogarty wanted to go to the Blue Place every day. He wanted to go there and wait, he wanted to be there when the things arrived, he wanted to see the magic. He wanted to see the Blue. He could hardly work for thinking about how he'd rather be at the Blue Place.

He'd rather be there or else just playing with his son. When he gazed into Moses's eyes, he felt that everything was perfect, ev- erything was fine, everything has been, is, and would forever be just wonderful.

Both things were a distraction to him, a man not used to dis- tractions. Both were inexplicable, both were fascinating, irresist- ible. The Blue Place seemed to manufacture things they needed: that cradle hadn't been there, and that high chair hadn't been there, and that baby hadn't been there, and then all of a sudden they were. They just appeared, and he hadn't seen anybody coming or going or lurking around in the dump. It mystified Fogarty, and he thought about that Blue Place the whole time he worked in the garden.

As soon as he was finished putting down the vegetables, with- out even taking the Sabbath off to rest, he set off to scavenge for the inevitable trip to town.

The first place he went was the Blue Place.

Fogarty had gotten there just after sunrise. He climbed a little mound of debris and looked around, surveying the territory, look- ing for new things, weird things, anything blue or magic or mov- ing. He saw nothing unusual, nothing but the normal speckled gray/white/rust landscape with its hollows and shadows, spreading out as far as he could see.

"Blue," Fogarty said. "Where are ya, Blue? And what are ya, anyway?"

The Blue didn't answer him, so Fogarty smiled, and shook his head, and stepped down off the mound, and as he did, he caught sight of something little and green, flapping in the early morning breeze.

He couldn't believe what he thought he saw, so he walked calmly over to it. It was a twenty-dollar bill, with one end caught underneath a stone, and it looked to be in exactly the same place the cradle had been. He picked it up and smelled it, then ironed it out by pulling it back and forth across his nose.

"Twenty dollars," he said. "Is that from you, Blue?" He looked up into the blue sky, and snapped off a salute. "My missus and my son thank ya, Blue." And he chuckled and pocketed the bill, then made his way back to the house, glad he didn't have to go scratching and picking for bottles and cans.

Mary Languished hadn't even seemed surprised. She just kept whistling, singing, and babbling to the baby in that silly little language she seemed to have made up, and Fogarty just smelled that twenty dollar bill and sat in his chair, sipping tea, feeling rich and making plans to set out for town the next day.

As the heat of the sun began to penetrate the heavy coat Fogarty wore to town, sweat that cooled in the fall morning began to trickle down his face. He walked along the street, smelling city smells, morning smells, and he saw people walking, talking, driving, laughing, working, eating, and suddenly he thought that his life was blessed indeed.

Who else has some kind of invisible Blue give them money? And babies? And furniture?

Nobody, that's who, Fogarty, he thought to himself, and suddenly he had to go to the bathroom.

He found himself a Shell station and went in, locked the door and sat down. Maybe there's something wrong with me, he thought. Things like this just don't happen to regular folk. He put his chin on his hand and his elbow on his knee, and he tried to remember anybody else he'd ever heard of that had things like this happen to them.

He couldn't think of any.

When he was finished, he flushed the toilet and washed his hands, and he felt better.

Maybe it isn't wrong, Fogarty, he thought. Maybe it's right. Maybe we are just blessed.

A frown wrinkled his forehead. He'd never heard of anybody being that blessed before.

He thought of his home, and Mary Languished, and figured that right at that exact moment, she'd be feeding Moses his breakfast. He pictured them in his mind's eye, Moses sitting in his little high chair, one of Lee and Donna's used-to-be-white kitchen towels around his neck, another one around his bottom. Mary Languished would be mashing up vegetables with the last bit of meat from a dented can, and feeding him, both of them laughing, Mary Languished speaking that strange little musical language, and the baby responding as if he understood.

The home scene seemed a little weird to Fogarty, as he looked at himself in the service station washroom mirror. Something wasn't quite right.

Yet it was all so normal when he was at home. Especially when he found himself speaking that same funny little musical language to his son.

Out here in the real world of Shell station toilets, that memory made him more than mildly uncomfortable.

He ran cold water on his hands, and splashed his face. "A family is a blessing, Fogarty," he said to his reflection. "And every family has its quirks. Now you go buy the things your family needs."

"Okay!" he said back to himself, and then he got serious, and pointed his finger at himself. "And no ponies."

He smiled, smoothed his eyebrows, and stepped back out into the sunshine.

By nightfall, Fogarty had acquired almost everything he needed. The filled pockets in the lining of his coat made it hot and heavy, and it floated awkwardly around his legs and banged into his calves.

He was pleased with the way the day had gone. He had scrounged in his usual spots and come away with some good things. He'd gotten a half dozen dented cans of tuna and another half dozen of corned beef for a dollar. He got diapers from the Salvation Army and Mary Languished's female things from the loading dock of the supermarket. A new boy had cut a carton too deeply and spoiled a couple of boxes. Fogarty was grateful to give the lad two dollars for them. The only thing left was cans of milk for Moses, and Fogarty worried how he would carry cases of cans of milk all the way home.

He decided to postpone the worry; to treat himself instead, to an extravagance—a hot dog from a red hot stand near the library. It cost a dollar, but he piled on the ketchup and mustard and pickle relish and threw a few good onions on, too, just to be sure he got his money's worth. Then he sat on the big lawn at the library and watched the traffic and the bicycles and the birds and the kids, and he thought about his day.

It had been a good day. He'd hardly thought of Mary Languished and Moses, except, of course, when considering the things on his shopping list. He sat on the library lawn and ate his hot dog and licked his lips and tried to imagine what the two of them were doing at his home right this minute, and he couldn't even remember what they looked like. He couldn't believe there were people in his house.

But, of course, there were.

Fogarty finished the last bite of bun, licked his fingers and wiped his mouth on the sleeve of his shirt. He stood up and took off his laden coat, folded it carefully and laid it on the ground. Then he stretched out on the cool grass and put his head on the bundle.

Ahhh, the freedom. The freedom felt so cool, so nice. He was free to go wherever he wanted, to do whatever he wanted. He still had twelve dollars in his pocket, and he was almost finished with his duties. He thought he'd have to spend two nights out, but now he had only to spend one. He could make it back to Lee and Donna's before they closed the restaurant for the night, and have a sleep there, then get the canned milk and go home in the morning.

Canned milk.

His brow furrowed. His freedom fled. How'm I going to carry canned milk on top of all this other stuff all the way out to the landfill? He wouldn't be free until he figured out how to take the milk to Moses.

He had twelve dollars, he could take a taxi.

A taxi!

The thought made him sit up and hoot. Everyone passing by turned to look at him.

"Take a taxi, I could," he said to them, then chuckled and lay back down on the lawn. "Take a taxi. That's good."

But the problem of the milk remained.

I could buy a cow.

A cow!

This time he rolled over on his stomach and laughed, and beat the ground with his fist. "Buy a cow!" He laughed until his cheeks hurt, until his stomach was sore, until his fist was bruised, until the tears ran down his face. Slowly, control came back to him and he wiped at his face, giggling still, and he looked up at the people watching him, and he laughed some more. "Oh what a blessing it is," he said to them, although he didn't think they could understand him through his laughter, "to have a little freedom, yes it is, yes it is." And he lay back down, and tried to calm himself, but his stomach still shook in silent waves of laughter when he remembered what a great laugh he'd just had.

Then he remembered Mary Languished and Moses, and the worry over the cleanliness of his home returned. The fact that there were people in his home waiting for him, depending on him, quietly vacuumed up his freedom.

He stood up, put on his heavy coat and began to walk toward Lee and Donna's restaurant. They might have a good idea about the stupid milk.

Fogarty had to stop and rest six times—he counted them, six times!—on the way home in the early morning heat. In addition to the hot, heavy coat he wore, he carried a big box of powdered milk from Lee and Donna and a case of canned milk on his shoulder. He'd told Lee and Donna that Mary Languished had a passion for drinking milk—for some reason he couldn't quite bring himself to tell them that they found a baby in the dump. They'd been very happy to send him home with a box of powdered milk, and he'd stopped and bought a case of canned milk at the last store outside the city.

He was happy to be bringing these things home to his family, but he'd never had to stop and rest before, not even after a hard morning's work at the restaurant.

He rested again as soon as he managed to put himself though the wires on the fence, and he set the box and the case down and mopped his brow.

"Almost home, Fogarty," he said to himself, and a little smile of home came to rest on his face.

Then he stood, and hefted his bundles, and with weak knees and a wobbly stride, made it down the home stretch.

"Mary Languished! I'm home! Oh, what a blessing it is to be in out of the hot, hot sunshine." Fogarty came down the stairs as quickly as he could manage, and he set the case of milk on the counter and the box of milk on the floor and shed his coat as he looked around his living room.

Mary Languished had moved all the furniture around. It looked a little strange, but it looked all right, if only she'd put the foot-stool in front of the right chair, and move it all back against the walls again, like it was supposed to be.

"Mary Languished?" Fogarty set the footstool back in front of his chair, then glanced inside the bedroom and the bathroom. All was quiet, and everything was as it should be, so he went to his chair and sat down.

"A drink of water would be a blessing, Fogarty," he said, so he heaved himself out of his chair and went to the kitchen to get the water jug.

It was empty. Fogarty held it up and looked at it. That meant he had to go all the way up and around the old boiler for a drink. He was too tired. He'd do it later. He set the bottle back down under the counter and as he did, something else caught his eye.

He pulled back the other curtain, and there, under the counter, was a case of canned milk, the cardboard pried up in one corner, one can missing.

Fogarty's mouth fell open as he stared. He looked at the heavy case of canned milk he'd brought all the way from town, dark spots on the top where drops of his sweat had fallen, wet handprint stains on the sides where he'd frequently changed his grip.

He looked back and forth between the two, and then went back to the living room and sat down in his chair.

A moment later, he saw a shadow cross over one of the sky-lights. His heart leapt into his throat, and then the shadow passed and he heard Mary Languished's voice as she came near to the front door. He stood up as the door opened and she came down the stairs, singing.

She seemed surprised to see him. Fogarty lifted his laden coat from the floor where he had dropped it, and moved it to the sofa.

She gave him a bashful smile, and Fogarty felt somehow be-trayed as he looked at her. He felt a vague uneasiness about her being in his house, moving things around, risking security by wan-dering around the landfill, making him go out on wild goose chases for canned milk she never even needed.

"Fogarty," she said softly, and she brought Moses up from where he'd been resting in his sling at her side, and she held the baby up to Fogarty.

Fogarty's hands automatically took the baby from her, and he broke his gaze from Mary Languished's face and looked at Moses.

His son.

Those clear blue eyes looked back into Fogarty's eyes and Fogarty felt rested and well. His mind cleared of all its anxiety and poisonous thoughts, and nothing mattered in the whole wide world except the nourishment and happy home life of this perfect child with the clear eyes.

Moses.

His son.

Fogarty awoke in the still darkness. Moonlight shone in through the skylight in the bedroom. Mary Languished breathed deeply beside him; Moses made little cooing noises in the basket at the foot of the bed. Fogarty sat up and looked down at the baby, who was gently playing with his toes and quietly amusing himself. Moses had thrown off his quilt, but he didn't seem to be feeling cold, so Fogarty let him be. He laid back down on the bed and pulled the covers up to his chin. The frost was definitely on; snow would be flying before Thanksgiving. He snuggled down and felt the warmth from Mary Languished's body beside him.

That weird feeling of things not being normal began to creep over him again, like a slow rush of goosebumps.

Mary Languished had found the case of canned milk in the landfill at the same place he'd found the money. The Blue Place.

Fogarty shook his head. He just didn't understand any of this. Somewhere in the back of his mind he had memories of a woman and a baby, and he sort of remembered, and that made him smile a lot when he was at Lee and Donna's, because they had their baby, and the baby cried a lot...

The baby cried a lot...

The baby cried a lot and the baby slept a lot.

Moses never cried. And rarely—if ever, now that Fogarty thought about it—slept.

Lee and Donna's baby cried a lot and slept a lot and Lee and Donna spent a lot of time with their arms around each other and their noses touching. They goo-gooed to their baby, and all of it made Fogarty smile as the little memories buried back there in the landfill of his mind shuffled around a little bit, not exactly springing forth to be recognized, but he remembered. Sort of.

There was no physical affection between him and Mary Languished. They never touched, or cuddled—she was too shy. And they never discussed their pride over the baby with each other, they seemed to discuss it with Moses. In his own language.

Fogarty ran his hand over his face in the dark. Something's really strange here, he thought.

Then he raised up again and looked at Moses in his cradle, and Moses stopped his playing and looked back at him, directly at him, those clear blue eyes looking deeply into Fogarty's soul.

Everything is okay, Fogarty thought, and he laid back down and went to sleep.

In the morning, Mary Languished fed Moses and rocked him, while Fogarty watched. Her eyes kept shifting around the room; she seemed restless and couldn't meet his gaze. Finally, he put on his coat and went up to forage for a while. Then he saw the hose.

A long patchwork hose made up of lots of little hoses hooked together stretched across the top of the dump from the deserted hydrant and disappeared into the trash next to his house. Fogarty was sure it went right into the kitchen, where Mary Languished could use it at will instead of having to walk up and out and over to the hydrant for water.

Anger burned up through Fogarty. That woman's going to get us discovered here, he thought, and marched right over to the hydrant. He turned it off, then disconnected the hose. He walked back toward home, disconnecting and burying pieces as he went. She didn't even try to cover it up, he thought.

"Roamin' the landfill during daylight hours, drawing a straight line toward the house, sending me out on wild goosechases..." Fear of discovery turned quickly to anger and rumbled out of Fogarty's mouth in a monotone of discontent.

He reached the blue Pontiac door and pulled it open. Mary Languished stood there with Moses in his sling, Fogarty's clock under one arm and surprise on her face.

"Fogarty!" she said.

"Mary Languished," he said, and bowed his head. "Where are you about to?"

A blush came up her neck into her cheeks. "This clock's for the Blue, Fogarty," she said. "For thanks."

Fogarty was stunned. "My clock?"

Mary Languished nodded.

"Does the Blue want my clock?"

She shrugged.

Fogarty stepped aside, and Mary Languished looked down, then came out. Fogarty went inside, closing the door after him. He descended the stairs and watched her shadow cross the skylights, then he looked at the spot on the wall where his clock had hung for six, going on seven winters. He'd foraged that clock and set it to working right. He even sold pop bottles and beer cans for money to buy brand new batteries for it.

The house didn't look right without the clock. What did the Blue want with the clock anyway? Maybe it would have been just as happy with a can of milk or a rag.

Fogarty found the hole in the wall next to the sink where the end of the hose came through. It was all wet; she'd just turned the hydrant on and let it leak inside the wall. He pushed it back up gently, then went back upstairs and pulled it out of the ground. He went to the old boiler and buried the hose up next to it.

Instead of patting the old boiler and listening to its wonderful hollow sound, Fogarty scowled at it and went to the hydrant for a drink.

When Mary Languished returned, Fogarty was sitting on the couch staring into space, waiting for her, his bowels churning. He saw her shadow pass across the skylights, and a knot tightened in his stomach. Then the door opened and closed and she stepped gingerly down the stairs.

She came into the living room, unslung Moses from her side and sat in the big chair, the baby in her lap.

"Did the Blue come, Mary Languished?"

She nodded, but did not look up at him.

"You saw it? You saw the Blue come take the clock?"

She began to pick at her fingernails.

"Did it take the clock?"

She shook her head and pulled at her hat.

"Where's the clock? Didn't you bring it home?"

This time she looked him squarely in the eyes. "Can't take back a gift," she whispered.

"If the Blue didn't want it…"

"Belongs to Blue," she said, and picked up the baby from where he'd been resting on her knees and brought him to her chest. She began to rock him.

"I took the hose apart, Mary Languished," Fogarty said. "You oughtn't have done that. It was like a trail, right to our house."

"Never left nothin' new, Fogarty," she said.

"What?"

"Blue never left nothing new."

"Maybe you oughtn't go there in the daytime any more."

"Why?"

"Because we're gonna get discovered, that's why. You can't just leave a hose trail and go traipsin' about all day long, Mary Languished. Someone's going to see and get suspicious." Fogarty felt heat come up his chest.

Mary Languished looked hurt, as if he'd insulted her.

"And they'll throw us out," he said. "Or maybe put us in a home."

Mary Languished stopped rocking and stared into her own memories.

"And take Moses away."

Mary Languished hugged the baby tighter and started rocking fast "No, Fogarty, you don't know."

"Know what, Mary Languished?"

"Blue decides."

"Mary Languished, the Blue don't decide about the County guys!"

Mary Languished stood up and walked over to the couch. She held the baby out for Fogarty to see, but Fogarty pushed her away.

"I don't want to see the baby," he said. He knew that if he looked into Moses's eyes, that everything would settle down again, everything would be fine again. No, he would only think everything was fine again, but nothing would be fine unless Mary Languished understood what he was saying.

Mary Languished turned again, and held Moses up in front of Fogarty, and somehow, against his will, Fogarty looked at that sweet, clean baby face, and those clear, clear blue eyes, and all his fears fled, and a sense of security and well being settled over him.

The next day she took his footstool. The day after that she took the quilt from the bed and replaced it with an ugly old stained, torn blanket.

Fogarty began to mourn.

He stayed in the house because he couldn't keep Mary Languished from going out and he didn't want too many people roaming the landfill. He stayed in the house and watched her feed Moses and carry him around and talk to him in that stupid little language they had for each other. He stayed in the house and watched her loot his little home, piece by sentimental piece, and he didn't say anything. He stayed in the house and watched Moses grow healthy and strong and begin to crawl around the floor, and his emotions skidded up and down like they were on a roller coaster. He stayed in the house and stayed in the house and stayed in the house. The longer he stayed in the house, the deeper his depression grew.

Every now and then, he would look into Moses' face, and the depression would dissolve. Happiness surged through him and he felt strong and good and wise. Then Mary Languished would swoop down and pick up Moses and they would laugh and laugh together and the feelings Fogarty had only lasted for a few more moments, then they slipped away and he plunged further into the pit of desolation.

He suffered in silence for a long time, and then he couldn't stand it any more.

When Mary Languished returned home after taking his porcelain chamber pot to the Blue Place, as soon as she started fixing dinner for Moses, Fogarty got up out of his chair, put on his coat and went outside.

The air was crisp and cold, the shadows long. He smelled snow on the air, the fresh, delicious air, and he ran in place for a moment, feeling his muscles freeing up after being inside for so many weeks.

He held his arms out and looked around his little domain, then set off to the Blue Place. He wanted to have a little talk with the Blue.

As he came over the rise, the first thing he saw was his beautiful chamber pot, atop a little pile of his possessions. Fogarty squatted down and examined each thing. It was all there, it was all intact. The quilt was a little damp, but that was no problem. He'd just pack it up and take it home.

Then he looked around and wondered if the Blue would come if he left a present for it. If the Blue came he could talk to it. He fished out the penknife he'd kept in his pocket for as long as he could remember, gave it a kiss and put it inside the chamber pot, then he sat down to wait.

He watched very carefully, because he wasn't sure how blue everything would get. Even the air came blue, Mary Languished said, so Fogarty watched very carefully for any signs of blue.

There were none.

He waited a long time. He waited until after the sun was down and the stars came out. He waited until his muscles cramped, until his joints ached from the cold. Then he stood up, shook out his limbs and retrieved his pocketknife.

"Why are ya doing this to us, Blue?" he shouted. "Why do you give us things and then make everything so confused? Here. Take the pot. It's our thanks for the milk and the money and the baby. Take it. Take it. We want ya to."

Only silence answered him.

"How come Mary Languished wants to bring ya things ya don't want? How come you only come when she's here? How come you're doing all this to us? We're good people, and you're not doing nice things."

He stopped to catch his wind. Only the breath of an evening breeze came through.

"I'm mad, Blue," Fogarty said, then stomped off toward home.

He got madder when he saw all the lights Mary Languished had put on. She must have lit every candle and lantern in the place. Light turned the skylights into beacons.

Time to go to town for a while, Fogarty, he thought to himself. Time to go see Lee and Donna. Time to go see the city and work in the restaurant and do some normal things, live a little normal life for a while.

But he was afraid to go. Afraid of what might be waiting for him—or not waiting for him when he got back home.

Fogarty awoke in the middle of the night. He got up and used the old rusted bucket that had replaced his beautiful porcelain chamber pot and then wandered though his little house. He didn't feel like getting back into bed with Mary Languished. He didn't want to listen to her breathe, and he didn't want to listen to Moses singing to himself in the cradle at the foot of the bed. Instead, he sat on the sofa and wrapped up in the soft knitted afghan that had so far escaped Mary Languished's offerings to the Blue.

The moon shone down through the skylights, and Fogarty felt his bottom lip pout out in absolute despair.

He looked across the room to his favorite sitting chair, already naked without its ottoman. "Hey, yo, Mister Chair," he whispered in the darkness. "How long before she takes you out to the cold?"

He wrapped the afghan tighter around his thin shoulders and gripped handfuls of it in his bony fists. "And you, Missus Blanket," he said. "You're the prettiest thing I have left. Soon you'll be out there warmin' up the chamber pot while I'm in here shiverin' and peeing in an old no-account bucket."

The pout deepened. His head sunk down lower into the hollow between his shoulders. The closed-in feeling wrapped around him again, tighter than the afghan, tighter than his skin.

"Time to move on, Fogarty," he whispered to the night air, and sadness pushed behind his eyes. He thought of packing up his few precious things and carrying them out of the landfill. He saw himself, looking old and skinny, just a haggard old man, standing at the main road trying to decide which way to turn.

"I'm too old to start over again," he said, and the tightening feeling squeezed out a tear that ran down the side of his nose. He looked around the patchwork walls, and remembered how hard it had been to build this little underground house all by himself. He thought of the years he spent scavenging household items—finding, fixing, replacing—until he had his home comfortable and perfect. He probably didn't have that many years left all told—he certainly wouldn't if he had to start all over again.

"What's the use?" he asked the pillow that sat next to him on the sofa, then he let go of the afghan and touched the pillow's worn velvet. "Might just as well up and die right now. There's nothing left for me."

A second tear followed the first, and Fogarty swiped at it with the pillow.

Then he got an idea that made his heart pound. He sat up straight. "I could move into the boiler, yes I could," he said. "I could move into that nice, clean old boiler, and I could move my things over and be closer to my water, and Mary Languished could live here with Moses, and she could give all her own things away. She could give it all away and I wouldn't care, because I would have all my own stuff in my own place." He smiled. "She could even give away my things and I could just go pick them up."

He sat back, shivering in anticipation of his new, good idea. "She could even give Moses away, yes she could, she could even give Moses away, and I wouldn't care. I'd just go pick up the stuff I wanted to keep. She could give Moses away and I wouldn't pick him up at all."

His smile became a grin.

And then he thought about Mary Languished traipsin' all over the landfill, carrying the baby, running water lines, and he knew that before long they'd be found out.

The smile evaporated.

They could take Mary Languished away and he wouldn't mind, but he would give up for sure if they took him away and put him someplace stupid like they sometimes did with old men.

Depression pressed him back into the couch. He bunched up the little velvet pillow and squeezed it. "I wouldn't care at all if they took Mary Languished away," he whispered, and then he got another idea, a great idea, a horrible idea, an idea that he didn't like, an idea he tried to push away.

"I could just give Mary Languished away," he whispered in the dark. "I could just give Mary Languished and Moses both away, just take them to that Blue Place and leave 'em for the Blue. And I'd make them stay there, too, I would, I would make them stay."

Thoughts of Mary Languished and her soft brown eyes and her shy manner trying to make Fogarty reconsider made him bunch up his fist.

"I would make them stay there, yes I would, yes I would."

It wouldn't go away, his idea, it was too good, but it was so awful, and it made him feel so bad, so guilty, that finally he went to bed to snuggle up next to Mary Languished's warm body to see if her sleeping sounds would make the idea go away.

It didn't go away, and it stayed with him all the rest of the night.

It was with him the next morning, too, and Fogarty couldn't look Mary Languished in the eyes. He just put his head down and went about his business, bringing in the food, foraging a little bit out toward the east, just him and his idea, alone in the world.

By the time his stomach told him it was time for dinner, Fogarty had taken control of his idea. It was a bad idea, and he felt guilty that he'd let it play so long in his mind. He stood up from his diggings and rubbed his aching back. It was time to go make a nice dinner for Mary Languished and Moses. He could never confess the thoughts he'd had about them, but he could make it up to them by fixing them a nice hot dinner. Maybe some nice vegetable soup and he'd even open a tin of meat.

He walked and walked to get home, surprised at how far away he'd gone during the day. By the time he spotted the blue Pontiac door, his heart gave a little leap. Home and hearth. "She's a good woman, Fogarty," he said to himself. "What a blessing it is to have such a fine family."

He opened the door and went down the stairs, noticing that it was bone-chilling cold inside. Mary Languished hadn't even started a fire. At the bottom of the stairs he smelled dirty diapers and noticed that the woodbox was empty.

He knew by the coldness of the house that no one was home, but he called anyway. "Mary Languished?"

There was no answer.

His favorite sittin' chair was gone. And so was the knitted afghan. It was like she heard him out there whispering in the privacy of his own nighttime. Eavesdropping on his own sleeplessness. Taking his privacy, his sleeplessness, his chair and his afghan in one slap.

Anger burned in his stomach. The bad idea returned with full force. It began to feel like a good idea.

Fogarty stomped up the stairs, hands stuffed in his pockets. He headed west, then circled around south, avoiding the Blue Place, and he just stomped and talked to himself in anger, kicking things as he went. Eventually he ended up by the old boiler and before he recognized the old crate as firewood, he gave it a kick that splintered its old slats and Fogarty grabbed it with his bare fingers and ripped it the rest of the way, driving slivers deep into the palms of his hands.

The pain brought him back to reality, and he looked at the pieces of crate, broken and twisted at his feet. He gathered them up and went home to build a fire.

By the time he got back, dusk had deepened and there was a faint light coming through the skylight.

Fogarty found one candle burning in the kitchen. Mary Languished stood in the middle of the living room, holding Moses, rocking him.

Fogarty threw the wood into the woodbox and dusted off his hands. He pulled two of the largest splinters out and left the rest for later. There was something that had to be done first.

He went to Mary Languished and took the baby from her and set him on the sofa. He put his hands on both of Mary Languished's shoulders and turned her to look him in the face.

"The chair, Mary Languished, you took the chair and the warm blanket. There's no wood and no food and too much...this is too much, do ya understand?"

"Never left nothing new, Fogarty," she said.

"Did it ever take the stuff you left it?"

She shook her head.

"Then let's go get it all and forget the Blue," he said.

She shook her head at him with a determination set to her jaw. "Can't," she said.

"Yes, Mary Languished," Fogarty said, and his hands burned with the slivers, "we can and we're going to. Right now."

"Blue protects us, Fogarty."

"Well, that's fine. It can do that without all my stuff in a pile out in the weather. You make a fire and some tea, all right? I'll go get the stuff."

"No," she said, and turned to the sofa to pick up Moses.

"I don't want to look at the baby."

"Here." She struggled against him to get to the sofa.

"No." He held her arms firmly.

"Here!" She lunged.

"No!" He held tight.

"Aaaaaaaaa!" Mary Languished began to scream and Moses began to sing and the whole room began to turn blue.

Fogarty let her go and he dropped to the floor. The room looked eerie, unreal, as if he were looking through a pair of blue glasses.

"I been a good man, Lord," he whispered. "I been a good man, yes I has."

A gentle calm washed over Fogarty, and he relaxed on his knees, feeling safe and warm. Then he felt a tingling in his hands and looked at his palms and noticed that the slivers, almost black in the eerie blue light, were disappearing, and the skin healed and grew smooth as he watched.

He looked up and saw Mary Languished, barely breathing, rapture on her face, eyes open but seeing nothing, standing with feet apart and arms stretched out wide.

And Moses was laughing

When the blue faded away, so did Fogarty's sense of well-being. Mary Languished, still enraptured, picked up Moses and swung him around the little living room, and then she took him into the bedroom, while Fogarty pulled himself up from the floor and onto the couch, his old joints creaking like never before.

"The Blue protects them, yes it does, yes it does," he said to himself, still marveling at what happened. He shook his head and looked around, and suddenly found it hard to believe that it really had happened.

He sat on the sofa and he thought about it, and thought about it and thought about it.

He thought about having something looking over him all the time like that—something so powerful it could melt the slivers right out of a man's palm. Something so powerful it could be summoned just by a little yell. Something so important it could change him from blood-freezing fear to calm security in the space of a heartbeat.

He thought about it and he didn't like it.

Mary Languished liked it. Mary Languished loved it.

Moses liked it. Moses loved it. Moses *was* it.

Barely a slip of a moon shone down through the darkest of night when Fogarty made his decision.

Very quietly, he arose from the sofa, stretched out his legs, rubbing out the cramps from sitting motionless for hours, then put on his jacket. He went into the bedroom and saw Moses, wide awake as always, looking at him with shining eyes from the crooked arm of a sleeping Mary Languished.

"Come Moses," Fogarty said, trying not to look directly into the child's eyes. "Come to daddy."

Fogarty picked him up gently, and Mary Languished sighed and rolled over in her sleep. Fogarty grabbed the bedding from the cradle and took it to the living room, where he wrapped the baby up tightly, determined not to look into those eyes that would immobilize him—or at least mesmerize him into inaction.

When he had Moses snugly wrapped, Fogarty took the little bundle in his arms, mounted the stairs and opened the old blue Pontiac door into the freezing night air. His breath plumed out before him. The ground was frozen and covered with frost. Fogarty stepped gently until he was sure he was out of earshot, and then he walked quickly, even ran in places he knew were flat and without hazard.

At the Blue Place, Fogarty held the baby tightly to his chest. "I've come to give him back, Blue. It's too much, do you understand? We're grateful and all, but it's too much."

He lay the baby down in the same place where he had first appeared, and then stood back to watch.

Nothing happened.

Fogarty began to shiver, and he thought maybe he would cry. "C'mon, Blue," he said. "Please?"

But then he remembered that the Blue never came for him anyway, and he left Moses there under a slip of a moon and went back to the house.

"Mary Languished," he whispered as he shook her shoulder. "Mary Languished, you must come with me. Moses has gone back to the Blue Place."

Mary Languished's eyes snapped open and she looked around wildly for a moment, then focused on Fogarty.

"Come," he said. "Moses is out in the cold."

Mary Languished looked down into the empty bed where the child had lain moments before, threw the covers off and leaped out, fully dressed. She pushed past Fogarty, ran through the house and up the stairs without bothering for a sweater or a jacket, threw open the door and ran out without shutting it behind her.

Fogarty was cold and winded, and couldn't keep up, but he followed her beeline to the Blue Place, and when he caught up with her, she was holding the bundle that was Moses and pulling at the bedding to uncover his face.

"You have to stay here now, Mary Languished," Fogarty said. "You and Moses are my offering to the Blue." He began to pick up his things and pile them in the big chair...the afghan first, then the porcelain chamber pot and the clock. He could come back for the other things.

"Fogarty," she said, her voice as soft as a spider on a web. "Fogarty and Fogarty."

The sharp edges of broken promises carved into his belly.

He turned to look at her, and she stood in a little hollow of trash, wearing the wedding dress he'd given her, her knitted hat, and a dozen pair of old socks up and down her legs with unlaced boots open at her feet, their tongues lolling in the cold. She held the bundle to her chest, and looked at him with those soft, those wonderfully soft brown eyes, and Fogarty thought he heard the sound of sixteen wheelers crossing over the sky.

"You'll be a blessing to the Blue, Fogarty," he said to her, then picked up the chair, an old frail man proving a point, and he staggered under its weight as he carried it with a light heart and a sweaty brow toward home.

Early the next morning he went to fetch the rest of his things, and there was no sign of Mary Languished or Moses.

He put all of his belongings back where they once were, cozying up his little home, and made a little daylight fire in celebration of his freedom. Then he went and packed up the little suitcase with Mary Languished's belongings and Moses's things and set them just outside the Pontiac door.

He took himself a shower and made himself a cup of tea and proposed himself a toast to Mary Languished Fogarty and Moses Fogarty, long may they live in peace.

The following morning he awoke while it was still dark. A sunrise for Fogarty this morning, he thought. He got dressed up in his warmest and warmed himself up by the stove, then went upstairs and into the crisp, starry early morning. He found an old suitcase by the door and carried it toward the east.

He carried the old suitcase past the old boiler and he gave the boiler a pat on the side, loving its deep hollow ring. "Hello, Mister Boiler, Sir," he said to it. "Such a nice old boiler you are." He continued east and when he found a suitable place, he put the suitcase down and sat on it. Then he bounced up and down a couple of times. "Hey," he said. "this suitcase makes a good chair. This suitcase makes a good old sunrise chair." He admired the old suitcase for a while longer—and decided to keep it. It might fetch fifty cents or so in town, but then he'd always wanted a sunrise chair.

He sat and watched the sky lighten and expand into a blaze of glory, and was enthralled. "Such a blessing, to have a sunrise like this, Fogarty, such a blessing on such a beautiful morning," he said to himself, his freedom feeling cool and nice, but then just a little tickle of sadness slithered in to confuse him. It felt a little like loneliness, and somewhere in the back of his mind was a memory somewhere, of a wife, and a child, but he couldn't quite place it.

※

Suspicions About Death

This is the big one, isn't it? Death. Isn't it the fear of what might happen to us after we die that keeps us interested in how we live our lives? Isn't this how most religions control us?

And speaking of religion, don't you think we would all do well to continually ask the uncomfortable and arguably rude question, of all those who would pontificate about the validity of their religion and their particular afterlife:"Just *exactly* what is the source of your information?"

Can we come back after death? Under what circumstances? If so, to whom are we able to speak, and why only to *them*, for god's sake? That is very suspicious indeed.

Is there a heaven? A hell? Is Evil loose upon the world? Could we really be doomed to repeat our mistakes ad nauseum until we do it right—without knowing what it was that we did wrong to begin with? Or is this literally Sandbox 101?

I guess the real question is this: Why all the secrecy?

MusicAscending

I stood at the top of the crumbling steps, gagging in the foul breath of the undercity as its stench rose to dance with the early morning street fog. Within moments, I would go below to capture one last sound, and I dwelt on the morning's strumming to quell the fear, to settle the bile, as I thought of going down there, down those slimy stone stairs into the pit, into the filth.

I cleared my mind of its fears and took a minute to think of the raw, melodic strains of the packets as they were this morning when I strummed them. I strummed them every morning for sustenance.

It was also my custom to run my thumb along the tops of the packets after each successful capture to hear the new addition, the new harmony in their song, and each time, the symphony has become clearer but still incomplete—and so I came for the final sound, came to stand at the top of the stairs. The stairs of the damned.

I am a designer of experiences. Clients seek me out to enrich their lives; they contract for a particular sensation. By use of higher mathematics and the nature of substance vibration, I collect the ingredients—sounds—which, if mixed correctly, will trigger chemicals in the human body and provide my clients with the desired event.

I have given the experience of a happy childhood to those deprived. I have given barren women babies to nurse. I have given grandchildren to young, terminally ill fathers, and I have given sight to those who are blind.

Most requests are basic, simple, and to the point. And so it seemed with this one, at first.

He had seemed such a harmless gent. This commission had come so innocently, seemingly spontaneously, on the wings of a wish during a Sunday after-church stroll through the park. He wished out loud. He saw his mortality and wished for more time.

Time for what, I asked. For a life richer in experience, he replied, and when I confessed my livelihood, he challenged me—
"Are you for hire, then?"

"I've retired."

"So young?"

"Young and bored. People want simple, ordinary experiences, and I'm tired of those. On my last commission, however, I published an entire circus—complete with elephants, calliope and smell of roasted peanuts, mind you—within the brain of a blind deaf-mute child. Ha!" I clapped my gloved hands together, recalling the experience. "A crowning glory to my career. After such an achievement, I could never go back to marketing the mundane."

We walked along in silence. The man was a stranger to me, a mild and gentle person, well dressed, with soft smile and manner, and I was restless in my retirement and eager for a fresh ear.

"Have you ever a bad experience? Have you ever erred, or harmed someone?"

"Harmed? No. Erred? Only in judgement," I replied. "For a short while I gave the experience of adulthood to adolescents, but then I decided that was unwise. From that point on, I refrained from administering any experience that might frighten, disappoint or depress. Bad PR, you know."

He chuckled in agreement. "How does this system of yours work?"

"Basic stuff. I design the experience, paying particular attention to detail. That's my trademark: exhaustive detail. Then with my gift of understanding substance vibrations and my propensity toward mathematics, I identify the ingredients, the sounds. When the desk work is done, I search out and capture the sounds, storing them in papers. I'm very particular about each phase of my work, but the collecting is most important. One must resist the impulse to substitute an inferior sound for the sake of convenience, or expedience. The collecting can take an enormous amount of time, if it is done properly.

"After the collecting is complete comes the most crucial step, and the test of my true genius, if I may say so. I mix the sounds, delicately blending with a fine ear and a practiced hand. Then I administer the distillation, which stimulates the client's brain chemicals, and they sally forth to create the hallucination. And I sit back and observe."

"Have you ever administered one to yourself?"

"Never."

"Where do you find these sounds?"

"Everywhere!" I stopped, and listened, and after an extra step, he stopped too, and we both listened.

"Once I gave a bedridden old woman a bareback horse ride through the woods," I whispered.

"Yes?" I saw the intrigue on his face.

"I collected all the required sounds—every ingredient—from a farmer's market and a bakery."

"But one has nothing to do with the other!"

I smiled and began walking again.

"I wish to hire you."

"I'm sorry."

"Please. I promise this commission will challenge your creativity."

Our stroll had been pleasant, but I had had enough. "I must go now."

He named an impossible amount of money, impressive enough that it offered me pause. He interpreted the pause as weakness in my resolve and doubled the amount. I turned slowly to face him.

He seized my shoulders and fired intensity into my eyes. "I wish to experience death," he said, his gloved grip conveying the seriousness of his intent. "Experience death and live to tell of it. I will pay you whatever amount you want, if you think you can accomplish it." He pressed cash and a business card into my hand.

I started to refuse, but recognized the obsession in the man and anticipated his mindless persistence, so I took his card and departed, expecting a few hours of research—a week maximum—before I could, with good conscience, return his money with a regretful report. Instead, by the time I reached my doorstep, I had a glimmer of an idea as to how to proceed. That very night I worked through until sunrise—the first of many such nights.

The weeks flew by as I delved deeper into geology, astronomy, mythology. I sweat for months upon the design. Reference books cluttered my desk, my floor, the top of my refrigerator and my tables. I slept with crystals under my pillow to open my mind to new possibilities. I became completely caught up in the speculation of the myriad possibilities. I could feel my imagination stretch until it warped out of shape. When it became loose-fitting and easily maneuvered, I reveled in newfound freedom of conjecture. Boundaries were no longer identified. Indeed, such was the nature of the task that common boundaries no longer held true.

My entire life centered around this one task. It seemed that the premature experience of death must somehow be either readily available to the masses merely for the asking, or else it would be completely forbidden—yet I kept seeing progress in my design. Always, just at the edge of despair, my hope was nourished by a glimmer of progress, and the project was saved at the expense of everything normal in my life.

It was always just after those moments of encouragement that he would come to call, to assess my devotion to his commission. And he would gaze upon my desk, at my research notes, and he would look deeply into my eyes, and then depart, leaving a taint in the air.

This agony continued for years—years!—until one night I awoke and sat straight up in bed, throwing aside the book on spatial isomerism I had been reading until exhaustion had overtaken me, and I realized that the design was already complete.

I ran to my desk and brushed all debris from it, leaving only the musical score. I checked and rechecked my calculations. Hope rooted and began to sprout. By the time dawn etched its rude violins on my windowsill, I knew that the design was finished—I had completed it weeks before, but it was a solution so brilliant that it had almost passed me by. Even I was astonished at my own genius.

My energy reached massive proportions. I felt I could go for months without sleep maybe I would never sleep again. Quickly, I began jotting down a list of ingredients, marveling at the symmetry, anxious to be finished with the paperwork and on with the collecting.

Eventually, I fetched hat and coat, list and score, and set out.

It was years again before I found myself at the edge—the edge of sanity, the edge of my own history. Only one ingredient had yet to be captured, and I stood at the lip of living hell, where below my feet had been cast the errors of evolution, where they have continued to exist and evolve along their own mutant designs.

One sound remained to be caught, and the stuff of it moved restlessly below my feet.

I stared down into the blackness, willing my feet to take the first step down, paper in hand and ready to catch the final sound, and I thought: of what use is the old man's cash if I must face a pit filled with the wretched excesses of an amoral humanity? What is the value of satisfaction in a job well done when the jaws of terror threatened to shred my psyche?

Yet the collecting begged for completion. The project was too important. Envelopes, precious envelopes in my hotel room contained the first whimper of a woman upon the birth of her third stillborn child. I had captured the thud of the fifth clod of dirt to fall upon the casket of a Satanist at a Christian funeral. I had the groan of an oak branch as it swung the body of a black teen. I had seen madness spit from a machine gun, and captured the sound of splintering bone. I held the final heartbeat of an abortionist and the death rattle of a drug addict.

But there was more. Beyond. I had reached into the future, and into the past to fill the musical score. I had spent years extrapolating figures that led me to lay in wait to capture the pant of a rabbit whose blood will grow a deadly strain of warfare bacteria in a petri dish. I had plucked from the air the black belch of a bus that will figure into the misinterpreted dream of an evangelist, whose political maneuvers will soon become clear.

And I had sealed into my papers the stomach gurgle of a world terrorist at his first newborn suck.

If mixed with accurate proportions, all of this would delicately balance on a minute particle of tincture drawn from the sound of a virgin's lips as they brushed the pillow in smile on the eve of her wedding day.

For a base tone, for the underlying heavy note upon which all else would rest, in order for my music to rise, I had yet to sink to the depths, descend into the fetid fields of filth below me.

My stomach churned, the trembling in my hand crinkled the delicate papers.

For what?

I stood ready, my sudden introspection daring to defy the clock. If I tarried too long, my opportunity would be lost, and all the years of work and preparation, the interminable waiting, not to mention the frustration of the design itself, would all be for naught.

But for what? For what have I worked this hard? Certainly not the money. The foolish old man who hired me could have easily paid ten times the amount—I had only to ask for it. No, it was not the money that carried me onward.

Was it to certify the genius of my design? No, my experience told me that my design was solid.

For what, then, I asked myself, as the optimum time drew nigh. My descent must begin or the opportunity would be forever lost.

I had become jealous of the experience I would create. I cared not to see the old man thrill at the result of my labor. He was a cowardly old man, selfish, wanting this experience only to better prepare himself in his few remaining years. He was a dastardly individual—Satan himself, I had come to believe, with his unfailing smile and soft words of encouragement—while I toiled night and day on his salvation. I had come to detest the senile old man.

If anyone deserved to die unprepared, it was he.

But this...this...*this* was the orchestration of a lifetime! When I completed my journey under the street, and had the final envelope vibrating in my pocket, when I returned to my hotel room to run my thumb across the tops of all the papers, raw collecting complete, I wanted to mix the experience for my own enjoyment. I was younger than the old man. I could mix the sensation stronger. I could take full advantage of the hallucination. The old man would need it weak, like his tea, like him.

I could make it last a miniature lifetime, and I would have what no man has ever had before.

It is far too important to waste on him. And besides, the Gods had given *me* the gift, had entrusted the design to *my* genius. My obligation was to them, not to him.

Dread surrounded me like a moist blanket. If I survived the depths here, if I obtained the final symphonic note, I would have to make a choice. If I did not survive, then I would compare my design with that of the Creator.

My body shifted forward; my shoes ground grit on the wet street. One step down, then another. I towered over the hole, fear grinding grit on my heart.

I would capture the final tone, and then decide.

My breath caught behind my breastbone. I had seen this place on paper, as numbers, and I had seen its result on a musical score, but the reality clogged my senses. I felt the denizens sliding about, shifting with anticipation as they sensed my intrusion.

I descended carefully, fingertips of one hand barely grazing the mossy rock walls as I went down, one step at a time, knees trembling.

I reached my foot out—no more steps. I was at the bottom. They gathered around, pressing close, awaiting their treat, and my breath caked in my throat as I wished I had brought something to distract their attention. After a moment, I felt my aura of health radiating out from me, repelling their sickness.

To the left, as I remembered my computations. To the left.

The stench was an entity. I walked seventeen steps to the left of the stairs. The stench and its loathsome steaming cloaked me in darkness. I had to deliberately breathe.

Seventeen steps, turn to the right, face the canal and wait. I heard my heart, the blood pulsed in my veins, pressure built in my nose, in my head.

I am the maestro, I thought. The maestro in the maelstrom, and my art is enriched by my every experience.

The time drew nigh. I readied the papers. I felt the two approach.

They passed me so close I did not even need to reach out.

Their twisted souls bumped together in obscurity, and I nipped the sound with my paper.

Anticlimactic. The collecting was complete, and I did not perish. *My design was not forbidden after all.*

Could I have erred?

No. The paper vibrated in my hand, and I felt it to be the one.

Carefully, I loaded it into my pocket, and my fingers touched the extra paper. Never before had I felt the necessity to bring an extra paper, but this time, this time...

I drew it out, and as I did, I heard a laugh, a wail, a wretched howl, a sound so devious that it threatened to release chemicals within my own brain—I felt on the verge of dementia. I felt—oh God—as if I had been *expected.*

My delirium passed, and still within the laugh that reverberated in the humidity, I heard the song that sustained life below. I heard genius misrepresented and thrown to tragedy, come to power through sickening manipulation. I heard bitterness and revenge, and an acceptance that shamed me to my marrow.

My hand whipped out and caught the first echo of the horrible noise, and I held that sound of genius turned insane vibrating in my hand. I held it to my heart as the wretches moved on, and when I had calmed myself enough to walk, I retraced seventeen steps and mounted the stairs.

Fresh air! I bounced up the last few steps and ran from the entrance. I leaned against the alley wall, blood pulsing behind my eyes, hot breath rasping through my throat. The stench of the underworld arose like steam from my clothes. I breathed deeply and tried to calm my heart. I had descended, and survived. I had won.

I held the envelope, vibrating with wrongness, to my sweating face and it buzzed my cheek. It danced in my hand. It lived.

I could give this to the old man instead of the other. The effect would be...

Would be...

I could not be sure until I had redrawn the entire formula, but my experience told me that the basic result would be the hell of perpetual torment, not the reality of death.

Then how would the old man prepare for his eventual demise? If he thought death would bring raving insanity, how would he proceed with the rest of his life? A most entertaining thought. A most attractive experiment.

And I could mix the potion strong. And charge an extra premium.

But I would use the entire mixture, if I betrayed the old one's confidence like this, and the actual experience of death, the experience as first designed—would be forever lost.

The Gods allowed me the recipe, and I collected the ingredients. I had been chosen to administer the preview of death to the person of my choice, whether it be the old man or myself. I had been entrusted by the Gods with this grave and important task.

But like the collecting, the experience itself would surely be anticlimactic.

No. This idea was far superior.

I looked at the paper containing the echo of the laugh.

It lived.

It begged to be used.

I took the other paper from my pocket. It seemed so small in comparison. So important, yet so pale. Inconsequential, in the light of my new endeavor I opened the seal and it escaped with barely a sigh.

Pleased with my decision, relieved of my burden, I pocketed my fortune and walked through the silent streets.

Anxious.

Eager.

※

Undercurrents

"This was a stupid idea," Cecily said to the heat, her heavy backpack, herself and her mother as she slogged through the jungle undergrowth. "'Go on a trip,' she said," Cecily mocked her mother's voice. "'Take that trip to Ecuador you always wanted. Go hiking. See some jungle.' Well here I am, Mom. Wish *you* were here. Instead."

There was supposed to be a trail, but it had been indistinct at best, and Cecily hadn't seen any sign of it for hours. She imagined that the jungle claimed anything left untended. Claimed it, absorbed it, and probably did it fast enough to be observed.

Cecily stopped and looked around. There was daylight, but the heavy overhead canopy hid the angle of the sun. She had no idea what time it was or how long she'd been walking. Birds and monkeys screamed at each other from secret places amongst the trees. Steam curled up from the composting jungle floor. The place smelled like hot loam. Rich, earthy, moldy.

She bent over at the waist so her back could take the weight of her pack for a moment instead of her raw shoulders. She dared not take the pack off; she might be tempted not to hoist it back on again. Sweat had soaked through her trendy papaya-colored polo shirt and the straps of her backpack, so it rubbed salt into her raw blisters with every step. Her khaki jungle shorts were too new, too stiff, and were beginning to chafe in the crotch.

At least I've got good shoes, she thought as she bent over, relieving the pressure on her shoulders and looked at her feet. Two hundred dollar hiking shoes. Worth every penny, if they'll get me out of here.

"I must have been insane," she said to herself again. She should have brought someone with her, but no, she had to travel alone, independent. Always independent. Too independent. Ready for an adventure, ready for something different, something she could do that would make her feel good about herself. Something she could *accomplish*. She should have stayed at the InterContinental Hotel and written post cards telling all about her journey through the jungle, amazing her friends. She could have *made up* a better adventure than this. Shit.

She stood up straight, and each of the backpack's twenty-three pounds settled deeper into her sore shoulders. She wasn't going to be able to do this much longer. She looked around. Especially since she had no idea where she was.

When sweat trickling down her face had awakened her that morning, she looked down from her camping hammock to see her backpack open and the contents strewn about. Panicked, she tumbled out of the hammock and went running around, gathering up all her things.

Her freeze-dried ice cream, in three little foil pouches, was missing. So were the dog tags her big brother had made for her as a joke. "Slogging through the jungle, eh? Can't slog through jungle without dog tags." He'd been in Vietnam. She laughed, and had brought them along, but they were impractical. This trip was miserable enough without things jangling around her neck, knocking her in the chest.

And her compass. Her compass was gone.

She could live without ice cream and dog tags. But the critters monkeys, probably—that stole her compass, had stolen her life.

Cecily winced as she raised her arms to pull the hair up off her neck. She readjusted her ponytail, took off her sopping headband and threw it on the ground.

"C'mon, kid," she said to herself. "You're not a quitter." That was a phrase that her father had repeated to her over and over her whole life. She began walking again, wondering if there was any glory for not being a quitter, or if quitting was sometimes a good idea.

She was no quitter, that was for sure. She'd stayed in that loveless, emotionless, sexless, affectionless marriage for fourteen years. She wasn't going to quit, she was going to wear Billy down. And she hadn't quit. Billy finally told her, flat out, that he wasn't interested any more. Hadn't been, in fact, since he stopped sleeping with her, stopped touching her, six years before that.

No, sir, she was no quitter. It had taken a major shove to push her away. It took the emotional equivalent of a steel fire door, slammed in her face, to make her stop.

And she didn't see any such obstacles in front of her now. Just more banana leaves and monkey shit.

She pressed on, the heat cloaking her like damp Turkish towels. The air was hot fog, and sweat poured down her legs so fast at times it felt as though she were wetting herself. All she could think about was finding a lush resort hotel around the next corner. A classic place with gorgeous, white-jacketed, brown-faced waiters and cold, fruity rum drinks with lots of ice. Lots of ice.

She didn't know she was crying until a sob surprised her. The sweat that ran stinging into her eyes felt the same as the tears that ran out. She stumbled a few more steps, then stood and cried. With each breath, her pack straps bit into her shoulders, her resolve weakened, her fortress tumbled.

She was alone and lost and would probably die out here. And without her dogtags—she began to giggle in the middle of the crying—nobody would even be able to identify her. She laughed a little more. The jungle would claim her, and some research scientist, looking for a cure for the common cold, would come upon her bones. She began to laugh harder, the hysterical tears coming faster. He'd think he'd found the missing link! She howled, laughing, and a warm afternoon rain began to mist down on her. She took off her backpack and set it down, feeling almost dizzy with the relief from it. She did a little dance in the rain, laughing and crying, howling and yipping.

When she was finished, when she had danced and yelled and screamed out all her frustrations and fears, she sat down, feeling a little foolish, on a big, flat rock and leaned back on the round rock behind it.

The rock vibrated.

Waterfall.

Probably one of those majestic, awesome waterfalls, the kind of thing she'd always wanted to see. The reason she came to Ecuador in the first place.

And probably cold water, to boot. Luxurious, bone-chilling cold water. She'd had enough of sweltering heat and warm sweat to last her a lifetime.

She stood up and hugged the big rock. She felt the power of the waterfall thundering on the other side of this outcropping. She pressed her body to it, felt the coolness on her skin. She wanted to absorb it, all of it. When she backed away, she noticed that her nipples had hardened and were poking her shirt.

She wanted fresh, cold water.

Keeping one hand on the chilled granite, she walked around the rock. About twenty feet from where she had done her little rain dance, a stream trickled out from under the giant boulder which actually looked more like a cliff face. She knelt down and peered upstream, through a narrow tunnel under the rock.

She could fit in there.

She lay on her back in the stream. The water was cooler than the rain, which seemed body temperature. It stung her raw shoulders, but in a moment, it felt good. She liked the coolness wicking up through her clothes, raising goosebumps as it rose. It felt marvelous. She felt tears threaten to choke her again, but she pushed them away and craned her neck to see into the tunnel, the tunnel she intended to crawl through.

It was so small.

On her back, she inched her way up until her head was inside it. The ceiling was barely above her nose. Cecily had never liked small, closed places, but that wasn't going to stop her now. Going in head first, it was unlikely she would get stuck, and if the opening became too small, she'd just inch her way back out again.

She knew what was in the jungle—she knew what had been in her marriage. She didn't know what lay beyond the tunnel, beyond the marriage. The adventure was the allure.

The tunnel smelled dank and mossy. It was cooler, in fact it was downright cold, once she got entirely inside. The ceiling was so low that she couldn't bend her knees far enough to give herself a good scoot each time, so she just inched along, inched along, hoping there was enough air, desperately trying not to think about lack of air or tropical spiders or snakes or...

When she tried to stop thinking about her breathing, when she stopped hearing her breath and only her breath as it echoed off the tunnel ceiling just above her nose, she felt it again, the vibration of running water. Waterfall. Big waterfall. The ground thrummed with it. Cecily found herself oddly aroused and more eager than ever to see this place that probably damned few tourists got to see.

She kept inching, inching, inching along. There wasn't enough room for her to turn her head to see ahead of her, and she wasn't sure she wanted to see ahead of her anyway. She just kept going. She kept going on faith.

Then the stream deepened and gave her more headroom. The water grew colder and deeper, and then the tunnel widened enough to bring her arms up and then the bottom dropped out all together. She took a big backward stroke with her arms and she swam out of the rock and right into heaven.

Both the cold water and the beauty of the place sucked her breath away. She stroked swiftly to a side of the pool and climbed out on the rocks. Then she stood, dripping, mouth open in awe as she viewed her surroundings.

Cliffs, a thousand feet high, surrounded her on all sides. A gigantic waterfall tumbled down one side into a clear, deep pool a hundred yards across. Big, flat rocks were strewn about the area like a giant's toys, and one of them was close enough to catch the mist from the waterfall and the sunbeam that zeroed in through the telescoping cliffs. This rock was covered with green.

Cecily made her way over to it. The moss was six inches thick, soft and spongy. She sat down on it and luxuriated in the softness and the coolness of the mist that wafted her way from the waterfall.

The falling water was so loud she could hear nothing else, even if there were something else to hear. The sound vibrated her bones, it pressed like sheets of electricity on her skin, it rattled her brain. It was wonderful.

Gone was the muggy jungle feeling. Here was fresh water, cooling mist, and sun! Real sun!

She stripped off her soaking clothes and lay down on the mossy rock, reveling in the hot sunshine. She let the dry heat soak through her skin as she looked around.

Totally deserted, this tropical paradise. Bunches of bananas hung from fat-leaved trees. Tall papaya trees with their clusters of yellow fruit towered everywhere. Little, stunted guava trees sported their pink fruit, and lilikoi vines wound a tangled web like a screen, from tree to tree.

She could live here. She looked closely at the ground. No trash. Not a cigarette butt. Not a footprint, a candy wrapper, a film container. Nothing.

She got down from the rock and pulled two yellow bananas from a bunch, then scrambled back up into the sunlight. She peeled and ate the first one quickly, hunger rushing at her. With the second one, she stood and looked around her, slowly turning, slowly eating, trying to imagine her good fortune in finding such a spot.

This was the stuff of real vacations.

She lay the banana peels carefully on the edge of the rock. She'd begin a compost area and dig a latrine later. The jungle would reclaim her insignificant refuse probably within minutes.

First, a nap.

She lay on the soft moss, and as the sun warmed her and the waterfall's mist cooled her, she toyed with the living green mat and marveled at all the tiny creatures that lived in it. Then she drifted off on a cloud of sleep and dreamed about trespassing on sacred ground and of gods long undisturbed, gods with an appetite for the warmth of mortal flesh.

When Cecily awoke, she was in pitch blackness and she felt the startling sensation of things scrambling out of her way. She sat up, trembling, her heart pumping the breath right out of her. She pulled her knees to her chest and wrapped her arms around herself. She tried to listen, to hear, but the presence of the waterfall dominated all sound. The night was so black she couldn't see her feet. And she was still naked.

She dared not move from the rock in the dark, she didn't know her way around. She cursed herself for not preparing. She should have prepared some sort of a covering for night; the air was warm, but mist from the waterfall chilled her.

She talked to herself, her insignificant mewings lost in the thundering of thousands of gallons per second, but she kept talking nevertheless, slowly and with reason. She calmed herself. There was nothing to be done now, she had to live with her mistake. Night wouldn't last forever.

She lay back down, willing her skin not to shiver, trying instead to feel the jungle heat between the drops that landed on her. She tried wrapping herself in a feeling of safety.

It worked. Her heartbeat returned to normal, she warmed up in the humid tropical air and she felt a sense of peace. Eventually, she slept.

She dreamed she was sleeping. She saw herself from a tremendous height—the top of the waterfall—as a tiny dot of warm humanity curled up on the sacrificial rock. She looked too naked, too alone, too vulnerable, too warm.

Then she was back in her body, sleeping, her mind awash with pleasantries, when she felt the first tickle. Her toes. Something was tickling her toes. Suckling her toes. All of them at once, she giggled, someone was sucking her toes, and it tickled. Then something warm and firm rubbed her feet. It wasn't like Steve's hand, when he used to do that, and it wasn't like a stick, but something in between, yielding yet firm. First the bottoms, then the tops, then the Achilles tendon pinched just to the brink of pain and then backed off. The massage continued up the calves of her legs, both legs at the same time.

Cecily moaned in her sleep. Her feet and legs were so sore from hiking, she needed this rub, and it was delicious. It was deep, but not too deep, it was hard, but not too hard, it was empathetic, and just right. Just exactly what her muscles needed.

Then it was sucking her toes again, and she felt as if she were being swallowed as it enveloped both her feet.

Her legs were gently parted as both thighs were massaged and the backs of her knees were—what, kissed?

"No," she giggled, this was too personal, but her protest was without conviction, and she arched her back and put her hands up over her head.

Something began to suckle her fingers.

Cecily giggled. She found it hard to concentrate on everything that was going on at once. There were so many hands, but they weren't hands, they were like tentacles,

tentacles?

and they were in her and on her and over and under her. She felt possessed by them, they surrounded her with slick, syrupy sensations as they massaged, kneaded and probed.

Open your eyes, she told herself. *This isn't right.*

But she couldn't open her eyes, she didn't want to open her eyes, it felt too good, it felt wonderful, it had been too long since she had been touched.

She heard the waterfall, felt it thundering through her, she heard murmuring, but she didn't know if the sounds were in the air or in her head. She began to move with internal rhythms as her arousal built. The tongues

tongues!

licked at her breasts. Lips

lips?

covered her throat with tender kisses. Her muscles were firmly massaged, the muscles of her face, her neck, shoulders, thighs, then she felt them probing her, deeper, deeper, it was so good, she rocked back and forth like a trusting child, she was ready, she heard her voice urging them on, encouraging them, her juices flowing. She felt flutterings in her stomach—then she became the waterfall as she went over the edge, the arms

they were arms

held her in loving embrace as she shuddered, the orgasm lasting and lasting and lasting as the fingers

fingers?

knew exactly what to do to prolong it.

I need this, she said, I need this, I need this.

"My god!" she said, and sat up.

She was alone. And cold.

Dawn spread a soft light throughout her private paradise; the sky high above looked milky.

That was a *dream*? Her nipples were still hard, her inner thighs sticky. She waited until her heart stopped pounding, until she stopped shaking.

With trembling legs and weak knees, she stepped off the mossy rock and walked back into the undergrowth, urinated, then waded in and washed herself in the cold pool. She ducked under, swam a little bit, shook out her hair, then climbed out, picked a couple more bananas and went back to the rock.

She sat cross-legged and viewed her domain as the dream faded to obscurity. She hadn't felt this good in years.

Yet, fantasize all she wanted about living the wild life in the jungle, she couldn't stay here. She needed more. She needed clothing, warmth, companionship. She might stay a couple more days, though

and then what?

but that would be all. It was her privilege to be able to spend time in a place like this.

She'd stay the day, and one more night—maybe she'd have another great dream. The thought gave her goosebumps—and then she'd shimmy her way out through the tunnel and back to reality.

Back to reality.

The thought of reality gave her a vague sense of unease, so she concentrated instead on peeling and eating a banana. She wondered how deep the pool was. The water looked clear, it was clear enough to see the rocks as they stepped their way down toward the middle, but she couldn't see the bottom. It was really deep, she thought. Probably really, really deep.

Appetite sated, she hung her wet clothes on tree branches to dry, then lay back down on the mossy rock and waited for the sun to slide up over the cliff and warm her. Eventually it did. Full strength.

Groggy from the sun and absolute laziness, Cecily slid down to the edge of the rock and dangled her feet in the water.

She remembered the sensation of having her toes sucked. She remembered the warm massage, the sultry feeling. Eyes closed, she swayed back and forth on the soft cushion of moss as she remembered her dream and began to feel her heat building up again.

Wait a minute, she thought, and kicked some cold drops up into the air where they sparkled at their zenith before dropping down on her browning skin.

She slipped gently into the water and felt it cool her floating breasts. She swam toward the waterfall and the cold water cooled between her legs with every kick.

In the center of the pool, in the shadow of the cliffs, in the cold water, that sense of reality returned. She spun around in the water, uncertain, suddenly, that she would be able to find her way out.

She had to get out of here.

Didn't she?

Was the tunnel under water? She looked toward the cliff face, but nothing looked familiar. She couldn't remember where she had come in, wondered if the monkeys had gotten into her backpack again, wondered if there was life after Steve or if there was only life with Mom.

She started to breathe fast, panic building. She tread water faster, tiring her arms, her overhiked legs. She should be getting back to shore, but the mossy rock looked so far away, she wasn't sure she would be able to make it. She'd swum out too far.

Stupid, she thought, stupid.

And then she felt a hand on her ankle.

Screaming, she kicked, and almost came right out of the water. She swam for all she was worth. For about a dozen strokes, then exhaustion threatened to sink her.

The hand came again, holding her foot steady. Strong, warm thumbs

thumbs?

caressed her instep, cradled her foot like a treasure.

Like a treasure.

She remembered what it had been like to be treasured.

I need this, she thought, and surrendered as it pulled her under quietly and gently.

※

One Fine Day Upon the River Styx

"First thing you need to know," the oarsman said as the boat skimmed the water close to the shore, "is that in this place, you become what you believe." Rushes that looked like they were made of barbed wire scraped the side of the boat, and Phil felt them as if they were rasping his flesh.

But he no longer had flesh.

He'd awakened on this flimsy excuse of a boat, disoriented and slightly nauseated. He tried to remember where he had just been, but his mind was fogged, it felt out of focus. He knew it had been important, he had been just a moment ago doing something very important. Horribly important. Of vast significance.

Oh yeah. Clutching at the pain in his chest on the floor of the men's room in a Chinese restaurant. Trying to rip out the white hot knot burning behind his breastbone.

And then, suddenly, this.

The sky (was it a sky?) swirled shades of gray, black and purple. If they were clouds, they surely housed acid rain. There was no indication that a sun shone from anywhere behind that massed mess, and Phil shivered, as if he were cold. But he wasn't.

Nuclear winter, that's what it made him think of. And some diseased wind blew right through his luminescence. To his right, the strange shore had receded out of sight. Now, water stretched ahead, behind and to both sides as far as he could see. It seemed like an ocean, but there was a definite current to it, a swiftness that suggested a river.

He took one look back at the oarsman, hooded and mysterious, and he put two and two together.

"So this is the River Styx," he said.

He leaned out over the boat's gunwale and felt the unstable craft tip. He drew back abruptly, overcompensating, sending the boat to rock wildly beneath his feet.

"Shallow and unbalanced," the oarsman said.

"I thought the River Styx was supposed to be on fire."

"Sometimes it is."

"Belching gas and smoke and shit. Brimstone, yeah, that's it. Fire and brimstone." Phil steadied himself, then leaned out, way out, too far out, peering down into the water. It didn't look like water. It looked thick and black, like heavily used motor oil. Stunk like old diapers. Definitely smelled flammable. He wasn't afraid of falling in; he was already dead. At least his body was. His old body. He still had his wits, and his curiosity seemed to be sharper than ever. His new shape suited him just fine. In fact, it felt just like his old body, without the aches and creaks of age. Without the malformed foot. Without the shortness of breath, the tendency toward obesity, the weak heart. He felt whole, light and ornery. He even noticed a little transparency to his... what was this, his soul? It was different. It even seemed to be a little bit attractive. In life, he'd not been particularly attractive.

Something eelish and toothy slithered past him in the water, turned and swam up to him. It opened its black mouth and a human-sounding laugh came gibbering out at him. Phil jerked himself back into the boat, sending the craft into another frenzy of wild rocking. What passed for perspiration popped out on what passed for his forehead. For the first time, he felt creepy. Really creepy.

"What the fuck was that?"

"A lie," the oarsman said. "Probably one of yours."

Phil wondered which one. There had been so many. He peered over the side of the boat, and the thick water burbled with activity. The indistinct light shifted and he saw that it was a ropy mass of the things, like a huge tangled ball of snapping, growling fanged snakes, roiling right next to the boat. Those that saw him, laughed, a chattering, horrible laugh that told him that they knew. They knew about him, they all knew. And more were joining the fray, swimming toward him, the surface of the river nothing more than a fluid highway of lies.

Phil wanted to hide, but he knew there was no hiding. His soul had been stripped bare, and this was just the beginning.

He staggered back into the center of the boat, where he would be in less danger of falling into the middle of the slimy morass. "How long until we get there?"

The oarsman smiled a mirthless grin, teeth gleaming in the shadow of his hood, and Phil realized it was a foolish question. Even if time did exist here, why was he in a hurry to get where he was going?

"This is your time to decide," the oarsman said. "Best you use this time wisely."

"Decide what?"

"What you believe," the oarsman said.

What he believed? He believed he'd like to sit down, that's what he believed. He never could think on his feet. He'd like to just sit down, relax and enjoy what might be his last time afloat.

There was no place to sit.

"You got a chair?" he asked the oarsman, but his question was met with silence. About three inches of river water washed back and forth across the bottom of the oddly constructed boat, and Phil wasn't eager to sit down in it. It looked and smelled acidic. But he was getting tired, and even his new head felt like it was brewing a tension headache. Too much stress. He could use a nap. A stiff scotch and a relaxing blow job wouldn't hurt, either.

The boat lurched and Phil lost his footing on the slippery deck. He fell to one knee, the sloshing water stinging his skin as his knee sizzled and smoked on contact. Something banged against the boat again, and Phil looked up to see the great knot of screeching, slithering things rise up over the edge of the boat. Serpents disengaged, tumbled over the side and immediately disappeared into the oily, sloshing water on deck. Phil scrambled to his feet and sought the help of the oarsman. He clutched at the cloak, but it felt like spider webs, and his fingers fell right through it, the fabric healing itself. The oarsman looked at Phil with dispassionate eyes.

Oh yeah. This wasn't just any river. Not just any water taxi. Not just any driver.

He could cower, or he could stand his ground. He imagined he'd do a lot of both before this was over. If it was ever going to end.

"Those things real?" He felt hysteria rising.

"Real as you believe," the oarsman said, and Phil knew there was a clue there, if only he could stop his panic long enough to consider what the man said. His lies had been real enough; he'd made a life out of lying. His whole business was a flimsy house of lying cards, stacking one on top of the other, teasing people, tripping others, fabricating scenarios in order to get what he needed from whoever he needed it from at the time. And the taller his house of lies became, the more intimidating he became, the more solid the illusion of his power, until people believed his forked tongue and accepted what he said without question. He became an authority.

What was worse: he had believed in his own self-fabricated authority.

He could also believe that in hell, those slimy, toothed lies would rip him wide open and laugh as they did it.

Or he could refuse to believe it.

"I made a lot of people happy," he said to nobody in particular and everywhere in general. "I made a *river* of money for people," he said louder. "They weren't lies," he shouted, "they were tools!"

The surface of the water calmed, and the swirling bilge water stilled.

A shiver ran up Phil's back.

"You learn fast," the oarsman said. "An angle man, eh?"

"What else?" Phil demanded. He was urgently intent to find out how the system here worked, and how he could use it to his best advantage. "What else do I need to know?"

"Study the boat," the oarsman said, and Phil caught a glimpse of the man's face in the muted light. He was more than a shadow, but not much more. A demon, perhaps. One whose face was slightly familiar. That sent another chill up what used to be Phil's back. Had he met this demon in life? Had he helped populate Phil's night-mares? "The boat, and everything else, reflects you."

"That's what you meant when you said 'shallow' and 'un-stable'?"

The oarsman shrugged. "You must make your decision before we reach shore."

"What decision?"

"What you believe."

"What I believe I am? What I believe I can be? What do you mean? What are you talking about? Speak straight to me."

The oarsman just stared out at the river.

"Can I grow? Can I change?" Desperation clutched where his bowels would be, had he any.

"Can you?" the demon asked back.

"Is it too late for me? Can I get out of here?"

"Mother, may I?" The oarsman taunted.

"Can you help me?"

"Help you? I've got no reason to help you." The demon took a long pull on the single oar. "I've already said too much." He lifted his chin and pointed with it.

Something big was dead ahead in the middle of the river. Some-thing gigantic. All Phil could see—damn the pale light!—was a smooth, round, black hump that rose and fell, rose and fell, as it approached the boat. "Jesus Christ," Phil said. "What is that?"

"Hard to say. Insincerity is pretty monstrous."

Insincerity had been his stock in trade. Looked like insincerity was about to swamp his shallow ass.

"Can I skate outta this? Can I deny it and make it go away like I did the lies?"

"Denying those lies was completely insincere," the oarsman said, and took a long pull on the oar as the humping creature in the river came closer.

"So *this* is real?"

"Real as you believe. Better hang on."

It can't kill me, Phil thought, I'm already dead. Can't hurt me, because I don't have a body. I've got nothing to lose; I'm on my way to hell. "Hey," he shouted at the monster, "Fuck you! You can't hurt me. I don't care about you. Swamp the boat. Munch me down. I don't give a rat's ass. I'm here for the duration, no matter what!"

The smooth glossy hump sank slowly, and the oily water closed over it.

"Well done again," the oarsman said. "Now *that* was true sincerity."

"Shut up," Phil said. His authority had saved him again, but all this fast-paced scheming was giving him a backache. Was he going to have to figure an angle for every goddamned event for eternity? Maybe. Well, if that was so, he was up for it, he had done it for every goddamned event in life. "What's next?"

"I don't know," the oarsman said, "but I'm detecting something very odd about this boat."

"Yeah? What?"

"It doesn't seem to be a boat at all."

"What do you mean?" But even as Phil spoke, the boat began to morph, right beneath his feet. Black, stinky water surged up and out of the bilges, covering his ankles. It stung, and acidic smoke rose up. "We're going to sink? Are we sinking?"

"What do you believe about yourself? Do you believe you're sinking?" the oarsman asked, working the oar, and as he did so, the hood on his cloak fell down around his shoulder.

Phil looked at him, did a double-take in surprise. Familiar. He looked so goddamned familiar. But it wasn't his face that was familiar, because he didn't really have a face. It was more his aura. His essence. Phil knew this guy, or, perhaps he'd known a thousand like him.

"How come you're not freaked out by all this?"

"I'm on staff," the oarsman said, pulling the cloak back up over his head, shadowing his face. "I work for the Man, carrying moral abortions like you across the river. That's *my* eternal hell."

"How do you get on staff? Can you get me a job?"

"No, stupid. I was recruited. You were damned."

The water clutched at Phil's lower legs with fingers of ice. It was bone-chilling cold. "What's happening with the boat?"

The oarsman just kept stroking, long, strong pulls on the oar. The boat was flattening out, becoming ever more unstable; the tiniest shift of Phil's weight shifted the slanted, slippery deck. A lie poked its head out of the water right by his crotch and bared its teeth, staring him right in the face before chortling and diving back into the water.

"The lies are back," Phil said, then tried to remember how he got rid of them in the first place.

"Look," the oarsman said, and the black hump in the water, like a huge whale, surfaced again and was making its way toward them.

Phil tried to think about getting rid of the lies before they ripped him to pieces. He tried to think about getting rid of the insincerity before it dumped them into the stinking water. He tried to think about what was making the boat melt, and how to fix that, all of that, all at the same time.

It was too much, it was too much. His closely held, tightly gripped confidence oozed out of him. "Arrrgh," he screamed in frustration.

"Land," the oarsman said.

Sure enough, on the dark, indistinct horizon there appeared a darker, low-level line that stretched way out. Could be land. Could be illusion. Could be some torturing monster. No telling in this place.

But the boat. The boat was melting right in front of his eyes. "Will we make it? What's happening to the boat?"

"I'll make it," the oarsman said. "I always do. You guys don't always make it."

"What's happening here? What can I do?"

"Seems you're not what you appear to be. The boat looks like a boat, and was a boat for a while, but now it's not. What is it?"

Fucking riddles, Phil thought. I played the big shot, a wheeler-dealer, but I wasn't. Never was. Always ran on guts and bravado, but what was I, really?

Liar.

Yes, but so is everybody. What else?

Scared little boy.

"What are you?" The oarsman demanded.

"Scared," Phil said as a portion of the deck evaporated and his foot fell through. Lies snapped at him, yammering and screeching, and that big humpy thing was so close Phil could hear its tremendous low vibration.

"What?"

"Scared!" he yelled, and the boat solidified, at least a little bit. It steadied, and the lies sank beneath the water.

"That's a start," the oarsman said. "You might make it."

Phil felt a little cocky with his latest success. "Are you here to make me better? Are you here to teach me to be a good person, an honest person?"

"Nope. It's too late for that."

"Then what?" The boat had melted down until it was nothing more than a raft on the river, and Phil stood in the middle, trying to keep his balance with nothing to hold on to, nothing to keep him from falling overboard. "Why are you trying to teach me these lessons, get me to confess my fears, show me the evil of my ways? If it's too late to rehabilitate me, then what's your point?"

The oarsman was silent for a long while, just sculling gently across the calm current. Phil shivered in cold. He thought hell was supposed to be hot, but it wasn't. It was cold. Colder than hell. No, he thought. Just exactly *as* cold as hell. And that was bloody cold. His whole being ached from the cold. His back felt stiff and uncomfortable.

"Part of your eternal torment," the oarsman said, "is in knowing how easy it would have been for you to be a nice person. You could have saved yourself all of this—" he gestured toward the approaching landfall "—by just doing the right thing now and then. Demonstrating that you knew all along what the right thing was."

"I know right from wrong."

"And you chose wrong. Every time. Until it got too big. Until you had so much of your personality invested in being the bad ass persona that you designed for yourself, that you didn't *dare* choose the right thing."

"I did good in the world," Phil whined. "I made people happy." He stretched, trying to crack out the discomfort in his back.

"You never made anyone happy. Ever."

Phil thought about that for a moment. *Was that true?* "You're kidding. Never? Ever?" Phil found this horribly disturbing and completely incomprehensible.

"Never. Ever."

"Not when I was a kid? Not when I was married..." No, not when he was married. Except for an occasional dry, unsatisfactory roll in the hay, and to pay her astronomical credit card bills, he didn't pay much attention to his wife at all. And he'd been a bully as a kid, so defensive over his gimpy foot that he kept his attitude in razor sharp fighting mode.

Nope, the oarsman was right. Whatever he did, he did for himself. And if anybody happened to mine a scrap of happiness out of his tailings, that was incidental, although he never failed to take credit for it.

He wasn't a nice guy. Never had been. And now he was reaping the wretched fruits of the bitter seed he had sown.

He felt that old attitude coming back. "So what do I do now?"

"You choose. Right now, you choose your fate."

"I choose outta here."

"There's no way out," the oarsman said, "but I can offer you a deal."

"Yeah?" Phil felt a surge of hope. He could do this hell thing, he knew he could, as long as he didn't have to be on the bottom of the pit. He could be a good administrator here. If he was smart, the Man in Charge would use his talents. Phil had many diverse talents, ruthlessness being one of his favorites. "A deal? Tell me."

The boat solidified under their feet, and the oarsman took the opportunity to scull swiftly across the current.

Land grew more distinct on the horizon. Here and there Phil could see the light of what looked like bonfires on the beach. And beyond, the smoky sky was illuminated by a soft orange glow. And he could smell land, but it didn't smell earthy and delicious, it smelled like... sulphur. It smelled like an oil refinery.

Fresh panic rose in Phil. This was real. This was as real as it gets. He was about to go to *eternal torment*, and there was nothing he could do about it. Regrets filled his soul. If only he had known. If only he had tried. If only he had been nice... maybe even just once...

"Tell me the deal," he beseeched the oarsman, but the oarsman would not be rushed.

As land neared, the sounds began to filter out to them. At first it was just the low moans, the droning of agony, now and then punctuated by a high pitched screech. But as they neared the shore, the sound grew in intensity and volume—a billion and more souls screaming for mercy that would never be shown them.

"Please," Phil said. "For god's sake."

"God's sake?" the oarsman said. He stomped on the boat. It was solid. "Okay," he said, and Phil felt like collapsing in relief. "The first thing is to get you to shore. If you don't make it to shore, there's nothing to talk about."

"We'll make it. I'll make it. You just tell me how. I can do anything."

"See how firm the boat is?"

Phil stomped on the deck himself. Solid.

"That means you are what you appear to be."

"Remorseful," Phil said, with what he hoped was a sincere look on his face. He felt a shiver squirm up his spine, but he wrote it off as just another of the weird sensations of this place.

"When we ferry someone with true regret, we can recommend they be sold into service."

"Sold?"

"At auction," the oarsman said. "Then you'd be working for someone torturing others instead of just being tortured."

An auction, yes. Phil had made a lot of money at auctions.

"Yes. Yes, that's for me."

"Not so fast," the oarsman said. "Torturing others is not nice. It's almost as bad."

"Anything. Anything you can offer me I'll take."

"You'll be hated throughout eternity."

"I was hated throughout life."

"This is different. Torturing others is one of the worst types of torment."

"I can do it," Phil said. "I'm cut out for that work." Again the tremor in his spine.

"Okay, then," the oarsman said.

Phil jumped to hug him, to kiss the hem of his cloak, but of course his fingers merely flowed through the fabric.

The oarsman slipped the boat silently into a current that brought them swiftly to shore.

A team of ugly ruffians met them as the oarsman deftly docked what was left of the boat, and when Phil stepped onto shore, it squirmed beneath his feet. Even the sod was built of the damned.

"Auction him," the oarsman commanded, and the joyful shout repeatedly ran through the terrifying crowd. A pathway opened before them as a smelly gargoyle with a vise grip on Phil's arm propelled him roughly and too fast to the auction block.

He was thrown on stage, which was comprised of a thousand sinners squished one atop the other. A mirror backed the stage, and for the first time, Phil got a look at himself.

While he no longer had flesh and blood, while his defective body and his none-too-attractive face now rotted in some grave, that which had been on his inside was now made visible to everyone with eyes to see. All the ugliness was made manifest, and he was as horrifying to perceive as all of those around him. They were misshapen, ugly, smelly and stupid, prone to howling and sniggering, and his horror at being amongst them was surpassed by the disconsolate knowledge that he was one of them. He was average here. He was no better, and he was no worse. He was of the masses.

His greatest fear in life had been to be merely average. Mediocre.

"What do you bid for this wretch?"

The bidding began, but Phil no longer cared. He couldn't do anything about it. He had cast his fate to these carcinogenic breezes, and they would blow him whichever way they would.

He thought about being the meat in an excruciating sandwich; he torturing others while somebody tortured him.

"I've seen the error of my ways," he shouted, but the jeering that came from the crowd laughed him down. Again, he felt that squirm up his spine.

"I'm sorry," he said, and fell to his knees, hoping that whoever was in charge would see his sincerity.

A quick glance in the mirror told him that he hadn't changed any, at least his face hadn't, but what the hell was happening to his back?

He was growing a tail, that's what, and as he watched in horror, he felt his mouth stretch and grind out of proportion as long, sharp teeth grew out of what used to be jawbone and slid into place.

"Please," he said, but it came out as a hiss.

"Just another lie," someone said in disgust, and the bidding whimpered to a halt. The crowd turned its back and began to disburse.

Phil flopped onto the stage as his legs shriveled, "Help me," he said, but it sounded like the cackle from a dying rooster. A last glimpse of himself in the mirror showed him that he looked like a fat tadpole.

"Just another friggin' lie," the oarsman said, and picked Phil up by the tail. "Thought you were going to make it, once you hit land." Phil caught a last glimpse of himself in the mirror, and his reflection now was more familiar to him than any reflection he'd seen in any other mirror.

He was a liar—always had been, always would be. He had been so good at it, he'd even convinced himself of his own authority.

And now he'd become that which he believed. A lie.

He belonged here, and he'd never even known it.

Life would have been so much easier, he thought, if he'd only known.

Phil felt himself being swirled around and around the oarsman's head—he felt himself getting longer and thinner with each pass. Then the oarsman let go, and Phil sailed through the air toward the river.

✳

The Cloak

Armando

Armando tiptoed around the room, dimming the lights, nervousness making him flit. He smoothed his hair, then his moustache. He went around the table to see to the comfort of his guests, touching each one briefly, ending up at the side of his gray-haired wife, whose eyes were closed as she rested, preparing herself for the ordeal ahead. He touched her softly, concerned.

"Mandalla, my sweet. Shall we begin?"

An almost-imperceptible nod.

Armando wished they had canceled this evening's seance. "Ladies and gentlemen, please to hold hands. My wife, Mandalla, she takes her power from you, from the circle. Please to not breaking the chain while she is in trance, for to breaking the chain may do damage to her. Please to remain seated and calm. I am assuring you that no matter what you see or hear, if you keep the circle unbroken, no harm will come." He folded his hands in front of him and smiled encouragement at the guests as they tentatively took each other's hands.

"I, myself, will not be in the circle. If you need assistance, call to me and I will come. I shall be here, attending my lovely wife. All right?" He smiled, and somehow he felt that tonight his smile was too toothy, his talk too slick, his pants too sharply pressed. He touched his wife gently on the shoulder and whispered, "All is ready, my sweet." Then he dimmed the last light. He took his seat behind and to the right of Mandalla, in front of his spinning wheel, and joined the rest of the people in wait.

Mandalla slumped.

"Sit," Armando said, anticipating everyone's rise in concern. It happened every time. "It is beginning," he said. He saw understanding on their faces, and they all settled back into their seats. He saw the beginning of the terror, the first chug as the roller coaster car caught on the chain that would take them to the top, to the beginning of the wild ride. He felt it, too. He felt it in his chest every time. He saw them look around the table at each other—spouses, siblings, in-laws, rivals, close friends—strange combinations of clients attended seances. It was a very peculiar experience.

Armando had to keep reminding himself that this would be the last seance. They should have stopped the night before. Mandalla was too old, too fragile to keep it up. Armando was afraid that one of these nights her heart would not bear the burden of such physical exertion. They had discussed their retirement, but they had nothing to keep them going—they charged little for putting people in touch with the netherworld, and they had no savings.

It had been several years earlier when Armando saw the writing on the wall—poverty—that he got the idea. It was a good idea, he'd turned it into a plan, and he'd followed through. Tonight was the last night they would need these seances, for after he finished the weaving, they would be rich.

Very rich indeed.

But now, as Mandalla entered her trance, Armando again felt they should have stopped with last night's session. Mandalla was still too tired. She awakened too late this morning, she entered the seance room too tired tonight, and he knew she would have liked to cancel; he knew he should have been the one to suggest it, but instead, he took her in his arms and convinced her to endure it once more. "The last time, my sweet," he'd said. "And then it will be just the two of us, doing as we please, making love all over the house, without concern. The last time is tonight, my love." And she had sighed and agreed.

Mandalla sat up straight in her chair, then threw her head back and laughed bawdily.

It was Shees the Whore coming through Mandalla tonight. Armando leaned close, and as the ectoplasm fell from her nostrils, he caught it, fed it into the spinning wheel and began to spin.

It spun beautifully. Armando was always surprised at the feel. He'd spun Mandalla's ectoplasm at every seance for years now, and he was always surprised at how cold it was. And heavy. And dry. And smooth. And pliable. It was like nothing else. He spun fast, for the stuff came faster and faster as Shees told her tales of gossip and lust in the afterworld, as those around the table asked their questions and listened to her replies, sometimes truth, sometimes lies. All the time the white ectoplasm ran out of the nose and mouth of lovely Mandalla and pooled on the floor around her feet until it was spun into fine yarn by Armando.

As each bobbin filled, Armando worked feverishly, breaking off the end and turning it under several times. Then he tied a loose knot and slipped the bobbin into a plastic bag and sealed it carefully. The ectoplasm would evaporate unless carefully sealed. Then he put a new bobbin on the spinning wheel, threaded it with a strand of ectoplasm and began treadling madly.

Eventually, he heard Shees the Whore tire of the stupid mortals and their stupid questions and she became surly and abusive. His guests were becoming offended. It was time for him to step in.

"Shees," he said. "You seem tired. Is there someone else there who would like to speak through Mandalla?"

"Armando, you pimp," Shees said, and Armando stopped spinning in shock. She had never before spoken to him, and these words were the last he would ever expect to hear. "You sleazy, greasy piece of dog turd." Armando was beside himself. He couldn't even begin to find the words to ask her...ask her...Why was she saying these things? "You've sold the services of your talented wife your whole useless life," Shees said. "And now when she's old and tired, you think you're going to sell your famous fabric and become wealthy. Tell me, Armando, what will happen to Mandalla then? Huh?"

Armando was beyond words. Guilt stabbed him and he bled. "She is my love. She is my life..."

"Yeah, sure. Just remember, you faggot pimp impotent greaseball, that when you make that stuff, it's got more of me in it than anybody else. Mandalla may retire tonight, but I won't. Ta-ta, idiots."

Mandalla's head hit the table with a thud. Armando, forgetting all about the ectoplasm, turned his chair over in his rush to minister to his wife. "Mandalla. Mandalla, my love. Please, someone, please to turning up the lights."

Someone did and Armando felt the cold ectoplasm swirling about his feet and ankles as it evaporated. He knew that the end of the bobbin would begin to go in a moment, if he didn't tend to it. Mandalla's face was ashen, but she breathed regularly, so he patted her on the head and secured his spinning. As it was, he lost almost one third of the bobbin. When it was safely in a plastic bag and sealed, he again attended his wife, who was returning to consciousness, a large red bruise on her forehead.

"Armando," she whispered.

"Mandalla, my love." Armando caressed her soft cheek, her arm, her shoulder.

"Did you get it? The ectoplasm, was it plentiful?"

"It was wonderful, my love. I spun three bobbins tonight."

"Good. Good. I'm so tired. Armando, I must go to bed."

This was most unusual. Armando's brow furrowed with worry, and he patted her. "Of course, my darling, of course." He stood up and began to usher out his guests.

"This has been a trial to my wife, who is not as young and strong as she used to be. I am sorry, but I must please to asking you to leave. Quickly, I am sorry. I suggest that you find a quiet place to discuss among yourselves this very night while the memory is still fresh, to discerning meanings of what Shees from the other world told you. Please, my wife... Thank you, thank you."

When he had locked the door and returned to the parlor, Mandalla was sitting up, her face still drawn and pale. "Come, my darling," Armando said.

"Put away the bobbins first," Mandalla said, her voice strangely flat. She made no move to rise.

Armando gathered the three bobbins in their plastic bags and rushed them to the closet. As he opened the door, his breath condensed and plumed out before him. The shelves were filled with bobbins of spun ectoplasm sealed in plastic bags, and they had turned the small room into a refrigerator. Armando placed the three packages on the shelf and closed the door.

Then he helped his wife to bed, where she barely had the strength to undress herself. Armando helped her, even asked if she would like to see a doctor.

"No, my darling boy," she said, looking at him with fondness and affection. "You're a good man." Then she closed her eyes and Armando's guilt raged.

In the morning, she was dead.

Instead of being hysterical, as Armando always thought he would be when his elder wife predeceased him, there was a sadness, an emptiness that grabbed his spine and shook the marrow in his bones. He went about making the arrangements for her funeral with a weight the size of an ocean in his soul. On the third day, she was buried. The graveside congregation was enormous. Mandalla had loved hundreds, had helped thousands.

Father Jake, the new young priest in the parish, gave the benediction, and spoke sparingly that all things were of the Lord, even those things that seemed mysterious.

Mandalla's sister Estella and her son Raymond stood next to Armando at the grave, but Estella would not speak to Armando afterward.

Raymond shook Armando's hand, and spoke sincere words of consolation, but there was no consolation for Armando.

After the burial, Armando drifted alone in their house, surrounded by Mandalla's things. The memory of her lived in the house through her many special little possessions, things that others had given her in gratitude. He walked through the house, looking, touching, smelling, remembering, grieving.

Then he walked down the hall and touched the closet door. Cold.

Her last request, he thought, was for the care of the bobbins. She knew the cloth was the future. Mandalla knew that above all, the path of the future must be preserved. He opened the door and felt the cold mist lap up around his ankles. He pulled on the light cord and illuminated floor-to-ceiling shelves, filled with rows of bobbins sealed inside plastic bags, thousands and thousands of yards of yarn, in various shades from creamy white to silvery gray.

Mandalla lives in this room, Armando thought. *I must make the fabric and do justice to her memory.*

He rushed to the attic and uncovered his family loom. It had been his mother's and his grandmother's before her. Armando had learned to weave on this loom at his mother's knee—weaving had been the family's business for generations. Now all that he had learned was about to culminate in the project of his life.

He sat on a box and ran his hands over the fine hand-carved wood. Where would he weave? And how would he weave it? He tried putting a rubber band around a bobbin of ectoplasmic yarn once, but within minutes, the rubber band had floated right through the yarn and hung useless on the bobbin. The yarn had healed itself unbroken, but it was plain that Armando would not be able to use just any kind of warp on this cloth.

What would he use for a warp, and how wide should the fabric be, and what would he eventually make of it, and how would he cut it, sew it, where would he sell it?

I'll warp it with the ectoplasm itself, he thought. *There is enough. And I will weave a plain rectangle. I can make a cape or a rug or a coat, whatever the fabric will allow. The design is not as important as the weaving, and I will work in the seance room itself. Perhaps the hand of Mandalla will guide my endeavors.*

He disassembled the loom and went to bed, but found no rest. He tossed and turned as feelings of guilt flew up from the night and told him that he had pushed Mandalla too far. It was his fault that she was dead. If only he hadn't insisted on that one last seance. His tossing and turning grew to thrashing and kicking, and when finally he did sleep, he heard the voices: Mandalla's myriad contacts from the trance world called to him as they lay trapped in the hall closet, bound up in cold skeins of yarn.

He couldn't quite understand what they were all saying, because he didn't have Mandalla's gift of translation.

Maybe the translation will be in the weaving.

He reassembled the loom, working quickly, the pieces of burnished wood feeling like old friends to his soft hands. *Mandalla, my love, Mandalla, my sweet. If I could speak to you one more time, you would know that it was never my intention to harm you, my love, my love, my love.*

The reassembled loom reminded Armando of a shrine as it stood in the center of the room. Armando took the photograph of Mandalla from his dresser and placed it atop the loom, so she could supervise his work.

He was afraid to start, for if the yarn would not be woven, he would be so disappointed he might not survive.

But the yarn behaved. Beautifully. As if it wanted to be woven.

Before the sun set, Armando had the loom warped. The only inconvenience was that the big loopy knots he normally put in the warp yarn kept falling out. Ectoplasmic yarn behaved like nothing else. Finally, he just left it where it muddled on the floor and appeared to pool, but when he lifted it, each strand was separate, just as he had spun it.

He began the weaving.

By midnight, his back was bent, his fingers felt frozen and stiff, he hadn't eaten, hadn't slept, and he was exhausted past all reasonable limits. Yet with each pass of the shuttle, the fabric became a reality, and the fire burned anew within him.

When he could no longer hold the shuttle in his brittle fingers, he made his way to the kitchen, drank a glass of milk, ate some bread, and fell into bed.

In the morning, he was dismayed at the slim progress he'd made the day before. At first he thought the fabric had evaporated in the night. But after closer inspection, he realized it was all there, he was just overly eager to have it completed.

With a fresh mind and new enthusiasm, Armando returned to work. The yarn was like nothing he had ever used before. The shuttle glided back and forth, and he barely had to beat it at all to get a nice, tight weave.

The yarn did not evaporate once it had been woven.

All day he worked, and at night he was rewarded with wonderful dreams. The next day he worked, and the next, and the next. Each night the dreams were more pleasant, more restful, more playful, and every morning they dissolved, leaving only a hint of better things to come, leaving Armando anxious to put in a solid day's work with the wonderful weaving.

The days passed. Armando ate when necessary, slept when exhausted, and worked on the fabric all the rest of the time.

The day finally came when he reached for the next bobbin of yarn and there wasn't one. He looked around, then tore through the piles of plastic bags, stacks of empty bobbins, but the yarn was gone. He had used it all. The fabric, apparently, was finished.

He felt a jolt—as if he had just awakened.

It didn't look like much fabric, yet the loom's breast beam sagged with the weight of it. Armando thought the floor must be bowed as well. With trembling fingers, he bound the edge and removed the fabric from the loom. It was heavy—God it was heavy—and so soft, so cool, it was music to his fingertips, and he couldn't resist, but swirled it around his shoulders and pulled it tight around him.

"Armando."

Mandalla's voice, as clear and serene as ever. He looked wildly around. "Mandalla?"

"Armando," she said again, and he knew that the voice was in his mind, a product of the fabric. "The weaving is a work of wonder, Armando," she said, and he almost swooned.

"I love you, Mandalla," he said, his words sounding empty. He felt foolish talking to a cape. There was no reply. He shrugged out from underneath the fabric and watched as it pooled at his feet. He grabbed hold and pulled it up and it returned from a puddle of whitish ooze into a heavy fabric. He dropped it again and watched it melt. It was magic. He picked it up once again and it solidified into material, cold and rich with streaks of silver and varying shades of gray. Magnificent.

He held it up until he could hold it no longer, then he put it back down onto the floor. What was he to do now? His life had been taken up with Mandalla, and now she was gone. There were the seances, and now they were over. There was the weaving, and now it was complete. He was to sell the fabric and retire, but he could never sell this fabric. Mandalla lived in this fabric. The fabric *was* Mandalla.

What was he to do?

Heart heavy, exhaustion overtaking him, he dragged the fabric behind him as he went to his bed, lay down, pulled the heavy cloth over him and began to dream.

In his dreams, he spoke with all the personalities that had spoken through Mandalla over the years. Hundreds of personalities. Some lost, some sad, some with a mission, some misdirected, some vindictive, some angry, some who just wanted to come back to earth, to life. Armando dreamed that he went from one to the next, moving through the crowd, and their voices all grew together as they insisted on speaking to him, each individually, but they were overpowering in their enthusiasm and he felt smothered, crushed.

"One at a time!" he yelled, but they would not be silenced, those who would not go on to their reward. They had unfinished business, and Armando was their conduit. *"One at a time!"* but they mobbed him, sucking the very air from his lungs. "Please," he begged with his last breath, but the heaviness of their grief, anger and intention overpowered him.

Mandalla's lovely hand reached out to him, but he could not touch it.

When he did not pick up his mail or his newspaper, did not answer his door or his phone, his neighbor called the police.

The coroner said he had died in his sleep. Died peacefully.

Died of a broken heart, the neighbor said.

Estella

Estella gripped her son's hand as they followed the realtor into Armando's home. The house felt musty and close, though it had only been four days since Armando died.

Even the realtor fell silent at the sound-absorbing qualities of the acoustics. The house was swathed in fabrics and overstuffed furniture. Flocked wallpaper and heavy draperies covered the walls, lampshades were ballooned with chintz, carpets were covered with rugs which were adorned with throw rugs. Stacks of pillows filled every vacant corner, as did heavy furniture covered with lace doilies and bric-a-brac.

It was claustrophobic.

Estella let go of Raymond's hand and lay a finger on the realtor's light-suited arm. "Just sell it," she whispered, putting a handkerchief to her nose and mouth. "Just sell it all and give the money to my boy."

"I want to see the rest of the place, mama," Raymond said. "Why don't you sit here," he guided her gently to a green velvet chair draped with doilies and filled with brocade pillows, "while Mrs. Nelson and I finish looking around?"

Estella sat tentatively on the edge of the chair. Raymond rearranged pillows and pressed her gently back.

"Close your eyes and rest now," he said gently. "This'll only take a few minutes, then we'll be finished."

Estella nodded. Mandalla had been her only sister, her baby sister. Estella was the final survivor of the six siblings, and she thought surely Mandalla, being the youngest, would bear the burden of being the last one left, but instead, the weight fell to Estella.

This was the first time she had been in Armando and Mandalla's house. Their mother had stricken Mandalla's name from the family Bible when she took to the spirit world—witch, their mother called her. Though they lived in the same town, barely five miles apart, Estella had not heard of or from Mandalla and Armando in over twenty years. To see Mandalla look so old in her casket, so see Armando look so thin and gray in his, had been a terrible shock. He hadn't looked that ravaged at Mandalla's funeral. The death of a mate can itself be fatal, she thought.

If Mandalla had died, could Estella be far behind? She sat up in the chair, certain the Reaper was crouching behind it. She didn't want him to catch her unawares.

She heard Raymond and Mrs. Nelson talking in the kitchen, their voices formless echoes. This seemed to be a huge house, Estella thought, and settled back again amongst the pillows. It would be more than a moment before Raymond-the-executor was finished with his work.

She sat back, but was not comfortable. This house has no warmth, she thought. It isn't cold, it's empty. Emptiness amidst all these possessions. She looked around the room for an afghan or something to put over her shoulders, but there were only heavy rugs and delicate doilies. Some silk scarves were draped over lampshades, but that wouldn't do, either. Besides, they were probably thick with dust. This whole place was probably an inch deep in dust, only one couldn't see it because it was covered so with tapestry.

She stood and walked gently, silently, her feet sinking deeply into the layered carpeting. She passed through the dining room, and averted her eyes from the large round table. "Witch table," she whispered automatically, and crossed herself. Everybody in the family knew what Mandalla and Armando did at that table, and it wasn't holy. She must have Raymond insist to the realtor that the table be sold with the house. She didn't want it, and she didn't want Raymond to have it, either.

Giving her bony arms a brisk rub, she started up the stairs, one hand appreciating the smooth polish of the banister, her feet appreciating the stealth, for while she didn't intend to snoop, Raymond would want her to stay put. She'd freeze to death in that living room. She was just going to look for a shawl to put around her shoulders. Just a shawl. Or a sweater.

There would be something upstairs, she was certain. Already her curiosity had begun to warm her.

She found the bathroom first, a huge room, tiled in tiny black and white octagonal shapes with a claw foot tub and ancient toilet. Estella pushed the old-fashioned black button wall switch and the light went on. Pink towels, pink bathmat, horrible with the black and white. What had Mandalla been thinking? She wanted to tinkle, but didn't want to flush. She didn't want Raymond to know she was wandering around. She turned off the light and continued her journey.

The door to the room at the front of the house, yes, that would be the main bedroom. The knob was frosted with ice crystals. Estella was afraid a window was out or something, but that was not her concern, that was Raymond's problem. She turned the knob and pushed open the door.

The room was sound, the windows secure. The walls were covered with more fabric, and the furniture was overstuffed and over decorated. There were more carpets on the floors, and layers of heavy draperies cloaked the huge windows that would overlook the street and the park beyond. In the center of the dark room was the bed. High, with a tall mahogany spiral at each corner.

This is where they both died, she thought, and went to the bed, which had been neatly made. She ran her hand along the brocade pillow sham, not knowing for sure if it was his pillow or her pillow, but feeling a softening in her heart. If they had loved each other, then surely there was some good in them, some good in their union. It didn't matter whose pillow Estella stroked, both of them had gone to their judgment.

All of the hardwood furniture was covered with crocheted doilies, silk scarves and minutia. Pictures, figurines, combs, brushes, feathers, artifacts, rocks, little pieces of this and that—

remembrances, probably. Estella moved silently, goosebumps on her arms in this frigid room, not touching anything, but not missing anything, either.

She moved to the windows and softly pulled aside the thick velvet drape. Underneath was a sheer white, and beneath that, next to the window, a lace curtain. She pulled them all aside and looked out into a rainy, gray spring day.

She shivered again and let the draperies swish heavily back into place.

At the foot of the bed was a grayish white rectangle. It looked light enough to throw over her shoulders. Then she could go back downstairs and wait patiently for Raymond, while she contemplated this Armando, an Armando she had never known. She could pray for his soul and feel at ease in his home.

The cold in the room seemed to emanate from the area of the folded blanket, but it was warm to her touch. And light. It was delightfully light. It was made of some filmy, slippery fabric that didn't have a discernable weave, probably one of those new miracle fibers. She swirled it around her shoulders and it was perfect. Exactly the right size, exactly the right weight, exactly the right fit.

She drew it closer around her, closed it at the throat with her fist. *I'll just take this home with me,* she thought. *Raymond will not mind.*

She went back down the stairs, feeling a little bit frisky, and went back to her place in the living room just as she heard Raymond and Mrs. Nelson come in from the kitchen and head up the stairs.

She felt naughty and that was good.

All the way back to her house, Raymond talked about Armando and Mandalla's estate and how he would be a good steward of the capital. He fiddled with the heater in the car and cursed it, pulling up his collar, wrapping his coat tighter around himself, while his enthusiasm for the financial project at hand went undampened.

Estella listened dreamily, cozy and warm within the snug affection of her new shawl. She didn't mention to Raymond that she had lifted it from Armando's bed. He need never know. She was eager to be rid of Raymond, and get back inside her tiny little apartment, where she could be alone to contemplate Armando's passing and exactly what that meant. She thought she might want to cry; she thought she might want to pray. But when they finally got there, what she really wanted to do was curl up on the couch with her new warm shawl and take a nap.

She snuggled down, amazed to discover that the shawl was long enough to cover her toes and stretch all the way up to bunch around her neck—more like a nice, small, lightweight cloak, actually—and as she fell softly asleep, feeling warm and well tended, she listened to the soothing voice and agreed with everything it said.

When she awoke, Estella found it odd to think that Raymond should benefit from all the money that Mandalla and her swishy Armando had tied up in that house. That money should belong to her, the next of kin.

Raymond must have duped her, she thought. She wrapped her new cloak around her shoulders and walked quietly into her little kitchen and brewed a cup of tea. Why would he have taken advantage of her like that? It wasn't like him.

Or so he would have her believe.

Estella's eyes gazed without focus across the rim of her teacup as she thought about Raymond. Things began to fall into place in her mind.

She remembered when he helped her buy this apartment. It was tiny. Cramped. She needed some space. She had money, she could afford something better, something with a little bit of an air about it, something more befitting a stately elderly gentlewoman.

She had money, didn't she? Or had Raymond cheated her out of her savings, too?

Her eyes narrowed to slits. She better get her money out of Raymond's clutches before he squandered it on fast women, potent drink and rich food.

She opened the cupboard and took out a box of graham crackers. She munched on the corner of one, then looked at it as if she had never seen it before.

She looked around her kitchen, at its meager, outdated furnishings. She swept the kitchen table clean, teacup smashing on the floor, tea splashing up the kitchen cupboard. The graham crackers hit the floor with a crunch and lay there, crumbs spilling out the corner of the broken waxed paper.

"I ought to have my own cook," she said. "And I shouldn't be eating graham crackers and drinking tea. I should have caviar with a glass of port."

Is that right? Is that my voice?

She tucked the cloak a little closer around her neck, as if a draft had come in to give her a chill.

Yes, indeed. That *was* right.

She ignored the mess, leaving it for the maid she would hire, and went in to the living room to call first the realtor, then her banker, her lawyer and lastly, Raymond, her son, the backstabbing, money-grubbing snake.

Backpeddling and playing the innocent, Raymond cut loose with her money, and within days, Estella moved into a fabulously expensive mansion on the hill. It had a view from every room. The realtor sent over a decorator, and the decorator brought a landscaper, and he brought a few friends, and soon there was more than upgrading going on. There was a party.

Lights ablaze all night long, Estella smiled and wandered through the house wondering what it looked like from town. She knew what it looked like. It looked like she was finally having some fun in her life.

Kimo, the young Hawaiian mason with rocklike arms and a back to match, taught her to drink scotch, and they spent their time on the terrace, the perpetual party loud and raucous behind them. Estella smiled when someone shrieked, or a bit of glass broke, because that told her that her guests were having a good time.

Kimo stroked her foot and talked of his tropical homeland and kept their drinks fresh. Estella pulled the cloak closer around her shoulders and listened to the sweet tenor of Kimo's voice and the soothing lull of the voices within the cloak, and realized she was the luckiest woman on earth.

Eventually, Kimo did more than talk. He awakened within her passions she never knew she possessed. He played her body like a fine violin—he had the hands and fingers of a master, and though she knew she was elderly, she was feeling younger and younger by the minute. When she looked at her face in the mirror, she was always surprised at the sight of it, because in her mind's eye, she was young, firm, redhaired, vibrant. If she applied enough makeup, and looked into the mirror long enough, that other face, that younger face emerged and smiled back at her.

Mornings were the roughest, when the maid got up and began loudly banging doors and cabinets, rudely trying to awaken those who had fallen asleep on the various pieces of furniture.

"Hush yourself," Estella would say to the twit, herself headachy and fragile. She would swallow two aspirin, take two more along with two black coffees, go back upstairs and gently awaken Kimo. The house was invariably a wreck, and of course the maid had plenty to complain about, but she was being paid to do a job, and part of her job was to get the house ready for the next night. She could do her job or quit. Or Estella might have to fire her. It mattered not to Estella, as long as her guests were having a good time, and she had Kimo to warm her bed, and her cloak to warm her shoulders.

Now and then Raymond would show up, either on a hang-over morning, when Estella would instruct the maid to tell him to go away, or on a night when Kimo seemed on the verge of propos-ing, and then Estella had no time for her son either.

One night, Raymond barged into her bedroom just as Kimo was warming the massage oil in his large, sensitive palms. Estella realized she better speak with him or he would never leave her alone.

She wrapped herself in a pewter silk robe she'd ordered from Japan, pulled the cloak close about her shoulders, and met Raymond in the library, far away from the laughing crowd and too far away from her young, enthusiastic lover.

"What is it?" she demanded, irked.

"What have you done to yourself?" Raymond asked.

Estella fingered her hennaed hair. It looked better than the old-lady gray she must have been crazy to wear all these years. She looked ten, twenty, maybe thirty years younger with a little color.

"You look like a harlot."

Estella's hand whipped out and slapped her son's cheek faster than thought. "You're trespassing here," she snarled, "and I have things to do."

He sat down to bring them closer to eye level. "Mother, these people are taking advantage of you."

"You're just afraid for your inheritance."

"No, I'm worried about you. This lifestyle isn't healthy for a person *half* your age. Look at you. Dyeing your hair, wearing all that crap around your eyes, drinking—" he picked up her glass and winced at the smell, "what is that, Scotch? Straight? What the hell has gotten into you?"

"I'm old, Raymond," she said, finding those words difficult to say, almost as if they were in a foreign language. "I'm having fun for the first time, and you have no right to come in here and accuse me of doing something wrong."

"I don't want you to get hurt."

He *is* afraid for his inheritance, Estella realized. He hasn't changed. He doesn't care for me. He only wants the money. "Get out," she said.

"What?"

"Get out of my house, leave my property and don't you ever come back. Don't you come back until it's time to put my corpse in the ground. Don't ever put your objectionable personality within the range of my senses. Ever again." She felt her face growing red, felt her hysteria building. "Do you understand me?" She could not believe the vehement hatred she felt for her son, the son to whom she had given birth, the son she suckled, adored, the son for whom she had sacrificed her youth. Now he was a terrorist. "Out! Out! *Get out!*" She shoved him back, and back, and back until he fumbled for the door and ran.

Estella calmed her heart, calmed her breathing. She was perspiring. Her hair, and probably her makeup, had become mussed. She hated confrontations, but at least that one was out of the way. Next up, she was certain, was going to be the stupid maid.

She knocked on the bathroom door, but carnal giggles answered her, so she went slowly up the stairs to her bedroom, freshened up, and then gently awakened Kimo so he could work his lomi-lomi magic on her.

The police were regular visitors to the house, called by one neighbor or another, usually complaining about the noise, usually around two o'clock in the morning. If Estella was up, she would flirt with the cops, flatter them, feed them if she could, and they would go away. If she was upstairs with Kimo, one of the other guests, usually the most sober one, would try to placate the policemen and convince them that the party was waning.

But one night, while Estella was upstairs in thrall with Kimo, her cloak, and passions she never knew the universe provided, the police came at the behest of the next door neighbor. When they arrived, they found seven naked people in the front yard, drunk and loud, ugly and disgusting. One woman was systematically breaking wine bottles in the driveway; one man was urinating on a woman who was dancing in hallucinogenic rapture. The lewd seven were arrested, and then the police swept through the house, advising everybody to pick up their things and go home immediately. Three bedrooms were occupied by girls turning tricks. They, too, were arrested, along with their johns. Eventually, a policeman knocked twice, then opened Estella's bedroom door.

Orange-lipsticked lips pulled back from her teeth when she saw his blue uniform. "Get the fuck out of my house," she said. Naked, she got out of bed and shoved him, then tried to close the door in his face, but he outweighed her by well over a hundred pounds, and he just shouldered his way in.

"You're the owner of this house?"

"You know damned well who I am, you prick," she said. "You've eaten enough of my caviar and drunk enough of my champagne. On duty."

"You're Estella Rodrigues?"

She ignored him and climbed back into bed where soft, warm Kimo waited for her.

"I'm afraid you're going to have to come with me, Mrs. Rodrigues."

"Fuck off."

"I'm placing you under arrest."

"Arrest?" Kimo jumped out of bed and pulled on his pants. "I didn't do nothin', man."

"Kimo, baby, come back," Estella said, waving her fingers at him. "You," she said to the cop, "get lost."

"Please get dressed, ma'am," the policeman said, then looked the other way while Kimo grabbed his shirt and skated out the door.

"Kimo! Kimo, get your hefty Hawaiian ass back in here!" Estella shouted, but Kimo was long gone.

"Come on, Mrs. Rodrigues. Don't make me restrain you."

"Restrain me?" Estella picked up a lamp from the bedside table. "Restrain me?" She threw the lamp at the policeman, and it crashed at his feet.

He just shook his head and spoke into the microphone on his shoulder. In moments, three other policemen were in the bedroom, and Estella was forcibly arrested. She grabbed her cloak from the pillow as they dragged her out of the bed. She fought like a she-cat as they wrapped her in her silk robe and carried her down the stairs.

Waiting, fuming, in the back seat of the police cruiser, she was glad she had her cloak to warm her shoulders.

Raymond

Raymond had barely closed his eyes, it seemed, when the phone rang. He opened his eyes and looked at the phone as if it were something evil. He sat up while it rang again, and made sure he was conscious enough to speak and remember the conversation, then he picked it up.

"Hello?"

"Mr. Rodrigues? Raymond Rodrigues?"

"Yes."

"This is Officer Bachman of the police department, Mr. Rodrigues. We have your mother, Estella Rodriguez, under arrest here."

Now Raymond knew for certain that the phone was an evil instrument. "Excuse me?" He didn't quite believe many things that had happened lately, certainly not this. And yet if he were honest with himself, it wasn't that much of a surprise.

"Your mother has been arrested, Mr. Rodrigues, on several counts of pandering, resisting arrest and failure to comply with curfews imposed. She's an old lady, Mr. Rodrigues, and we will remand her to your custody if you'll come get her. You can bring her back for her arraignment in the morning."

"Is she all right?"

"She's mad as hell."

Raymond signed the necessary papers to spring his mother from jail. They handed him a bulging manila envelope and told him to have a seat on the long, hard and scarred wooden bench. While he waited, he opened the envelope.

A pair of gaudy cut-glass earrings, the silk tie from her robe, and a light gray cloak. Her personal effects, he assumed, and waited calmly, fingering the soft fabric of the finely-woven cloak.

He closed his eyes. The one night when he actually had potential for a good night's sleep and his mother, his *elderly* mother, for God's sake, had to get arrested.

He leaned his head against the wall.

A chill came in from the door that revolved with people going in and out, in and out.

Raymond folded the belt and put it in his pocket along with his mother's earrings, then covered his chest with the cloak, closed his eyes and tried to relax. No telling how long it was going to be before they processed her release. If she was being difficult, it could take even longer.

He closed his eyes, trying not to think about the fact that his mother—*his mother*—had been arrested, tried not to think about the sleazy characters who were coming in and out of the police station at this time of night, who might see him, whom he might see. He just tried to relax.

He thought he heard some kind of a buzzing, like white noise from a television. He didn't know where it came from, but it was fine, it helped him mask out the reality of his situation. He listened to the fuzzy sound and tried to focus it, bring it in a little bit clearer. A sense of peace and well being began to come over him, and soon he was dozing, or it felt as though he were dozing. He startled awake a couple of times when things happened in the police station, but then he closed his eyes and sank quickly and easily back into his twilight dream state.

He thought of his family, this episode with his mother aside, and realized what a rich legacy he had been left. His aunt Mandalla, what a wonderful woman she had been. Her funeral had been enormous. People came from all over the country to pay their final respects. She had been a friend and healing mate to thousands.

That could be *his* legacy, he realized. Raymond could pick up where Mandalla had left off. He had the gift of translating from the other world—he knew it, he had always known it. He'd heard voices when he was a child, and it had alienated him from his friends. It was only by sheer force of his will, and the religious browbeating from his mother, that had slammed that door shut and then nailed it down tightly. Raymond had conscientiously stifled all that information, all those voices, that enormous genetic and spiritual gift.

But the door could open at any time. It had been closed by force of will, and it took even less than that to turn the knob, and the gift would open the door itself. It was his God-given talent.

He had always struggled in business, and while he made a fair living, who was he helping? Mandalla had helped so many. Raymond could help as many in his lifetime, if only he began.

If only he began now.

Now was the time.

Open the door, Raymond, he heard the voices in the white noise say. *Open the door. Let us help you help the people.*

"Let me the fuck out of this hell hole!" his mother shrieked.

Raymond's eyes popped open to see a garish caricature of his mother fly through the door, one hand keeping her silk robe closed around her birdlike frame. Her thin, orange-colored hair stood up like an aura around her head, her mascara had smeared and so had her orange lipstick. She looked horrible. She looked like a

Halloween creature.

"Give me that!" she snarled at Raymond as she strode past him, grabbing the cloak from around his neck so violently it pulled him forward with the momentum. "C'mon, Raymond, let's go."

The inside of the car was freezing. Raymond kept fiddling with the heater, but there was something wrong with it. It just wasn't putting any heat out. The steering wheel grew so cold it hurt his fingers to touch it. His mother didn't seem to notice. She just wrapped that cloak around her shoulders and muttered profanities to herself. Raymond had never seen her like this. She had been the epitome of a sweet, frail grandmotherly lady until recently. And now, she was terrifying.

And she had that lovely cloak. Raymond wanted a cloak like that. He wasn't sure, but he thought it would look okay if he wore it over his business suit. It was the perfect weight for him, it was just exactly the right amount of warmth he needed. Look, it kept his mother nice and toasty in this freezing car. He wanted the cloak.

"I want you to give me that cloak," he said.

She snorted in response.

"I mean it, mother, you've caused me no end of inconvenience and embarrassment, and I want you to give it to me in payment."

"Shut up and get me home," she said.

Reason flickered for a moment within Raymond. Maybe the cloak was the cause of all the trouble. His mother hadn't gone insane until after his uncle Armando died. And now he wanted to steal the cloak from his mother?

Did he want to steal the cloak?

Yes, he did. Yes, indeed he did. He wanted to take her home and wait downstairs until she was asleep, maybe even give her a handful of sleeping pills to help her on her way, chased by a big glass of scotch, and when she was out of it, he'd slip the cloak from her shoulders and put it around his. He could listen to the white noise, the voices, those soothing voices who told him that he was important to the world. He wanted to hear about the plan, he wanted to know what he should be doing next.

"Wait a minute," he said, put on the brake, and slowed the car.

"Get me home, dammit," Estella said, then whipped out a bird-like claw and snagged his wrist. "*Now*, before I beat you within an inch of your useless life."

"It's the cloak, mother," Raymond said. "It's the damned cloak!"

"I don't know what you're talking about, but I'll give you until the count of three to get this ridiculous BMW back on the road or I'll get out and hitchhike."

"It's the cloak that's causing you to behave like this."

"One."

"None of this happened before Uncle Armando died. Did you take it from his house?"

"Two."

"Okay, okay." Raymond put the heater on full blast, trying to warm his freezing hands, and got back on the road. He needed some time to clear his mind. He felt foggy-headed. He didn't know if he wanted to get the cloak away from his mother because it wasn't good for her or if he wanted it for himself.

At the bottom of her driveway, she didn't even wait for him to stop before opening the door. He chirped to a stop and she got out.

"I'll pick you up for court tomorrow," Raymond said.

"Eat shit," she said, and slammed the door.

Raymond sighed to himself and drove off. Two blocks later, he turned off the heater. It was roasting him.

He went home, but there was no sleep to be found. The radical transformation of his mother indicated some kind of serious mental illness. He ran his options back and forth, back and forth through his head: commitment to an asylum—or at least a 72-hour mental health watch at the local hospital—or send her away to some Betty Ford-type place, because surely there was enough alcohol in her system to fuel a race car. Maybe he could just ship her off to some relative.

Always in the back of his mind, he was thinking of separating Estella from that cloak. Raymond wanted that cloak, he wanted it bad, and he didn't know why.

When he finally admitted to himself that he was only thinking about getting his mother out of her house so he could get that cloak away from her, he got out of bed and dressed. If the cloak was the problem, it would be easier to remove it than to remove her.

He refused to think about how much he wanted it. He told himself he wanted it out of his mother's house, away from her. He refused to remember the soft voices, the lyrical prospects for his future if he would just sit at the seance table. He could stop struggling with life. He could have thousands at his funeral, too.

He didn't want to think about that. He wanted to help his mother.

When he got to the house, it was dark, the first time he had ever seen this house silent. He parked on the street and walked up the driveway. He had no key—she wouldn't give him one, but he tried the front door anyway. Locked.

He walked around the house, checking each of the doors and windows until he found what he was looking for.

A high unlocked window on the ground floor.

Quietly, Raymond removed the screen and slid the window open. It was an unoccupied bedroom. He jumped and wiggled through, landing, fortunately, on a bed.

He lay there a long time, heart pounding, listening to the noises of the house, listening to whether or not anyone was coming after him, or calling the police.

No sounds.

He took off his shoes and padded out of the bedroom in his stocking feet. The house was silent. It smelled of old booze and cigarettes, like an old tavern.

The kitchen had been cleaned up. Someone had stayed. Oh yes, Estella had hired a live-in maid.

He walked quietly up the stairs, hoping they wouldn't squeak. At the top, he gently turned the knob on her bedroom door. The cloak would be at her bedside, he was certain. His heart was pounding, and he didn't want to breathe too loudly, but he was scared half to death. He'd never done anything like this before, and for a moment, he couldn't remember why he was there.

The cloak. Estella's sanity.

His future.

He opened the door and looked in.

The barrel of a shotgun looked back at him.

"Hold still or I'll blow your fucking head off," Estella said.

"Mom," Raymond choked out, "it's me."

"Prowler. Not fit to take another breath."

"Mom, don't shoot me, I'm here to talk to you."

"Use the telephone."

Raymond's heart beat so hard and so loud that he was afraid he was going to faint. He couldn't breathe fast enough. Red bubbles danced in front of his eyes. "Mom, please, don't you see the change that has come over you? Can't you see that something isn't right here? Do you want to go to jail tomorrow? Will that make your life better?"

"You liked it when I was poor and you had all the money."

"It was always your money. You wanted me to manage it for you, remember? I always asked if you needed more, and you always said no, remember? Remember?"

No response.

"Put the gun down, Mom."

She lowered the barrel of the heavy shotgun and Raymond took it from her, relief making him weak in the knees. He pushed the door the rest of the way open and turned on the light.

The cloak was not on the bed.

"Where's the cloak?"

"I hid it. I knew you would come for it, you thief."

"I think it's that cloak that's causing you all this trouble," he said. "Where did you get it?"

"None of your business," she said. "You can't have it."

"I don't want it," Raymond lied. "I just want to take it away and put it someplace safe for a week. I need to know if that's what's been making things strange around here."

"It spoke to you in the jailhouse," Estella accused.

Raymond found that he couldn't lie to her, not eye to eye. "Yes," he said. "It's evil. Look at you. Look at what has happened to you—" He took her thin shoulders and turned her to face a mirror, "I think it is to blame. Let me take it away for a week. Just a week."

Estella seemed amazed at her reflection. She touched her hair that stood up like a cane fire.

"Okay," she said weakly. "It's downstairs in the hallway trunk."

Raymond raced down the stairs to grab the cloak before she changed her mind. But when he opened the trunk, there were only folded quilts inside. The quilts his grandmother had made. He dug through them, and soon Estella was standing next to him. "It's gone," she whispered.

"Gone? What do you mean gone?"

"I put it right on top there," she said. "And now it's gone." She began to smooth the quilts that Raymond had messed up, then she put the lid down on the trunk. Raymond sat heavily on it.

The cloak was gone. Loose in the world.

"I got it at Mandalla's house," Estella said. "It was on their bed. When you were with the realtor, I was cold and wanted something for my shoulders."

Raymond nodded. He knew it was his responsibility. Somehow, he knew that it wasn't the gift of sight or communication with the other world that was his family legacy, it was that scrap of fabric that was his family legacy. It was his to worry about. It was his life's work, now, to recover it and destroy it before it destroyed any more lives the way it almost destroyed his mother's.

Estella sat next to him on the trunk and smoothed down his hair.

Father Jake

The donations for the poor were kept in the coatroom of the church, and when Father Jake, the young priest, went looking for the draft that seemed to whoosh through the cavernous church all the way to the kitchen to cool off his breakfast oatmeal, he found the coatroom to be in disarray.

Forgetting the draft, he began putting everything right. There were bags of clothing, boxes of toys, stacks of dishes and more boxes of kitchenware, even some power tools and sports equipment. He'd have to call the ladies to come in and hold their sale, or disburse these donations, or whatever it was that they did with this stuff. It was accumulating faster than the little coatroom could hold it, and when autumn set in, the coatroom would be needed for more than just hanging up the choir robes.

He righted a couple of brown paper sacks that were overflowing, and as he did, his hand brushed something soft and warm and very pleasant.

For a moment he thought it was a kitten or something.

Then he was afraid it was a rat or something.

But no, it was white, or kind of a shimmering grayish white. He stood the bag up straight and pulled the item out and was amazed to find that it was a beautifully-woven stole, the kind that priests wore over their vestments during a service. It had no embroidered cross, no symbols at all. It was plain, but it was beautiful.

Who would have put such a thing in with the donations for the poor?

Father Jake put it around his neck, certain that whoever had donated it had done so by mistake—they must have meant to bring it to him as a gift—and he finished straightening up the room.

The cold draft disappeared.

Father Jake looked around the huge room and felt a surge of confidence. He knew he was young, he knew his parishioners missed Father Wilson, the old priest who had held forth in this church for thirty years, he knew he was inexperienced, but by golly, he was well trained and his faith was well placed. He could do this. He could benefit people by making this church grow, prosper, thrive. He could. He would. He was younger, and more in touch with today's youth and their problems than Father Wilson had been. He'd give them one winner of a sermon come Sunday. They'd see.

Meanwhile—he checked his watch—he had a counseling session in a half hour. Just time to shower, shave, slip into his new set of vestments and meet with the middle-aged couple who were having a difficult time with their marriage.

"He never listens to me, Father," the wife complained, holding a soggy tissue to one reddened nostril.

"I don't know what she's complaining about," the husband said. "I bring home a fat paycheck. I'm home every night instead of out drinking or chasing like a lot of my friends. I pay the bills, all she has to do is keep the house from looking like a pig sty and raise them kids." He looked over at her. "Too many kids—pardon me, Father you had too damned many kids, that's what the problem is."

The wife looked at Father Jake with a "See? It's hopeless" look, and he couldn't help but agree, in part. The husband was a dolt and needed a little bit of a shock to realize what a good thing he had going.

"Have you considered a little vacation from each other?" he asked.

They both leaned closer as if he was mouthing magic words, words they both wanted to hear. It gave him an oddly uncomfortable feeling of power.

"Sometimes a little space can give people perspective on their problems," he said.

"I'll go visit my sister," the wife said, "and you can take care of the cooking and the cleaning and the kids."

"Hey," the husband said, "You want to fight with the jerks on the line? You can go to work every day. I'd be happy to cook and clean and look after the brats."

She gave Father Jake that look again.

"Why don't you send the kids to your sister's for a week," he suggested. "Then you can each take a little time off from each other, and then maybe you can get back together for a little honeymoon before they come back home."

"She'll have to lose about a hundred pounds," the husband growled.

The wife stood up, graciously accepting Father Jake's suggestions, and he noticed that she did indeed have an ample rear end. But it was a long way from being unattractive. In fact, he couldn't quite keep his eyes from noticing her allover squeezable dimensions. They shook hands, and then she exited, the rumpled loser of a husband following along behind her.

Jake leaned back in his chair feeling pretty good. He'd never been married, never even had a woman, what with his vow of chastity and all that, but he could imagine what it must be like to be married, to have kids, to have a woman like that throw her leg over him in the middle of the night...

He stood up abruptly and went in to wash his face.

The next day she was back, her face puffy and her eyes red.

Before he knew it, he was sitting in the chair next to her, and he was stroking her hair. He'd never stroked a woman's hair before. It was shiny and silky.

Then they were on the couch, and he had his arm around her, and she was crying softly into his chest.

He put a finger up under her chin and brought her face up and those lips, those lips.

He put his lips on hers—they were incredibly soft, and then she had her hands on his belt buckle, and he had her dress up and her panties down, and... and...

and he saw God.

There's something wrong with a church that denies its leaders this fundamental act of pleasure and creation, he thought.

Did he say that out loud? Did she say it? Who said that?

She seemed to be weepy, but in a different way as they rearranged their clothes, and Father Jake felt an odd protectiveness toward her.

"Don't let him make you feel anything but wonderful," he said as he walked her to the church door. She smiled demurely, kissed him on the corner of his mouth, and then she left.

Wow, he thought. Holy shit. What have I done?

He knew it was wrong, he knew he should be ashamed, but he felt great. He felt good about himself, he felt good about his role as parish leader, he felt good about that woman and her future prospects, and he felt wonderful about life in general.

He walked back through the church to his quarters, saw his sermon still up on the computer screen where he had been working on it when her visit interrupted him, and he turned it off. He ought to finish it, but maybe he'd go get a haircut first.

He kissed the stole as he took it off and hung it up.

He felt naked.

He put the stole back around his neck and wrapped it like a long scarf to hang down his back. He knew it looked weird in the summer heat with his jeans and his shot-sleeved black shirt, but he didn't care.

On the way out, he grabbed twenty bucks from the poor box. Hey, he thought, a donation is a donation.

The barber made him hang the stole up on the coat rack, and Jake itched and jangled until the barber was finished and he could wrap his neck up again all nice and cozy. He paid the man, and then felt a gnawing hunger in the pit of his stomach. He knew what it was, and it wasn't a burger that was going to sate it. He remembered that feeling from when he was about twelve.

This time there would be no behind-the-bathroom-door guilty feelings. This time he knew what women tasted like and he liked it. He was going to have to taste a little bit more.

He walked downtown, and kept walking until he reached the seedy side.

Druggies stood in clusters on the corners, waiting for their drive-by customers. Young girls in almost-clothes leaned against buildings, pouting in boredom, hoping for one of their elusive dreams to come true.

Jake at once wanted to minister to their needs and wanted to rip their clothes off. He just kept walking. He walked down past the girlie theaters, went in and dropped a couple of quarters. About the time the sun went down, the hunger that had gnawed on his belly had turned into a raging need.

He went back to where he saw the prostitutes, the young ones, the ones with tight skin and firm muscles.

He grabbed one, a very young one, she couldn't have been more than thirteen. He paid an unshaven hotel clerk seven dollars for an hour's use of a room, then took her upstairs.

First, they got into the shower together and he scrubbed all that makeup off her. She complained when he shampooed her hair, but then she settled down like a little girl and let him bathe her all over.

He loved the feel of her young skin under his soapy hands.

And she knew all too well what to do with him, as well. Overly eager, ruthless and rough, Jake took that which he felt had been denied him for too many years.

Jake McGinnis, priest, saw God for the second time. He wrapped his arms around the girl, and covered them both with the stole that was somehow long enough and wide enough to cover them both from head to toe, like a blanket, and they slept together until the hotel manager stomped up the stairs and pounded on the door.

Jake was up in a flash, whipped open the door and landed a right to the guy's jaw. The manager flew across the hall, hit his head on the wall and slid down to the floor.

Jake closed the door and got back into bed with the girl, but she shrank away from him and the hair-trigger violence he exhibited. He saw the fear in her eyes and he kind of liked that, too.

Plenty of fresh experiences for ol' Father Jake.

He tied her wrists to the bed with the two ends of the stole, and that egged him on. He remembered those girlie magazines he and his friends had looked at when they were eight, nine, ten, those pictures that had never really been too far from his consciousness. He still dreamed about some of those pictures and felt guilt and shame when he awoke with an erection.

Ha! That was nothing. Here was the real thing, the real anatomically-correct, warm piece of ass right here in this bed, under his control, and he felt not one whit of guilt. He tied her and then he calmed her and then he took her again and again, feeling like a racehorse, feeling like a raging bull.

By the time he was finished, she was crying, but he had no time for that.

He had to think. He had too many choices, too many directions in which to go. He felt so much freedom. He wondered why he had ever felt that his life choices had narrowed his path so severely—he could see now that they had opened his life instead.

He dressed, untied the girl, wrapped the stole around his neck, threw whatever change was left of the twenty onto the bed, and walked back through the night toward the church.

He had way too much energy. Something inside told him that things weren't quite right, but then something outside told him that everything was perfect.

Back inside the church, he hung his stole on the coat rack in his office. Then, walking through the chapel on his way to bed, he stopped and looked at the crucifix hanging over the altar.

He genuflected, as was his habit, as was proper, and feelings of guilt began to flood him. His actions were wrong, were harmful, were inexcusable. He felt his soul swell with emotion as he began to repent. He had broken his vows. He had harmed another. He had stolen. He had broken the commandments. He, who was to be a pillar of the community, a beacon in the spiritual night of all lost souls, a model of God's goodness and pristine habits, had sinned in the worst possible way.

Pain in his gut doubled him over. He leaned so far over he began to bang his forehead against the wood floor, feeling relief in the external, self-administered pain.

He felt naked.

He ought to be praying for forgiveness while wearing his vestments. If he ever felt worthy enough to wear them again, he ought to never take them off.

That poor girl!

He stood up, ran back to his office, donned the black robe, the white stole, and walked, shamed, to the chapel.

But then he didn't feel like praying any more.

He felt like taking a hammer to those ugly stained glass windows instead.

Or that crucifix.

Father Jake stood looking at that model of Christ on the cross and he shook his head. Why did they always make him look so haggard, so thin, so worn out? Everything he'd ever read of Jesus said that he was always of good cheer, he was a carpenter, didn't that mean he probably had muscles? Wasn't he most likely a good looking, fun-loving kind of guy?

Or was that more blaspheme?

He didn't think so, but he didn't know. Whatever, that representation of the person that Christ was and the symbol he had become for Christianity offended Father Jake. That skinny, miserable wretch up there on that hunk of wood wasn't worthy of worship.

Jake got his hammer.

First he'd take down that ugly crucifix. Then he'd go after those stupid windows.

He hiked up his black vestment robe and climbed up on top of the altar. Hammer in hand, he was just ready to take a full-bodied swing at the Savior's kneecaps when he heard the church door open.

Damn. He should have locked the door. But who'd have thought someone would come to the church in the middle of the night?

His eyes narrowed to slits.

That bitch of a hooker better not have called the cops, he thought.

Juliette

Juliette hadn't slept at all since she stole the old woman's shawl and donated it to the poor box at the church. She lay awake in her bedroom under Estella's own roof, on this, the second sleepless night, knowing that it was likely her sins would see to it that she never slept again.

There is no rest for the wicked.

She could have just quit her job, she could have confronted Estella and told her that her lifestyle, the things she did, the things that went on in her house made it a place unfit for someone with Juliette's upbringing, it conflicted with her sense of morality, it was flat-out sinful, and she couldn't watch it or listen to it or clean up after it one moment longer.

She could have said all that, and then quit.

Instead, she stole the one thing that the old lady seemed to hold sacred, and then kept her job. It was an uncharacteristic thing for her to do, but that cloak seemed to instigate it.

Stop it, Juliette, she told herself. *That's ridiculous. Take responsibility for your actions.*

Juliette was no different than the sinful old woman herself. Well, if she were to find any peace at all in this life, she had to learn to put her wrongs right.

She got out of bed and dressed.

The house was silent. At least being arrested had shaken some sense into the old fool—she hadn't had that smoking, drinking, drug-snorting ilk around since she went to jail that night.

Careful not to make any noise, Juliette walked quickly through the house and let herself out the front door. The donations were kept in the coatroom, just off the church vestibule, and it wasn't locked. She just hoped the new priest hadn't disbursed them yet. She needed to give that cloak back and make amends to her employer.

She ran through the dark silent night, desperate, suddenly, for the cloak to be there. She chanted a prayer as she ran, begging God for the opportunity to make good for her evil ways. If the cloak wasn't there, she didn't know what she would do. She'd have to confess to Estella, and she couldn't imagine what the old lady would do to her. Beat her, probably, and Juliette had a good beating coming.

She was out of breath by the time she got to the church, but there were lights on inside. Father Jake was up and about. Thank God. Even if the cloak had been given to one of the poor of the parish, at least Father Jake could hear her confession, and maybe she'd get some relief and perhaps some sleep.

She pulled the great doors open and heard them grind on the stone floor. Then she peered into the coatroom, and her heart soared at the sight of it being so tidy and so full of donations, including the paper sacks she had brought. The cloak was safe, and she could return it to its rightful owner. She breathed a prayer of thanks and promised God that she'd try to be less of a willful girl in the future.

Then, curious about the handsome new priest and his nocturnal activities, she walked down the hall and opened the unlocked door to the chapel.

What she saw amazed and disturbed and confounded her.

Father Jake was standing on the altar, and it looked as though he was about to desecrate the crucifix. Stunned almost to silence, she said in a small, quavering voice that echoed through the room, "Father?"

But he was already looking at her. "Juliette," he said and smiled.

He was terribly handsome. And he remembered her name!

He stepped down from the altar and set the hammer down. He was wearing his vestments, so she thought this could be some sort of late night ritual, some part of the secrets the priests kept among themselves. She wanted to ask, but she had been sinful enough. She bowed her head and waited as he walked toward her, his skirts billowing behind him, his white pristine stole around his neck, his hands outstretched.

"Juliette," he said. "What brings you here at this time of night? Are you ill? Do you need help?"

The lack of sleep and the constant strain, and now the massive relief erupted from her in a single tear that leaked out of her eye and ran down her cheek. She tried to wipe it away before he saw it, but she wasn't fast enough.

"Juliette, my child, come sit down and tell me. Do you need to confess?"

"Not yet, Father," she said, knowing that her confession would come when she had returned the cloak. She let him take her hand

and lead her over to the nearest pew. His hands were warm and soft, and his teeth were so milky white and his eyes had such a sparkle to them. All the single girls talked about Father Jake, and though Juliette thought it was not exactly proper to giggle about a priest in that way, she went along with it anyway. She couldn't help herself from imagining what her girlfriends would say if they knew that she was sitting next to him on the pew in the middle of the night.

And he had his arm around her.

"Now tell me," he said, and another tear leaked out in spite of her, and he held her hand with one of his and wiped the tear with the other. She tried a brave smile, but it only brought another tear.

He kissed that one away.

And then his mouth was on top of hers, and that hand that still had her tear on a fingertip was under her dress.

Juliette pushed herself away from him. He grabbed for her, but she slid away down the pew, and then got up and ran.

Her sin had driven the priest insane.

"Juliette!" he shouted, but she was out the door. She ducked into the coatroom and kicked over the brown paper bags full of clothes, but she couldn't remember which one she had put the cloak into.

The church door opened. "Juliette, wait, please, talk to me for a moment."

She left the donations in a mess and ran out the door. She didn't dare let him touch her again. She had to get out of there. She had to go to Estella and confess to her. That would be the first step, and then they could go together to the church to find the cloak. Then Father Jake would have regained his equilibrium and everything would be fine.

She had to erase this sin from her soul.

She ran back through town toward Estella's house, she ran as fast and as hard as she could. By the time she reached the house she was out of breath and a searing pain stabbed into her side.

"Estella, Estella!" she called as she opened the door, then ran up the first few steps, clung to the banister and tried to catch her breath before continuing up to Estella's room.

"What is it?" Estella asked.

Juliette looked up and saw Estella as she had always known her, with her pale face and all that red washed out of her white hair. This was the Estella she had grown up with at church picnics, this was the Estella she had known since childhood. Whatever strange mental convolution had taken Estella over that had made her dye her hair and throw her morals to the wind had ended.

"Estella, praise God," Juliette said, then collapsed at the old woman's feet. "I took your cloak, God have mercy upon my wretched soul. I took your cloak in anger, I stole it, I did it vindictively and with forethought. Please do not hate me. Please forgive me. My act has caused madness in the church, and I can't put things right until I am forgiven. Please. I beg you." And then the real tears came and they dripped onto Estella's feet.

"Where, girl, where is the cloak?"

"I put it in with the donations at the church and now Father Jake is bearing the brunt of my sin. It's my fault, it's all my fault."

"Get up, child, we have things to do," Estella said, and went back into her bedroom. Juliette dried her face on her skirt and followed.

"Raymond?" Estella said into the telephone. "Wake up, Raymond. The cloak is at the church."

Raymond

Raymond hung up the phone, dressed and was out the door before he was even completely awake. He had just about given up on the idea of finding his mother's cloak. In fact, he had talked himself into believing it was all in his mind. He had begun to believe that there really was something wrong with his mother. She was elderly, after all, and perhaps there were some arterial problems in her brain.

But then she resumed normalcy after the cloak came up missing, even calling the realtor to sell that gargantuan house on the hill.

And now his beliefs had been tossed one more time. Maybe it *was* the cloak.

It hadn't traveled far. The church was less than a mile away.

The dashboard clock said 1:47 when he pulled up in front of the church. Every light inside was on, blasting light out through the stained glass windows into the dark, silent street. Raymond wondered what he could take with him that would provide him some protection, then realized that there was nothing. He just had to stay aware, stay conscious. Try to be immune.

He'd never been so excited or so afraid before. He was so vulnerable. He knew the cloak was the very definition of evil potential, but used correctly, couldn't it also propagate good? He didn't know, didn't think it mattered. It ought to be destroyed. He only hoped he had the wherewithal to accomplish that.

He pulled open the big doors and entered the vestibule.

The church was quiet, though it had a feeling of being filled with people. Raymond half expected to open the interior doors and see the church filled with parishioners, the choir in their white and gold robes, the organist in his loft, Father Jake in the pulpit. He could almost hear the restless feet on the stone floor, the subtle coughs, the dry stones sucking respiration moisture from a thousand lungs.

He opened the door. The church was empty. Cold and empty. Freezing cold and empty.

Father Jake stood in the pulpit.

Raymond strode up to him, and the priest came down to greet him. They shook hands, but Raymond saw a glitter in Father Jake's eyes that he had never seen there before. It was a familiar look, the look he had seen in his mother's eyes when she was in the midst of her madness.

Father Jake had gone mad.

"Hello, Raymond," Father Jake said, only he said it with a mocking tone, nothing like Raymond would have expected. "What brings you out at this time of night?"

"I'm looking for my mother's shawl," Raymond said, and it sounded weak and ineffectual and stupid.

Silver threads seemed to crawl around in Father Jake's stole. Raymond found it hard to take his eyes off it.

"Why would it be here, Raymond?" Father Jake asked, snapping him back to the present. "She hasn't been to church since…let's see, since Armando's funeral."

"No," Raymond said, "it was stolen." the stole mesmerized him. He reached out to touch it, and he swore it reached out to touch him, but Father Jake took a step back.

"You come here in the middle of the night to report a stolen cloak?"

Raymond looked up and his eyes locked on to Father Jake's. Father Jake knew. He knew everything.

"Yes," Raymond said, then reached out again for the stole, but Father Jake turned and strode away.

"Stolen goods? Donated, perhaps. Shall we look through the donations?"

"No. I don't know," Raymond said, following the priest through the chapel. Raymond was intimidated, and the last thing he wanted to do was paw through boxes of worn out clothes in the coatroom.

Father Jake stopped, turned.

The shimmering gray and white thing around Father Jake's neck wanted to be around Raymond's neck and he wanted it to be there. He wanted to feel the softness of that fabric next to his skin more than he had ever wanted anything before.

He reached out, but the priest took a step back.

"Please, let me just touch—"

The fringed ends fluttered like fingers. It wanted to touch him, too.

"I can't help you," the priest said flatly.

Raymond looked up at him, and it took all his energy to resist tackling him and ripping the stole from him. It was evil, Raymond reminded himself. It was the cause of all this trouble. Leave the church unscathed, he told himself. Just get out. "I'll come back," he said, and without looking down at it again, he walked away.

By the time he reached the vestibule, his clothes were soaked in perspiration. He felt as if he had escaped by a hair's breadth.

As he reached for the heavy outer church doors, he had a feeling that Father Jake and the entire invisible congregation inside were laughing at him.

Raymond still perspired, his heart pounded, his breathing was difficult all the way to his mother's house. Since he first encountered her cloak that night in the jail waiting room, it had been seducing him. He was obsessed with finding it. His dreams were filled with the thought of owning it; he couldn't work, couldn't eat, spent all his days aimlessly searching without a single thread of a clue as where to look. He was restlessly driven.

Now he knew where it was. Now he knew what it was, and who had it.

But how to deal with it? How to battle it?

As evil as it may be, he still wanted it. He wanted to lose himself in it, to bask in it, to succumb to it, leaving all of life's responsibilities and difficulties behind, and let the fabric master him.

*

"I couldn't do it," he confessed to his mother. "Father Jake has it, but I couldn't take it from him. I had to get out of there. It has power over me."

"And you over it," Estella said, her tiny cool hands gripping the ends of his fingers. "You have the gift, Raymond, it's been a known fact in the family since you were born. You spoke with the spirits before you spoke with your father or me. But I didn't want that for you, so I kept you from your Aunt Mandalla. I didn't want you to be influenced. I didn't want you to grow up knowing the power you have. Mandalla used it for good, but so many wield their power against that which is righteous."

Juliette crossed herself.

Raymond nodded his head. He knew he had his Aunt Mandalla's gift.

"You must perform the seance, Raymond. You can call the cloak."

Her eyes twinkled with health and intelligence and mercy and love. Sincerity showed in her face, and Raymond knew it was the only way. He was afraid, afraid of the spirit world blasting through the wall he had so carefully constructed to keep all those voices out, afraid that he might be persuaded to use his power in the wrong way, afraid for what might happen to his mother...he was afraid of everything. But he knew in his heart that evil had escaped after Mandalla's death, and he had to retrieve it. It was his family obligation.

He nodded, then hung his head. He felt as if he had sealed the fate of everyone he loved.

"Come," she said. "We must hurry."

With the still distraught and uncomprehending Juliette, they drove to Mandalla and Armando's old house. Fresh curtains hung in the windows. A new car was parked in the driveway.

"It's two o'clock in the morning," Raymond complained.

"Never mind that," Estella said. "This is an emergency." She led the way to the door and rang the bell three times.

"Excuse me for disturbing you," she said to the tousled man who opened the door. I am Estella Rodrigues, this is my son, Raymond, and this is Juliette. I am the sister of the woman who owned this house before you bought it."

"Yes?" the man said. Raymond knew they didn't appear to be any threat, but he was still uncomfortable disturbing a family in the middle of the night. He felt like an irritant, or worse, a curiosity.

"There has been an emergency at our church," Estella went on. "Does my sister's great round table still stand in the dining room?"

She moved past him before he could answer, and Raymond, with a shy smile, followed her in.

There it stood, burnished, scarred, beautiful.

A woman in her robe and two little girls in nightgowns stood huddled together at the top of the stairs. "Max?" she called.

"It's okay," Max said, then he turned to Raymond. "What exactly is it that you want at two o'clock in the morning?"

"Please," Raymond said. "We would never disturb you if it weren't an emergency."

"We need to call the spirits back," Estella said, pulled out a chair and sat down. She held out her hands for the others to join her.

"What?" Max said.

"Please," she said. "I have known the evil. I have *known* the evil. We have no time to waste. Ask your wife to join us. Please," she urged.

Raymond sat on one side of her and Juliette on the other. They took her hands and held out theirs.

"What is this, a seance?" Max said.

"You girls go back to bed," the woman said, then floated down the stairs.

"Please," Estella said. "Dim the lights and join us."

"Max?" the woman said.

"Please hurry," Estella said.

Max shrugged, turned down the rheostat on the dining room light and pulled out a chair for his wife. "This is Sonja," he said in introduction. They sat down and held hands. The circuit was closed.

A shiver ran through Raymond, and played about at the top of his scalp.

"Come," Estella said beseechingly to no one. "Help us."

Raymond felt an internal opening, almost as if his heart had flowered. A feeling like warm water rushed through his soul, and when he opened his mouth to exclaim the feeling, he heard his Aunt Mandalla's voice.

"Welcome friends. Raymond. Estella, my sister. Armando and I are responsible for this terrible thing, and we will put it right, but you must help me."

Raymond looked around the circle and all eyes were on him. He realized that Mandalla was talking *through* him. Her voice was coming out of *his* mouth. He was more incredulous than those who were witnessing this event, and their eyes were wide and their mouths hung open.

"You must not be afraid, no matter what happens. You must be strong and not break the circle. No matter what happens, you must not break the circle."

"Yes, Mandalla," Estella said, then squeezed Juliette's hand.

"Yes, Mandalla," Juliette said, fear turning her face pale. Max and Sonja mimicked Estella's words, and then Raymond felt his mouth open again.

"Very well. Hold tightly to each other and bind your strength." She raised her voice and it reverberated around the room as if amplified by a truckload of speakers. "I call to you, trickster spirits who have fallen from your element. Hear me!"

Father Jake's head snapped up as the female voice reverberated through the chapel. His eyes narrowed as he walked briskly down the aisle and mounted the stairs to the pulpit. He would meet this disembodied voice, this evil, head-on. One end of the stole crept up the front of his vestments and snugged itself around his neck.

"Hear me!" Mandalla's voice commanded.

"Be gone!" Father Jake said, but his voice sounded thin and weepy compared to the authoritative voice he was trying to rebuke.

"You have no power in this world," Mandalla's voice echoed with gentle power. "You know your rightful place. Say I now to you: *go there!*"

Her words seemed to emanate from every crevice in the chapel. Intimidated, Father Jake amped up his ire. He lifted his hands as if in benediction. "This is a house of God," he said, and the stole began to change shape. First it elongated into a cloak, and as he watched, transfixed, not able to bring his hands down from where they beseeched the heavens, the shawl took on weight and stretched into a heavy cloak. A terribly heavy cloak.

The cloak was heavy with voice, and personality, and power, and wrath. "Stop," he said, but he said it weakly, and he didn't know to whom he was speaking.

"Hear me!" Mandalla's voice commanded.

In agitation, the cloak began to move. It tightened its grip around Father Jake's neck, and he pulled at it. It was too tight, it was hard for him to breathe.

The ends of the cloak began to unravel, and long, white oozy strands wrapped themselves around his legs.

"Stop," he choked out, "stop. Let...me...go..." The pressure was building in his face as the cloak gripped him tighter and tighter.

"Leave this world!" Mandalla demanded.

The cloak clung to Father Jake in desperation. Eyes wide, he clawed at the fabric, trying to pull it off him, but his hands couldn't grip it. It was smooth, and cold and slippery, and whenever he felt he had a fistful of it, it slipped right through his fingers.

His blood pressure built to the bursting point, he felt his legs go weak, he saw dark swirls at the edge of his vision.

He also saw faces in the fabric, undulating, changing, each of them with an expression of fear, their mouths wide open, and if he could just get them to let him go, he could hear them, he could help them, but the noise of his own blood pumping in his ears was the only thing he could hear

The angry yelling of an invisible mob filled Max and Sonja's house, and the members of the circle clung to each other with a tighter grip. Raymond looked up and saw the two little girls hugging each other at the top of the stairs while madness swirled around them. There were no visual manifestations, just the horrible sounds of a thousand furious people.

"Leave us!" Mandalla shouted.

Father Jake felt his fingernails raking his own throat as he tried to free himself of the tendrils which had encased him in slimy strands of foggy ooze. He couldn't breathe.

He stumbled backward, trying to plead with the voices, the spirits in the stole, begging them with his mind, praying to them, but they weren't listening, they were clinging to humanity, to mortality, but he couldn't help them. He couldn't even breathe. He stumbled, reeled, and arms banded to his side by strands of unraveled cloak, he crashed into a rack of candles and fell.

Hot wax sprayed flame all across his vestments and the cloak, searing him, but he couldn't feel it. The cloak constricted in its own sizzling terror, and crushed what life was left right out of him.

Unearthly shrieking filled Max and Sonja's house, and all of those sitting around the table screamed in terror right along with them. They clung to each other's hands, fingernails digging, trying to shut out the horrifying screeching of the spirits, who sounded like a whole village of burning people.

Underneath it all was Mandalla's voice calmly saying, "Don't break the circle, don't break the circle, it's almost over, it's almost over, don't break the circle, it's almost over."

And eventually, as sirens outside took over the wailing, the howling inside the house diminished to just a voice or two, and finally, a last gasp, a sigh, and it was over.

It was over.

"Thank you, my darlings, my loved ones," Mandalla said to a tableful of exhausted people. "I bring greetings from all your kin who have gone before," she said to Max and Sonja. "To you, Estella my sister, I shall see you soon. To my sweet nephew, Raymond, make the most of your talents, and never hesitate to call upon me. And to Juliette, lovely girl, I see nothing but happiness in your future. Be confident that I will be there to personally welcome you all to the other side. Good bye now."

Raymond felt a greatness slide out through the top of his head, and all his muscles went slack. He was bone-tired, exhausted, as if he had been holding the weight of the world on his shoulders alone. He closed his eyes and let his head drop forward.

"I'm going to let go now," Max said as another fire truck sped wailing down the street. He broke the circle, then turned up the lights.

The burning church lit up the skyline, and everyone went to the window.

"I have to go," Raymond said. Distant firelight reflected off his mother's face. He was exhausted beyond all his limits. He was afraid he wouldn't be able to drive.

After he helped his mother and Juliette into the car, Raymond stood for a moment, listening to the sirens and watching the red glow in the sky. He felt a profound sense of loss. He felt as if he had been doing something important for the first time in his life, chasing down the whereabouts of the cloak. He felt as if he had a family legacy, as if his life had genuine purpose, but now that was finished.

He felt directionless. He leaned up against the cold metal of the car and couldn't imagine going back to work, to that dead end job. He didn't know what he would do now. He wanted more of the hunt. He wanted more of the thrill of chasing and vanquishing evil.

He'd seen evil. He'd looked into its grinning face and he wanted to smash it.

Raymond smiled to himself, a wistful, accepting smile. Should have been born a dragon slayer, he thought. But instead, he'd been born an accountant.

Too bad.

As her parents saw the people out, Susan grabbed her little sister's hand, ran down the stairs and hid under the big table.

There was a pool of cold, misty white stuff on the rug, under the chair where the strange man with the old lady's voice had been sitting.

Monica, the seven-year-old, picked up a handful and let it ooze out from between her fingers. "It's cold," she giggled, but Susan, afraid the grownups would hear them, hushed her with a stern face.

Susan, older and wiser at age nine, picked up a pinch of the ectoplasm she had seen run out of the man's mouth in a fine stream, and blew on it. It evaporated into a whiff of moisture. It was great. "Go get a Ziplock," she said.

Obedient Monica ran the errand, then held the bag while Susan scooped handfuls of the goopy stuff into the bag. When it was all cleaned up, Susan sealed the bag with red-cold fingers. They ran back upstairs, jumped into bed and Susan stuffed the bulging bag under Monica's pillow. "Not a word," she warned her sister.

They heard the tired footsteps of their parents come up the stairs.

"You girls ready to go back to sleep?" their mother asked.

"Yes," they said in unison.

"Good. We'll talk about all of this in the morning."

"Okay."

Their mother turned off the light and closed their bedroom door so that only a thin shaft of light fell across the ends of their beds.

Susan reached her hand out across the abyss between their twin beds, and Monica took it.

Susan could see Monica's eyes glittering in the dark, and she knew they had found something powerfully wonderful.

It made her smile.

❋

Suspicions About Sex

Sex is great. There's nothing better than two smooth bodies merging in heat and love and tenderness.

So why all the fuss? Why all the perverts and the censorship and the shame? Who's in charge of all that and why do we allow it?

We're animal by nature, but by all appearances, we deny it.

Is that because we suspect that others are having better/more/different sex than we are, and we either don't want to know about it or we don't want them to be enjoying themselves?

Or being "higher" creations, are we supposed to be "above" all that carnal stuff?

Or are some of us eternally pissed off because it's something that's available to everybody and not just those who can pay the tax or earn the privilege?

Two things are for certain: 1. We're complex individuals, and nothing speaks to that so much as our diverse sexual interests; and 2. Good sex is a function of trust. Are we looking for that trust in all the wrong places?

Sex is, after all, ultimately revealing. Maybe that's why it makes some people so nervous.

Hot Cheeks, Cold Feet

The bellman brought in the two well-used backpacks and set them on the webbed suitcase stand with as much reverence as he would have given to Coach luggage. He opened the draperies to let in the view, but Christina was in no mood to look at snow-capped peaks. She sat weakly on the edge of the king size bed and slumped, feeling overwhelmed, strange, rushed, almost numb. She needed to think. She needed to rest. She needed a walk in the woods with her dog, a long bubble bath. She was unprepared, and she needed to get her mind right about all of this.

The bellman, paid to be sensitive, cut short his spiel about hotel amenities.

"Are you all right, miss?" he asked. She put her cold hands up to her hot cheeks and nodded. "If you need anything, the concierge—"

"That's fine, thanks," Lawrence said and handed him a ten. The bellman left without another word.

"Hey, baby," Lawrence said, and sat down softly next to her.

"I need some time, Lawrence," she said. "This is. . . too much, too fast, too weird—good God."

"Hey," he said, and put a gentle hand on the back of her neck. She wanted him to leave her alone so she could think, just so she could make peace with herself, but she knew that by sliding out from under his touch, she'd hurt him, and she'd rather do herself damage. She just needed some time. Some space. Somehow, she had to slow down long enough for her awareness to catch up to her.

Here it is, she told herself. Right here. Space between the words, between the thoughts, the actions. Stop wanting space and take what's right here right now. Except that he's going to want to make love now, she thought, and I can't. I can't think about that, and I can't do that.

Relax, she told herself. He's just rubbing your neck, and that feels good.

Yeah, but—

"Better?" he asked.

Strangely, she was.

"Want something?"

Yes, she thought, I want to turn the clock back two, six, ten hours. I want to run, to hide, to escape, to go home to my mommy. But what she said was, "A bath and a Diet Coke."

He kissed her shoulder and stood up. A moment later, she heard the bath water running. Then she heard him call room service, and the sound of his voice was deep and resonant, it was the voice of the man she loved, the man she wanted to spend the rest of her life with—and all she wanted to do was scream.

Without looking up, she headed toward the bath.

He'd even added bubbles.

She pulled the sweater off over her head and dropped it into the corner, shucked her hiking boots and jeans, then turned off the horrid light and noisy fan and slipped into hot, soapy water. She ducked her head under and rubbed a bar of soap across her short hair and the makeup on her face. Then she ducked under again to rinse, and lay quiet in the dark, watching the stripe of light under the door as if on alert for an invader. She couldn't relax, she couldn't concentrate on what she had to think about as long as he was on the other side of the door.

Lawrence had married a maniac and he had no idea.

This trip had been fun and exciting and wonderful, just as their two years together had been, and then suddenly, after a rigorous early morning hike in the mountains and an uncharacteristic champagne lunch, he'd popped the question.

"Hey," he said. "Let's get married."

She raised an eyebrow over her champagne glass.

"Here," he said. "Now."

"You're nuts," she said and laughed.

"Come on. Let's do it."

"I dare you," she said, and instantly wished she hadn't, because he immediately got up from the table, and when he came back five minutes later, it had been arranged.

"Really?" She was astonished.

He shrugged. "It's Nevada," he said.

She scraped off the soapsuds then twirled the gold band on her ring finger. She hadn't meant to do it. She hadn't wanted it this way. She'd wanted her mother there, her brother, her girlfriends— Tears began to leak out and soon she was sobbing as if she'd just been deserted, not as though she'd just been married.

By the time she heard the room service guy come to the door, her crying jag had passed. Lawrence was probably going to bring her drink in, and she didn't want him to see her like this. "You're a married woman now," she said to herself. "Grow up." She blew her nose into her hand and splashed fresh sudsy water on her face.

A soft knock came at the door. She cleared her throat. "Hi," she said.

He opened the door and looked in. "It's dark," he said. "And steamy."

"Come," she said.

He closed the door behind him and sat on the toilet. She took the Coke and drank half of it right down. She felt dehydrated from the hike, the champagne, the hot water, and the cry.

"Did we do the wrong thing?" he asked, and she started to cry again because she had chosen a wonderfully sensitive man. "Maybe it was the right thing, but we did it wrong?" He so desperately wanted to understand her grief so he could try to make her feel better, and all it did was make her cry harder.

"Come here with me," she said, and his clothes came off in record time, he climbed in behind her and rocked her quietly in the heat, in the bubbles, in the dark.

I've known this woman for two years, Lawrence thought as he held her close and rocked her, and she is every bit a mystery now as when we first met. The water made little slapping, splashing sounds against the side of the tub and squished between her back and his chest.

He had no idea what she wanted or needed. He felt inadequate and guilty. Didn't every woman want to be proposed to? Didn't every woman want to be swept off her feet? Well, Lawrence had done all he knew how to do in that regard. Christina was the woman for him, he'd known that for a good while. He was her husband, her mate, and he wanted to fix her misery, but he had no idea how to do that, because he didn't know what had caused it. Somehow, he had caused it, but he was at a complete loss about it all.

As he held her, in the dark, in the suds, her freshly soaped hair in his face, he felt his penis fill with desire, but he was reluctant to let her know.

She was his wife, this was their wedding day, and he wanted to make love to her. He wanted her to know that he was a good man, he was going to be a good partner, a good husband, and everything was going to be fine.

When he came home defeated from a wretched day at work, nothing put him right again like that sly smile of hers that showed him that even if he felt like he was nobody in the boss's eyes, he was still king of her castle.

His erection grew more insistent and he adjusted his position to give it room.

Maybe he needed to make her feel like a queen.

He took the bar of soap and lathered his hands, then moved them slowly around her neck, down her shoulders, resisting the urge to kiss her. If the last two years had taught him anything about her, it was that showing her his erection did nothing but raise an eyebrow and elicit a "So?" No, he had to bring her around to his way of thinking, and he had to do it slowly.

The hotel soap had a fruity fragrance that matched the bath gel he had emptied into the tub, and the liquid sound of the water dripping from her as he rinsed her neck increased the heat between them.

He soaped up his hands again and ran them under her arms and cupped her breasts, her well-trained nipples responding exactly the way he hoped they would. He knew this body, and he loved it. Her flat, muscled tummy was next, soaped and then rinsed, and she arched her back and leaned against him, arms up and around the back of his neck.

Bingo.

"Come on," he whispered, his voice thick and foreign sounding, and she followed him up, even giggling a little as he wrapped her in a big towel before subjecting her to not only light, but air conditioning.

He'd already turned down the bed, and she knelt on the edge, silhouetted against the snowy mountains outside. He pulled the towel from her shoulders and looked into her eyes. There was something new there, some question that he didn't know how to answer, just as she didn't know how to ask.

The only possible answer was a kiss, so he moved close and with both hands on her face, touched his lips to hers. She made a noise that was almost a whine in her throat, and when he pulled away to see if he was doing something wrong, she grabbed him with both hands and pulled him over on top of her.

"Oh God, I love you so much," she said, emotion making her voice uncharacteristically high. With the slightest movement, she opened herself and he slid right inside, both of them gasping at the suddenness of it.

He lay quietly, kissing her, great long kisses where their lips met and their tongues met and didn't move, listening to her heart and her breath on his cheek. He moved only as much as was required to maintain his erection, and when they both had settled down, he let her take the lead.

The kisses she came back with began almost angrily. She kissed him and bit his lip, then his shoulder, hard until he flinched. Then she did it again. She was angry, and he let her go. She wrapped her legs around his waist and pulled him closer, grinding herself against him, kissing him with a wild desperation that was completely foreign to him. He didn't know this particular Christina, but she was one he found to be undeniably exciting.

And then she said it. "Lawrence," she whispered, and he knew she was ready to fly off into that mysterious land of the female orgasm, and he knew just what to do to send her there.

He thrust, matching her intensity of strength, again, again, and then he paused, feeling his own close at hand. She clutched at him, her teeth digging into his shoulder as all of her muscles contracted, lifting him clean off the bed—and then those vaginal muscles worked until they pulled the gush out of him. He heard his own voice, louder than ever before as spasms sent his seed seeking ova.

Still she wasn't finished with him, wanting to wrestle every last ounce of will from both of them. As the colors returned to his vision and she began to relax, and he started fighting the sleep that automatically began to overtake him, he marveled again at what a wonderful creature she was.

No matter what she said or thought, he was glad he'd snagged her and made it legal.

He put a hand on her round, muscular butt and rolled over onto his side, pulling her with him.

She clung, and that was fine. That's what husbands were for.

Lawrence blew gently on the tiny stream of perspiration that flowed between her breasts, down under the left one and wicked into the sheet. She felt one cold drop follow another, and when he blew on her, goose bumps rose in waves across her hip.

She wished they'd turned off the air conditioner. "Sheet," she said, and he pulled it up by first grabbing it with his toes and then his free hand, fulfilling her request without moving away from her. She appreciated that, because she'd never felt so clingy, so needy.

If he gets up or turns on the television, she thought, *I'll die. I'll divorce him and then I'll die.*

But he didn't. He held her and their sweat mingled with left-over bath water and their skin stuck together with a suction force.

Can't get much closer, she thought. His penis softened, and with the sheet-raising action, began to slide from her. They read-justed their position to maximize square inch of skin magnetism and she pulled him closer to her with an evil feeling of despera-tion.

Relax, she said to herself. *Why are you behaving this way?*

She didn't know, but couldn't deny it or stop it. She just knew that if she could climb inside his skin with him, she would.

Gently, idly, he began to pull wet strands of her hair from her forehead. She responded by hugging him tighter, poised on the verge of despising herself for being so totally at the mercy of her insecurities.

"I'm glad," he whispered. "I know you're not, but I am."

That helped, but only a little. She mustered some kind of a noise from deep in her throat that ended up sounding non-com-mittal.

"Better, worse, richer, poorer, sickness, health," he recited. He grabbed the back of her head with his big hand and moved it until her forehead was in kissing range. "'And if God so choose, I shall love you even more after death.' Know where that line comes from?"

She shook her head no. What happened to the til-death-do-us-part stuff?

"That's Elizabeth Barrett Browning. I asked the minister to put that part in."

Christina had no response for that. He asked the minister to change the vows? From death to eternity?

"I probably should have asked you first," he whispered, then ran his thumb down her spine and his soft hand over her warm buttocks. "Next time."

She snorted. *As if.*

"Really," he said. "We've done it my way, next time we'll do it your way."

She frowned, pulled away from him and looked up at those soft, greenish eyes, that tousled, little-boy hair cut, the mustache that had already sprouted a few stray strands of gray.

"When." It was more challenge than question.

"Whenever you want," he said.

"June."

"Okay."

"Church. White dress."

"Okay," he said, and started to laugh. His jiggling made her giggle, and her heart grew lighter as she realized that he *would* marry her, marry her for real for real, in front of all their family and friends and not as a private secret with no pictures to prove it.

"Lots of flowers. Big flowers. Everywhere flowers."

"Lots of flowers," he agreed.

"Invitations and bridal showers and bridesmaids dresses and champagne at the reception and everything will be very, very expensive."

"No problem," he said.

"Really?"

"Really. Whatever you want. I heard you say 'I do' in jeans and hiking boots, and that's all that matters to me."

"*Really?*"

"Really. So you plan the wedding of your dreams and we'll do it."

Christina thought about this marvelous man, and the way he had looked at her when he said his vows. He'd meant them, just as she'd meant hers. It hadn't been marriage on a dare, it had been the real thing. He loved her, he meant for them to be together for ever.

For eternity.

The thought was a stunner.

"No thanks," she said, pushed him over onto his back and nestled her head in the crook of his arm. "You only got to think it was your idea, getting married on this trip."

She heard him gasp in mock amazement as he played along, and she steeled herself for the tickle which would surely come, and so it did.

❅

In a Darkened Compartment

Friday. The moon-faced clock ticked its minutes off like centuries as I finished my reports and anxiously pulled at my polyester uniform in the wet Italian heat. That last Friday took longer to pass than the entirety of my three weeks at Naval Base Naples and I was more than eager to finish my assignment and get out on my own—I was desperate.

Finally, I had the Captain's handshake, a fat paycheck, my well-worn uniforms packed into a box to be shipped home, and I waited for the taxi that would begin my real European adventure.

"*La stazione*," I said to the driver, and held on as he drove like an insane man through colorful streets whose traffic lights worked even less often than the people. Naples. I always felt a bit naughty when I said the name, as if I would slip and say Nipples, or as if Naples meant nipples in Italian. I didn't know, but the sound of the word always took my tongue by surprise.

The taxi slammed to a loose, shuddering stop at the train station with my heart in my throat and my passport clutched to my chest. I paid him, mumbled a "*grazi*," and got out.

Free. Alone in Europe, just me, my carry-on, my passport and my Eurailpass. I felt powerful and lusty with potential. I breathed my last of richly-scented, unwashed Naples and stepped into the sweltering train station. *Switzerland*, I thought, *here I come*.

The train, like Naples, was shabby, threadbare and in marginal working order. I grinned, watching the tired, mustachioed conductor deal with emotional people and their overly dramatic language.

My reserved seat was in a semi-private compartment that smelled of cigars and old socks. I stowed my bag in the overhead rack and sat down, watching tearful, extravagant goodbyes on the platform.

With a crusty lurch, the train set out, and I grinned again as my adventure began in earnest. I relaxed and put my feet up on the seat opposite, luxuriating in having a compartment to myself.

The wildly-colored city passed by my window with its brown children, laundry hanging between crumbling buildings, traffic snarls and open markets. The landscape changed dramatically as we picked up speed and entered the countryside.

I thought country was country—American, Italian, what could be different?

Everything. Even the greens were a different mix. Sheep and vineyards, stone buildings and peasants captured the novelist in my soul and I watched in complete fascination as the background details of my new book flowed before my eyes.

Then the conductor showed his dour face as he opened the door to my silent, contemplative compartment. The clicketing of the train's wheels filled my room and then did he—a passenger, with his tweed valise and musky cologne.

"*Bueno sera,*" he said to me, his accent as bad as my own. I smiled and nodded, as he slammed the door closed, sealing the noise outside, the pheromones inside. He put his valise in the overhead rack, shrugged out of his suitcoat. Dark rings showed under the arms of his blue dress shirt. He hung the jacket on a pull-out hook, then sat down opposite me with a copy of the *New York Times.*

American.

I'd always fantasized about an erotic encounter on a foreign train with a mysterious stranger. But for the first time, I realized that I could be that stranger. I could engineer someone else's fantasy and thereby satisfy my own.

This man, this American, was attractive, wore no wedding ring, we were alone. . . Everything was perfect for my scheme.

Outside the window, lights began to appear in the windows of country homes as daylight began its golden wash toward evening.

I brazenly watched him read. He looked up occasionally and smiled in discomfort as he saw me looking at him. Always looking at him.

What a study! One bushy eyebrow crawled like a caterpillar across both eyes. His head was round and smooth and brown. In my mind's eye, I pressed both palms against its warmth, against its shininess. His beard, now probably twelve hours long, darkened his face into mystery around lips that were full and soft.

He turned the page, folded the paper, smiled uncertainly at my scrutiny, and turned on his reading light, which cast his face into even deeper shadow.

His nails were finely manicured. Thick black hairs wired out of his knuckles and the backs of his hands, up his wrists and curled around his gold watch. I wondered if he could smell the two of us as distinctly as I could.

Finally, he folded the paper and set it next to him. He looked at me. "Do you speak English? Um. *Parle Englaise?*"

I just shrugged and smiled, but I wonder to this day if it looked like a smile. He shifted in discomfort, clicked off his reading light and looked out the window.

The lights we passed reflected in his shining eyes, and I saw when they shifted over to my reflection in the glass, first in tentative glances, then in bolder strokes.

Finally, he gave up on the window and looked at me directly. We sat gazing at each other, the heat in our bodies warming the close room, the tang of arousal thick in the air.

"I don't know what you want," he said, surprising the silence with the deep tenor of his voice.

An executive-looking hand passed over his head, his face, and his chin in indecision, then with a deft movement and without unlocking his eyes from mine, he locked the door and drew the curtain.

I caught my breath and felt my pulse in my panties.

He sat up on the edge of his seat, his knees apart, his hands clasped and dangling between them, as he helplessly sought my approval or at least a nod of acknowledgement.

He spread his hands in the typical American male signal of helplessness. "Here we are," he said. "Every man's fantasy. Beautiful Italian woman, foreign country, anonymous encounter. On a train, no less. I wish you spoke English."

He became more attractive by the moment.

"I could say anything to you. You wouldn't understand me, no matter what I said. I could tell you lies or say terrible things. But the truth is, I would die to make love to you."

It was a terrible effort to maintain a deadpan expression.

"You're so beautiful," he continued. "You Italian women are extraordinary. I'd give my whole world to just hold you, kiss you, stroke you. I'd kiss your eyelids, suckle those lovely young breasts. I'd hold you and cherish you. . ."

My heart was pounding so loudly I was sure he could hear it.

He sat back. "Who am I kidding? A paper salesman from New Jersey. Old. Divorced. Bald."

I slid forward on my seat and captured one of his knees between mine. I moved it back and forth as we stared at each other with expressionless faces, eyes flashing with the passing lights outside the darkened window, the rhythm of the train matching my pulse.

He moved closer, brought his knee between my thighs, kissed his fingertip and laid it on the inside of my knee. With gentle pressure, he opened my legs.

"There is a god," he breathed.

Fresh air chilled the damp lace of my panties and I ached with vaginal dew the way ice cream made me ache with saliva.

His finger drew up my thigh and I felt the fluttering of deep feelings begin a long way off.

I pulled back and snapped my knees together.

He looked at me questioningly, moisture in his eyes. I stood up and did the long-awaited act. I placed both my palms on his beautiful shining head and it was warm and soft and smooth—like nothing I had ever felt before.

I kissed it as I heard his belt buckle, then his zipper. His warm hands caressed the backs of my thighs, ringed the lace, lingered on the inside, and with a slow, deliberate stroke, pulled my panties to my ankles.

I stepped out of them, put one knee on the seat on either side of him.

One of his gentle fingers stroked my wetness, and I saw a glistening finger disappear into his mouth.

My hands and lips on top of his miraculous head, I allowed him to guide himself into me. I lowered completely, in one slow and deliberate stroke. I felt the soft hardness of him fill me until the air rushed out of me in a moan from heaven.

"It feels as though it's been years," he breathed. "It *has* been years. . . oh, God. . ."

The flutterings came back again—this time I heard them as clearly as I heard his teeth click against the buttons of my blouse. I held absolutely still, filled with his warmth, and the thousand butterflies of my passion neared, beat harder, and still I pressed my lips to his dampening head.

"Oh God, I want to take you home with me. Say yes, please say yes."

The pulsations deep within became little birds beating their wings, flapping closer and harder, millions of them with their diaphanous wings seeking release. His hands gripped my thighs—and then he moved—and my cage door opened. I heard a harmony as he and I both called to our maker and the winged creatures flew out in waves, flew out of my heart in flocks.

My lips, I noticed, had slipped down his forehead and were velcroed tightly to his eyebrow, my hands resting on the handles of his ears.

"My God," he said, "I thought it was only men who did that. I've never experienced anything like that before. You're amazing."

Feeling overwhelming affection for this stranger, I wrapped my arms around his wonderful head and pressed him to my chest. His penis softened and allowed his seed to seep out, tickling me and wetting his trousers.

"You're extraordinary, so young, so tender, so soft. I didn't hurt you, did I? This skin, this gorgeous skin. You feel so fragile. I was afraid of hurting you, but I just had to taste you, to feel you, to have you wrap yourself around me, my God, you're the loveliest thing I've ever seen."

I slid around to lie on the train seat, pulling him over with me.

"I know you don't understand English," he mumbled against me. I saw the moisture in his eyes as the train rocked us. "And I am sure you would never understand this even if you could." He put both hands on the sides of my face and tender, soft thumbs caressed my cheeks. "But for you to find me attractive in this way after—well, after everything I've been through—well, you'll just never know, you could never imagine what this means to me."

There were tears in this man's eyes. My heart squeezed. I kissed his soft lips, our first kiss, amazingly enough.

He covered us with his suitcoat and enveloped me in powerful arms.

With my cheek against his chest, I could feel his voice as well as hear it.

"I live in a modest house in the suburbs. It's a nice place but it could use a woman's touch. I could use a woman's touch. You. Your touch. You could come to America. I would teach you English, and we would grow babies in that lovely belly of yours. Oh man, think of the beautiful babies we'd make."

Now it was my turn for throat-catching emotion. This encounter was turning into something far more than I had expected, and I had deceived him. I was still deceiving him. He didn't deserve that.

"I wish you could understand me," he whispered into the intimacy. "I wish I could understand you. I wish we could talk. I want to know more about you. I want to know all about you. I want to see you again, oh my God, I want so desperately not to lose you."

This was beginning to hurt.

"I wish I knew where you lived. I'd go there right now and ask your father for your hand."

I squinted my eyes and a tear leaked out and ran down to my hairline.

"Where do you live?"

I took a deep breath. "Wisconsin." I squinted my eyes and waited for the reaction. I expected anger.

But what I got was silence. Stunned silence.

Then, "Wisconsin?" And a small, snorty laugh. "*Wisconsin?*" he asked in disbelief, accompanied by a little chuckle, and then it grew into a deep roaring laugh. He hugged me and squeezed me hard, until I began to laugh, and then it got out of control until we were both laughing so hard we couldn't breathe. Then real tears came and we held on to each other, laughing and crying. Amidst the emotion, I felt the doors of our hearts open wide and we became brand new with each other.

And through the night, our train sped across the Italian countryside.

✳

The Goldberg
A Love Fable

"I have a young maiden who wishes to enter into marriage," the Keeper of the Virgins said. "She is fair of hair and skin, has learned her domestic skills well in her seventeen summers, and is intended for her husband in the morning."

The king had been told all of this well in advance. This announcement was part of the formal ritual; the girl waited nervously outside, and he did not want to add to her anguish. "Bring her forth," he said.

The woman bowed. "Yes, my king," she said, and backed out of the doorway. A moment later, a tall blonde girl swished through the cloth curtain.

The king appraised her. She was lean, with appealing lines. Small, high breasts, flat stomach, flaxen hair twisted into droopy curls. Her blonde pubic hair shone with coconut oil and had been cleverly combed. Her blue eyes stared at some infinite spot over the king's head. She seemed to be tightly wound with anxiety.

He picked up her hand and her frightened eyes clicked onto his in surprise. "Don't be afraid," he said. He led her gently to his soft bed of rushes and moss, made fresh for this evening ritual. He bid her lay on the soft moss, and when she was comfortable, and as relaxed as she could be considering the circumstances, he kissed her.

Her lips were full and giving. "This is how your husband is to always kiss you," the king said. "With love and tenderness."

She nodded, her eyes wide with uncertainty.

He let his fingers wander across her forehead, down her cheeks, linger a moment on those lips, then down her long neck, across her breasts, down her stomach, and then with an easy movement, he parted her legs.

The Keeper of the Virgins knew her job well. The girl's passageway was slick with heavily scented coconut oil. He touched her with a gentle stroke.

"And he is to always touch you," the king said, "with reverence and respect."

The girl closed her eyes and he felt the tension whoosh out of her. With one hand on each of her thighs, he brought his face down to taste the oil mixed with the girl's natural juices, and felt her squirm slightly under his tongue. He didn't want to spoil her more than was necessary; *that* was for her husband. He only wanted to set the standard.

He untied his robe, lifted her hand and put it on his penis. It arched high and twisted slightly to the left. "You will also touch him with reverence and respect," the king said, and with a gentle hand, taught the girl how to bring him pleasure.

After a moment, he parted the girl's pubic fur and slowly, gently entered her. He knew the first time for most of them was not the most pleasant experience, but it was too important to leave to the grappling, eager, insensitive young men. This was the king's way to promote harmony among his people, and it had worked for many years.

It had perhaps worked too well, for among this blue-eyed, fair-haired, light-hearted people, many of the children bore the piercing brown eyes of the king.

He moved with the girl slowly, gently, teaching her as he went, and she, as had all of those who preceded her, learned what he had to teach with a passion for learning. When they were finished, the king again kissed her on her lips. "While you and your husband will sometimes grow angry," he said, "you must never touch each other in anger. Touch is gentle, always and forever." She nodded, her eyes glistening, and he saw her out the door. "Be happy," he said, "in your marriage and in your life, for that is the one thing you and only you can control."

"Yes, my king," she said, and backed out the fabric door.

After the girl had gone, the king returned to his bed, but sleep eluded him. He questioned everything, over and over and over again.

It had been many years since the ship of forty schoolchildren with their teachers had blown off course and crashed onto the rocks of his island. He risked his own wretched, lonely life to save those he could, and suffered from nightmares to this day with the memories of having to choose who to save in the turbulent, storm-tossed surf. Thirty children and two teachers survived.

Ten years before the children and their teachers arrived on the island, his solo sailing adventure had been cut short by a freak squall. His boat sank, and he washed up on the sandy beach. As the only inhabitant of the tropical isle, the man jokingly named himself king, and invited the newcomers to refer to him as such. At first they did it out of respect for his selfless saving of their lives, and as they grew more toward becoming a community, a tribe, they bowed to his wisdom of island survival and actually began to look upon him as their king.

He didn't like it, but he accepted it.

And now the brown-eyed offspring of his young female initiates were going to begin coming into his hut for their initiations, and he knew that was improper. Many of them looked so much like him he was amazed that nobody else understood. Or perhaps they did. Perhaps they didn't want to cause a rift in the easy peacefulness of the status quo.

The king tossed and turned all night, falling into a fitful sleep toward dawn, wherein he rescued the children from the sea again and again and again, and kept the exhausted teachers from going out into the surf to drown while trying to grab one more child from the clutches of the cold, salty undertow.

In the morning, the Keeper of the Virgins brought him his breakfast, but the king had no appetite. She sat in front of him, familiar after their long association, and he looked at her face with great affection. "We have another initiation tonight, my king," she said.

He closed his eyes. He didn't want to do this any more. "Who?" he asked.

"Imira is betrothed to Savoy. She has begun her preparations this morning."

The king nodded, his heart heavy. "She is fair-haired?"

"She is."

"The tribe lives peacefully?"

"It does."

The king nodded. "Very well, then," he said.

That night, when Imira was brought to his hut, the king was tired and ill-tempered. The sight of the beautiful young girl lifted his spirits, but he felt for the first time as if he were removing something from thier marriage instead of adding to their union.

He had her sit across from him, then ran a finger down the side of her face. He knew she was nervous, but she had been listening to the tales of his initiations for years now, and knew she had nothing to fear. He kissed her. "This is how your husband is to always kiss you," the king said. "With love and tenderness." The girl nodded. "You are to never touch your husband in anger, nor he you." The girl nodded, and sensing she was about to be dismissed, became more alert. "Be happy," he said, "in your marriage and in your life, for that is the one thing you and only you can control."

The girl nodded and smiled at him with affection. "Yes, my king," she said.

He dismissed her with a kiss on the forehead, and she scampered away, forgetting, in her youthful exuberance, that she was supposed to back out the doorway.

It was time to do away with that stupid rule, the king decided.

A few moments later, the Keeper of the Virgins sought entrance.

"Come in," the king said. There would be no peace for him this night, either.

"Are you well, my king?" she asked. "Imira tells me her initiation was different, less than complete."

The king looked at the woman and noticed how her green eyes sparkled in the candlelight. One of the original teachers, her hair had silvered like his. She was a hard worker who kept her body muscular and brown, still appealing, though it was beyond childbearing age. "I am old and tired," he said.

"Not to my eyes," the woman said. "To my eyes, you grow ever more wise and desirable."

The king sighed.

"Perhaps it is time I showed you my Goldberg," she said.

The king sat up, his attention caught by this surprise of all surprises. "You have a Goldberg?"

"I do, my king," she said, eyes demurely downcast.

For a moment, he thought she laughed at him, but he knew her heart, and knew she would not do that. "By all means, I must see it."

"Then come to my hut tomorrow night and it will be ready for you," she said, with a sly look. "Rest well until then." She backed out his door, leaving the king to contemplate this most unlikely turn of events.

During the ten years the man had been alone on the island, for his amusement, he had devised a game, which grew steadily more elaborate as time wore on. It utilized a complex maze of vines and pulleys, stones and water, clickety-clack sticks and sand. It fell into disrepair as he spent his days building a village for his people, but once the community was settled, he resurrected his contraption for the enjoyment of the children. It became an annual tradition as he unveiled it for the tribe during the Festival of the Mango. Once a year was enough to keep their interest, maintain his status as tribe genius, yet not often enough for the older children to understand the simple structure that it was. Choosing the person to drop the first stone that set the entire apparatus into motion was one of the most hotly contested aspects of the festival, and that person was revered until the following year, when the next person was chosen. All they had to do, once the king set up the device, was to drop one stone into a tiny cup, and the action began. It took half an hour and covered almost an entire acre of garden for the Rube Goldberg contraption to run its course. The king had built in many noise makers and as much entertaining silliness as possible, and while it took him almost a month to set it up every year, the joy on the children's faces as it worked its magic was worth all the trouble.

And now the Keeper of the Virgins said she had a Goldberg of her own.

The king contemplated that with no jealousy. His gadget had been borne of boredom and a need to use his ingenuity. He was sure hers was the same.

Again, sleep eluded him. He couldn't wait to see what the woman had up her sleeve. He slept fitfully toward dawn, and when he woke to a bright sky and the sounds of happy children and birds, he gave thanks for all that was good in his life.

The day waxed with agonizing slowness for the king. He saw much activity around the Keeper's hut, women coming and going, and both raucous laughter and modest giggles emanated from the flurry of activity within. He busied himself playing with the children, and helped the men repair the water system.

Toward evening, his level of anticipation began to rise. He bathed carefully, although he didn't know why. He changed into a clean cloth and then paced in his hut until he felt the time was right.

As he walked across the yard toward the Keeper's hut, he realized he had never been inside her territory. Not once, in all these years.

She greeted him at the door. Her hair was shiny, like silver wires, in the diffused light of a dozen coconut candles. Her face lit up with affection as he came in, and he looked around the floor for evidence of her machine.

"It is not on this plane of existence, my king," she said, and led him gently by the hand to her bed, which had been made fresh with rushes and moss. "And you must listen carefully to hear what happens when the first ball is dropped."

"Listen?" said the king. "To what? Where?"

"Shhh," she said. "Listen with your heart." She slipped out of her gown and lay next to him.

With gentle motions, the woman brought her love to him, bringing his passion to ebb and flow. At first, he wondered where her experience came from; she had been such a young lass when she came to the island, but then he realized that he had heard the first ball drop and that their give and take had become the Goldberg. It had a life of its own, which had nothing at all to do with experience.

The exchange of affection between them was energizing; it had been the one thing he had missed, with taking care of the tribe and seeing to the happiness of the marriages. One night with each of the girls had done nothing for the internal knot of loneliness that lived under the king's breastbone.

The Keeper's Goldberg lasted much longer than the whimsical half hour his own contraption took to complete its course. And as the evening wore on, the king could identify each click and clack, each musical rift, each sigh and gasp.

And at the end, just like in his own Goldberg, where a boat was dramatically launched from its mooring to swoosh out into the central lagoon, a warmth was launched from her heart, and it swooshed out into the central lagoon of his soul, finally melting the iceberg of loneliness that had always floated there.

"Oh my god," the king said as he sought to drown himself in their delicious mixed juices.

"Please," she whispered, putting soft fingers on his lips. "My name is Anna."

❊

Crosley

I have always been fascinated by evil. I've flirted with it, been tempted by it, but only once have I fallen in love with it.

I live on an island in the south seas. How I came to be here is a story of young love, foolishness and weakness—both his and mine—and therefore a tale for a different time.

I pour drinks in a poor man's bar. In the tropics, no walls are necessary, just a good roof and a room at the back where Godfrey used to live. The liquor shelves have a lockable grate to keep out the monkeys and the thieves. Daily rain washes the island and the open air dance floor which, at the time of Godfrey's ownership, hadn't seen a dancer in years—not since the tour boats stopped docking here.

Godfrey was a harmless old drunk who began each day with an impressive head of optimism and a mug of thick black coffee, and ended it with a rant of some sort and sometimes a roundhouse punch at a hallucination.

Many times I hauled Godfrey to bed, locked up the booze and slept on the couch next to his bed, afraid he had finally taxed his liver to the maximum. Surely he couldn't survive this level of toxicity much longer. But he had done so since long before I met him, and God seems to look out after old drunks for some reason.

I worked for Godfrey. I poured drinks, mopped the floor, received shipments of liquor, collected overdue accounts from the locals, endured their hard luck stories, listened to their weary tales, parried amorous advances and generally did whatever was called for, including tending Godfrey. I did all this, outwardly patient, while inside I seethed, waiting for the next adventurer to sail into the harbor and bring either news of something familiar, something of my old life perhaps, or an offer of something magnificent, a gateway to a new life.

They came, the adventurers, not frequently, but steadily. We had a protected anchorage and a stocked bar, the locals were skilled handymen, and UPS knew our address.

But when they came, they mostly came in couples, and they shared what adventure they had in their souls, but it was either not enough, or of the wrong kind, or pointed in the wrong direction. And when they hoisted their main and caught a freshening breeze out of the bay, their names and faces faded immediately into obscurity and I would go back to fixing something that the jungle was trying to reclaim.

The morning that Crosley arrived, Godfrey and I sat at the bar drinking coffee and watching deluge rain soak the already sodden earth. It fell as a solid sheet from the gutterless roof all around, splashing mud from the rain-gouged trenches to mix with the water that splashed up from the dance floor, bits of grout and other evidence of its deterioration floating closer to our bare feet.

I felt the tropical depression in my soul and sipped coffee silently, feeling desperately claustrophobic, penned in by the humidity and the liquid walls, the vinyl of the stool sticking uncomfortably to the backs of my thighs.

Godfrey, on his second cup, was full of enthusiastic remodeling talk, but his enthusiasm was not infectious—I'd heard it all too many times before.

And then, characteristic of many tropical storms, the rain ceased abruptly, and Godfrey was caught mid-sentence. My thighs peeled off the stool without thought as we both stood at the sight of the long, sleek black yacht at anchor in the center of the bay. It had appeared as if by magic.

An astonishing array of seaworthy and not-so-seaworthy craft came and went from this bay. Generally they came one at a time, but occasionally cruisers would arrive in tandem, and now and then, enough showed up at once to raft up together. Their drunken parties could wake even Godfrey.

But never had such a craft arrived with such little fanfare nor during such a storm. The entrance to the bay through the coral reefs was treacherous during the best of times. Who would chance it during such a blinding downpour?

Someone stupid. Someone stupidly lucky. Someone with supermortal navigating skills. Or perhaps someone who had been here before.

And the boat itself sixty feet if it was an inch. Sails were neatly furled under black covers, and what lines we could see from this distance had been coiled at their ends. No gear was visible on deck. The boat looked not as if it had been sailed at all, but as if it had been freshly groomed and polished, ready for a show.

All hatches were tightly closed.

"Know that boat, Godfrey?" I asked, entranced.

"Nope, and not the type of thing I'd be likely to forget," he said, and he was right, of course, even with his cheesecloth memory.

It floated, mysterious, anonymous and somehow untouchable—not even the local islanders roared out to investigate—for two days with no visible signs of life.

I went about my normal daily duties, but with a difference. There was a spark of excitement in my soul. There would soon come an alteration to my mundane routine, brief though it was sure to be. My eyes drifted out to that floating yacht, dark like a hole in the brilliant blue of the bay, and my imagination, long dormant, came alive.

On the second night, when the regulars drifted in for their beer or tequila, to retell old jokes, reopen old wounds, and reignite old jealousies, the topic was exclusively The Black Yacht. Godfrey had come to believe it was the Reaper's yacht come for him, and the idea that the Reaper had a yacht fueled the hilarity for most of the evening.

But when Godfrey's head hit the bar and he began to snore, a man stepped out of the dark, thick tropical night and sat on the stool next to him.

Conversation faded as we all observed the outsider. That he belonged to the black boat was obvious. He looked like the yacht. Tall, swarthy, with black hair just beginning to silver, dressed in black shirt and black cotton pants, he smiled a charming, white-toothed smile at me and ordered a grappa.

As it happened, a bottle of grappa collected cobwebs under the cabinet and I opened it and poured him a shot.

"Grappa for all," he said quietly, and he became an instant hero to these drunken fools as I set up a row of shot glasses and began to fill them.

Mingo was the first to thank him, patting his shoulder and trying to include him in the ring of camaraderie, but the stranger merely flicked his eyes in acknowledgement at the procession of gratitude and kept his attention focused on me.

I wished I had fixed myself up a little more, but the light was dim and he seemed to like whatever it was he saw in me, so I warmed to his attentions.

And why not? It had been two years since I had the attentions of a man, and my femininity suffered for it.

He savored his grappa, though the others drank theirs as fast as he bought and I poured, and soon they all stumbled home. Someone had seen to Godfrey, and we were alone. I could tell it was going to be a long night—I hoped it was—so I ran myself a shot of espresso and slugged it down. "Last call," I said.

"A ballad," he said.

"Pardon?"

"I call for a love song," he said, and held out his hand.

Damned if I couldn't hear Stardust coming from somewhere. I took his hand, came around the bar and he twirled me into his arms.

"I am Crosley," he said, and I had no response for him, my senses were completely overwhelmed. He smelled like a spice I couldn't identify—something exotic. His hands held me firmly, competently, self-assuredly, and he directed our dance in a slow, comfortable rhythm, completely in time with the music in my head.

His broad chest, the hard muscles of his arms, his breath warm in my hair made me want to lose myself in him. *Take me,* my mind ordered my mouth to say. *Take me away from here. Give me a new life, an easy life, a pampered life, a loved life.* But I said nothing. I merely swayed with him.

When the music ended, Crosley held me steadily, then disengaged himself, his hands on my hips pushing me gently away. He kissed my fingertips with warm lips. "So lovely," he said, then he turned and disappeared into the night.

I stood alone in the center of the dance floor and for one awful disorienting moment, wondered if I had imagined it all. Did I just dance by myself to music in my head? Were Godfrey's drunken hallucinations contagious? Or was my own loneliness and dissatisfaction with life pushing me over the edge?

Then I heard a small splash in the bay, as if from an oar, and I heard his voice in my heart as clearly as I heard the music, and I didn't care about the consequences of loving this man, this drifter, this unconventional sailor. I only knew that I must have him, some way, some how, no matter how briefly.

Godfrey woke me the next morning, and I was surprised to find myself sleeping on the old sofa in the bar. He handed me my coffee and he paced back and forth on the dance floor. "Bet that guy's got money," he said. "Bet he'd be smart enough to invest in an operation that could give him a good return on his investment."

"What guy?" I asked, but I already knew.

"That black boat guy."

"Crosley," I said, and sipped my coffee.

"You met him?"

I ran my fingers through my tangled hair, damp with tropical moisture. "He came in last night and we fed the home team all the grappa."

"Money, you think?"

I shrugged. I wasn't about to get in the middle of one of Godfrey's schemes. "Stay awake tonight and you can ask him yourself."

"Think he'll come?"

I did. I did indeed. "Where else?"

"Do we have any steaks? Let's cook him a steak. Think he eats meat? Is there any grappa left?" Godfrey made another pot of coffee and stuck with it all day long. Perhaps Crosley would make a difference in everybody's life.

I found it difficult to concentrate, and ended up wasting most of the day on daydreams of dark hair, dark eyes and an exciting life of sailing the seas with Crosley. When the sun went down, I went home, showered, shaved, powdered, perfumed, and made up my face. There were a few whistles and knowing elbow jabs among the regulars when I got back. They knew who had captured my eye and my imagination and they couldn't help but approve. After all, he had bought drinks for the house.

They all teased Godfrey about going on the wagon, too, and he took their ribbing good naturedly. They'd seen Godfrey sober before, always when he rode high on a fantasy. His sobriety ended when his dream—which was never based on reality—ended. This one was no exception, and we all knew it. I suspected Godfrey knew it as well.

Talk was of the usual nonsense, the locals sensing Godfrey and me both pegging a dream on Crosley and not wishing to interfere. But it was clear that a sense of excitement ran through their conversation. Many brought their spouses, hoping the free booze would run again.

The party was wild and rambunctious when he stepped out of the night and into the circle of warmth.

An involuntary cheer went out, and people moved aside so he could take his former barstool—an honor among this group of barflies.

Godfrey slid right over and placed a napkin on the bar. I urged everyone to quit gawking and get back to drinking. I poured a few more, opened a couple of sweaty beers, my heart pounding and my breath coming hard at the sight of him. And when I glanced at him, he was looking at me.

I had to hold on to the bar to keep myself from floating right over to him. I smiled, a smile I hope looked full of promise, then busied myself with Godfrey's business while Godfrey talked with Crosley. He talked earnestly and passionately, with many gestures, and I tried not to look, although I stole a glance now and then. Crosley's drink sat before him, untouched.

After a while, Godfrey came over to me, poured himself a double shot of whiskey and slugged it down. "Fully invested," he muttered, and took over my end of the bar.

I was glad. I'd never throw my lot in with Godfrey on purpose, but the bar paid me enough to live simply in this simple place.

I wandered toward Crosley, although I'm sure it was more like a making a beeline to him.

He picked up his drink, held it up to me in a toast, then drank it.

A moment later, he was gone.

I was disappointed beyond reason, and blamed Godfrey. I was tempted to walk down to the water and borrow one of the islander's boats to go to him to explain—explain what? Godfrey?

I wouldn't. I wouldn't be chasing after a man like Crosley.

Instead, I went home.

Disappointed and distressed with my choices in life, I crawled into my lonely bed and cried.

In the night, when the banana moon turned the jungle black and silver and the nightlife was at its noisiest, I heard a step on my porch. A human step.

I kept a small bat by my bed and a machete between mattresses for self defense. Although it had never happened, one of those drunken locals could get an idea. . . And then there were always the transients, the cruising sailors with no resume, no history, no real accountability.

I grabbed the bat, and the book of matches. In my heart-pounding haste to light a bedside candle—my little shack had no electricity—I kept crumbling the humidity-damp matches.

Then a lighter flicked open and a flame illuminated my bedside table. Crosley lit the candle and sat down next to me.

My hair was a mess, my eyes were swollen, I had a terrible taste in my mouth.

"I must leave in five days," he said, and I moved over and held open the covers for him.

His skin was cool and smooth and felt good next to my sleep-warmed body.

His hand moved slowly from my knee, across my hip, waist, around my breast to my neck and lay quietly on my cheek, leaving a trail of fire in its wake. With studied slow, self-assured movements, he manipulated my passions and drove me to a frenzied wildness like I've never known before. By the time our bodies merged, our mouths locked together as if transferring our souls, the orgasm that had threatened to overwhelm me burst forth in all its Technicolor glory.

We continued the dance as if we'd done it a thousand times before, until he slid from me with a sweat-slick sigh and entwined my fingers in his.

"From the first moment I saw you. . ." he whispered, then his breathing slowed and a soft snore took its place.

Likely a line used a thousand times on a thousand women, I thought, but that did not diminish its effectiveness.

For five days, I never set foot inside Godfrey's bar, as Crosley and I lived, loved and spoiled each other. We explored my island, swam naked, gorged on native fruits and licked the juices from each others' bodies. His boat was as dark, mysterious and as free of affectations on the inside as it was on the outside, and though I longed to learn more of Crosley—his history, his family, his aspirations—there was nothing to be gleaned from his possessions. Nor from him. He remained an enigma, revealing everything of his exterior, revealing little of his substance.

We slept together in my bed, on the beach, in his stateroom, in the jungle, on the hills under the stars. We made love and laughed, swam in the lagoon with the dolphins and whiled away rainy afternoons, making up silly poems. We wove garlands of flowers for each others' hair, and buried ourselves in the warm sand. We showered together and made soapy love in the flimsy, tin shower stall. We melded.

And every morning, when I watched the sky grow light with the fire of dawn, the fire of panic grew within my gut as it was another day closer to his departure. Desperate to not cling to him, I clung to his words, his gestures, his amusements, his kisses. I let his actions speak, and they eloquently spoke of love and desire and delight.

Surely he would never leave me.

We didn't speak of the future, but it was not far from my tongue. Five days with Crosley was not going to be enough—perhaps a lifetime of him would not be enough—and my heart broke on an hourly basis for five days as I knew he would, eventually, leave.

And then he said it.

We lay together in the lee of a rock outcropping on the beach. We had picnicked and finished a bottle of wine, then thrown the leftover food to the crabs and engaged in what seemed to be the next event of our continual lovemaking on the chenille bedspread I laid out. We had discovered gourmet sex, funny sex, quickie sex, instant sex and slurpy, delicious sex, but this was emotional sex. We both cried when it was over, and he kissed the tears from my cheeks and told me he loved me.

We lay quietly together after that, watching the sun sink, his arm protectively around me, until the chill came over us, and with one thought, we got up and slowly made our way back to my cabin.

We showered, crawled into bed and held each other, neither of us speaking of the fact that this was our last night, if it was. There is always hope, I told myself. Always hope.

With hope in my heart and our arms and legs entwined, we slept.

In the morning, when I woke, I was alone. At first, sleepy-brained, I thought he was in the bathroom, or he had gone to fetch breakfast. But when I sat up and saw the fresh gardenia leaning next to the bedside candle, I knew.

"No," I wailed. I jumped out of bed and threw on my clothes, desperate to make him stay, to remind him that he loved me, to convince him that I could sail with him, to beg him not to abandon what we had created.

By the time I was out the door and running for the bay, I was desperate only to say goodbye. I had to hold him one more time, to kiss him once more, to tell him how he had restored me, to wish him well on his journey.

But the bay was empty.

Far off on the horizon, I saw a black sliver with its mainsail illuminated in the dawn.

I felt gutshot. Numb. Dead.

I wandered to Godfrey's bar, made myself some espresso and mixed in some Jack Daniel's. After two drinks, I eliminated the coffee. After two more, I began to cry.

My name is Winston. I came to the island on the run from the law when I was only twenty-four. Today I am twenty-nine and hopelessly in love with Francine, the bartender. I am short and dark like a chimpanzee, and a deep scar runs through my right eyebrow and down my cheek, pulling my nose out of alignment. It would be so romantic to tell of some knifefight over a noble cause, but the truth is, I stumbled off the path and fell into a ravine one night while drunk, and lay unconscious at the bottom with my face impaled on the sharp edge of a banana stump until morning. Infection raged, and this scar is the result. On my best days I tell myself that my look is unique, particularly among these beautiful Polynesian locals, and on my worst days I view myself as a deformed Quasimoto, barely fit to breathe this fragrant air.

I am short, I am ugly, I am unskilled, but I am also devoted. I work at the landfill, and every day after work I bathe and then go to Francine's bar. She is always there, smiling and pouring drinks for the regulars, the home team she calls us, cracking jokes and buying rounds for the house.

Francine was here when I arrived. She is somewhat older than I am, but age on her makes her only more beautiful. Age is not the only difference between us; while my upbringing was dictated by the toughs in the streets, she led a white bread life of privilege. When I left North America, it was to escape the law, and no one has ever missed me. When she escaped North America, it was to escape from her parents, and toward Eternal Bliss, and mail arrives for her every week in the pouch without fail.

Everyone on the island has a crush on Francine, but all except mine are fanciful, for Francine beds no one.

No one, that is, but the boy who brought her here ten years or so ago, and the European devil who sent her into the depths of despair. This man came shortly after I discovered Francine's bar, although at that time it was owned by a drunk named Godfrey. I had already lost my heart to her. I had lost that upon first sight.

And my crush on her is not fanciful, because I love her, and have vowed to protect her regardless of the frivolous antics that bring her nothing but heartbreak. Some day she will see me for who I am, and until that happens, I can be patient.

And it is because of this love I have for her, and my self-sworn duty to protect her, that I, and only I, know what happened that night. I know, and Francine knows. And we are the only two.

The story begins with Godfrey's yellow death.

Francine, still heavy with grief over the European, came to work one morning to find the coffee pot cold and Godfrey even colder. He had been turning yellow the last few months, and when she came upon him in his bed, he was the color of urine. His face wore not the mask of peaceful repose, but a grimace of pain, and he was doubled over and frozen in that position.

Francine called Mingo, who gathered several of the home team together. We built a pyre on the outcropping that formed an arm of the bay, and it was there we set fire to Godfrey and sent his spirit to its reward. Mingo danced and spoke in his native tongue, while Francine sat numbly watching the flames, smelling the ambiguous odors of roasting meat and roasting Godfrey. And when we had all had enough, I helped her up and walked her back to the bar.

She took her place behind the counter, and I put a bill on the bar and bought a round for the house, in Godfrey's name.

She bought the next round, and it wasn't long before everybody began patting her on the back and congratulating her on inheriting the bar.

She didn't understand at first, but after a moment, she realized it was true. Godfrey had no family, no heirs, there was no paperwork, the bar just passed from him to her and that was that.

This is what brought her out of her grief for the devil.

I began coming by on weekends and doing repair work around the place. I regrouted the dance floor, and strung up tiny fairy lights as she began to plan her grand opening. Apparently, the bar brought in plenty of money, it was just that Godfrey drank up all the profits. Francine had a different business sense.

Every week UPS brought some other prize she'd ordered through a catalog, and she was selling raffle tickets, and getting the community organized. There is a poor mission not too far from here, and once a year doctors come and minister to the sick children. Francine was raising money for them—they need so much— and it was a good thing for the community to rally behind. Soon the island women were coming around as well. When Godfrey owned the bar, the island women hated the place. Of course, their men would come in, get drunk and go home and beat them and their kids, no wonder they hated it.

But now, Francine wouldn't let the men get that drunk in her place. It was clean, the women were welcome, and she sat and chatted with them while their children played on the fresh dance floor with their toys. The women arranged flowers, so the bar always had a festive, tropical atmosphere.

The day of the grand opening dawned sunny and clear. Francine was up and about early, pouring coffee for all her workers, the same people who would later attend the party in their nicer clothes, but in the morning they were wearing work clothes and breaking their backs to launch her new enterprise right.

Women delivered elaborate flower arrangements, men set up tables to display the gifts, boys mixed juices for the refrigerator and stowed fresh kegs for chilling. Another crew put up a small stage in the corner of the dance floor for the band, who was to arrive later, and even the priest from the mission came by and had a cup of coffee, and ended up sweeping the floor. A couple of cruising sailors who happened to wander into the bay joined in, and Francine put them to work preparing food.

I had appointed myself foreman for the whole remodeling project, and wandered around with a coffee cup, making suggestions and helping everywhere I could. Francine joined me periodically, wiping a sweaty lock of hair from her forehead, and consulting with me on a point or two. Whenever she did that, I felt as though we were doing it together. A joint project. A couple. It made me feel important.

Then, when everything looked ready, and all the locals went home, it was just Francine and me taking a final look around before going to our respective places to get cleaned up.

"Francine," I said, and she turned those lovely eyes on me. She was dirty and sweaty and never lovelier. She looked at me with familiarity born of long association and respect. "May I have the first dance tonight?"

Her face softened at the question, and she smiled. I know there was affection in her heart, but I also recognized that she didn't want to foster any false hopes of romance between us. "Sure," she said, and put her hand on my shoulder. "We've done a good job here, haven't we, Winston?"

"You have," I said. She gave my shoulder a squeeze and I went home to get ready for my dance with the love of my life.

And it was every bit as wonderful as I imagined.

The crowd was young, the band barely warmed up, but I knew that Francine would be frantically working after a few minutes, and if I was going to get my dance, it would have to indeed be the first.

The sun had gone beyond the horizon, but the clouds still blazed. The fairy lights seemed like a net of jewels over our heads. Those who had come early stood around the edges of the dance floor, watching the band hit their stride, and when they played "Stardust," I held out my hand, and Francine accepted.

The crowd yelled and applauded, and she moved into my arms gracefully.

She is taller than I am, so I didn't have the pleasure of her face against my chest, but our cheeks did touch and I rested my hands on her hips and she put her arms on my shoulders. I felt everybody watching us for the first part of the dance, and it felt wonderful. Soon, other couples swarmed the new floor, and I was proud that so far, Francine's evening was perfect, and the new dance floor was having a fine inauguration.

Then a hand on my shoulder. I smiled. Someone wanting to cut in. Yeah, sure. No way. I held her tighter and turned to refute the friend, but it was no friend.

It was the European, and Francine froze in my arms, an expression of stunned pleasure on her face. An expression that struck terror into my heart.

I had no intention of giving her up, yet he moved right in and took her from me. My face heated and I had to walk away, out into the jungle to calm my rage. He had come back to hurt her one more time, and I couldn't bear it. I wouldn't bear it.

After an hour or so, I went back to the bar, and Francine was dancing around her guests like a young girl at her coming out party. She looked lithe and youthful, more beautiful even than she had when the party started, and my jealousy burned ever brighter at the thought that it was this wretched womanizer who made her feel thus, when my love only turned her gaze to one of pitiful tolerance.

She danced and she flitted, and she smiled and she laughed, and never far from her was the devil, smiling and acting the host, the role that I had intended to play.

The party wore on, and I watched from the sidelines, but before it was over, Francine got one of the boys to bartend, and she and the European slipped off the far end of the dance floor and escaped into the night. I followed them to the bay, and watched as he rowed her to his black yacht, almost invisible in the dark night.

I went home and tried not to think about her in his arms. Tried to think, instead, of the day she would be in my arms, but my dreams were flat and without substance. Francine would never be mine, not as long as she could still be so tempted.

What did I want with such a woman, I kept asking myself. But she was not to blame for her weakness. She was a good girl, a clean girl, she just had a soft spot for the rogue. And he capitalized on it. I hated him with the all the hate that was in me and all the hate that should be in her. I cast about, trying to imagine what I could do to rescue her, but I could think of nothing. She was an adult. She was her own woman.

When the devil smashed her heart again, I would be there to hold her and kiss away her tears.

It was this thought that consoled me in the night, and toward morning, when I knew they slept exhausted in each others' arms, I, too, eventually slept.

I didn't mean to watch them. I didn't mean to follow them. It was never my intention to spy on them. But they were so easy with one another. Francine laughed so easily, so gaily that I was attracted beyond my willpower. I watched the European effortlessly make a lei of flowers for her head with deft fingers, the type of romantic thing that I imagine all women love, but I would never have thought of it. That he did intrigued me as much as it pleased Francine. He was physically affectionate, always touching her. His white teeth flashed in the tropical sun often, and she put her face down in modest shyness just as often. What did he say to her to elicit that type of response?

I felt completely inadequate as a man.

And I could not take my eyes off them, I could not keep from studying them. All hope for a romance, a relationship, a marriage with Francine vanished as I watched the magic he wove about her head and into her heart. I wanted to run and shake her and say, "Don't you see? Can't you see what he is, what he is doing?" But I couldn't do that, because I was as entranced as she was. The European, Crosley his name, was busy teaching us both. He taught her what it meant to be a warm and wonderful, delightful woman, and he taught me what it meant to be an ugly scar-faced runt.

Still I could not stop watching them.

I followed within the cover of the jungle as they walked up the beach that first morning, to the party-ravaged bar. She fixed them each an espresso, and then arranged for Kenny, one of the home team, to take over the bar for the next five days. She said she was going to take some time off.

Five days.

That concept immobilized me with dread. I would have to watch them together for five days. On the other hand, Crosley was sure to leave after the five days were up, and so my agony, while intense, would be short-lived. And then I would hold her while she healed. Perhaps she would come to me then, tired of the razzle-dazzle which ends in heartache, preferring instead, the solid and steadfast.

Hope is a strange and wonderful thing.

Five days turned out to be an eternity—an eternity of waiting in the weeds. Waiting and watching as they made love, as they talked and laughed and spent endless idle hours together. I barely ate, barely slept, didn't work, didn't bathe. I was afraid to leave them, afraid I'd miss the moment where he revealed his nature to her, the moment when she saw the truth of him, the moment where what they had fell apart and I could swoop down and rescue my damsel from the evil one.

I waited and I watched, tirelessly, with undying devotion, and all I saw was more love and more affection and more touching and more kissing and more madness grew inside my head until I spent all my time hating myself for watching. "She would never look at the likes of you," I said to myself in disgust. "Look at you!"

And still I followed and watched.

Now and then I thought of the home team's opinions of Francine and her affair. They were surely crude about it all, and while I was tempted to go to the bar and defend her honor, I could not leave her. For five days I watched from the doorstep of the eroding shrine of love I had built for her in my soul.

And on the fifth night, when they were back at her shack, I went home. I bathed and shaved and tried to ignore the wildness in my eyes. Then I went to the bar, ate a decent meal, and tried to ignore the prodding questions from the regulars. I tried even harder to ignore the things they said about Francine. They were not mean things, these were her friends, but they were hurtful to my ears.

And so, dressed for the occasion, I went back to her place to await the final hour, when the evil Crosley would drive a spike through my beloved's heart and I would be the first one she would cling to upon its completion.

Five years later, he returned. Could not stop thinking of me, he said. Could not forget the silken feel of my skin, the amber scent of my hair. Could not escape the way the dimples in the small of my back fill with perspiration when we make love. Lies I lived to hear, lies that rolled off his tongue so smoothly and delicately and sounded so sweet when I listened only to his words and not to his duplicitous soul.

Godfrey failed to wake one morning, so I inherited the bar by default. I cleaned it up and changed the menu, instituted some policies and began making it the social center of our side of the island as it should have been all along, instead of a smelly drunk's hangout. I had the dance floor fixed, and staged a gigantic grand opening party, including a dance band and a raffle. It was a great party, and it had barely kicked off when Crosley swept me into his arms for a dance.

I had been too busy to notice the arrival of his yacht, and my surprise was authentic and overwhelming.

I'd been expecting him. I'd expected his return since the moment he left me. I'd expected to see his smile at the end of my bar every night for five years, but when I actually saw him, smelled him, felt him, and then tasted him, it was a sight, a smell, a sensation totally beyond that of my meager imagination. He was dark and pungent and his hands strong and familiar and bold. When he tasted me, I felt as though I had never been tasted before. My spirit soared. He could not have chosen a better time than my grand opening ceremony.

I continued acting the hostess for the night, but as the party wound down, I set others to see to the wrapping up of it all, paid the musicians, grabbed the dusty bottle of grappa I had stashed in the back of the cabinet for just exactly this anticipated event, and let myself be led to his boat, to his bed.

Again, I was stunned into silent submission by my own inadequate fantasies of what Crosley had been like. What Crosley had been to me.

After stormy, insistent, almost desperate lovemaking, we lay quietly in his bunk listening to the snapping and popping of little creatures as they fed on the boat's bottom growth. The anchor rode squeaked as the yacht pulled on it, and somewhere high above, a halyard clanged.

My fingers toyed in the thick curly black hair that grew in a line downward from his navel. The cabin smelled like seafaring, like diesel, like weathered teak, like lovemaking.

"I must leave in five days," he said softly.

I had expected that, but the sound of it sliced my heart. I took a steeling breath and vowed to make the most of these five days he allowed me.

Early the next morning, I delegated responsibilities around the bar, and told the home team that I was taking a few days off. Then Crosley and I set about recreating who we had been five years previously. We did many of the same things of sensual pleasure. He had five years worth of new seafaring stories to delight me, and his storytelling skills had sharpened.

I was like a young girl. I knew I could have Crosley for five days and survive. I had decided long ago that if ever given another chance, I wouldn't ruin the poetry of the moment by superimposing the inevitability of the future. Whenever the sinking feeling would come into my belly at the thought of either his string of women, all in five-day increments, or at the thought of his leaving me yet again, I squashed that thought and put it right out of my mind. I had business at hand. I had to make these five days last a lifetime. I needed to experience the depth and breadth of all that he brought to me. I was experiencing myself for the first time, and it was through the catalyst of Crosley's attentions.

I wondered continually if his other women whined about his leaving them and what he thought or did about that. Perhaps he came back to me simply because I never mentioned it. But while I was young and free this time, not whining internally or externally, Crosley was not. Perhaps it was exactly my lack of concern for the future that made him nervous. Perhaps he was falling in love with me. Perhaps he was feeling the accumulation of years. Perhaps his cast aside litter of broken hearts was beginning to wear on him. Regardless, Crosley had become paranoid.

It began the very first night, as we lay in each others arms in his stateroom. "I feel as though someone is watching us," he said, and twice during the night he took his binoculars topside and scanned the edge of the bay.

He has dealt with too many cuckolded husbands and jealous boyfriends, I thought to myself.

And the next day, as we swam in the ocean and made love in the sand, then, too, he felt as though we were being observed. But nobody was interested in two middle-aged people having sex on the beach. If they saw us, they went about their business. It was the island way.

But Crosley was not convinced of that.

And after a while, I began to feel it, too. Eyes. Desperate eyes fronting an unsettled mind. "Crosley," I said, "please stop this. You're making me afraid in my own home."

"I'm sorry, darling," he responded, "but there is something not right. There is a harmful energy here. Deeply bubbling. Your lover?"

"Of course not."

"You're sure."

After repeating that same conversation in what must have been a hundred different ways, I stopped responding. I had no desire to be infected with his fear.

And a tiny voice of hope spoke through the tangled mess of my emotions that asked if Crosley was considering me for a lifetime mate and wanted to make certain that I was unencumbered.

But I knew that wasn't the case.

On the fourth night, I sat straight up in bed out of a sound sleep and said, "Winston." And then I knew. Winston was afraid for me. Shy, reclusive, scarred Winston. Lonely Winston. Winston had a little crush on me, and I knew it, I knew it when he started coming to the bar after Godfrey's death, looking for work and then accepting no pay for what he did. I did nothing to encourage his ardor; perhaps he encouraged it himself, and needed no help from me.

Winston. Winston was keeping an eye on Crosley to make certain Crosley behaved in an honorable manner. Winston should not have wasted his time. Crosley had no honor.

That Winston was looking after me was a comfortable feeling, and I felt just a tiny twinge of shame to know that Crosley and I had made love so openly, so blatantly, so passionately in full view of poor little Winston's feelings. Yet I was not responsible for Winston's clandestine activities, nor his uninvited attentions.

On the fifth day, Crosley and I spent the day tangled among each other in the hammock, reading. Plates of fresh fruit and bottles of wine kept us company, and we dozed and touched and dozed and read. My mind began to flirt with the bar, wondering what had transpired since I was last there a week ago. I wondered if Carola had had her baby; I wondered if Pico got his promotion. I wondered if the bar was being kept clean, swept and mopped daily. I wondered if anyone was stealing the receipts, or guzzling free booze. I didn't worry; I had chased worry from my life when I moved to this slow-moving tropical place. I was more curious. I missed it. I was eager to get back to it in the morning.

And that said a lot about my relationship with Crosley. Maybe he was right to keep his affairs to five days. Five days was perhaps enough.

As evening drew near, he began to get restless, looking behind him all the time. That, too, was becoming tiresome. "Is there a lock on your door?" he asked.

"No," I said, although I had a way of locking it when I felt unsafe. This was the fifth day. Crosley would be leaving me before dawn—without a word, without a goodbye—and I felt like tormenting him a little bit. "Put it out of your head, Crosley," I said, "and come make love to me."

He did, and it was the transcendental experience of souls merging that every woman longs to have. We spent half the night murmuring to each other, stroking softly, urgently, gently and then stopping to talk and laugh, only to begin again, slowly building. That peak, when finally attained, left me disoriented and fragmented. Words from different languages, partial thoughts from what certainly must be different minds shot through my head like stray bullets. I saw colors I'd never seen before, and could not follow a concept. I'd never had an experience like that before, and while at first afraid, I thought perhaps sleep would heal it. Crosley was already snoring.

Afraid I would sleep through his departure, I got up and moved a chair in front of the door. And when I next heard the scrape of that chair, Crosley was dressed and making his escape.

"Crosley," I said softly.

"Yes, darling?"

"One last kiss?" He looked at me; I saw the reflection in his eyes from the indistinct starlight that shone through the large windows in my shack. "Please?"

He slipped off his shoes and got back into my bed, clothes and all. I held him to me, the emotion rising up from my belly to clog in my throat. I unbuttoned his shirt and kissed his chest, then rested my head against his breast.

"Francine. . ." he began.

"Shhh," I said, and spent a long, concentrated moment memorizing him, for this would be the last time his heart would beat against my cheek.

My plan was to confront him as he slipped away like a coward during the early morning hours. It doesn't take a lot of intelligence to count to five, and I sat not far from her front door in those the pre-dawn hours, waiting for that door to open. I didn't know what I would do with him, I just knew that if he wanted to cruise the world breaking hearts and wreaking emotional havoc, he could do as he pleased, but not on my island, and not with Francine.

But when the door opened it wasn't Crosley standing there, it was Francine, dressed in that gauzy white fabric she was prone to wearing. "Winston," she said, and my astonishment could not have been more complete. More paralyzing was the shame that she had known. She had known that I watched, and yet she acted in that wanton way—it was too much to think about. I had to have time to ponder all the ramifications of that one word spoken clearly in the dark. Her summons. "Winston," she said.

I stood up and walked calmly to the door, as if entirely by pre-arrangement.

"I need your help," she said, and it was then I saw the blood on her hand. She saw it, too, and rinsed her hand in a bucket by the front door that had captured rainwater, then threw the water on the banana trees.

Crosley was in her bed, dressed. His shirt was unbuttoned, and the stub of a bamboo shoot protruded from his chest. Blood leaked out around the wound and stained his shirt.

"There is a consequence for every action," Francine said to me, her eyes calm but sad. "Crosley's has come and gone. I will wait for mine."

Together we carried him to his tender, and Francine drove it to his yacht, while I followed in my whaler. With difficulty, we loaded him aboard his boat, weighed anchor and motored out of the bay to the calm, deep green water. Not a word passed between us.

I secured Crosley in his stateroom, then opened the seacocks on both toilets, and together she and I sat in my boat and watched the black yacht settle ever lower in the water, until with great burbles and gasps, it sank beneath the surface.

I motored us back to the bay just as the rain began. We ran through the deluge for the bar, and arrived soaking wet. Francine made us each a double espresso and threw in a shot of Jack Daniel's.

We clicked coffee cups and made our private toasts silently.

The morning that Crosley left, Winston and I sat at the bar drinking coffee and watching deluge rain soak the already sodden earth. It fell as a solid sheet from the gutterless roof all around, splashing mud from the rain-gouged trenches to mix with the water that splashed up from the dance floor, bits of confetti and other leftover party debris floating closer to our bare feet.

I felt the tropical depression in my soul and sipped coffee silently, feeling desperately claustrophobic, penned in by the humidity, the liquid walls, and my self-limiting choices in life, the vinyl of the stool sticking uncomfortably to the backs of my thighs.

※

Fates Entwined

When the plane began its descent, her heart began to pound. She didn't know if he would be at the gate to meet her, shyly smiling, wearing a baseball cap and his purple Patagonia jacket. Maybe he'd be at baggage claim, keeping an eye on the Jeep at the curb and the airport police who were so generous with their citations. Maybe he'd be waiting inside the curbside Jeep, watching for her, ready to jump out and grab her luggage, give her a peck on the cheek, a quick squeeze, then sweep her out of the airport tangle and back to his place.

Then again, maybe he had to work, and the key in her purse would fit the car parked in Lot 3, close to the Hertz cars.

As soon as the seat belt sign came on, she grabbed her toiletries case, and ignoring the look of disapproval from the snooty flight attendant, she went into the rest room. Four hours of dry airplane air had reddened her eyes and fried her skin. Or so it appeared in the harsh light.

She repaired her makeup, brushed her teeth and hair, spritzed perfume and pocketed some mints.

The plane slowed. The attendant knocked on the door. She finished with some lipstick, nodded at the overall effect, and went back to her seat. She hoped he'd be at the gate, but she wasn't counting on it.

Wyoming. Ohio. Wyoming. Ohio. She lived in Wyoming, he lived in Ohio. They had met in Chicago. A warm buzz started up between them immediately, but uncertainty kept them reluctantly apart. When she said goodbye to him, it was with a warm, total body hug and a kiss open to interpretation. Sister? Lover to be? Friend? Ship in the night?

Then he called, two weeks later, and two weeks after that, and two weeks after that until she invited him to Wyoming. He wasted no time in acting on her invitation.

More reluctance.

Wyoming. Ohio. Wyoming. Ohio.

He stayed in her spare bedroom for a week, every night it was more difficult than the previous one to kiss and hug goodnight in the hallway and go to their respective beds.

The final night, he came to hers.

"Can we sleep together and behave ourselves?" she asked.

"I don't know," he said, and climbed in beside her, wearing only his jockey shorts. She had already decided that sex was not an option at that stage, good Lord, they'd only known each other a week plus a couple of days, plus a bunch of phone hours.

They did sleep together that night, rubbing each others' backs and taking comfort in another body in such proximity. He respected her boundaries, and that softened her heart. She was cautious not to overstimulate him, because her hold on the reins of her own chastity were so tenuous.

In the morning, her favorite time for lovemaking, she ran fingers lightly across his shoulders and broad back, feeling the freckles and textured terrain. She felt his rise to consciousness, along with the rise of her passion and knew she had to stop touching him if they were going to survive his visit with their priorities intact.

The plane touched down. She popped another mint.

She was glad they hadn't made love then. They got closer with their souls instead of their bodies. They communicated their lives instead of their lusts. They could have stayed in bed all week and learned so little of each other, really, instead of touring parts of Wyoming and learning each other so well.

And after his plane left? After that wonderful hug and kiss, he left and she cried. And their calls became weekly events. They shared their lives and their longing long distance, laughing, talking, purring into the phone to each other, always ending with one of them saying, "Wish you were here."

"Wish I was, too," the other would reply, and they gave vague murmurings to holding each other, or kissing, or tickling secret places. Usually she hung up laughing, but with misty eyes.

Wyoming. Ohio. Wyoming. Ohio.

There was no doubt about the agenda of this trip. They were compatible on all the long-distance and short-term levels. Were they compatible physically?

They had to be. She'd already fantasized it to complete success. They had to be.

She spotted him before he saw her. He was looking at his fingernails when she came off the jetway, pulling her wheeled suitcase behind her.

He was every bit as delicious as she expected, and felt a little squeeze in her lower belly. His whole face broke into a grin when he saw her. In Wyoming, she'd worn boots and jeans, but in Ohio, she had on a long, yellow dress with lace trim. Just the way to his heart, this sweet man with hopelessly old-fashioned values.

His hug lifted her clean off her feet and his kiss almost sucked the soul out of her. "God, I've missed you," he said. "You look great."

Exactly the right thing to say.

She was the one who ended up smiling shyly as he took her hand in one of his and picked up her suitcase with the other.

They stood silently at the baggage claim, holding hands, all their conversation too private for a public place. She grinned, her small hand in his big one, feeling ever so superior to be with him. Just being by his side made her feel feminine. The yellow dress doubled the ladylike sensation.

In the car, they grinned at each other before starting off. Then it was all small talk—how was your flight, the food was awful, are you hungry, no are you, no I just ate.

By the time they got to his apartment, it was ten o'clock and long dark. He carried her bags to the bedroom and then came to her with his arms open for a hug. The closeness re-energized her. She felt tired from the travel, from the anticipation, from the expectation, from the worry of how it was going to be.

There was nothing to worry about.

He held her close and they breathed each other in—she vaguely thought she must smell like an airplane—and the embrace wasn't sexual at all, but comforting. "Shower," she whispered.

He pulled back. "Take your time."

She did. She shampooed her freshly-washed hair, shaved her already-smooth legs and then creamed her skin. She dried her hair, decided against makeup—you're going to *bed* for God's sake—and put on the white cotton Victoria's Secret nightie she'd just bought. Oops, the price tag was still on the sleeve.

She touched on a tiny bit of perfume and turned off the light.

Would he be in bed already?

She opened the bathroom door.

No. He was sitting on the couch. In the dark.

She felt uncertain. He ought to be in bed. Should she have put on clothes?

She sat next to him and saw his eyes shine in the dark as they surveyed the white v-neck of her nightie. "Hi," she said.

"Hi," he said, and she was glad he wasn't in bed, because she wanted to help him get there.

He leaned over, smelled her hair, then kissed her so softly it almost hurt her to let him lead. She wanted to suck in his lip, she wanted to climb all over him, but she retained her self control. *Let him do it*, she told herself.

And he did. He stood up, and pulled her to her feet with one of his fingers on one of hers, then led her to his bedroom where a single candle burned on his antique bureau.

Every place he touched her was a surprise. She, feeling anxious, wanted to overcome the anxiety with aggression, but stifled it, more successfully at some times than at others. She knew there would only be one first time for them, and she wanted to be present and conscious and aware so when she was back home in the Wyoming loneliness, she'd have this full-bodied memory to keep her company.

No stranger to a variety of men's hands, kisses or techniques, she appreciated his style for its uniqueness. It was genuine. He was genuine. He seemed reverent somehow. This was a special night for him, too, and that realization made her skin ultra-sensitive and her fingertips ever more curious. Some day, familiarity would bring fun sex, but tonight it was romantic sex, and that meant emotional sex.

She slipped her hands under his shirt and lightly scratched her nails down his back. He pulled the shirt off over his head, and she pulled at the hairs on his chest with her lips.

His hands felt appreciatively all along her curves—back, sides, breasts, butt, and he pressed her closer to him, the hardness of his erection becoming more and more evident.

In a bold move, she pulled out the front of his jeans and plunged her hand down into the humid interior. He gasped, then moved to accommodate her. His penis felt smooth and ready, and she wanted nothing more than to kiss it, a weakness growing in her knees as her pulse began to pound between her legs.

She fumbled with his belt, felt him watching her. His jeans fell easily to the floor, and when he pulled off his dark blue jockey shorts, his penis sprang forth.

She cupped his warm scrotum in her cool hand and led him the few steps to the bed. In a swiftly efficient move, he pulled her nightie off over her head and they stood looking at each other in the candlelight. He looked so sincere, if she hadn't been in such a hurry to get his hands back on her skin, she might have laughed. Or teased him. But this was nothing to laugh at, this was falling in love. Serious business. They could laugh later.

She sat on the bed and scooted over to make room for him. He lay down next to her and ran his hands over her, from her neck down her breast, around her nipple, across her ribs to the small of her waist and the swell of her hip and then back again. She lay down next to him, closed her eyes and luxuriated in the softness of his fingertips, the hardness of the callouses on his palms, the tenderness of his breath. She touched his face and lost herself in the sensations of arousal, both his and hers, but when the time came, when the place opened within her that could be filled only by him, his penis had softened and lay like a wounded thing on his leg.

"Sorry," he whispered. "Sometimes. . ."

She kissed away his apology and then kissed awake his passion, worrying for only the briefest of moments if he would think her just a little bit too skilled in those maneuvers.

Then he was ready and she was ready and when they merged, she felt whole.

His rhythms were slow and considerate, give and take, his body talked with hers in a language that was beyond concepts and symbols. She understood him. For perhaps the first time in her life, she knew she was completely in sync with another human being, as if living a deja vu on purpose.

Then the urgency began, and she felt her psyche come back to her—they parted into separate entities and while she didn't want to leave the intimacy, her body was calling. Reluctantly, and then eagerly, she followed its urgings.

They peaked together, holding, squeezing, groaning, gripping, tensing, then easing, easing, easing, coming in for the softest landing together. She was barely aware of the cooling down twitches and tics, only focused on the colors and rhythms of the symphony, sliding slowly back into the body she had escaped for the briefest of moments to dance with him somewhere in the ether.

They slid apart, and as if she were too raw yet to expose herself to him, turned on her side away from him, facing the candle. He turned on his side behind her, and brought the sheet up over them both, then put his arm around her, one hand protectively cupping her breast.

The thought briefly fled through her mind of why she had married small men. Maybe because they danced well together, as good as reason as any to marry either of them. But this man was a big man. Tall, broad-chested, long-armed with size twelve feet, enormous, working-man hands and a glorious, generous penis to match. Lying next to him, she felt small and safe. It was okay to be vulnerable with him, she thought, because he could take care of her. He would take care of her, wouldn't he? She was so tired of doing it all herself.

The tears that threatened to swamp her when she gave in to that orgasm now leaked silently out of her eyes. She figured he was sleeping, but refrained from sniffling and carefully controlled her breathing just in case he wasn't.

Quietly, and in solitude, all the worry, fear and desperation leaked out of her along with those tears, and when her private emotional storm had passed, she wiped her leaking nose with her fingers and brushed the tears off the bridge of her nose. He'd be horrified if he knew she'd been crying, and she would never be able to explain why.

"What are you feeling?" he asked, his whispered voice a comforting surprise. Maybe he did know. Maybe he knew and he just let her have her space. Affection swelled up inside her.

She wiped her nose and eyes on the pillowcase, then turned around to face him, tucking one arm under his pillow, the other hand resting gently on his arm. The candle illuminated his face and she knew she'd see love and tenderness and affection and devotion and all those things she ached to see if only she'd look at his eyes, but somehow she couldn't make herself look at him. Not yet. She was too vulnerable. She didn't know what he'd see in her face. She didn't know herself what she felt.

Being alone is easier than this, she thought. This is way too revealing.

Easier, yes, but unfulfilling. If you want him, be real with him.

"I'm not sure," she finally said. "Scared."

"Of me?" He pulled her close, put his chin on the top of her head.

"No, of me. Of us. Of this step." She spoke into his chest.

"Are you sorry?"

Sorry? Oh no, god no, never, she thought, but she couldn't say that, because the tears were back and they were clogging up her throat.

She took a ragged breath and his big arms tightened around her. He kissed her forehead. They lay like that for a long time, snot leaking out of her nose as his seed trickled down the back of her thigh.

His arm relaxed into heaviness and a soft snore rumbled in his chest, but she wasn't ready for him to sleep. Not yet. She moved, sniffing, wiped her face again on the pillowcase and he relaxed his hold on her enough for her to do that. Then she kissed him, a long, exquisite, motionless kiss, tongues lightly touching, and when she opened her eyes and looked into his, it was all there. All that she hoped to see and more.

"Mmmm," he said, and snuggled her down, then pulled up the covers and tucked them around her chin. "I was just having a little dream."

"About what?" she asked.

"Wyoming," he said, and she smiled into the night.

✳

One Afternoon in Hana

The beach was exactly as her friend had said. Looking down from the top of the switchback, the red sand beach was a study in subtle reddish browns, swirled with white shell-sand and fine black grit. Stunted, wind-bent kiawe trees grew out of the cliffs, their feathery green breaking the striated red rock pattern. A wall of tall volcanic spires separated the bright blue swimming area from the crashing waves of the Pacific. The sea surged in through a break in the wall, washed through the pool and out the other side, washing with it a handful of people, whose whoops could be heard all the way to the top of the cliff, carried along on the salt spray.

The whole scene sparkled in the bright tropical sun.

The beach was not heavily populated this late on a Tuesday afternoon, but there was one unmistakable, undeniable fact.

Everybody down there was naked.

"Hey," he said. "Swimsuit optional! Cool." And he began down the trail.

"Wait," she said, uncertain she wanted to participate.

"What?"

"Are we going to get naked down there?"

"I can't speak for you," he said, then smiled gently and took her hand. "C'mon. It'll be all right." Hesitantly, she followed him down the switchback, and he attentively helped her over the dangerous spots where the trail, held up only by tree roots, had fallen through.

She carried the towels; he carried the drinks and a backpack full of snorkeling gear. With every step, she tried not to think about taking her bathing suit off in front of him. She didn't have to; there was no pressure. Surely there was somebody on that beach wearing a swimsuit.

She stopped and looked. No swimsuits. Just flesh. Tanned, firm flesh. One island beauty paraded down the beach, her brown breasts looking young and perfect above a flat stomach and thick black pubic hair. Oh, man, there was no competing with that. Twenty years old—Forty years old. No children—Three children. Perfect weight—Twenty pounds over. Firm and tan—Not so firm any more, and sunburned on Minnesota-winter-white skin.

And she didn't know *him* all that well, either, although she'd like to. This was the second time they'd met at this annual symposium, but the first time they'd spent any real time together. Certainly the first time they'd gone sightseeing.

But as the days passed and they got to know each other, both single, both available, she hoped that they would shed their clothes by candlelight, or by the indistinct light the hotel torches provided, scented breezes flowing through his room, the sound of the surf in the background. She spent her days fantasizing about their last night at the symposium, when it would all happen, she was certain. The attraction between them was too great. And that last night, well, that would be tonight.

First, they would have a private farewell dinner together, maybe attend a party or two, have a couple of cocktails, then go to his room to raid his mini bar for munchies and more wine, and at one point, he'd lean over and—

And he'd grab the remote to see if the game was still on.

No! No he wouldn't.

She knew what blouse she'd wear, the one with all the buttons up the front. Buttons, she'd heard, were tiny little aphrodisiacs to a man, each one a little problem to be solved, each one a little mystery to uncover. No panty hose. Men hated panty hose. Bare legs, freshly shaved and oiled. The lighting would be low and romantic. She'd smell lightly of the expensive Hawaiian perfume she'd bought at the hotel gift shop.

He'd kiss her neck and then he'd say—

"God, could you believe that pompous ass who gave the keynote?"

No! No he wouldn't. He'd whisper something soft and sweet and appreciative. His lips would be soft, so soft pressed against hers, and heat would begin in her belly and shoot both ways.

"Here," he said. "Be careful of these rocks." He held out his hand and she took it as he guided her over a dozen carelessly tossed boulders, and then their feet hit the red sand.

Naked people everywhere looked up to see them. These strangers were going to watch them take off their clothes together in bright sunlight with no wine, no perfume, no buttons, no romance, no romance at all.

He took the towels from her and spread them out side by side on the sand, then lifted off his t-shirt. Wearing only his swimming trunks, he rummaged in his backpack until he came up with his mask and fins and a squeeze bottle of waterproof sunscreen. He handed it to her with a question mark on his face.

"Sure," she said, happy to have something to do except stand by, quietly agitated. She rubbed sunscreen across his freckled back, wishing, desperately wishing that she were rubbing massage oil into his glorious skin, getting it all over the sheets, getting it all over each other, in their hair, on their faces, in their mouths.

"Thanks," he said when she finished. "You all right?"

"Yeah."

"Want to snorkel?"

"Not quite yet."

"Okay." He reached down and whipped off his swimming trunks, grabbed his fins and mask and walked into the water.

She demurely averted her eyes as he faced her, but she had no shyness about watching him walk into the water. His butt was round and muscled, his thighs hairy and handsome. She watched him walk in, stumble around as he put on his gear, then he submerged and became only the orange tip of a snorkel and white mounds of buttocks as he swam out toward the open ocean.

She stood in the warm Hawaiian sun, wondering how men could be so casual about such things. Then, with his eyes safely focused on other things, she slipped out of her swimsuit and lay down on the sunwarmed towel.

The cool water splashed across his back as he swam out from the beach. The bottom of the ocean was swirled with colors—yellow coral, black lava rock, red cinder. The fish looked hand painted as they went fearlessly about their business, whatever business that might be, dodging predators, finding food, searching for a mate—no different, actually, than anyone else in life.

The temptation of the open ocean was great, but instead, he decided to float weightless in the safety of the lagoon, where he could watch the fish and think about the woman, hopefully naked by this time, sitting on the beach waiting for him. The sun warmed his back and he could still feel the gentleness of her soft fingers as she'd applied the sunscreen. He should have her put some on his butt, but he was afraid for her to touch him there when he was naked in front of all those strangers.

She was something. He had liked her the minute he'd met her at the previous year's symposium. That she was back again this year, and still romantically unattached was his great fortune. If only he could make the right decisions, make the right moves, convert some of this attraction into something more substantial. On the surface, she seemed to be everything he was looking for in a mate.

But she lived in Minnesota, and he lived in Tennessee, and that wasn't exactly optimal conditions to incubate a growing relationship. Better to not even start?

Tough call.

He tried to concentrate on the school of little yellow fish that were congregating around a hole in the lava, but the thought of her lying naked on the beach was just too invasive. They were both leaving the island in the morning. If he was going to make a move—and it seemed to him that she was entirely willing to entertain such an event—it was going to have to be tonight. This afternoon. Now.

Not now. Tonight.

Maybe he'd take her out for a nice dinner. Maybe they could find a good waterfront place that served up a nice risotto. They'd share a bottle of wine. It being the last night, there were sure to be parties, and dressing up and looking good and having social time with colleagues always seemed to put a woman in a good mood. He could casually suggest something to get her back up to his room later—a phone call, perhaps, or maybe just an outright invitation. He didn't need to play any games, he didn't need any seduction subterfuge, they were both adults. They were adults and they were wildly attracted to each other. It was obvious, and not only to the two of them.

He'd wear that silk knit polo shirt that women loved to touch. And linen slacks. He had one last fresh pair of boxers.

He couldn't wait to see what kind of underwear she wore. Something lacy, he imagined. Something matching. Something flimsy and of no practical value. Maybe, if he were lucky, something tear-away. No, not her, not on the first night. On the first night, she'd want romance, not play.

He'd give her romance. He loved romance.

A long, moonlit walk on the beach after dinner. He'd casually take her hand at some point, and from then on, they'd be a couple. It would be only natural they'd go back to his room, the softly scented breezes blowing through, the sound of the surf, the light of the tiki torches around the hotel grounds. . .

He swam around to the other side of the volcanic wall, being careful to stay away from the sharp rocks. The surge wasn't as dramatic as it appeared from above. The wildlife was more interesting, the color variations more dramatic in the deeper blue of the water. He had a greater feeling of weightlessness; it was almost like flying.

They'd come in from their walk, pleasantly heated from the warm, humid nighttime air. He'd close the door, and she'd stand next to him in the dark hallway. He'd brush the hair from her forehead, and she'd move in close. Their bodies would touch for the first time in a full-bodied embrace, and he'd kiss her forehead, kiss her cheek, then their lips would meet for the very first time.

Electric.

Soft. So incredibly soft. He'd pull back, look into her eyes and ask the question with his, and she'd say—

"Got any Diet Coke?"

No! No, she wouldn't.

He'd lead her by the hand to the bed. They'd sit, smiling at each other with the awkwardness of teenagers, not exactly knowing how to proceed, knowing only that they *must* proceed, they *required* closeness, they ached for the magic, for the mystery, for the touch of another human being.

He'd begin to unbutton whatever she was wearing, for surely she would wear something with many buttons, and she would put one of those soft hands on his shoulder and lean into him. She smelled like tropical heaven, and she'd say—

"I'm so sunburned I can barely move."

No! No, she wouldn't.

But speaking of sunburn, he could feel his back tightening up, and he was beginning to get kind of cold. He swam back toward the beach, took off his mask, then his fins, and walked up out of the water toward her, suddenly self-conscious.

She was lying on her back, her hair wet, with drops of water scattered across her nude belly. Her nipples knotted up with the chill his shadow cast over her. She looked up, shaded her eyes and smiled. "See anything?"

Man oh man, he thought. Do I ever. "Yeah, it was great."

He dropped his gear, then lay down on his towel next to her before biology began its irreversible course and she saw the effect of what he saw.

"Did you swim?" he asked.

"Lovely."

They rested for a while, safe in each other's company.

"Hand painted fish," he said.

"Hmmm."

"It's getting late."

She turned over on her side and adjusted her sunglasses. "The shadow from the mountain is about three inches from your head," she said.

"Let's go."

She needed no more encouragement. He, ever the gentleman, turned his back while she pulled her sticky swimsuit on over wet skin, but she watched shamelessly as he stepped into his trunks, sandy feet and all. They quickly packed up their gear, then he took her hand to help her over the boulders on the way to the trail.

"How about getting cleaned up and then having dinner? Maybe hitting a couple of farewell parties after?"

"Sounds good," she said, smiling shyly.

She tried to disengage her hand once they were on the trail, but he wouldn't let her.

Definitely the blouse with all the buttons, she thought.

Definitely.

❊

Suspicions About Friends, Family, Love, Work, Technology, the Government, and Everything Else

Not all those topics are addressed in these stories, but they ought to be. I'm suspicious of them all.

The government seems to top the list of most peoples' suspicions, and rightly so. Ditto tree-hugging, tofu eating, recycling, composting, green environmentalists, although I'm one of them. Sometimes. When I'm not a Republican. I reserve the right to change my mind about almost anything at any moment. Very suspicious behavior, if I do say so myself.

I hate being suspicious of my family members, but I am. And of my friends. I guess I've been disappointed too often. Had my heart broken too many times to dive into a new friendship with all portals wide open, only to have poison flood my chambers. Searching for love (either romantic or friendship) is tantamount to navigating a mine field. Is it worth all the trouble? You tell me.

It gets back to that whole motivation thing. It's liberating to investigate our own motivations, yet not good to look too hard at other peoples' motivations. I'm intrigued, and yet a little bit afraid to see them too clearly.

While I delight in toying with my suspicions, writing about it keeps me from the prison of living a suspicious life.

And I think it makes great fiction.

Mothballed

The girl was a little bit too drunk to be in a rowboat, and Danny hadn't realized it until she stood up, bottle in hand and tried to make her way back aft, to where he was.

"Sit down," he hissed at her. "Sit down and be quiet."

"Oops," she said almost losing her balance. She giggled as she regained her center, the boat rocking, then she sat down hard on the bench. "Sorry."

"You have to be quiet." He took another long pull on the oars, and soundlessly, a giant chain appeared from out of the fog and passed within a few feet of their boat. Strands of seaweed clung to it all the way up to the high tide mark, and barnacles bred clumping colonies right at the water line. Each link was as big as Danny's head.

The girl's eyes grew solemn as saw this mysterious chain that seemed to tether the ocean to the heavens, and then the ship, big as a walled city, darkened the fog.

Danny shipped the oars and put his hand out just in time to fend off. The big gray monster was cold.

"Wow," the girl said with reverence.

"If we get caught," Danny said, "we'll both go to jail. Do you understand?" He could barely see her from four feet away, the fog was so thick, but he saw that headful of blonde curls bounce as she nodded. He also saw the glint of the bottle as she upended it and drank the last of the Southern Comfort.

Perhaps this wasn't the best idea he'd ever had.

"I'm cold," she said.

"Okay." He took off his jacket and handed it to her, then picked up the grappling hook from the floor of the rowboat.

He moved as far from her as he could, and then he began to swing it, around and around, letting out more line every time, knowing that landing this hook would be an incredible long shot. He gave a mighty heave, saw the rope disappear into the fog over his head, and then heard a loud clang.

He ducked, expecting the hook to come speeding down toward him, barbs first, but it didn't. It held. He waited a minute, listening for the sound of a motor and to be pegged by a searchlight. Nothing. The fog had muffled the noise.

"First try," he said, smiling smugly to himself. He tied the row-boat to the end of the grappling hook's line, shrugged into his heavy backpack, put the coiled rope ladder over his shoulder, put on his leather gloves and kissed the bimbo on the cheek.

"I'm going to go up there and let down this rope ladder. You climb up it, okay?"

She nodded, subdued by the cold, gray monolithic wall next to them that rose up and disappeared into the mist.

Danny took a hefty grip on the knotted line and hand-over-handed. He was a little drunk himself, and though he'd been thinking about this adventure for almost a year now, he hadn't really thought about how it would feel to actually climb up a rope again, sneakered feet walking up the wet, slippery side of a ship. In the dark. Hands freezing.

But once he was twenty feet up, he couldn't stop. He didn't have the strength to climb back down. If he fell, he'd crash through the boat and it'd take less than a minute for them both to drown in that ice cold seawater. He had to go ahead. He was in shape, but not this kind of shape. He felt his strength waning, the rope was burning into his hands, but he had to keep going. He had to keep going.

And he did. Below him, the rope disappeared into fog. Above him, the rope disappeared into fog. There was only the segment of rope right in front of him, and the slippery gray side of the ship next to him, and the heavy rope ladder and backpack that he was carrying. The backpack got heavier with each passing minute. Its straps bit into his shoulders, it banged his back, throwing his balance off. If he was certain he could miss the rowboat, miss the girl, he'd jettison the blasted thing.

Instead, he kept going.

He should have trained for this. He should have spent some time in the gym, climbing a rope.

But that would have meant preparing for a felony. This was just spur of the moment stuff.

Sure. He just happened to have a grappling hook in the boat and a rope ladder over his shoulder. And a backpack full of the proper tools for the job.

His head bumped something, taking him by surprise.

Catwalk. The hook had snagged the catwalk.

Danny grabbed it, then heaved himself up and onto it. He lay there, gasping for breath, feeling his hands ache. The muscles in his arms and shoulders twitched and burned.

The network of rusting metal sketched cold artwork into his skin.

He'd actually made it. "Fooled you, you stupid, useless hunk of metal," he whispered.

After resting for a moment, he heard a low whine coming up from the rowboat. The blonde.

He ignored her and listened to the water lap at the edges of the ship, heard her old steel plates creak and groan as she moved sluggishly against her moorings.

He secured the rope ladder and let it down.

"Okay," he whispered loudly. "C'mon up."

He didn't think his voice carried all the way down, but he saw the rope ladder tighten, and it swayed a bit with her weight. Little moans of terror wafted eerily on the breeze that ruffled his hair.

Wind inside the fog.

Then he grabbed her jacket and helped her aboard, tears of fear moistening the corners of her eyes. She brushed them away with tiny red fingers that protruded out of the long sleeves of his jacket. "What are we doing here?"

"This is my old ship," he said. "I wanted to show it to you."

"You were in the Navy?"

Danny looked around at the mist-enshrouded deck. Faint moonlight shone through the fog. "Yeah. I lived aboard this crappy damned ship for four fucking years." The deck was slick with salty moisture. Rust bubbled the paint everywhere. He scuffed the deck with his shoe and the gray flaked off. "C'mon." She clung to the back of his shirt as he made his way forward.

He expected to find all the doors and hatches welded shut; he'd heard that they sealed up the mothballed fleet pretty tight. But the first door he came to was ajar. It seemed to invite him in, and that made the hair on his arms prick up a bit. "It'll be warmer below," he said, and pulled a small flashlight from his pocket.

He shouldered the door open another few inches with screeching difficulty, wincing at the noise. Then he slipped through the squared-oval opening. "Watch your head."

"Danny..." she whined, but he was beyond her now, the memories overpowering him with that unmistakable Navy ship smell. Shipmates. Foreign ports. Exotic women. Puking bad booze. He shone his light down a ladder, then ran down it as if he had been doing it right up until yesterday. His body remembered this ship, too.

"Dan-ny!" He heard her hesitant footsteps following him in the dark.

He shone his flashlight briefly on the ladder so she could see, then he flashed it around. The ship looked weird, with all the useful stuff gone. It had been gutted. Corroded ends of wires hung out of the bulkheads and down from the ceilings, where their fixtures had been removed. The farther forward they went, the drier it got and the more preserved the paint, but somewhere, water dripped and echoed tinnily. Even their breathing echoed in the vast emptiness which used to hold hundreds of exuberant, sweating, cursing, working men.

"What is this place?"

"They mothball the old ships. The Navy is superstitious about scuttling them, so they just leave them out here to rot. They're worthless. Useless."

"Superstitious?" The girl touched the wall with a reverent fingertip.

"Yeah, the Navy's full of ritual and history that they think is so important, but it's just superstitious crap. 'The ship never forgets,' they say."

"Forgets what?"

"Never mind. It's stupid."

They walked through passageways, the light of his small flashlight showing the way, ducking through the short headspace of the doors and stepping over their lower edges. Then down through another hatch in the deck, down the metal ladder, ever deeper into the belly of the ship.

He could navigate the interior of this ship in total darkness. He had *done* it in total darkness.

He could do it in his sleep. He still *did* it in his sleep.

"Here," he said, shining his light into a small empty room. "This is where I slept. With thirty-nine other guys." Unbelievable. This room was way too small for that. He shone the light up to the number stenciled on the I-beam. Sure was. This had been his berthing room.

"Let's go," she whined.

"C'mon, I'll show you the galley." Danny felt strangely euphoric. He felt as though he was putting something over on the Navy, something he had never felt before, not really. He'd sabotaged a few gas masks, sure, and slept through a few watches, but nothing like this. He was trespassing on their property, and they didn't know about it, and they couldn't do anything about it. He

was free to go anywhere and do anything, and there were no officers or chiefs to stop him.

He could even go into officer country.

Officer country!

The thought took his breath away.

Another level down, through long passages, a dozen doorways,
across a few rooms, and there they were: officer country. Sacred
ground, or so they would have you believe.

It looked exactly the same as the rest of the ship. Even the
Captain's quarters, while roomy for only one man, was small and
cramped. The paneling had been removed, and the bulkheads were
bare gray metal, just like everything else. The wardroom was small,
too, not like the area where the enlisted people—the working men,
the guys who ran the goddamned ship—ate.

Danny remembered standing in the chow line on his first cruise
out. He had been lost a half dozen times already, and the lower
ranking petty officers seemed to delight in sending him on wild
goose chases, getting him even more lost. When it was time for
chow, he stood in line, starving, he couldn't ever remember being
that hungry before, and then out of nowhere it seemed, came the
snipes.

Covered head to toe in black oil, those sweating men with white
circles around their eyes walked into the chow hall and the place
went silent. The line parted automatically. Danny stepped away
from the food and let these men, these enginemen—these sailors
who never saw the light of day and worked in hot oil all day every
day, from eight until late—eat first.

He kicked at the wardroom bulkhead.

There had never been a snipe in here. Officers were too pure to
hang out with those who beat their brains out making their ship
run. Making them look good.

Danny had never been in officer country before, and assumed
it was palatial. Of course it couldn't be, it was still a fairly small
ship, but they kept it shrouded in so much mystery, they kept the
division between officer and enlisted such a vast abyss. . . and yet
the officers were really no different than anybody else. Most times
they were less intelligent, they were more prone to fuckups than
the seamen.

But would they ever admit it? Hell, no.

"Dannny. . ."

"Stop whining!" His voice resonated nicely in officer country.
He sounded like an officer here. He could have been one. He should

have been one.

"Danny, I'm cold. I want to go back."

He clicked out the light.

"I'm cold," he mocked her. "I want to go back."

She made a tiny girlish noise of worry.

"You're a sailor now," he said. "Your country and your ship-mates and the safety of this vessel depend upon you. There is no going back."

"Danny. . ."

"Dismissed."

"Turn the light back on. Please."

"No whining. Stop your whining or I'll write you up. Article fifteen. You'll go to Captain's mast."

"You're scaring me."

"You'll get sent to the brig. Bread and water. Or better yet, the Big Chicken Dinner. You know what that is, don't you? Bad Conduct Discharge. BCD. We call it the Big Chicken Dinner around here."

"Danny. . ."

"Get out of here," he said, tired of her

"I don't know where I am. This place is so confusing."

A long groan shimmied the length of the ship; the weary complaint of a dying behemoth.

Danny smiled. "I'm going to sink this fucker," he said, and took off out the door, leaving the whiner behind.

He went to another place he'd never been on this ship: the engine room.

The machinery had been cannibalized. What was left looked incomplete, pipes and ducts reaching dramatically to nowhere, holes in the catwalk grid where something ought to be, but vacancy lived there instead.

The dripping was louder down here.

Danny shone his light down into the bilges. They were full of oily water. It stunk of diesel fuel. "Oh, no you don't, you wily bitch," he said to the ship, and his voice echoed and sounded tiny. "These fumes would blow me up along with you."

He could punch a hole in any part of the ship, as long as it was below the waterline. The weight of the incoming water would settle the ship lower and lower, until the goddamned thing finally sank. It wasn't going to take a very big hole, either. And Danny was in no hurry.

He left the engine room—it was too vast, too creepy, too dangerous, and chose the Chief's quarters instead. That was fitting. It would be that goddamned Master Chief Watts who would have had a fit over a hole in the hull. Well, Danny thought, let him have a fit over this one.

Holding the maglight in his mouth, he opened his backpack and pulled out all the newspaper wadding he'd put in there for protection. The battery, the wires, the small wad of plastique. He'd been pinching plastique from his job site, one pea-sized piece at a time until he had a wad the size of a golf ball. That should do the trick. The ship was steel plate, but it was old. Stressed. Rusted. Barnacled. This should make a nice, tidy little hole.

Danny fixed the wad on the cold, perspiring hull next to a rib, stuck a blasting cap in it, then ran the wires back to the battery. He'd seen enough explosions to know that this was going to cause some major damage, and it would be immediate. Shrapnel would fly, water would pour in through the hole, he'd have to get his ass out of Dodge, and he'd have to do it in a hurry.

Still holding the flashlight in his teeth, he fixed one wire to a battery terminal, then careful to hold the other wire far away from it, he stood up and played out the wire. He'd touch this sucker off from two compartments down the passageway. The explosion would happen under water—at the most, it would be a loud burp at the surface. By the time the patrol came around in the morning, they'd just find an empty parking spot in the row of mothballed ships.

He grinned at the thought of it, and saliva dripped down his chin. He rubbed his chin on the shoulder of his shirt, but that knocked the flashlight cockeyed. In working his lips to right it, it fell out of his mouth, glass shattered, and everything went dark.

"Shit."

"No kidding," the girl said, then slammed the compartment door.

Danny dove for it, and before she had a chance to turn the rusty dogs down to lock him in, he had the door open and a fistful of her shoulder. He threw her into the compartment, stepped out into the passageway and dogged the door down.

He stood sweating in the dark dampness, listening to her yell and beat ineffective fists against the thick metal door. She was locked in the dark room, not a good place to be, but better her than him. Bitch.

This put an end to his plans of sinking the goddamned ship. Maybe it was just as well. Maybe he'd wait until they were both just a little bit calmer, then he'd open the door and they'd get back into the rowboat, he'd take her home and they'd never have to look at each other again.

The girl pushed against the door with all her weight, but it didn't budge. She knew when she was had. She was locked in tight.

Danny had been fairly easy to find, making all kinds of racket, talking to himself, with the little beam of light flashing all around the place. She'd followed him as best as she could, she even kind of started to get the hang of this place, even in the dark.

Then she saw that he was planning to blow them up.

No way.

In fact, she better disarm that mother right now.

She put her hands out in front of her and walked slowly toward the wall where Danny had squeezed the plastique into a crevice behind the support rib.

But one tennis shoe stepped on the end of the wire the same time the other tennis shoe kicked over the battery. The terminal hit the salty metal deck just inches away from the end of the wire.

Closed circuit.

The blast blew the hole in the side of the ship and it also bent up the bottom of the door to Master Chief Watts' quarters. Danny had only closed one of the six dogs, enough to keep out one skinny little girl, but not enough to keep out the ocean. And it poured in, flooding the ship so fast he barely had time to get out of its way.

Jesus Christ, Danny thought, and began running. The deck slipped and tilted alarmingly right under his feet. The ship was taking on tons of water and it was doing it right fast. He had to get up and get out.

He ran up a ladder but the hatch at the top was welded shut. He backed down, and then had to slog through knee-high water to the next ladder. He made it through the next door, closed it, dogged it, and that bought him a minute or two while he tried a different hatch.

Found one.

Up the ladder.

Locked.

The ship groaned and metal screeched as the old destroyer settled lower in the water, turning onto her side. Danny slipped and slid around, trying to get a grip on the bulkheads, trying desperately to find a way up and out.

"Should have dogged the door properly, Seaman Richards," Master Chief Watts said.

"I meant to," Danny said, "I just didn't think. . ."

"You didn't think," the Master Chief said. "You never think. You're a poor goddamned excuse for a sailor. The worst I've seen."

"We're sinking!" Danny yelled.

"Your shipmates will all die and it's your fault," the Master Chief said. "How many times have I told you that you can't fool the ship?"

Danny pushed past him, but his shoes slipped off the bulkhead and the surface of the water closed over his head. He pushed off and came up, gasping, swimming desperately against the current, looking for a way out, his heart pounding, his eyes bulging in the dark, feeling his way along, finding it harder and harder to breathe. . .

Draft. He felt a draft.

He tried to calm his nerves long enough to ignore the roar of the water and the screech of wrenching metal. He closed his eyes, held his breath and tried to gauge the direction of the breeze.

Left.

He turned and swam with all the stamina he had left, making for the opening. Where there was airflow, there was a way out.

Please God, a way out, and not just an air vent.

It was a hatch, rusted partway open. Danny stuck an arm through, put his foot on the ladder and heaved. The rusted hinge gave a little, but not enough. Water caught up with him, the current raging around his torso. He took a deep breath and hoped that he wouldn't burst a blood vessel with the attempt. He saw red globes in front of his eyes as he grit his teeth and shoved on that rusted hatch with all the strength in his legs and his back, and it gave just a little more. Enough more. Danny made himself as thin as he could and slithered out of the opening.

Outside.

He rewarded himself with a deep breath of fresh air, before the sky exploded into fire.

Shipmates ran past him single file, the heavy snake of a hose under each right arm. Men scrambled frantically trying to keep their footing on the slanted deck. When they slipped, they slid over the side and fell, yelling, into the burning water.

Another fireball in the air.

Another explosion on deck. Pieces of burning metal screamed past him and the blast left him flash-blind and almost deaf. Danny's feet slipped out from underneath him. He grabbed onto the hatch cover and kept himself from going over the side.

"Deploy the lifeboats," the captain's voice hollered over 1-MC. But Danny couldn't see any lifeboats. He just heard the planes dive bombing them. He heard the explosions and saw them light up the night sky behind his clenched eyelids.

"They're bombing the whole fucking fleet," someone yelled, and an explosion of ice-hot metal blinded him and sliced off his legs as clean as a guillotine.

Funny, he felt no pain.

"This is all your fault," Master Chief Watts said. Danny looked up and saw the big man looking down at him.

"My legs. . ." Danny said, and saw them tumble down the slanted deck and fall through the hole that the explosion had left.

"You should have dogged that hatch," Chief Watts said. "Piece of shit sailor if I've ever seen one."

The waterline slid quickly up the deck. Sailors lost their balance trying to scramble up away from the flaming fuel oil that covered the harbor. Some made it as far as the catwalk and held on until their arms gave out, then fell straight down into hell. Others windmilled their arms, saw that they weren't going to make it and just gave up, diving right into it, hoping to swim under it and come up on the far side. Fat chance. The suction of the sinking ship pulled them in, pulled them under, pulled them to their graves.

This ship deserved to go down in glory, and nobody knew it better than the ship herself.

Danny, legless, helpless, watched the water rise. "Help me, Chief," he whimpered.

But the chief wasn't there.

And the explosions had stopped.

The water still rose, but it was a silent starry night and Danny's legs were pinched tight in the partially-opened hatch. Pieces of the girl floating in diesel fuel belched up and out of the opening as the ship went down, violently, powerfully, heavily, sucking all of Danny's secrets down with it.

He struggled, but he knew there was no use to it. The ship was in control. As he had meant to have the ship, it now had him.

Pinned to the deck like an insect, the water rose up over his chest to his chin. He stretched and struggled, but there was no hope, and he knew it even as he tried.

As cold sea water filled his lungs, Danny looked wildly around one last time.

Master Chief Watts knelt next to him. "This ship deserved a courageous ending like she just gave herself, son. But you. . . Well, some men just ain't made to be sailors," he said. "The ship never forgets. You did good to get away the first time, acting the way you did in uniform. Too bad you pressed your luck."

This ship he'd kicked and swore at and sabotaged and finally bombed: she'd invited him in, confused him and then held him underwater while she made herself a courageous exit.

Too bad Danny was her only witness.

As his eardrums imploded and the pressure forced the last of the air from his lungs, Danny finally understood the meaning of respect.

※

Reggie

In those murky days after Reggie's suicide, my mother buzzed through my life like a noisy, nasty fly. When the sedation haze lifted, I found all trace of him erased from the apartment. She'd sent his clothes to the Goodwill, shipped his tools to his brother, packed away our photo album and love letters and put them in the attic.

Just as I was about to swat her, she left.

She meant well, but I would like to have packed Reggie away myself. The deed done, however, I wasn't about to unpack him— I was too fragile.

I was left with a cold and lonely apartment, populated by grief and guilt, tears and heartache.

Ten nights after he died, I turned over in dream-entangled sheets and felt his warm smooth skin. His breath was sweet, like strawberries, and at my touch, he turned me over, snuggled my back and covered my breast with his large, warm hand. I slept easier and less afraid of the night.

I forgot about that dream until about noon the next day when I took my sandwich and apple to the courtyard to watch secretaries in their summer frocks preen and flirt with young executives. I ate my apple first, then reached for the sun-warmed brown bag. At first touch, I remembered the night, and the thrill of his skin on my fingertips. My nipples hardened at the memory and pressed against my clothes as aching soaked my belly and the familiar grief lay heavy in my chest.

Imagination can be cruel, I said, and dropped the apple core on top of the poor sandwich, refolded the bag and threw it away.

Work was no consolation. I couldn't concentrate. I heard his voice in the hall. I saw the back of his head as the elevator door closed. I smelled his after shave in the lobby.

I feigned a headache and went home early, drew a scented bath, lit a candle and soaked until the water chilled. I remembered when he used to join me in the tub.

I turned on classical music and remembered our mutual love for the symphony. I cooked a chicken breast and remembered the orange sauce he created one inspirational snowy day. I wrapped up in the terry robe he bought me for Christmas, crawled between yellow sheets we bought one carefree spring day, and cried myself to sleep.

At two a.m., he was there, snoring softly, his long legs, weighted by huge feet, moving restlessly, like a dreaming puppy.

I reached out, tentatively, fear overcome by longing. Yearning.

Tears came again, but I choked back the sob and pressed my breasts to his back, my tummy to his butt, my thighs to his hamstrings. I wrapped one arm around his torso and let the other slide under his pillow.

I breathed in the campfire scent of him, kissed his neck. He stilled his restless legs, twined his fingers with mine and we both slept.

In the morning, I was alone. I grabbed the pillow with the desperation of a woman afraid for her sanity. It still had the imprint of his head. It still smelled like him. He *had* been here. He *had*.

He came to our bed every night after that. Every night, I tasted his saltiness, smelled his uniqueness, touched him and let his arms enfold me with comfort and tenderness.

But I never heard his voice. I never saw his face. I never looked into his eyes, and I couldn't stand that. One night I forced the issue.

I awoke on a sultry summer night and he was with me, one arm thrown over his face, one hand resting on my thigh. The thick air pressed close.

I felt that hand on my leg and remembered how well that hand knew my reactions, understood my responses. I moved slightly under the fingers; felt them flex.

Reggie made a small noise.

Wide awake now, and aroused by memory, I covered his hand with my own and moved it up my thigh, higher until the black curly hairs on his fingers were indistinguishable from my own.

He turned away, tried to draw his hand back, but I was awash with my idea and not about to let him leave me now. Too long I had been without him. Too long I had been without.

I moved his hand deeper and more forcefully, feeling my heart flutter as his fingers automatically began to probe in the skillful way that was his second nature.

I moaned in pleasure and he tensed, then withdrew his hand.

"Reggie," I said, my heart breaking again, "please."

And he was gone, the light sheet that had covered us slowly sinking, like my passion, to the bed.

I cried until I had no strength. Then I got up, washed my face and made a pot of coffee.

Then I got mad.

I had a right to get over him.

He had no right to string my emotions into a never-ending thread. He needed to stay dead and keep his soft, hairy fingers out of my bed and off of my skin.

I said it. I felt it. I believed it, but it was killing me all the same. I missed him so badly.

When he came back the next night, I hugged him.

The following night, I kicked him and told him to leave. I got up and began to think.

Why was he there? What did he want? Was it something about his suicide? Could I help him on his way? I hurt for him, hated his unrest, vowed to help my man find peace.

The following night I slept fitfully and came wide awake the instant the space next to me began to fill. The covers raised as if pumped full of air. Then he had heat, and texture, then color.

"Reggie," I said, laying a gentle hand on his shoulder. Why did he always face away from me?

He moved. He was not asleep.

"Reggie, look at me. I need to see you, your face, your eyes. Reggie, honey, why are you here? What do you want? Tell me. Show me. Let me help you."

His hand shot out and gripped mine, then he began to fade.

"No," I cried. "Please. Stay."

His hand tightened as if he didn't want to go, but we were both powerless to stop it. I grabbed his shoulder to turn him toward me, but it was too late. My fingers slipped right through him.

Why wouldn't he face me? Had death turned him ugly? Did his face show something in death that it had not shown in life? Was he ashamed? Had he come to make peace with me for something—his suicide, perhaps?—and literally could not face me until I had forgiven him?

To my female intuition, this felt solid, felt right. Of all the wild things I could imagine Reggie doing, suicide was never among them. I never understood. I thought I would never understand. Except now, perhaps, when he needed me to understand. I had to discover the source of his shame, confront him, forgive him and let him go to his reward or his hell—whatever his release was to be.

The next day I opened a bottle of red wine—it goes well with grief—and got the box down from the attic. Our box of history. It was the only thing I had left of Reggie, and if there was a clue, it had to be there. I said a silent prayer and peeled back the wide cellophane tape.

A brown paper lunch sack was right on top. It was filled with the letters he wrote when his Army reserve unit had been called to Panama. For six dark, lonely months, our daily letters crossed in the mail, time lag giving answers to long forgotten questions. I didn't need to look at the letters; they had become part of me. Some day, maybe, when I had forgotten what his handwriting looked like.

Under the bag of letters was our photograph album. I'd pasted in, dated and annotated each fond entry. I didn't need to look at the photograph album again. Some day, maybe, when I had forgotten what he looked like.

I set the album aside and all that was left in the box was an envelope with my name on it. I'd never seen this envelope before.

A sob caught in my chest as I looked at the three things in the box. Mom packed away this envelope. She packed away this envelope and used the letters and photo album as an excuse. Why?

I picked the envelope up by a corner. It had power over me. It had the power to hurt me, I knew it. Maybe it also had the power to heal me. To heal Reggie.

I set it on the coffee table and went to the kitchen for a cup of tea to settle myself. But my mind would not settle. I returned to the living room, choosing to gulp down the glass of wine instead.

There it sat, that cursed envelope, innocent in and of itself, while I viewed it as the instrument that might tear my world apart.

No, that had been a shotgun. This was just an envelope.

I picked it up and ripped it open. A single sheet. I unfolded it.

Jean.

I am lost. Please forgive the spiritual disease that has sucked the life from me. Forgive yourself and don't waste grief on my sorry soul.

Love, Reg.

His suicide note. So there *had* been one.

I would forgive Reggie, no matter his crime. I would forgive myself, for emotions are human.

But I would *never* forgive my mother for keeping this from me.

My face burned with indignation as I reread the note, trying to understand. Spiritual disease? What did that mean? Drugs? No. Gambling? Not to my knowledge. Infidelity? Perhaps.

It was well into the night that my mind stopped spinning. At three o'clock, I dialed my mother's house. Her sleepy voice answered the phone. "Hello?"

"It's me," I said.

"Jean?" I heard her sit up, clearing her throat, looking at the clock. "My God, honey, the time. What is it? Are you okay?"

"Not really. I found Reggie's suicide note."

"Oh." There was more to that flat response than an innocent protecting of one's offspring. "Did you read it?"

"Of course. Did you?" I knew she hadn't, the envelope was unopened.

"No."

"Why did you hide it?"

"How did you find it?"

"Oh, Mother, didn't you know you couldn't hide something like that for long?"

"What did it say?"

I felt no need to tell her.

"I wanted you to heal."

"You were afraid?"

"Yes. For you. For me. For us."

"Why?" It came wailing out of me.

"Jean—how can I answer that? I don't know. Things happen. They just happen."

I waited.

"I can't expect you to understand. I'm not sure I understand myself why I why we—why people do the things we did—they do."

I was no longer sure we were both talking about the same thing. I held on to my silence.

"I never meant to hurt you."

I began to shake. I didn't want to understand. I didn't want to hear more.

"It had nothing to do with you, darling—I had no idea Reggie would—what we did was wrong, but—"

I slammed the phone down. I tore my hair. I screamed, kicked, cried, pounded my belly, trying to stop the hurt, the pain, the awful, awful, awful.

Sometime, I guess, I fell on the bed.

Reggie woke me. I sobbed into his back, tears of pain, tears of sorrow, tears of remorse. Finally, tears of forgiveness.

Then he turned and held me tightly, his strong hands stroking my back. I clung to him as to life—my history tossed and rewritten in a gush of maternal betrayal and confession.

He pulled away and looked deeply into me, his eyes clear and bright, his soul more apparent than ever before.

"I love you," I said.

He closed his eyes in relief and hugged me close. "Even so?" he whispered through my hair, his voice ethereal and echoing.

I nodded, my emotion too terrible to trust.

He sighed and the sigh blew straight through me.

I caught my breath, held the scent of his essence, and when I again breathed, he was gone.

※

Gemphalon

The call came mid-sun. It was like a bell, or a chime, something Gemphalon had never heard before. He put down the piece of slate he'd chosen for the roof of his house and looked east.

Desert wasteland stretched as far as his eyes could see, all the way to the yellow horizon. The suns were at their zenith, crossing overhead, the little one closer this time of year, but no less intense. Gemphalon rotated again, reached for the piece of slate, but then the call came again, scrolled right up the screen of his mind, and it was so clear that he could not ignore it.

He straightened up and looked around. His house was almost finished. His design was sure to attract a suitable mate, and he would be of breeding age by swarm this year. He didn't want to leave his house, because the moment he did, some sexually-mature interloper would move in, make use of it and then make use of Gemphalon's mate when she arrived.

No, he couldn't leave. He wouldn't leave. Swarm was his right, it was his duty. He had spent his entire life preparing for it. He wouldn't miss it, especially not this, his first year.

But he'd been called to the east. He had to go east.

No. He ignored the call, and picked up the piece of slate.

But this call was like no other. It was a hunger so deep that Gemphalon felt weak in its shadow. He was filled with an unidentifiable longing. It was much like the longing for swarm, which had increased steadily in the past few months, only this was a thousand times, a thousand thousand times stronger. This could not be denied.

He *would* deny it. He was preparing for swarm. Its what his greater had done, and his greater before him. It was what every breeding-age male in the colony was doing. The females would come within two weeks, and Gemphalon would be prepared. His house was better than most; he would attract a fine mate.

Then the call washed over him so completely that the slate dropped from his grip and shattered on the ground.

East.

He looked again at his house, and it had lost all importance in his carefully prioritized life. He barely had will enough left to fetch his walking stick before starting out.

First stop was the tree, where he gulped a bubble of water. Within the short minute he paused on what was already his journey, the hunger pawed at him again. As soon as he began walking, it eased into a constant gnaw. No one from the colony accosted him, no one asked him where he was going. Every one was intent on getting ready for swarm. When swarm ended and life settled down to egg tending, someone would ask after him, surely, but until that happened, preparations were the priority and Gemphalon's whereabouts were of no importance.

Gemphalon walked among the toilers of his colony, all his eyes straight ahead, going from certainty into mystery without enough will to stop himself. By the time he had left his clustermates behind, he didn't even doubt that he shouldn't have any doubts. All his priorities had been rearranged. All he thought of was going east. Going east was the only thing that settled his soul. He wanted what was there, though he had no idea of what that was. Something to sate this craving. Everything else would fall into place.

And so it did. Sun after sun, when hunger came upon him, he found an abundant supply of lessers to catch and eat. The occasional tree held a bubble of water, and into his mind began to flow ideas, many ideas, concepts that were above the colony and beyond the stars. Those ideas came in gushes, giving Gemphalon time between flows to try to digest their meanings, although most of it was beyond his ken.

Gemphalon made his way slowly east, eating when hungry, drinking when thirsty, never doubting that those needs would be cared for as he went about his greater purpose, whatever that purpose was to be. For the moment, it was putting one foot in front of the other toward the eastern horizon.

The moons were the nicest. The impulse eased off—not enough to allow doubts to enter, just enough to allow him peace. He squatted in the desert and watched the twin shadows lengthen as first one sun and then the other set over the hills. Then he watched the moon with its slender-shadowed satellites rise, giving the whole landscape a black-and-silver sheen. He secreted lubrication and oiled his joints, then rocked back, locked his hips into place, closed his eyes and shut down so the sleep mystifiers could have their way with him.

When he awoke, the hunger was with him so desperately he barely had time to unlock himself before starting out again toward the east.

The mystifiers had never given him such strange messages in the past. Gemphalon knew nobody who'd had such mystifications. Relating unusual mystifications was a common form of entertainment at the colony, but though unusual in their details, the mystifications all centered around colony life. These, though, were different. These had to do with. . .with. . .cosmic citizenship. Those words popped into his head as clearly as the chime that called him to the east. Gemphalon wished he knew enough to be afraid, but he didn't. He wasn't.

He had no time and energy for fear. He had survived to adulthood, and that was test enough of his wily character. In fact, many of his cluster had survived, a tribute to his greater, who tended them. Many of the greaters ate their lessers instead of nurturing them. Gemphalon was going to be a good greater, feeding his lessers instead of having them feed him.

Next year, maybe, he would have a cluster of his own larvae to tend, and a pang of sorrow over his missed opportunity came upon him. His first swarm, and he would miss it. He would be a lesser for one more year.

He wanted to let his mind wander into the familiar speculation about his mate, what it would feel like to be chosen, and to fertilize her ova. How he would feel as a greater, following the steps of those who had gone before him. The urgings as swarm approached brought with them increasing speculations until that was all any male could think about for weeks before the females arrived. When they did arrive, the males were consumed by the madness. For season after season, Gemphalon watched with his envious clustermates as the greaters went insane with the delirium of it all.

But he couldn't concentrate on that fantasy any more. It was as if swarm had passed, and sanity had returned to the colony, and life was filled with the business of eating, sleeping and tending, with no time to think about mating. He thought only of something fine waiting for him in the east.

He saw the dust trail of another long before he saw the other's form. This one was coming from the southwest, and soon their trails would converge. Gemphalon took a tighter grip on his walking stick. He may have to defend himself. But when they met on the trail, there were no words between them, neither of greeting nor of challenge. They just walked during the sunlight hours and squatted side by side during the moonlight hours. Gemphalon was filled with questions, but they were not for this being, so he held them inside.

The following sun another joined them, and within the week, they were a silent marching brigade, headed in a long trail, not quite single file, through the desert, toward something extraordinary.

The horde of females passed by, boiling a dust storm behind them, but none of the pilgrims gave them a second glance.

Neither did Gemphalon, and he thought it was mighty strange.

The terrain began to change from hot, dusty desert, until there were a few trees and bushes. Water was more plentiful, and the lessers were of a different type, and far more plentiful. Soon there was grass beneath their feet, and occasionally, bogs. Gemphalon had never imagined such abundant water. He never failed to oil himself every moonrise, because though the sand was hard on him, the dampness was worse.

They saw others who didn't look like them, who sat and watched their parade, but there was no terror among the pilgrims, and they were not accosted. Still others joined them, others of Gemphalon's type, with subtle changes to their color and structure. And no one spoke, intent only on the journey, yet the level of excitement grew with each freshening of the scenery. Every sun brought mind-expanding wonders, until Gemphalon felt that he was silent merely because he had no words to express his amazement. There was barely room left for anticipation, he was so filled with astonishment during the sun and mystifications during the moon.

But the aspect and nature of the pull was changing, and Gemphalon gravitated toward the minor course corrections and the others followed. He knew they neared their destination. The others knew it, too, and while they didn't quicken their pace, they put more energy into their footsteps.

Ten sunrises plus another eight had them weary and approaching the top of a long hill. They made little headway every sun because none of them was used to walking. They weren't designed for long distance travel on foot. And they were desert-dwellers. Soggy ground, morning dew and rain all took its toll on their exoskeletons. They lost a few by the wayside, and Gemphalon hoped that they'd regain their health and eventually continue the trek. If they were like him, they would have no choice. Gemphalon would have crawled if he had to.

But cresting this tall hill was a trial for the whole line of marchers. The hill was bathed in grass and wildflowers, it smelled of a freshness that Gemphalon had never known. In fact, he discovered portions of his sensory receptors that had never been activated. The grasses were filled with all manner of lessers, and the entire troupe ate their fill, then locked down in exhaustion, well before the moon. They would crest the hill the following sun. Surely going down would be easier.

The mystifiers woke Gemphalon mid-moon. His eyes extruded slowly and looked around. All the way down the hill, along the pathway, his comrades were squatted and turned off for the night. There were no sounds except for a soft breeze that ruffled the tall grasses.

He unlocked his hips and stood up, grabbed his walking stick and headed for the crest of the hill. He felt, or perhaps the mystifiers had told him, that the thing which pulled him lay just on the other side. He wanted to see it.

The going was slow, and he missed the comforting sounds of his companions. Thoughts strayed differently as he walked under the moon, and he wondered if the females would swarm if he and his traveling companions settled in a region such as this. Would the females object? Could they find the new colony? Could the larvae be brought up in such a climate? Would their lessers survive?

The terrain leveled off as Gemphalon contemplated all these things, and he walked through the darker shadows of trees that topped the hill, anticipation like nothing he had ever known working on him. He left scent periodically to guide the others, and when he broke through the other side of the woods, he could see down into the valley.

What he saw astonished him beyond imagination.

There were stars in the ground. The ground itself was carved into geometric shapes, and there were structures, square structures, not round as he and his people made.

Gemphalon was startled and alarmed and charmed and intrigued all at once. He didn't know what to think about any of it. He squatted, locked himself, and waited for the sun.

As the suns rose, the colony in the valley came to life. Gemphalon, resisting the urge to head down the hill ahead of his mates, waited, still locked in place, and he watched.

They were strange creatures, and they went about doing strange things.

Both suns were high before the first of the travelers met Gemphalon at the top of the hill, and they too, were stunned with the sight spread below them. For as far as they could see, both north and south in the valley, the vegetation was broken into different colored squares. Unlikely looking bipeds wrapped in colors moved about at random but with the stride of purpose.

Gemphalon's traveling companions lined the mountaintop and locked themselves into place, eager to be down there to quench the thirst that had compelled them to make this journey, yet cautious of the unknown. They stayed there for the rest of the sun, none of them leaving their posts long enough, even, to eat. When the stars came out of the ground, there were gasps all around, and they began to talk among themselves for the first time.

The chatter lasted almost all moon long. Gemphalon listened to the speculation and the wonder in their voices. There were no arguments, no fights. His breed was quick to anger and just as quick to kill and eat an antagonist, but they were subdued by the enormity of their quest. They talked quietly, well into the moon, and in the early morning, a cloud appeared, sending water down upon them.

All the travelers woke at this unpleasantry and got busy lubricating themselves. Then, as suns lightened the sky, Gemphalon unlocked himself, took up his walking stick and became the first to head down the mountain.

The others followed, single file.

Avonia was the first to spot them coming down the mountain, and she trilled in thrilled anticipation. Her work mates looked where she pointed, and there, like a line of ants, the local citizens came down the mountain trail. Avonia had served on a hundred or more of these biological upstep commissions, but seeing the best of the species answer their summons was always a wonderful sight.

This project was different, because this planet was a decimal planet, and therefore all the life forms were experimental. Nobody expected that it would be an insectile life form that would exhibit moral behavior first, and this was a tremendous surprise. Many long nights were spent discussing this upstep project, and it was difficult to create consensus for the obvious answer.

Regardless, all the preparation, the permissions, the petitions, the bureaucratic nonsense and the hassle of planetary administration was lost in the joy of seeing the best of the best walk, slowly and with some discomfort, down the mountain on what would be the last leg of their arduous journey.

What lay ahead for them was so wonderful that Avonia could barely contain her excitement. These creatures would soon become people—real people. Their lives would transform completely, and they would have so much, *be* so much more. And they had no idea. They would come in afraid, as usual, and reluctant, as usual, but when they were released to go back to their colonies to affect radical change and improve their way of life, they would be elated. Their spirits would soar for years. For generations. Avonia had seen it, time and time and time again.

She was particularly intrigued with this task, because on all previous assignments, they had worked with mammals. She had no idea how it would work with the insects. Or insect-like creatures, which was the truth of it.

"Avonia," her supervisor said. "Back to work now."

She knew they would be watching her. She had a tendency to go a little bit overboard, she knew it. She'd been reprimanded in the past by getting too close to the pilgrims as they were headed to the chambers for treatment. But they were so afraid, most of them, most of the time, and there wasn't enough counseling for them. Nobody spent the time to sit down and explain to them what was about to happen, and why they shouldn't be afraid.

She understood her superiors' reasoning for this. It was almost like sacrificing the one for the good of the whole. The process that would be effected in the chambers would upstep the indigent creatures' genetic material, and that would bring expanded awareness and spiritual potential, but it lacked wisdom. Wisdom came with experience, and it was only after several generations that wisdom made its appearance. The personal touch could never be passed along, unfortunately, so in the quest for expedience and so as to minimize trauma, the locals were herded into the chambers, recombined with the upstep genetic plasm, and released to return to their colonies. All without explanation, all without counseling of any kind.

"It has never made a difference," she was told when she complained. "It has never helped. These are but animals, Avonia. We're making them human, but genetic material does not make for immediate morality and instant ethics. That has to come from within them. And social evolution is a slow process. You cannot rush it."

Avonia thought they were probably right, which is why they were her superiors. But still, her heart went out to the pilgrims, especially when she saw that they were afraid. Afraid and not in control of their actions.

She went back to work, weeding vegetables, but her mind wasn't completely on it. She kept glancing up to gauge their progress. It was slow progress, but then they weren't built for this type of traveling. Surely they were weary. Would the garden administration even feed them? Or offer them beds? She didn't know.

But she did admire the way the leader of the group held his head up and strode with great purpose. This creature seemed unafraid, and bravely led his fellows into the garden to confront their destiny. Avonia felt a kinship with him. She, too, was unafraid, and always had been. Sometimes what people in the gardens did wasn't exactly the way she would do things if she had the power. So she circumvented the rules a little bit and made things better.

It got her into trouble all right, but it wasn't serious trouble, and Avonia knew in her soul that she had done the right thing.

Yet the supervisors were wise to keep their eye on her. She wasn't above doing something stupid. Her wisdom didn't quite match her energy level. She was young and impetuous, but her heart was in the right place.

She kept on weeding.

By noontide meat, the pilgrims were almost to the valley floor. She went to the supervisor and asked that she be chosen to escort the leader to the chamber.

The supervisor looked long and hard at Avonia before responding. Then he merely nodded, and went on with his meal. Avonia's face flushed with excitement, and she went back to her place, though she no longer had an appetite.

Escorting the leader was a privilege. This meant that she was again back in the good graces of the administration, and she was once more allowed to prove her reliability. If she continued to make good, solid, sound decisions, she would again begin to advance her status. This was a wonderful opportunity.

She finished her meal early and went back to the vegetable garden, weeding with increased vigor, anticipation fueling her energy.

She was also the first one to put down her hoe and begin the procession line to greet the newcomers, lining the path they were to take so that they didn't scatter and become lost and disoriented. The garden was a marvel, but it could be confusing to those who didn't understand the layout, particularly the concentric rings of pathways with their interconnecting spokes. Anyway, she got there early, and when Gemphalon, the leader, first came into the garden, she began the applause that would welcome home the whole group.

She saw the mesmerizing effect of the summons drop from their eyes the moment they stepped into the garden, and saw the fear take its place. That was another thing. Couldn't the Powers lower the level gradually? It was like these innocents suddenly found out that they had been sleep walking for months and had traveled halfway across the planet, only to wake in a completely foreign land without an idea as to how they got there, why they were there or anything about the strange species of people they discovered upon awakening. It was cruel, Avonia thought, and she would change that system if she could.

When she could. As she moved up in planetary administration, she would effect some of those changes.

But for now, she saw the fear take hold of Gemphalon the leader, and she clapped harder, and cheered him, and tried sending out all the psychic signals she knew how to send in order to bring him some peace. But she didn't know if insect people received psychic signals, and she didn't know if clapping and cheering might even seem like an act of aggression to them.

To his credit, he didn't bolt. He just faltered a few steps, and then kept going on down the road, lined all the way to the governor's mansion by garden helpers clapping and cheering their arrival.

She tried to make eye contact with him, but all his eyes were on the ground, and he just kept steadfastly walking.

He was hers. He was the best that this planet had to offer, the most highly evolved so far, and she was going to escort him to the chambers.

She was in love.

The soft-shell bipeds put down their tools and watched the procession down the hill, and slowly Gemphalon and his weary travelers made their way toward them. Gemphalon got himself ready for confrontation, but when they finally made it to the colony, the bipeds began slapping their extremities together in greeting. Gemphalon lifted his mandible and led his group right into the midst of them. As he did so, he felt the urgency of the call diminishing. He had nothing to replace it but fear, but he wasn't about to succumb to that. They had made a mighty pilgrimage, and they all needed to stand tall and accept their fate.

The noisy crowd lined a pathway, and it was obvious where Gemphalon was to go. He heard them, but could make no sense of their communication devices. He bravely followed the pathway, which ended at the steps of a huge structure, the likes of which Gemphalon had never seen. It had square corners and an angled upward path. He stopped at the bottom of those steps and waited. Surely a king or a god would come out, and then they would receive their fate.

But nobody came out. The stragglers of his troupe continued to accumulate until there was a great lot of them all together in the area in front of the structure, and the suns were going down. The bipeds brought stars on sticks and set them around the pathways. Gemphalon, not knowing what else to do, locked down and shut himself off.

The mystifiers came to him immediately, filling his mind with all manner of wondrous visions. Gemphalon, even in his dream, tried to pull away and stop it, but it was as if a gentle, calm hand was laid upon his fevered forehead, and he relaxed and let them talk with him.

An uplifting, they said. For the lessers. More brain power, larger spirit receptor glands, healthier, less warlike. Gemphalon didn't understand all of what they tried to tell him, but when he awoke to the sunrise, he had a profound feeling of being a necessary part of something enormous.

But still when the soft bodies came to get him in the early sun, he resisted. Fear descended upon Gemphalon. He screeched a war cry, and his brethren awoke, tiny wings emerged from within their shells, and they sprayed scent and flapped their ineffectual wings with dangerous emotion. It didn't seem right, this war cry, with these softbodies that appeared to be peaceful. The aggressors retreated, and Gemphalon felt shame that he had reacted that way, but he knew no other way to react.

They could only want to eat him. What other use would they have? He was a lesser, after all.

The crowd silenced in a wave, and Gemphalon swiveled his head to see the great doors open. Out stepped a tall blue softbody. It was a king. Or a god. But nobody bowed, nobody fell down, everybody just turned their attention to him.

He spoke into Gemphalon's mind just as the original call to the east had come to him.

"Be not afraid. You and your fellows have exhibited the finest genetic traits of your species," the king said. "It is now time for those traits to be enhanced. You have been chosen and gathered here in order to upstep the biological status of your race. Please. Go in peace with your handlers. They will treat you well."

Gemphalon felt a touch, and looked down to see a small, light blue softbody. "You are their leader, Gemphalon," she said into his mind. "The rest look to you for your example of bravery, so you shall be first. Come." As it seemed he had little choice, he followed her, but he had grave reservations, and wished he could be elsewhere. He didn't understand any of it; it was all new and horribly frightening.

But the small blue softbody had an attractive scent of her own, and Gemphalon, not immune to the awakening within his body that he attributed to the time of swarm, followed. She led him to a side door of the big building, and with a final glance at his fellow travelers who stood agape at his display of calm compliance, he entered the hall.

"Do you know what a cocoon is?" the softbody asked, her voice soft and cool in his mind.

Gemphalon nodded. Of course knew what a cocoon was.

"This is much like a cocoon, and you will sleep for a short time. During that time, your life plasm will be harvested, combined with that of my species, and then replanted into your system. You will make a transformation, but it will not hurt. I promise."

"Swarm?" he asked.

Her eyes were flush with her head, but even so, they could exhibit much emotion. "Kind of," she said, an understanding look entering those eyes. "Swarm will be different from now on, at least for you." She put a hand on his arm and led him to a table. "Can you lie down?"

"Lie down?"

"Well, then, get up on this table and make yourself comfortable, whatever that means."

Gemphalon stepped up onto the table with the aid of his stick, squatted and locked. The softbody looked at his position. "Are you comfortable?"

"Comfortable?"

"Can you stay like that for a long period of time?"

Gemphalon nodded.

"Don't be afraid. I will be with you again when you wake. Now sleep," she said, and though he had just awakened from a moonsleep, Gemphalon felt a thick drowse come over him. He barely noticed that she was with him on the table, and turning him, and pressing herself to him before the mystifiers came and stole his mind.

Avonia knew she was going to get into big trouble for this, but she just couldn't help herself.

She had taken many indigenous creatures to the chambers, and the rules to follow were precise and clear. It always happened the same way. Avonia liked to think she added a little of her personality to the task, in soothing them, and talking to them. Sometimes they were on a compatible communication channel and could actually converse, but most of the time, she had to pantomime and move slowly and calmly with efficiency, and from that, they gathered that she knew her business, and that always put them somewhat at ease, though they had no idea what was happening to them. Other than being a little bit extra nice, and maybe making a little joke now and then, she followed the outlined procedure exactly.

Except this time, and she knew she would get into big trouble.

Just as she was getting herself out of trouble.

Oh well. The deed was done.

Generally, she brought the creature into the chamber, got them on the table and began the anesthetic. When they were asleep, she placed a small open container of the new life plasm to be combined with their genetic information, then initiated the cocoon.

She didn't know how it worked, but in two planet weeks, she went back, disentangled the genetically-enhanced creature from the strands of silk that the cocooning process always creates, discarded the empty vial of plasm, and gently awoke the new citizen of the cosmos.

Usually, all of those who had made the pilgrimage awoke at about the same time, they were fed and then released to make the journey home, carrying with them a whole new biology with which to populate the planet.

It was a simple project. This genetic upstep was perhaps the most important thing that they did on every evolving planet, yet it took so little of their time and energy. The rest of the time the team had hard work, preparing for the day when the hundreds of thousands of biologically superior offspring of these initial implant recipients instinctively came back seeking knowledge.

The garden had to be ready for that teaching project.

And that had been Avonia's job, readying the gardens, slowly moving up the hierarchy of administration, taking two steps forward and one step back, always impetuous, eager, and with barely a shred of the patience that the elders were always admonishing her to cultivate along with her crops.

And here she was again, acting impetuously.

Oh well.

There was something heartfully appealing about this large, young, slow-moving creature. His nature spoke to her, both figuratively and literally, in that they were fortuitously channeled on the same frequency, so they could communicate. His was a simple mind, free of the extraneous silliness that seemed to overwhelm her thought processes most of the time. She readied him, and wondered at the product of this transformation. From insectile to human. He would never be totally mammal, but his value system would change with his enlarged spirit receptor. What would that be like? Instead of laying thousands of eggs as insects did, they would have nuclear families. How would that work?

What would they eat, if they didn't eat each other?

The questions came at her faster than she could ignore them, and then before she knew what she was doing, she had an overwhelming compulsion to add her *personal* life plasm to Gemphalon's, and to be an actual part of this extraordinary occurrence, not a mere bystander. She knew that the elders would be very angry, and it could in fact get her expelled from the life implantation program she was interning for. But it would be an experience like no other. It would be a radical achievement, and perhaps change the way that things would be done from then on out. Who knew? Maybe she would be cited for bravery and given a promotion.

And she had no idea what would actually happen to her. She knew that Gemphalon would become more like her, but would she become more insectile?

The reality of that eventuality flitted through her mind as she had already initiated the process, just as she had entwined her limbs with his, as the anesthesia stole her consciousness. Her last thought had just a twinge of panic in it.

Oh boy, I've really done it this time, she thought.

The mystifiers had some unusual tricks this time.

They took him places he didn't know existed, places that eventually he began to suspect were within him. It took Gemphalon a long time to realize that he was awake and aware, and that the mystifiers were not still spinning strange stories to his inner sleep. He had been going on a guided tour, it seemed, of himself. He was awake—his eyes were open—but he felt disoriented and odd. He was not the same as he was when he first entered the chamber, got on the table per the request of the small softbody, and fell asleep.

Everything about him was different.

He looked down at all his various parts, and they all appeared to be the same. He felt as if he hadn't eaten in a long time, and the smell of food attracted his attention right away. On a table to his right was a vast array of things, and with difficulty, he stepped down from the table. He took a moment to lubricate his joints—he had been idle too long—and then he viewed the things that had been laid upon the table.

There were a variety of green things, things that had grown. There were soft-shelled things and green things and brown things and things that smelled pungent. Nothing moved.

He picked up and smelled a variety of objects, and one small round purple thing looked intriguing, so Gemphalon bit it.

Sweet juice squirted into his mouth, and he gobbled the fruit down greedily, then looked for more.

He found an abundance of delicious foods on the table, things he never would have tried eating before. Before, he ate lessers, and the quicker they moved, the tastier they were.

But now he seemed to have lost his taste for the lessers, and gained an appreciation for things that grew out of the ground.

How odd.

Starvation temporarily sated, he looked around for the next adventure, or an exit or something, and he saw the small blue softbody wrapped in a protective covering, lying on a different table.

He approached her and felt a disturbance in his stomach. At first he thought it was the foreign food, but as he got closer to her, he felt glad to see her, as he would a long-ago friend. He felt affection and concern. She looked pale and weak. Unconscious. The last time he had seen her, she was vibrant and sparkly, competent and authoritative.

He touched her, and her eyes opened, but they didn't see.

A moment later, those dark blue eyes focused on him and she shrank away from him in fear.

He took a step back in surprise. He hadn't frightened her before.

She clutched the blanket to her chest and drew away to the end of the table, fearful eyes on his every move.

"I won't hurt you," he said, but what came back to him on the circuit was a horrible mind-chatter that screeched and scratched, so he shut it down. He looked around for help, but there was no one. Just the two of them. He went back to the table, picked up a piece of fruit and brought it back to her. She ate as if she was starving, the juice running down her chin and dripping onto the blanket. He brought more food, and the more she ate, the calmer she became.

Gemphalon was pleased. He felt a compelling attachment to this softbody, and he didn't know why. He just knew he didn't want her to be hungry or to be afraid.

He approached her slowly, but the terror returned, so he backed away again.

Then the door opened, and the king, or god, or whatever he was, the tall blue being in charge walked in, followed by a half dozen small blue softbodies.

"Greetings," he said into Gemphalon's mind. "I know you don't appreciate the significance of the change that has transpired in you, but it is vast. Your job now is to go forth and procreate. Your progeny will be of such a superior order that all others will either be admixed or else will expire. You and the other brave souls who made this treacherous journey have been noted on universe records, and your contribution to the mortal races of this planet will not go unrewarded in time. Go forth, now, and bear offspring vigorously."

Gemphalon didn't have any idea what he was talking about. He only understood that he was free to go.

In response, he looked at the softbody.

"Ah, Avonia," the tall man said. "Such youth. Such curiosity. This has never happened before, and it will take us time to study the effects of your joint life plasma exchange. Clearly, you received the better byproduct. Perhaps her condition can be reversed. We have yet to find out."

"I'll take her," Gempahlon said.

"Oh, no, no, you are to go back and breed with your own species."

"I will care for her," Gemphalon said simply. He would not leave without the little soft one who had in some manner sacrificed herself for him.

The tall one turned to another small softbody like Avonia and they spoke quietly. "Bold. . .success. . .remarkable. . ." were the only words Gemphalon understood, and he gathered that they were all somehow pleased with his request. He looked back at Avonia, and she seemed to be less afraid of him than of the others.

"Avonia will remain with us," the tall one said.

"No," Gemphalon responded, and he was, to his own amazement, firm on the matter. He thought about his colony, and how empty it seemed. Far, far away in more ways than one, and destitute. He thought that Avonia would add life to the colony. He thought Avonia would add to his life.

The tall one looked at him in silence for a prolonged moment, then said, "We will confer." With that, he exited the room, closing the door behind him.

Something was wrong with Avonia's mind, but she couldn't identify it. She remembered, or thought she did, being able to understand the things that went on around her, and for now, nothing that was within her sight or smell or taste or anywhere in her range of reality made sense. It was discombobulated, disjointed, meaningless and frightening.

She felt guilty. She felt that punishment—for what, she didn't know—was imminent. Harsh punishment. Strong, severe, life-threatening punishment.

She thought she might be eaten.

Strange creatures were speaking in foreign tongues, and now and then it felt as though someone entered her head, poked around and then left.

After the tall dangerous one and his fierce cohorts left, she took a deep breath and tried to make sense of it all. It seemed that understanding was just around the corner. It was something she had had, but had been taken from her, and she didn't know how or why.

The big bug knew, though. He had fed her, and then he protected her from the giant. For that, she wouldn't kill him. If she even could.

There. That was it, wasn't it? The tiniest thought of things the way they used to be—before what?—that kindness, that sensitivity. She used to have that. She used to have nice thoughts about others, and now it just seemed like so much excess baggage.

Eat or be eaten, that's how it was, and to think anything else is mere foolishness.

But right now, she had to wait for the bug, because it was somehow in control of their escape.

Gemphalon would have liked to sit for a season and contemplate all the new thoughts, concepts, ideas and emotions he seemed to have acquired. There was an entirely new structure to his perception of things, and he needed some time to sort through it, in his careful, methodical manner, and come to terms with the discovery.

But he hadn't the luxury. The soft thing, Avonia, the elder called her, approached him with wariness and urgency. He knew that she must be desperate indeed to come to him when she was so afraid.

He would never hurt her, but she apparently didn't know that, and he didn't know how to tell her. He tried opening his mind to her again, but there was just that awful screeching static, so he closed it again.

She hesitated in her slow approach when he did that, but it didn't stop her.

He wished he knew what the elder was doing, or going to say. He was clearly free to go, but he had taken a protective stance over this Avonia, and he would not falter.

Strange that he felt like succumbing to the authority of this elder. He had never felt that before.

Avonia came still closer, mindless fear on her face. He squatted quietly, motionless, waiting for her. He wanted to touch her. He remembered, vaguely, being locked in place on the table when she had touched him, and in his memory, her touch had been so confident, so gentle, so compassionate, when he had been so afraid.

He wanted to touch her like that now. But he dared not. She was making forward progress on her own.

As she came nearer to him, a level of excitement grew in him. There were odd emotions surrounding this young thing, as if she were a part of him in some way. He could no more leave her here than he could leave a piece of his body.

But what if they told him she had to stay?

He pulled his mandible down to his chest. Then he, too, would stay.

But what if they wouldn't let him?

Avonia crept around on her hands and knees until she was in front of him. She stood up on her knees and held her extremities together. Then with what must have been a tremendous force of will, she entered his mind with one crystal clear concept: "We go now." Then the static came back and she shut down the communication.

Of course, he thought. He needed no approval. He unlocked his hips, quickly lubricated himself while she watched with rapt attention, picked up his walking stick and walked out of the room, out of the building and into the bright mid-sun.

The elder was nowhere to be seen. Those of Avonia's breed stopped their work and waved, and called, but Avonia clung tightly to Gemphalon's extremity, and without faltering a step, he strode along the path, past those who shouted, and on out of the garden, up the side of the hill.

No one followed them.

They stopped halfway up the side of the hill the first moon. Gemphalon, not designed for long walking, was of particularly poor design for walking uphill. It had taken him less than half a sun to walk down, but it would take two suns to walk back up.

Avonia walked by his side, and when he locked down for the moon, she sat next to him on the ground, and together they watched the stars come out of the ground in the garden.

The next sun they crested the hill, and the garden was lost to view.

When that happened, a transformation came over Avonia. She made unnatural sounds with her mouth, and she ran around with her extremities flapping. She ran around Gemphalon in circles, and she lay on the ground in the grass and rolled around. He had no understanding for her actions; he merely kept walking. They had a long way to go. She ran here and there, but never got out of his sight.

He worried about her at first, then realized that she was all right; she would come back to him, and she did. They were tied together in some cosmic fashion, and she would always be drawn back to him, just as he could never leave her.

He thought of her living in his colony, but as he could no longer remember the colony that clearly, placing her within that society made no sense. If she didn't fit in there, they would simply make their home someplace else. He had ideas about building her a house. A fine, stable, substantial house. And he would provide for her. He wasn't certain yet about the things she would eat, but the desert was full of wonder, and there would surely be things to her liking there.

Would there be things to his liking there? His tastes seem to have changed. Perhaps they could grow the plants they liked to eat, right next to their house.

As the suns dipped below the horizon, Avonia brought him a handful of small round red things. She ate one, and then he ate one, and it was good. She took him to where they were growing in a field, and together in the lengthening shadows, they ate their fill.

Gemphalon felt a kinship, a growing closeness with his odd little softbody. He felt a profound affection for the inept, vulnerable little creature.

They traveled for four suns, finding food when they needed, resting during the moons, Avonia always sleeping at Gemphalon's feet. Every day, Gemphalon's fantasy grew more distinct, as they neared their destination, he knew how he would provide for her. He began to think of her as his mate, although surely they would be incompatible when it came to raising lessers. That didn't even matter to him any more. Odd. That which had been of overwhelming importance to him at the colony, now seemed almost barbaric. He remembered what the elder had told him about going forth and multiplying, but that was no longer his destiny. Tending thousands of eggs every year no longer appealed.

No. He wanted to learn to communicate with the little blue female who had given him his spirit.

During the fifth moon, Gemphalon woke. Avonia was shaking, and her eyes leaked. She clung to his leg and he put his hand on her head, his heart breaking for whatever it was that hurt her, but he didn't know how to fix it. Her pitiful mewing strengthened his resolve to take care of her. This traveling was no life for a fragile female like this. We'll pick up the pace, he thought. She needs a home.

The call came mid-moon. It was like a bell, or a chime, or something Avonia had never heard before.

She didn't know what it meant, only that she could not ignore it. She could not disobey it. She dare not.

And, in fact, she didn't want to.

Yet she couldn't leave the big creature who had rescued her from that place, and who took such good care of her.

Well, yes, she could leave him.

Loyalty, while a concept she vaguely remembered, seemed like such a waste of energy.

They approached. She had to go.

She touched the creature and he awoke. She began to tell him about the call, but she had no words, and then the last of her emotion rose up like a giant bubble that at first cut off her air, and then rose up her throat to explode in a spasm of sobs and tears. She cried all that there was to cry, and when that was gone, so was the rest of her humanity.

She could hear them now, thundering closer.

She stood, all thoughts of Gemphalon completely erased. Somewhere in the back of her consciousness she recognized his presence, but that was all. He was no threat, therefore he didn't exist.

Avonia stood straight and tall, chest out, chin up, eyes wide open, and she waited to be absorbed. She saw it from a long ways off on the horizon, and waited with calm restraint. It moved fast, as fast as the wind, and she felt electricity crackle about her as it neared, a cloud of boiling dust like a small tornado.

The screeching static in her mind focused into voices, a million or more voices, chattering their excitement, and involuntarily, she began to chatter as well, her mind merging with theirs long before they scooped her up into their whirlwind and headed for the next colony of males.

Swarm.

Heaven.

Gemphalon watched her go, his dreams crushed, his heart broken, his future a vast wasteland stretched out like the desert before him.

Chasing after her was not an option; the females fairly flew in their hormonal cluster, and he was but a flat-footed, slow witted, dirt-simple male. He watched the whirlwind and luxuriated in its fragrance until it was out of sight.

He missed Avonia, but most of all, he grieved for her more immediate destiny. She may have thought she was one of them, but she wasn't. She was different. She was a softbody. She would be eaten.

He lifted his walking stick and began again the long journey back to his colony. In his mind's eye he tried to visualize exactly what was going on there in his absence. They would be egg tending. They would be jealous and fighting, stealing and eating each others' lessers.

It seemed so horrible. So difficult. How could he possibly change anything there?

Who would he talk with? How could he make sense of the new thoughts, feelings, insights he was having without someone who could understand? He had an overpowering need to share this information. But there was no one to listen.

He had a mission, he reminded himself. For the eventual good, for the ultimate good of his colony and all others. The life of the one was not as important as the lives of the many. But that was a vague concept at best.

What he did understand was that he had been changed. For the first time, he felt loneliness. Profound loneliness. He was a solitary pilgrim and there would be no companionship back at the colony.

He walked on, trying not to question the gift he had been given, the gift that had created a different hunger inside him. This was not a hunger that could be satisfied by walking a thousand or more miles.

This was a hunger that could only be satisfied by—he didn't know what, he only sensed that it would burn him as long as he was alone.

He looked at the vast wasteland of the desert before him and knew, with a spirit-crushing certainty, that he was to serve his kind, but he would serve in isolation.

He wondered if, in their best of intentions, they knew what they had done to him.

He kept walking.

✳

The Shyanne Letters

Paul snapped open the newspaper to the personals ads, took a quick glance around the coffee shop to make sure nobody was close enough to see what he was doing, folded the paper down to a manageable size, took out his pen, and began to read.

Nothing. . . Nothing. . . Nothing.

They all wanted guys who were "fit" or "financially secure" or "emotionally available." Paul wasn't fit, wasn't financially secure, and he didn't know what emotionally available was, but he was pretty sure he wasn't it. What he was, was lonely. And horny, although it had been so long since he'd had sex, he sometimes wondered if his idea of being horny wasn't just that—an idea. Most of all, he was just flat-out lonely.

Wait. Here's one.

Paul's heart began to pound. He'd never seen an ad like this before.

> I'm so lonely
> and so afraid.
> Write to me, please.
> Shyanne

There was a local post office box number.

Writing was Paul's job. He wrote technical how-to manuals for the computer illiterate, but it was still writing. In fact, he could write better than he could call and leave an off-the-cuff message on the usual voice mail things.

The coffee shop had a card rack. Carrying the paper with him so somebody didn't steal it, he squeezed between tables and chairs and picked a nice blank-inside card with purple flowers on the outside.

Then he bumped his way back to his seat, mopped his forehead and picked up the pen.

His hand trembled.

This was no ordinary woman. But then he wasn't looking for an ordinary woman. The ordinary women who placed these ads were not for him. He'd tried placing ads himself, but his size always put women off. He always felt if somebody ever took the time to get to know him, they'd see that he wasn't his fat, he really wasn't.

He went back up to the counter and got a croissant and a scone and two big spoonfuls of strawberry jam, then sat back down and thought about what to say.

Shyanne. What a beautiful name.

He indulged for a moment in visions of exquisite prose and poetry passing between them, warming their hearts, soothing their tortured souls, meeting after an extended time, recognizing each other across a crowded park ala the "Maria" sequence in West Side Story. She was small and blonde, petite and shy, and he would be wearing a brand new blue suit that brought out the color in his eyes. He'd have a huge bouquet of flowers, and she would be searching the crowd, her beautiful eyes restlessly searching, and when she saw him, she would smile and the world would light up.

She'd step down and into his arms and he would pick her up and owing her around, flower petals flying as they laughed

By the time they met, they would know each other so well, they could go right to the preacher. He could even propose to her through the mail.

He dunked the end of his croissant into the jam, mushed it around then stuffed half of it into his mouth. While he chewed, he thought.

Might as well be honest, he thought. No sense starting this relationship out on a lie.

He licked the jam from his fingers, wiped his hands and mouth on a napkin, then picked up the pen again.

I'm lonely, too, but I'm not afraid.

Hmmm. Good start. He munched down the rest of the croissant, went back for more coffee, more jam, then started in on the scone.

By the time he was finished, his table was a mess of crumbs and slopped coffee, but the card was beautiful. It said: *I'm lonely, too, but I'm not afraid. Share your burden. Your way of reaching out is as beautiful as your name. —Paul* He added his address, then sealed it in the envelope, addressed it, bought a stamp from the cashier, and dropped it into the box on the way to work.

As soon as the letter box door clanged shut, anxiety hit. He wondered if it sounded too fey, the way he worded it. He worried that she'd get so many responses she wouldn't choose his. He worried that somebody else would respond that he was afraid, too, and they would have that in common, closing him out.

He dragged depression and anxiety around with him for three days.

On the fourth day, he came home from work and there was a lavender envelope in his mailbox. The return address said simply, "Shyanne."

He was afraid to open it.

See, Shyanne? I am afraid, too.

He took the card into the kitchen and propped it up against the microwave while he boiled a pot of spaghetti, browned a half dozen Italian sausages, microwaved spaghetti sauce right in the jar and threw it all together in a big mixing bowl. He toasted a split loaf of frozen garlic bread, then took his dinner to the living room. With Shyanne's card set carefully out of the way of any splattering red sauce, he ate.

When finished, he sat back against the couch, burped quietly, and felt settled and ready for whatever she had to say. Amazing how a little food could take the edge off anxiety.

Oh, Paul. Are you really as sensitive as you sound? My fear is that no one will ever understand me, that no one will ever understand my loneliness. Could you? Would you? —Shyanne.

The answer to all of the above was yes. *Yes!*

Paul felt a tiny flowering of hope, and it felt a lot like fear. It also felt a little bit like indigestion. Or maybe hunger.

After eating a pint of Jamocha Almond Fudge, he again put pen to paper.

I do understand, Shyanne. I am not that good with words, but if I could hold you for just one long moment, I believe our souls would touch, communicate, and perhaps we would both find strength and understanding. —Paul.

By return mail, another envelope.

Paul, if I asked you, would you loan me money? If I needed you to fly to—say Missouri, would you? Could you devote yourself to me, body and soul, for ever? Could you do what I ask, love me without reservation, without condition, without restraint? Dare I hope? —Shyanne

Without hesitation, Paul opened his wallet, withdrew five twenty dollar bills, folded them into a blank piece of paper, wrote "Paul" as the outside return address on the envelope, and put it back in the mailbox. It was no more than he would spend taking her out to a nice dinner and a movie.

For the next three days, Paul refined his fantasies.

She wore tiny little satin ballet slippers and a long, flowered print dress made of some flimsy fabric fluttered about her tiny feet as she waited for him, nervously clutching her tiny black purse. Two tender strands of braids were caught up behind her head with flowers woven in. She was a little too pale for her own good, but he'd help her fix that. And when she saw him, her face would light up the world, and those big baby blues would fill with tears as she melted into his arms. . .

Four days later, the money came back exactly as he sent it. *My needs are so great*, Shyanne wrote. *Your selflessness gives me hope. But I must know more. Tell me about your women.*

His women.

Paul set this letter aside for a couple of days while he thought about it. There was nothing to be proud of in his association with women.

He supposed there was nothing to be ashamed of, either. He wasn't a virgin, and he wasn't a womanizer.

His women.

There had been three.

The first was his high school sweetheart. Carla dumped him one beautiful spring day right in front of the high school.

Skinny, her hair newly dyed Rit red, wearing black leather and the new addition of a denim jacket with the sleeves torn off, she was headed for the street after class, when Paul stopped her.

"Please don't go with him again today."

Carla shook her arm out of his grasp. "Don't tell me what to do."

"Those people aren't good for you, Carla."

"I don't think you're in a position to know what is or isn't good for me."

"I care about you. We're. . . you know. . . I mean, aren't we?"

Carla stopped popping her gum long enough to give him her complete attention. "Listen, Paul. We're neighbors. We grew up together. We've had sex a few times, but just because I popped your cherry doesn't mean you own me."

Paul's heart hammered hopelessly. "Go with me tonight," he said, but it came out a strangled whisper.

Someone kick started a motorcycle, and Carla glanced over her shoulder. "I've got to go."

"Please. . ." He felt like he was begging and he hated himself for it.

The motorcycle revved. She looked back at the older guy waiting for her on his bike. He jerked his head impatiently.

"It's okay, Paul," she said, and he never knew what she meant by that.

She ran, jumped on the back of the bike, showing the embroidery on the back of her denim vest. The Black Diamonds.

The Harley thunked into gear and they took off together, their red hair the same color, wearing the same jackets, the same sunglasses. Paul stood watching them go, and he felt his shoulders stoop in an irreversible way.

Carla.

Paul stood up and went to the telephone. The number for the pizza place was written on the wall.

Then there was Becky. College.

Becky dumped him in the middle of their junior year.

He was over at her dorm room, sitting on the floor between the twin beds, leafing through her physics text. Paul had gone from high school pudgy to college fat. Becky was still pudgy. Becky emptied out the tiny refrigerator and laid out the array of leftovers and snacks on the floor.

"You've got one hell of a brain," Paul said.

"Yep," Becky said, dipping a cracker into some kind of dip. "The lord gave me a good scoopful. He gave you a pretty good one, too."

"Yeah, but not like this. You understand all of this math? I thought math was supposed to be a guy thing."

"I love it," Becky said, and popped the cracker into her mouth. She dipped one for Paul and handed it to him. "Math is my life." She stopped chewing, and looked down at her fingers. She swallowed with difficulty. "Math and Nicole Clark."

"Huh?" Paul looked up, grabbed another cracker and scooped dip.

"Nicole Clark," Becky said, but couldn't meet his eyes.

Paul couldn't believe what he was afraid he heard.

"You know you and I are more like brother and sister than. . ."

Paul's hand fell to his lap, the dip falling off the cracker onto his pants. "You're kidding."

Becky started to cry.

Paul slid the food aside, threw the book on the bed, and took her into his arms. She sobbed as if her heart were breaking. "Listen, Becky, these are weird times. These are our college years, the times we're supposed to be experimenting and making choices, but Jesus Christ, honey, let's keep a little perspective."

"I love her."

It was a steel rod through his chest. "I love you," he said.

"I love you too, Paul, but it isn't the same. There's no. . . passion. With Nicole it's. . ."

Paul pulled away. "I don't think I want to hear about it."

"We're getting an apartment together."

Paul shoved her the rest of the way from him. "When was this decided? When has all this been going on? While we've been going out? While we've been sleeping together? You've been two-timing me with Nicole Clark?"

Becky began to cry and reached for him, but he pulled away. She slumped over and sobbed into the carpet. He picked up a box of crackers and left.

Becky.

The doorbell rang. Paul paid the pizza man, got the roll of paper towels and took a Pepsi from the fridge. He sprinkled the pizza with salt, then with chili pepper flakes.

There was a hole in his soul the size of this pizza and he couldn't eat it fast enough to try to plug that leak where the cold wind blew through.

But once he began to reminisce, he couldn't stop.

And then there was Crystal. The third and most recent woman in his past. He could never forget Crystal. She dumped him when he was thirty-seven. Thirty-seven and obese.

Crystal was one of the most beautiful women he had ever seen. She had three children, aged 4, 5 and 6, but that didn't matter to Paul. He liked kids all right. He hoped that he and Crystal would have one or two of their own to add to the pile.

One day he picked them up from school, came home, made dinner, but Crystal didn't come home. She was gone all night long.

And the next night.

Paul called the police, the hospitals, her mother, her friends. Nobody knew anything. He panicked, but he had his hands full taking care of the house and the three screaming children, making sure they were fed and clothed and got to school and that he got himself to work.

Another day passed, with no word. And then another.

And finally, on the fourth evening, when the television was blaring and the children were screeching and running around, not listening to him, mocking him when he asked them to please, *please* settle down, there was a timid knock on the front door.

Crystal opened the door and peered inside. "Hi, guys."

"Mommy!" The children mobbed her. She knelt and hugged them, kissed their heads and made eye contact with Paul.

"Hi, Paul."

Paul was sincerely sorry she wasn't crippled or in a cast or something. He had hoped there would be an excuse good enough, but he could see that there wasn't. There just wasn't. "You've been gone four goddamned days, Crystal."

"I know. I'm sorry."

"You could have called."

"I know. I'm sorry."

"I worried about you. I called the hospitals, the police—

And then a young guy who looked like he ought to be on an afternoon soap opera stuck his head in the door.

"Need help, Crystal?" he asked.

Without taking her eyes from Paul's, she said, "No. Wait outside, okay?"

He pulled back and closed the door.

Paul's soul took its third plunge toward the bottom of the well. It was the well of hope, and it was empty. "That's the recycling guy, isn't it?"

Crystal huddled the children around her close, her eyes wide with fear. The children looked at him with what appeared to be hatred.

He had to admit, the anger was beginning to build in a pretty scary way. "That's the guy who picks up our old newspapers, tuna fish cans, and milk cartons, isn't he? He's what, twenty years old?"

"Twenty-two."

"Yeah, right. Fine." He shook his head, but he didn't know why. Disbelief? Not really.

Crystal kissed the kids' heads one more time then said, "C'mon, kids, we're going to go sleep in a new place tonight."

Pain squeezed his eyebrows together. He looked up at her. "Just like that."

Crystal shrugged. "I guess."

Crystal.

When he let it, that one still hurt.

By the time Paul fell asleep on the couch, a grungy hand-knitted afghan pulled up over him, a three-page hand-written letter to Shyanne was safely tucked inside an envelope.

He dreamed of holding a slim, frail, blonde, tortured Shyanne in his arms, smoothing away her fears as she lay trembling against him. His small, neglected penis responded, and when he awoke to its bothersome presence, he got up and ate a couple of bowls of granola to calm himself.

And your family?

Paul felt that he was being interrogated. He felt on the defensive all the time. What was *she* revealing? She was getting to know everything about him and letting him know nothing in return, nothing.

Be patient, he told himself. She is cautious, as well she should be. She has been damaged. She placed the ad; she is screening the replies. Good things come to those who wait. If you are patient and honest with her, you will have her in her entirety.

Paul's elderly mother lived in a rest home, his father had been dead for many years. His older sister was married and lived in Texas with her rocket-scientist husband. There was not much family closeness, not much family contact.

Did any of your past relationships resemble your relationship with your mother or your sister?

This is getting to be pretty silly, Paul thought, and he put this card aside.

That night he dreamed that Shyanne's post office box had been stuffed with mail on the first day the ad ran, and as she answered each letter in turn, demanding, asking, probing, the replies dwindled until only one envelope continued to show up in that little glass window.

Paul would persevere. Shyanne would be his.

He got right out of bed, made an omelette, then sat down and compared his love life to his family life. It was an uncomfortable process. The three women he had romanced had all seemed exactly like his sister. They even sort of resembled each other. Each one of his lovers had been just a little bit out of his reach, like his big sister. He was always running to catch up, jumping to get their attention, settling for the pizza crusts they left on their plates.

As distasteful as it was, Paul honestly admitted all of this in a letter. I'm not afraid of a little discomfort, he thought. I can be uncomfortable in order to grow. Can she?

Then, for the first time, he challenged Shyanne. *Tell me about your men,* he wrote.

On the fourth day, there was no letter. Nor on the fifth, sixth or seventh.

Paul began to panic. He wrote her a dozen letters of apology, and tore them all up. He ate everything in the house, filled a grocery cart full of food and ate all of that, too.

After two weeks, he decided that if she couldn't accept his relationship history, or his gentle probe into hers, then she wasn't worth having.

After three weeks, he began to worry about her.

He couldn't work. He'd boot up his computer and filled the screen with her name. He missed deadlines and had more than one talk with the supervisor about it.

After a month, he was willing to do anything. He decided he'd take some vacation time and go to the post office, wait, and talk to her face to face when she picked up the mail out of her box. She must go there every day, or at least every other day.

Then the letter came.

I'll meet you on the 23rd. I'll stand on the third stair from the bottom on the east side of the sculpture in Brown Park at 10:30.

He hugged the letter to his chest and tears of relief squeezed out the corners of his eyes. She was all right; she hadn't fallen prey to some mail order predator.

Even more than that, he'd passed her tests. The fragile Shyanne was willing to trust him.

It was a grave responsibility.

On the heels of his relief was fresh panic. This was the 20th. The meeting was three days away. He had only three days to prepare, and so much to do.

First, he wanted to lose weight. He knew his bulk put women off, something he should have thought about when they first started this correspondence. Something he should have taken seriously a year ago. Two years ago. Ten years ago. If he lost two pounds a week, it would take him almost two years to lose it all. What a dummy. He'd never even notice losing one pound. If he starved, he'd lose maybe three pounds before their meeting.

Since losing weight was out of the question, the next burning issue was what to wear. All his clothes were outdated, misshapen and most of them had food stains on them. Paul hated to shop for clothes, because he hated mirrors.

He agonized over it so much he ate two cherry pies in one evening. The next day, trying to work was like trying to read a book written in Chinese characters. He had no concentration. His boss called him in and asked if everything was all right in his personal life.

"Yeah, sure," Paul said.

"When was your last vacation, Paul?"

Paul couldn't remember ever taking a vacation. There was nowhere to go. He didn't fly because the seats were too small; he hated driving long distances. He couldn't go to the beach, or to the pool. Traveling was for thin people.

"I don't know."

"We want you to take some time off, Paul," the supervisor said. "Your work hasn't been up to your normal standard of excellence."

"I know. I'm sorry. I've been distracted. . ." Paul felt the flush crawl up his neck and into his jowls. He wanted a Boston cream pie, he wanted one bad.

Work was all he had. If he lost his job. . .

Sweat popped out on his heated forehead. He could feel it trickle down the side of his face. He looked at the supervisor and for the first time he felt as though he really needed a friend, he really wanted someone to confide in, needed somebody to talk about Shyanne with, his fears, his worries, his unbalanced life. He looked at the supervisor and opened his mouth to speak.

The man looked up at him and Paul knew that he was not the one. He was a supervisor, not a friend. Shyanne. She would be his friend.

"I'm sorry," Paul finally said again. "You're right. I'm overdue for some time off."

"Good," the man said. "You're a valuable employee, Paul. When we see your work slip a little bit, we're concerned. We want to keep you with us for a long time."

"Thank you, sir," Paul said, stood up and shook the supervisor's hand. "I'll come back brand new."

"Good man, Paul. Rest up, now."

It took a Boston cream pie, six eclairs and a box of Fannie Mae before Paul got used to the idea of not working for two weeks. He pulled the draperies closed, locked the door and vowed not to answer the phone, as if it ever rang.

The next day, the 21st, he got up early, showered, had a hearty breakfast at his usual haunt and went shopping for clothes.

The salesman with the European accent in the Big Men's Store downtown greeted him as a customer, completely without prejudice. It was as if he saw people Paul's size every day.

And he probably did. There were lots of clothes there Paul's size, which meant that he wasn't alone. He didn't have to shop at the freak section of K-mart, as he had always done.

It took most of the day, but by the time they were finished, Paul had a new suit, slacks, jeans, shirts, shorts, shoes, socks, ties, and underwear. And he looked good in these clothes, too. Paul felt as though there was some new kind of designing technique that made him look good in these store mirrors. He modeled for the mirrors, turning back and forth, back and forth, smoothing the fabric over his bulges. He looked good. He looked damned good. Shyanne would like what she saw.

He would twirl her around and around, lifting those tiny feet right off the ground. She would giggle and flowers would fly out, and he would kiss her on the cheek, her bright teeth flashing in the sun. People in the park would see them and love them, smile and nod to themselves and each other, remembering what it was like.

He burdened his credit card with these purchases, but what the hell. It was less expensive than a vacation.

He went home and hung up all his new clothes and admired them.

The next day, the 22nd, he put on new sport clothes and went to the same coffee shop for breakfast. It might have been his imagination, but it seemed as though the girl behind the counter flirted with him and his new image.

He read the paper, skipping the Personals section entirely. As he left the coffee shop, he saw a little girl sitting out in front with a basket of puppies. She handed one to Paul and tears came to his eyes as he held the warm, sweet smelling little thing.

Shyanne would love cuddling a warm, wiggly puppy. She could name him.

When he got home, the puppy was following him on his new leash, and Paul carried a bag of puppy food. Paul opened the curtains, picked up the all the old newspapers, did the dishes and aired out the apartment. Then he played with the puppy and took him for a walk. He strode confidently, smiling at those he passed, and felt good about getting smiles in return.

At dusk, Paul returned, put the puppy in the bathroom with lots of newspapers and his water dish, then collapsed on the couch. He turned on the television, then looked at the stack of letters from

Shyanne. He clicked off the television, picked up the letters and leafed through them.

He opened the last one. *I'll meet you. . .*

Dully, Paul went to the phone and ordered lots and lots of Chinese food. He ignored the whining and scratching of the puppy.

The morning of the 23rd dawned cool and lovely. Paul let the puppy in, who ran around and ran around, then climbed up into Paul's lap and licked his face. Paul wondered that he had never thought of getting a dog before. He wondered if he should take the puppy with him to meet Shyanne.

No. Just him. Him and his new blue suit and a huge bouquet of spring flowers.

He wondered how he was going to survive until ten-thirty.

He walked the dog to the coffee shop, then ate a good breakfast. A good healthy breakfast. He had a bran muffin, a bowl of fruit and two cups of coffee. He was going to lose this weight. It was time. He'd lose it for Shyanne. He was tired of it, and if he concentrated for a year or two, it would be gone and that would be the end of that.

Over his second cup of coffee, he figured his morning time line. He'd be at the park at 10:15, which meant he had to get in his car at 10:00. He'd allow himself an hour to shower, shave and dress, just to make sure everything was perfect. So he had to begin all of this at nine o'clock. And it was already eight forty-five. Perfect.

He untied the dog from the tree and walked it back home, feeling pretty good about himself.

Back at the apartment, he showered and shaved, paying close attention to a good, close shave.

He was perspiring by the time he finished.

Then he powdered all the areas that chafed, and went to the closet.

He pulled out the new blue suit and held it up. It was a beauty, he had to admit.

New socks, new underwear. 9:30.

He flossed and brushed his teeth, snipped a couple of nose hairs.

He put on the crisp shirt and struggled with the tie. He did it over and over again, and when it was finally right, the shirt was no longer crisp.

He got into the pants and discovered that his old black belt no longer fit. He didn't even think about buying a new belt.

Perspiration trickled down the side of his face. 9:45.

He put on his shoes and immediately stepped into a little pile that the puppy left on the bathroom floor, right on the paper, right where he wanted the puppy to go.

Paul was afraid he was going to blow it.

Gently, he picked up the dog and put him in the back yard, trying not to get puppy hair or puppy smell or puppy poop on his new clothes. He picked up all the papers in the bathroom and threw them in the trash, then cleaned his shoe and put it back on. 9:55. She'd be there in a half hour. She'd be standing there in a half hour, waiting for him.

He shrugged into his new suit coat and buttoned it.

He turned back and forth in front of the mirror, but something wasn't right.

He smoothed the fabric down over his rolls of fat, but they still showed. They didn't show in the store. In the store, he looked cool and sleek and clean. Now he looked damp and fat and lumpy.

This wouldn't do.

He ripped off his suit, throwing it into the corner. He pulled on a pair of jeans, but the fat around his waist rolled down over the top. Had that happened in the store? He couldn't remember that it had, but it would not do. He took them off and threw them into the corner too, and put on a pair of gray slacks.

They were awful. They made his butt look like an elephant's butt.

His shirt now stuck to his back. His moussed hair had been messed up, wetted with perspiration and then frozen again at an awkward angle.

Stop this, he said to himself.

10:10.

Go with the suit.

But the suit was balled up and in the corner. He picked it up and shook it out, but it was beyond salvage.

He went back to the closet and pawed through. Nothing was good, nothing was right, nothing would work.

10:15. And he still had to buy the flowers.

He stood in the middle of his apartment, and the panic began to build.

He grabbed a pair of shorts and a new sport shirt. He took off the dress shirt and tie and put on those clothes.

But all he had were ugly, worn out sneakers to go with.

10:20. He would be late. And he wouldn't have flowers.

He tried on the shorts and shirt he'd worn the day before, the time the girl at the coffee shop flirted with him.

They were wrinkled. And they smelled.

10:25.

Paul stood in his underwear in the middle of his small apartment, surrounded by an explosion of clothes at his feet. The puppy whined and scratched at the back door. Perspiration dripped off his nose. He heard the howling of the wind as it blew through that hole in his soul.

He reached over and picked up the phone. He ordered two large pizzas with the works and a 2-liter bottle of Pepsi. He let in the dog, then sat with it on the couch. With the puppy licking his face, he thought about Shyanne waiting on the step, waiting, waiting, then turning, silently, and walking back up the stairs.

✳

Empty Walls

Karen slammed the door shut behind her and listened to the echo throughout the barren apartment. She collapsed against the empty wall without energy, without motivation, without a future. At least now she was home and didn't have to act normal, or brave, or as if everything were fine.

A lick of flame in her guts flared up. Her white shoes squeaked on the tile foyer floor as she tried to take a deep breath. *Breathe*, she said to herself. *Breathe.*

The stomach cramp eased and she collected a long, ragged breath of stale, abandoned air.

Without the distraction of work, the scenario began to run again, for the zillionth time, right from the beginning.

All the evidence laid out on the dining room table.

"Here it is. Look at this. You must have *wanted* to get caught."

"What is this," he said, "a fucking trial?"

"If you like. Exhibit A: Lipstick on the shoulder of your shirt. Not mine. Exhibit C: *Smell* this. I would never wear perfume like this."

"That's enough. A secretary's lipstick over a birthday hug. Sometimes I come home smelling like cigarette smoke, too, but that doesn't mean I smoke."

"Exhibit C: Receipt for flowers. When did you ever send me flowers?"

When did you ever send me flowers? When did you ever send me flowers? When did you ever send ME flowers?

"I never sent anybody flowers. Let me see that."

"And you charged them to *our* goddamn Visa card. What the hell is the matter with you?"

"I swear to God!"

"Exhibit D."

"What is that?"

"My diary. Times you said you were going someplace and then didn't go there. Things you said you were going to do but didn't, because you were with *her*."

"What did you do, follow me? Check up on me? Spy on me?"

"I built a file, is all. Here it is, all laid out. Pretty, isn't it? You're guilty as hell."

Guilty as hell. Guilty as hell. Guilty.

"You're nuts."

"And you're leaving."

"You're throwing me out?"

"On your ass, buddy. Your shit is already packed. But before you go, I have one question. Just one. What kind of woman does this? What kind of woman sleeps with another woman's husband, hammering an irreversible wedge between them? What could you possibly find attractive about a woman who would do that? What kind of woman does that?"

What kind of woman does that? What kind of woman? What kind?

Karen unbuttoned her white uniform with a tired hand and shrugged out of it, pulling the syringe out of the pocket before letting the fabric pool at her feet.

Even her presence echoed in the empty apartment.

In the kitchen, she opened the refrigerator and stared inside. She had no appetite, but her body needed fuel or she wouldn't be able to work tomorrow. She needed to work tomorrow. She needed to work. She needed to do something to take her mind off the despicable woman. . .

She set the syringe on the refrigerator shelf, grabbed a tub of yogurt and a spoon and wolfed down a couple of mouthfuls, then stuck the spoon in it and put it back on the shelf.

She could feel the yogurt echoing in the emptiness of her stomach. She closed her eyes and told it to stay there.

She closed the refrigerator door and made her way slowly through the empty living room to the bedroom. The worst thing about an empty apartment was the square marks on the walls where framed pictures, photographs, paintings and prints used to hang. Walls gave an apartment its personality. A completely empty room with art on the walls was still decorated. Fill the apartment with furniture, and if the walls aren't personalized, the apartment isn't finished yet.

This apartment had been personalized, had been finished, had been filled with family and fun and memories.

But not now.

Karen walked through the living room, and if she'd had a pencil in her hand, she would have drawn frames around those square dirt marks on the walls, and then she would have drawn people, happy people, inside the frames.

But she didn't have a pencil, and she didn't have any energy.

Her bed was a futon mattress on the floor in the corner of the bedroom. Her brother's sleeping bag was on top of it. It was all she had. All she had. It was all there was. That and dirt marks on the walls where pictures used to hang.

It shouldn't be like this, Karen thought to herself. It's not supposed to be like this. I shouldn't be alone, not at this stage of life. She felt like there were square dirt marks on the empty walls of her mind, the empty walls of her soul, where portraits of loved ones used to provide personality.

She pulled her slip off and let it fall to the floor. Panty hose followed. She shrugged into an oversized t-shirt and pair of cotton panties. As she passed a mirror, she glimpsed what looked like a hollow-eyed little boy. She didn't stop to investigate. She had no time.

The scenario continued.

"Don't you love me? Don't you respect me? How could you do something like this?"

"All right. You're right. I did have a fling. But she meant nothing to me."

"She meant nothing? How could you do something so serious, so seriously damaging to me, to our marriage, with someone who meant nothing to you?"

"I don't know, darling, I'm sorry. What would it take?"

"Does *she* know she means nothing to you?"

"I'm sure she does."

"I'm sure she does *not*. What kind of a woman would do this? A woman with no soul, that's what kind. A woman with no self esteem, a woman with no life of her own. A terrible, horrible, awful woman, that's who. And you carried on with her, for. . .how long?"

"Can we get beyond this?"

"I don't know. I don't think so. I don't think I know how."

"Please?"

"How long?"

How long? How long? How long?

Satisfied that the yogurt had finally settled, Karen went back to the refrigerator, thinking about adding something to it. The door opened and the light echoed in the cold emptiness. Even the refrigerator was cold and empty.

Yogurt. Grape jelly. Syringe.

She was going to do that home wrecker, that bitch—that *woman*—some harm.

There were lots of things she could have picked up at the hospital. Karen could kill her easily with some drug or some infectious disease. She could have picked up a vial of blood that was HIV positive. She could have gone to the lab and gotten any one of a number of things, including herpes, or yellow fever. Those were her first choices, but then she got a much better idea.

Oh yeah, a much better idea.

The woman was a slut. She had no moral fiber at all. She seduced husbands and ruined marriages all over town. She needed to be punished, but punished periodically for the rest of her life. She didn't need to be dead, and she didn't need to be giving herpes or AIDS to all the men around. No, Karen had a better plan than that.

She picked up the syringe and walked back to the bedroom, flopped down on the futon and held the syringe up to look at it.

Simple. Innocent. She handled a hundred, sometimes several hundred syringes a day, and they were nothing. A tool. A tool to heal.

But not this baby.

The aching, the longing, the pain wrenched her gut and she pulled her knees up to her stomach and turned on her side. The syringe fell from her fingers and rolled across the floor.

"How long?"

"I don't know. Three weeks. A month."

"A month?! You were seeing this bitch for a month? What, you—you'd fuck her, come home and sleep with me? You felt no remorse, no guilt?"

"Of course I did."

"You're an animal."

"Listen!"

"I no longer listen to you. Where did you meet her?"

"That's not important. She's gone now, she's out of my life, I'll never see her again."

"As of when? Just this minute? Just now, when you got caught? Is she expecting to see you tonight? Is she somewhere, right now, waiting for you?"

Waiting for you. Waiting. Wait.

Karen could have procured a syringeful of instant death or slow death, but what she finally opted for was intermittent death.

Malaria. A new strain. An exotic. The worst yet.

The fever came on unexpectedly, like weakness. Like an affair. Like lust.

She'd seen the results of it, too: delirium, sweat, muscle spasms, helplessness. Like sex. Like heartbreak.

But this was severe. So severe, those stricken usually prayed for death. And it lasted two, three weeks, sometimes. Like a cheap affair. An affair that meant nothing.

Karen reached over a thin hand and picked up the syringe. She held it up to the light again and marveled at how calm it looked to her professional eye, yet she knew quite precisely the devastating chaos it would effect on a home wrecker.

She visualized the little microbes, like tiny lobsters with giant pincers jumping with glee into the bloodstream, headed for the brain, the eyes, the liver, the vagina.

It would sting, but the sting would be nothing. Comparatively speaking, the sting would be nothing. Compared to the anguish of the fever, compared to the anguish she caused—

"Where did you meet her?"

"Can we stop this?"

"At the hospital, right? What is she, a *nurse?*"

Before she could change her mind, Karen pulled off the pink needle guard, stabbed the needle deeply into her thigh and pushed the plunger.

It did sting. "Ow," she said, then plucked it out and threw it across the room.

She lay back on the futon. Her first round of punishment should begin well before morning.

Then maybe she could relax. Then maybe she could stop hating herself. Then maybe she could stop imagining the homewrecking scenes between her lovers and their wives. Then maybe she could stop acting on those impulses that hurt her, hurt them, hurt them all.

Karen lay quietly imagining the activity in her veins as the microbes went to work.

To pass the time, she looked at those square dirty marks on the walls of her new apartment and tried to visualize what kind of pictures used to hang there.

A real boyfriend would paint them over for her.

※

Harvest Home

By the time Roman had hauled himself out of bed, dressed, slogged down a cup of coffee while shaving, grabbed his lunch box and made it slowly, tiredly out the door for work, Cindy was agitated to the point of dizziness.

The minute the door slammed behind him, she roused the children. "Get up! Get up! C'mon, we have an adventure today. Five minutes. C'mon, we have to leave here in five minutes." She pulled the covers off each of the kids and shook their shoulders. "C'mon Freddie. C'mon Kewpie. We're going for a ride."

Freddie's eyes opened and he rubbed them, but Kewpie just screwed up her face and reached for her teddy bear.

"Get her up, Freddie," Cindy said. "I've got to dress."

She ran a brush through her hair and smeared on some eye shadow. She didn't need to be beautiful for this transaction. She just needed to be present. And on time.

She pulled on a pair of slacks and a sweater, spritzed some perfume to mask the scent of sleeping next to Roman all night, brushed her teeth, and pulled the suitcase from the back of the closet, where it was packed and ready to go. Roman never even noticed that her side of the closet was empty.

"Get up!" she said to Kewpie, grabbed the little girl by the ankle and pulled her to the bottom of the bed.

"Don't pull her," Freddie said.

"Then you get her up," Cindy countered, checking her watch. "And get dressed. We have a plane to catch."

"An airplane?"

Even Kewpie's eyes opened at that, and she sat up.

"Yep," Cindy said, now realizing how to motivate them. "We're going on a trip."

"What about Daddy?" Kewpie asked.

"He'll meet us later," Cindy lied.

"Where are we going?"

"Florida."

The children's eyes widened. "On an airplane?" Freddie asked again.

"Yes, but only if you hurry. Get up, now, get your backpacks and pack two pairs of fresh underwear and a change of clothes. Don't forget socks."

Freddie got their backpacks from under the bed.

"Freddie, you can help Kewpie. Two changes of underwear and one change of clothes. And you can each bring one toy." Cindy walked out of their bedroom and into the kitchen, but she had no taste for breakfast. She'd had no internal battle over this situation until just now, just this moment, when the children looked at her with such trust in their eyes.

Too bad. Too late. The wheels—whatever they were—had been put into motion.

The children were dressed and ready to go in record time. Cindy handed each of them a bagel, checked again to make sure she had the tickets, hustled them out of the apartment and into the frigid car.

"How come Daddy never mentioned going to Florida?" Freddie asked.

"Know how you can never sleep on Christmas Eve?" Cindy said. "We didn't want you to get so excited you couldn't sleep. Today is going to be a big day, you needed your rest."

"Mickey Mouse lives in Florida," Freddie said to Kewpie, and Cindy's heart gave a squeeze.

She parked the car and hustled the kids through the airport, and they made the gate just as the flight to Miami was boarding. The children were wide-eyed and excited, and they made sure the flight attendant knew they were going to Florida. The pretty girl smiled at Cindy with an "aren't you a lucky mom" smile. Cindy scowled back. If she liked the children so much *she* could entertain them. Cindy plugged in the headphones and turned up the music.

The idea of having a family seemed like a good one at first. Roman was big, handsome and a hard worker. Cindy was heart-broken and damaged and saw no future for herself. Roman needed a mom for his kids, Cindy needed something to cling to, so they married and Cindy moved in.

Within a month, she knew it had been a bad move.

Freddie at seven and Kewpie at five were incredibly high maintenance projects. Cindy didn't have enough energy to care for herself, much less two little kids. Roman worked two jobs just to pay the bills, so she never saw him and had to do all the work by herself. And there wasn't even enough money left over for any of the sweet things. Like jewelry. Or trips. Or a winter coat, like a husband ought to buy his wife. Life for Cindy became a steaming pit of resentment.

When Roman went to his night job, Cindy put the kids to bed, locked their bedroom door and went to hang out at the CyberCafe. A cute guy had shown her how to log on and chat with a variety of interesting people, people she felt she had more in common with than her husband. Soon, she was hooked.

And that's where she met Della. Online.

Della seemed to understand everything Cindy was going through. She understood how frustrating step-children could be, she understood an inattentive husband, she understood having not enough money to buy a fresh lipstick. She became Cindy's best friend. Cindy poured out her heart and soul to Della, who responded with sympathy and empathy and love.

Over a period of time, Della convinced Cindy that she ought to take the kids to Miami for a visit. There were investment opportunities. There were things Cindy could do to climb out of that pit. Stay with Della and let her take over the kids for a couple of days. Cindy had made an investment in Roman and his family, a hasty, unwise investment, and perhaps it was time for her to consider her own needs. Cut her losses, liquidate her assets and get on to the next adventure.

Everybody would be better off. Everybody except perhaps Roman, but he'd survive. Some day he'd thank her for helping him shed a little baggage.

Della talked softly and sweetly about it to Cindy, and before Cindy knew it, a packet of airline tickets showed up in the mailbox. A round trip for Cindy and two one-way tickets for the kids.

Must be a mistake, Cindy told herself, rationalizing that she didn't know what she was getting into. She hid the tickets, and from that moment on, everything Roman or either one of the children did made her want to scream. Everything, every little thing, reinforced her decision to go spend some time with Della.

The plane touched down at Miami International and Cindy felt her heart pounding in her chest.

It's not too late, she told herself. *I can turn right around and put the three of us on the next plane to LaGuardia and be home by the time Roman gets off work.*

But she knew she wouldn't.

Della met her at the gate.

She looked like someone's well-tended grandmother, not at all the good-times soul sister that Cindy expected. They hugged like old friends, then Della squatted and hugged each one of the children and gave them Disney toys. She carried a briefcase.

"We'll walk you to your gate," Della said.

Cindy looked at her ticket, then up at the wall clock and realized with a taste of panic that her return flight left in forty minutes.

Della engaged the kids in spirited conversation about their flight. Della knew exactly how to talk to kids. Cindy had never acquired that enviable skill.

They got to Cindy's departure gate as the plane was boarding. "I'm going to take the children to the rest room, while you board," Della said softly. "No goodbyes." And she handed Cindy the briefcase. Then she turned with the children and walked down the concourse, leaving Cindy lonelier than she had ever felt in her life.

She dully handed her ticket to the agent and boarded the plane. In the tiny airplane restroom, she opened the briefcase and found it full of packets of twenty dollar bills. It was more money than she had ever seen before. It was more money than she could ever have imagined having.

It didn't help. Somehow, it didn't help, and tears leaked out of her eyes, ran down her cheeks and fell onto the cash.

"Where's Cindy?" Freddie asked Della when he came out of the men's room.

"She's gone back to fetch your daddy," Della said. "You're going to come home with me and they'll meet us later."

Kewpie wrapped her arm around Goofy's neck, stuck her thumb in her mouth and grabbed Della's hand with her other. It was clear to Freddie that Kewpie preferred Della to Cindy, and, in fact, so did he.

They rode in a blue van and looked at palm trees and blue sky with soft clouds. They'd never seen palm trees before. Freddie had a feeling that something wasn't right, but Della kept talking to him, and the longer they talked, the more he liked her.

She took them to a big house, and gave them their own bedroom. It had twin beds with matching blue bedspreads and curtains. There were games and puzzles and toys in the closet, and clothes in the drawers. "When do we get to see Mickey Mouse?" he asked Della.

"Soon," she promised. "Now get into your jammies."

"Why?"

"Because a doctor is going to come and talk to you in a little while, and he wants to see you in your jammies."

Kewpie did as she was told, and Freddie reluctantly followed her example. Something wasn't right about this. He wanted to see his dad.

Somebody was crying. Somebody in the house. Some little kid. Freddie got out of bed and went to the door, but it was locked.

A little while later a doctor and a nurse came in and told them that every person's fingerprint was different, and he inked up each of their forefingers and pressed it to a card to show them. Then he put a rubber band around Kewpie's arm, stuck a needle in her vein and filled up tubes with her blood. Kewpie screamed, and when it was Freddie's turn, he tried not to cry, but it hurt and he was scared. "It's called tissue matching," the doctor tried to explain, "it's just like a fingerprint," but Freddie wanted to see his dad, and he wanted to see him *now*.

The nurse gave both of them something cherry-flavored to drink out of a tiny plastic cup. Kewpie settled down with a baby doll and a red sucker, and soon Freddie had a hard time keeping his eyes open. Kewpie slumped sideways over her new doll, a spit bubble blowing in and out of little lips still red from the liquid she drank.

Freddie closed his eyes. In spite of himself, he liked the feeling of this new bed, new sheets, new pajamas, but he still hoped that when he woke up, he'd be back at home, hating Cindy all the way to hell.

Cindy's plane touched down in New York about the time Roman would be getting off work. Her stomach was in an uproar. She could no longer deny the fact that she had foreseen this outcome—a briefcase full of cash and no more kids—and she found out that she didn't have a plan to take from here. If she had been smart, she would have just taken off for Rio or somewhere, right from Miami. Why did she use her round trip ticket? It didn't make sense. Some kind of a homing device, she thought. Her suitcase full of clothes was in the trunk of the car.

She got off the plane in the stream of passengers and looked around the airport full of people with purpose. She was too antsy, too agitated to get on another plane. Maybe it was good this way. She could drive. She could drive across country. She could drive to Canada. She could put the pedal to the metal and get out of town under her own power. She could drive fast and hard and sing loud along with the radio. Somewhere along the way she'd ditch the car. Maybe she'd just drive down to D.C. and leave it in the airport parking lot there. Maybe she'd fly to Paris or Zurich and make a fresh start.

She squealed tires in Roman's old beater, and headed south.

With hands shaking from cold and guilt, and trying not to think about the nausea that was building like a volcano, she fiddled with a recalcitrant heater and a shorted out AM radio as two lanes merged. While her attention was desperately elsewhere, a Volvo sideswiped her rattletrap car going seventy-five miles an hour.

The car spun across four lanes of traffic, hitting everything and everyone in its rush hour path. Nightmare Bumper Cars. Ultra Pinball.

Cindy screamed with what breath was in her as terror squeezed her throat. She was bashed, rolled, flipped and tossed.

Roman's car ended up slowly spinning on its crushed top, the steering wheel embedded in Cindy's chest, packets of twenty dollar bills littered all around her.

The phone began to ring as Roman stared blankly, unseeing, uncomprehending, at Cindy's empty closet. Somewhere in the back of his mind he knew what had happened; it had been inevitable, really. She'd been too young, too much of a free spirit for him to tie down with kids that weren't hers and who resented her. But that didn't mean that the sight of tangled, empty hangers didn't sear his soul.

Oh well. Kiss marriage goodbye. This was his third-time-charm effort. He'd be disinclined to try again. Not until the children were grown and gone. He didn't want to put himself through this again, but he *really* couldn't put the kids through it again. They'd never learn how to trust.

Hookers and day care. His life would be reduced to hookers and day care and working his ass off. What a charming thought.

Speaking of day care, Cindy must have left a note telling him where to pick up the kids.

He walked out of the bedroom and into the kitchen, where logic told him a note would be. There was no note. He picked up the ringing telephone more to quell its relentless noise than to talk to anyone, but habit made him put the receiver to his ear and say, "Hello?"

"Mr. Daniloff? Mr. Roman Daniloff?"

"Yes?"

"New York police, Mr. Daniloff. Your wife has been in an accident. She's at Good Samaritan Hospital."

Life clicked into focus and Roman could count the microseconds float by. "Is she hurt?"

"You better come down right away."

"The children?"

"Children?"

"Were the kids with her?"

"No, sir."

Thank god.

Twenty minutes later, he was sitting beside Cindy's empty bed while she was in surgery. On his lap rested a paper sack full of money.

When he first arrived at the hospital, he began going through the things the police brought in from the twisted wreck that had been his car. The suitcase, full of her cheap floozy clothes. Her purse. Her passport. Her address book.

And a big paper bag full of twenty dollar bills.

He went through her purse, but there was nothing extraordinary in there, either. No clues to where the kids might be. Nothing.

He dumped the cash out onto the hospital room floor and picked up each blood-soaked packet of twenties, fanned through it and put it back into the paper bag. One hundred thousand dollars.

Good god, what had she done?

Hours later, they wheeled her bed in.

Cindy was pale, cut, bruised and hooked up to a variety of machines, one of which was keeping her heart going. Her ribcage had been crushed, they'd removed one lung, and her heart was damaged beyond repair. Her only hope of survival was a new heart. The doctor told Roman she'd been bumped to the top of the priority list. She could be saved if she remained stable long enough. If a heart could be found.

Roman didn't know about all that stuff. He only knew that something had happened to his kids, and this faithless bitch and this bag of money were all part of it.

When a nurse came in to check on Cindy, Roman asked if she could be awakened.

The nurse looked at him pityingly as if he were an idiot and shook her head. Then she left the room.

Roman thought he was going to lose his mind.

He opened the closet to put the cash and the suitcase in there, and saw a plastic bag with Cindy's torn, cut and bloodied clothes. He emptied that out and went through it. Nothing.

But her stained coat hung in the closet, and in its pocket, he found a paperback romance with two airline ticket stubs stuck in as bookmarks. LaGuardia to Miami, Miami to LaGuardia. Today.

Roman looked over at her—small, pale, every breath initiated by a hissing machine in the corner. *Wake up, you evil bitch,* he thought. He wanted to jump up and down on her ravaged chest and have her spit out the information with her dying breath.

He talked to the police, but they were only mildly interested. They had too many things to take care of right there in New York. They didn't have the time or the resources to track down a couple of kids who may or may not be missing. And without any further information, it would be futile for Roman to fly to Miami.

His only hope was for Cindy to get her new heart. Hopefully, they'd replace the hard lump of stone she had in her chest for a real flesh and blood heart. Then she would wake up and tell him what she'd done for one hundred thousand dollars.

He'd go to Florida, return the money and pick up his kids.

Roman set his jaw and sat down on a plastic chair, listening to Cindy's various monitors and ventilator. He was prepared to wait.

When Freddie woke up, Kewpie was gone. A lady brought him a tray of breakfast, but he wasn't hungry. He was homesick and worried about his baby sister.

"I want my daddy," he said and started to cry.

"I know you do, honey," the lady said and sat down on the bed. She had a nice face, and Freddie knew she would help him. She held him and rocked him and cooed to him until he was all out of tears and only hiccups were left. Then she gave him another drink of that cherry syrup and Freddie fell asleep.

"We have a heart," the doctor said. "It's young, very young, but we are optimistic that it will continue to grow, and will serve your wife well for many years. It's an unusually good tissue match, and the timing is amazingly fortuitous. But your wife's movement will be restricted for a length of time—she'll probably be confined to a wheelchair for as much as two years, while everything adjusts. And of course, there are the anti-rejection drugs which take their toll." He leaned forward. "This is outrageous good fortune," he said. "Unheard of, actually. Five years ago, your wife would have died. But with today's technology—"

"Just wake her up," Roman said.

The doctor handed him the consent forms, and Roman signed.

"The heart will be here tomorrow," the doctor said. "I'll notify the team."

When Freddie awoke, he didn't know what day it was. It seemed to be dawn, and Kewpie still wasn't in her bed.

He pulled the covers up over his head and tented his knees so he could see around in his dark little bed cave and tried not to cry. He tried not to be afraid. He tried to figure out what he could do. He wanted to get dressed, and when they came in to bring his breakfast, he could just push the lady over and run out the door. He had his own clothes. He even had fresh underwear.

He thought about what was in his backpack.

A cell phone.

The cell phone! He always kept it in his backpack in case he needed his dad. It was so small and light, and it was kind of fun. Best of all, he could beep his dad any time day or night, if he had a nightmare, or if he missed the school bus, or whatever. He never had, but he knew he could.

He snuck out of bed, opened the closet, unzipped his backpack, and grabbed the phone, then zipped it up, closed the closet door and dove back under the covers.

He didn't want to screw this up.

He opened the phone and turned it on. Then he pressed Memory#1, and heard the phone dial. Just as the beeper operator came on, there was a soft knock on his door, and it opened.

Heart pounding, he clicked off the phone, hoped nobody heard the beep, folded it and peeked out of the covers.

"Good morning," the doctor said. "How are you?"

"Where's Kewpie?" Freddie asked, sliding the phone under his legs.

"She's helping someone right now," he said.

"How long are we going to be here?" Freddie asked. "I want to go home."

A nurse came in with a tray full of tubes and packages and sat on Freddie's bed. "We need to take some more samples," the doctor said, and Freddie began to cry.

"I hate this," he said.

"I know, sweetie," the nurse said. She was so nice, and so pretty that Freddie wanted to trust her, he wanted to trust her so bad, but he just couldn't.

He got out of bed, leaving the cell phone under the covers, and peed into their jar. Then he got back into bed and grit his teeth while they took a tube of his blood, thinking not of the needle, but of the cell phone underneath him. It would be terrible if his dad remembered the phone about now and gave him a call.

"Someone's going to come and help you take a shower," the nurse told him.

"I can take my own shower," Freddie said. "I'm no baby."

"Of course you're not," the nurse cooed. She gave him a Tootsie Roll pop for bravery, and while Freddie was unwrapping it, the doctor stuck another needle in his arm and gave him a shot.

The doctor left, and the nurse stayed, smoothing his hair and talking quietly to him, and Freddie felt woozy and sleepy. He wanted her to go, because he needed to call his dad. He didn't want to close his eyes, but she kept telling him to close his eyes, and so he thought that maybe if he did, she'd leave.

He closed his eyes and began to have little dreams about his room at home.

He opened them again, and she was still there, speaking softly, her fingers cool on his hot cheek.

He closed his eyes, afraid, and little dreams of Kewpie played about in his head.

He felt the nurse get up off the bed, and when he heard his door open and close, he reached for the phone under his covers.

But his eyes weren't working quite right, and the dreams kept imposing themselves upon him with his eyes wide open. His fingers felt thick and stupid.

He opened the phone and dialed the Memory number again, and this time when the beeper lady answered, he pressed 5555, or thought he did, or hoped he did, and then he hung up, just exactly the way he and his dad had practiced. That was their signal.

Freddie clicked off and held the phone to his chest, his eyes closing. *Please call right now,* he prayed. *Please call me before they come in with breakfast. Please call me before—*

Roman's beeper went off as he was dozing in the plastic chair in Cindy's room. First, he cursed it, then he looked at it, and then he jumped out of his chair so fast that he almost tore down the flimsy curtain that surrounded her bed. He went directly to the pay phone in the hallway and dialed Freddie's cell phone number.

God, he had completely forgotten about the cell phone.

After Roman's second wife abandoned them, Freddie, then five and fearful, was terrified that Roman would go to work and not come back. So Roman had got one of those cheap cell phones for $9.95, had the air time activated and they practiced a signal. Whenever Freddie was feeling lonesome or scared, he could dial Roman's beeper, and Roman would call him back.

Freddie kept it in his backpack all the time, but never used it. Roman paid the minimum charge on the damned thing every month, it was a security blanket for the kid—and for him, too, he supposed—and he never considered canceling. Now he was grateful he hadn't.

The phone rang once, then clicked on. In a whisper, he heard his son say, "Dad?"

Relief flushed through Roman like a tidal wave. "Freddie, where are you?"

"Um. Florida," but there was something wrong with his voice. It was slow and low, not like Freddie at all.

"Hold it together, Freddie. Are you all right? Do you know where you are? Is Kewpie with you?"

"They took Kewpie."

He sounded as if he'd been drugged. "Okay, son, don't hang up. Just put this phone somewhere where nobody will find it and I'll get the police to trace the signal. Are you okay?"

Freddie croaked out a "Yeah."

"Don't be afraid, boy, I'm coming for you."

"Yeah."

"You have a place to put the phone?"

"Yeah."

"Good. Do that now, and I'll see you soon."

"Um. Hurry."

"I will. I'll come get you and The Kewp. Okay?"

Freddie nodded. Roman knew he was nodding. He could see his brave little boy and the thought tore his heart out. "Put the phone away now, and I'll see you soon." He listened as rustling sounds came over the phone. "Freddie?"

"Mmm?"

"I love you, boy."

"Me, too," Freddie said, his voice fading.

Roman's throat filled up with hot emotion as he lay that receiver on the ledge and picked up the receiver from the pay phone next to it. He dialed 911 and hoped to god the NYPD or the FBI or somebody knew how to handle something like this. And handle it before the cell phone battery went dead.

Within an hour, the hospital corridor was filled with police.

Freddie looked at the closet. He should get up and put the cell phone back in his backpack, zip it up and they'd never find it.

Or in between the mattresses.

But his legs wouldn't work and his fingers just twitched when he wanted them to do something. The cell phone sat on his chest, in full view of whoever might come in, and the dreams he kept having were interfering with the task he knew he was supposed to perform.

Gotta do it for Kewpie, he said to himself, but it didn't help.

Against his will, his eyes closed, and the dreams played about on the inside of his eyelids.

When he woke up, the maid was cleaning his bathroom, he was dressed in fresh pajamas, and his sheets had been changed.

"*Buenos Dias,*" she said when she saw that his eyes were open.

It took Freddie a minute or two to remember just exactly what was going on. He couldn't seem to keep track of everything.

The phone!

He rummaged in his bed, still feeling like his head was out of focus.

"Your toy is on the nightstand," the maid said, and pointed at it with her elbow as she wrung out a cloth into a soapy bucket.

Toy?

The phone.

"It fell out of your bed when I changed your sheets," she said.

Freddie grabbed it—it seemed as though his arm stretched out a mile. It was still on. The red light still glowed. He almost put it to his ear, but he didn't want the maid to know it was a phone. How could she not know it was a telephone?

He pulled it under the covers, hugged it to his chest, rolled over onto his side and closed his eyes.

The next thing he knew, someone was yelling. Somebody ran past his door, then what sounded like a whole bunch of people ran by. He heard whispering just outside his door, then more yelling downstairs.

Then people walked up and down the hallway, up and down, up and down, and he heard that kid crying again. He wrapped his arms around his knees and prayed that nobody was going to bust through his door, but if somebody did, he hoped it would be his dad.

"Mr. Daniloff? FBI. We have your son."

A sob of relief broke out of Roman's chest. "Is he all right?"

"He's fine. He's eating ice cream here in the lounge with thirteen other kids."

"And my daughter?"

There was a pause so deep Roman could have fallen though it. "No word on the girl yet."

That took away most of the relief. "Who are these people, anyway? What were they doing with my kids?"

"Let us get back to you as soon as we find out about your daughter, Mr. Daniloff."

"Tell my son I'll be down to pick him up."

"I'll do that, sir. He's a smart and very brave boy."

With a trembling hand, Roman clicked off the cellular phone the police had given him and looked over at Cindy, whose ventilator continued to aspirate in a maddening rhythm.

Special Agent Monroe had a five year old daughter himself, a precious little blue-eyed blonde that was the essence of his late mother. He believed it was no accident that he was involved in this disgusting case. He made it his personal mission to find that boy's little sister and rescue her from these monsters.

It had to be done soon. They certainly wasted no time processing these children—he couldn't afford to waste any time, either.

He mustered the city and county uniformed police and had them canvass every hospital, every clinic, every veterinarian. He wanted them to inspect every inch of any place where surgery could be competently performed. And he wanted it done within an hour.

They caught his urgency. They caught his desperation. He told them about five-year-old Kewpie Daniloff, whose name alone was enough to strum their heartstrings. Most of those uniformed cops were in the right age bracket to have five-year-old daughters themselves.

He had a ray of hope. A slim, solitary ray, but it was better than absolute darkness.

Roman watched a crew of scrub nurses wheel Cindy's bed out of the room. Apparently, her new heart had arrived.

"Would you like to walk along with us?" one nice nurse asked.

Roman shook his head, respectfully declining. The thought of it made him sick. The thought of Cindy made him sick.

They wheeled her out and down the hall, and the room was uncomfortably quiet. He wanted to go get a cup of coffee, but he didn't want to move. He just wanted to sit, solid, until he heard that his baby girl was safe.

His phone rang.

He picked it up, clicked it on, pulled up the antenna. "Yes?"

"Daddy?"

It was Kewpie. Roman started to cry. "Hi, baby," he said. "You okay?"

"My back hurts. . ." He heard her voice fade out.

"Special Agent Monroe here, Mr. Daniloff. She's fine, or as well as can be expected. It appears as though she has donated a kidney, but otherwise she's just fine."

Donated a kidney?

"Tell her I'll be down to pick her up tonight," Roman said, then without waiting for the FBI guy's reply, he hung up. He had something to do.

Surging with energy, he got up out of that damned plastic chair, ran down the hallway, pushed through doors, followed signs to the operating rooms and finally caught up with Cindy. He grabbed the metal-jacketed chart from the end of her bed, flipped it open, and ripped out the consent forms. "No consent," he said to the assembled people in green masks and gowns. "I *forbid* you to operate."

"Mr. Daniloff," some masked doctor said. "We have her heart. We have the team. We *have* to operate."

"No operation," Roman said, tossed the chart onto Cindy's blanketed legs and ripped the consent forms into little pieces.

The speechless medical staff watched them flutter to the floor. "She'll die," someone said.

"Fine," Roman replied, and walked away. He had a plane to catch. Then he and his kids had some money to spend. First stop: Disney World.

❈

Riding the Black Horse

The little girl sat down in the seat next to Mick, a pretty thing with long straight brown hair that shined in the dim airplane overhead reading lights. She clutched a brown-haired dolly that looked much like she did, though she was dressed in shorts and t-shirt and the doll wore a long white gown of sorts.

"Hi," Mick said. He knew that children should not talk to strangers, and that strangers should not encourage communication, but she surprised him by looking straight into his eyes and responding.

"Hi," she said. Then she looked down in a very attractive, completely unselfconscious bout of shyness.

"This will not do," her mother was saying to the flight attendant. "I need to sit next to my daughter. She's only ten, for God's sakes, this is like having her fly alone. It's worse, having her sit next to. . .next to a strange man."

The flight attendant, pushed from behind and already beginning to fray around the edges of her coif, looked at Mick. "Would you be willing to switch seats?"

"Sorry," he said. "No can do."

The mother glared. "Why not?"

He opened his inflight magazine and successfully ignored her.

The little girl tugged at her dolly's hair. "Put your seatbelt on," Mick whispered to her. "It's going to be a bumpy ride." She smiled up at him as if they were conspirators in some as-yet-unrevealed scheme.

While the flight attendant went about begging other people to give up their seats, Mick settled in, closed his eyes and felt around his psychic arena for her aura. It was there, fresh and innocent. He loved that. He loved kids. He was going to have fun with this one. He hoped she was adult enough to have a sense of outrage like her mother. That would be fun.

"I'm sorry, Ma'am," the flight attendant said to the mother. "I need you to take your seat."

The woman crouched down next to the little girl. "I'm only two rows back on the aisle," she said. "I can see you. If you need anything, just turn around and I'll be there."

"I'll be okay," she said.

The mother pinned Mick with a killing stare, then went to her seat.

"I'm Mick," he said, and held out his hand.

"Monica," she said, and shook his hand in the shy, limp way that ten year olds do. He loved the feel of it.

"Can I buy you a drink, Monica?"

She smiled with sparkling eyes, and Mick was afraid he was falling in love.

"Gin and tonic? No, that tastes awful. Vodka martini? No, that's worse."

She started to giggle.

"Rum and coke? Beer? Wine? Or how about just a cup of coffee?"

"No, thank you," she said, and went back to straightening the doll's hair and clothes.

"What's your dolly's name?"

"Lucinda."

"Monica and Lucinda," he said. "You ought to be living in a British school for girls, having tea every day at four o'clock and making fun of the headmistress."

"I've been to England," she said.

"You have? You're a world traveler. And where are you going now?"

"To my grandmother's house. We're going to have to live there until she dies."

"And you don't want to?"

"I hate it there."

"Is your grandmother mean?"

"No, she's sick. She smells bad. My mother's the mean one."

"She looked mean to me, too. I'm glad she's not sitting with us."

Monica looked up with surprise, amazement and delight in her eyes. "Me, too," she whispered. "I was hoping the plane would crash."

"Well, then," Mick said, loosening his tie. "We've got a long flight. Let's have some fun."

"I know a game," she said, and retrieved her purple backpack from under the seat in front of her. She cast a glance behind her, at her mother, but as the seatbelt sign was still on, they were safe. "My mother doesn't like me to play this game," she whispered.

"Well then, by all means," Mick said. "Let's have a go at it. I love games. I especially love games that mothers don't like."

She pulled from her pack a deck of blue Bicycle playing cards.

"Oh, good," Mick said, thinking Old Maid, Slapjack, War or on a good day maybe some Rummy. "Black Jack? Strip poker?"

"No," the girl said, but she was interrupted by the attendant coming by for drink orders.

"Let me buy you a drink," Mick said.

"I'll have what you're having," she whispered.

"I'm going to have a Bloody Mary," he said.

"Me, too."

What could it hurt? Mick thought, and ordered a double. Monica ordered tomato juice and held out her glass for him to pour in a small bottle of vodka. Oddly, Mick felt as if she had an old soul, and he could confide certain things in her. They were already sharing secrets.

"I was hoping the plane would crash, too," he said.

"Why? Is your mommy mean to you, too?"

He laughed. He liked the adult sparkle in her eye. No way was this girl ten years old. She was irresistible. "No, my wife. She divorced me and took everything. I have nothing left. No house, no books, no dog. Barely a job, and lots and lots of payments." And court dates, he thought, if he ever went back to California.

"We could probably crash this plane if we wanted to," she said.

Mick sipped his drink.

"I could just go up there and open that big door. The loss of pressure would suck me out, of course, and probably kill me instantly. But the plane would have to go down, and the funny oxygen things would dangle from the ceiling and the pilot would make an emergency landing somewhere, and with any luck, the plane would rip in half, and some hot metal would cut my mother's head clean off, leaving her body still strapped in by the seat belt."

"Keep drinking," Mick said, startled by the girl's admission, and the detail with which she had fantasized it. He liked her. Maybe they could run away together.

The girl took a swallow. "This is good," she said, and patted her pouty little lips on the napkin. "Too bad there isn't someone here that you'd like to kill."

"Just me."

"No," she said, "not you. You're nice."

"I'm not so nice," he said. "Let's play your game."

She looked around behind her again, then pulled the cards out of the cardboard case and set them on top of the tray table. "This is a good game," she said, "but you have to take it seriously."

"How seriously?"

"Dead seriously."

"It's just a game, Monica."

"Maybe. Okay. Pick a card."

"Is this a trick?"

"No. Pick a card."

He cut the cards and pulled one from the middle of the deck. "Do I show it to you?"

"Of course." She took it from him, looked at it, looked up at him, frowned, looked at the card again, then sipped her drink. "This is the heart attack card."

"I'm sorry?"

"Heart attack." She showed him the seven of spades. "That's how you're going to die. Want to know when?"

Mick thought he could feel his chest beginning to seize already. "Not particularly."

"You don't look like a heart attack," she said. "You exercise, right?"

"Yeah."

"Must be in the family."

In fact, it was. Mick's father, mother and brother all died from heart disease at ages younger than he currently was.

"Hey," he said. "You pick a card."

"I already know my card."

"Yeah? What is it?"

She smirked up at him. "Plane crash. So's my mom's."

Was that a change in the engine's pitch he heard? He downed the last of his drink, and watched as she downed hers.

"This will probably be it," she said, and daintily wiped her mouth on the cocktail napkin.

The flight attendant came by and picked up the detritus of the cocktail hour, and Monica set her dolly up on the tray table.

Mick no longer wanted to play with her. He was too busy listening to the sounds inside his skin and the sounds outside the airplane's skin. His anxiety grew as the sky darkened outside and the reason for the seat belt sign remaining on became evident. Turbulence.

"Better hold on to Lucinda," he said to her.

"It won't hurt," she said. "It might be a little scary at first." She thought for a minute. "But I guess a heart attack does hurt, doesn't it? You'll die before we do. Still feeling okay?"

In fact, he wasn't. Cold sweat trickled down the side of his face and he felt as though there wasn't enough air in the plane to breathe. He closed his eyes and listened to Monica sing to her dolly, and then the dolly was sitting on his chest, and Monica was breathing boozy tomato juice breath into his ear. "She's heavy, isn't she? Lucinda is very, very heavy."

"Help me," he squeaked out, and she laughed and bounced the dolly up and down on his chest in rhythm with his labored heartbeat.

Bum-bump. Bum-bump. Bum-bump.

"Please," he whispered. "Call the flight attendant."

"She can't help you," Monica said. "The plane is going down in a minute."

Mick tried to concentrate amid the burning pain that enveloped his left arm and chest, and the band that squeezed the breath out of him. *I'm sorry, Lord,* he tried to articulate clearly in his thoughts. *I've not been a nice person, and I hope it isn't too late to ask for forgiveness.*

An explosion of some kind rocked the plane and blew out a line of windows directly across the aisle. The lights went out. People began to scream. The plane headed down.

In the midst of the madness, Mick regained his calm. He heard Monica's mother desperately calling her name, but Monica was laughing, and he thought he'd take that sound with him to the grave and beyond.

He was a little more successful with his prayers after that, as his concentration focused on the very important task at hand. His wife, his daughters, the series of little girls he had terrorized in his past.

Monica was his just desserts, he knew. And as he fell down that black rabbit hole of unconsciousness, as the plane fell through the black sky toward obliteration, the only sound that he heard chilled him worse than death taking his pulse.

"Whee!" she said. "Whee!"

It was a sound he had made himself in the company of little girls way too often.

✳

Genetically Predisposed

I first walked into that tattoo parlor on my fortieth birthday. Struck dumb by the horrid graphic visuals—the walls in the waiting room were papered with tattoo designs, typical red-and-black, violent, sadistic and macho designs—I almost backed out as quickly as I had come in.

I stilled my heart. Nobody had touched me with needle and ink yet. I clutched my purse tighter and began to look at the individual drawings. There were many skulls, knives, fists and bloody claws for sure, but there were also beautiful flowers, birds and mythical creatures drawn and colored with a delicate hand and fine sensitivity.

I didn't know what I wanted, I didn't even know that I was seriously considering a tattoo until I found myself walking through the door of Sailor Mike's. I just knew I was terribly unhappy with life, *terribly unhappy*, and I need to show a little spunk, a little individuality, a little rebellion of my own, for once.

My husband had fallen in love with someone else. Our marriage was only a shadow. We continued to live together, and we kept our money in the same pot, but it was only a matter of time before that changed. Our nest was empty and so was my life.

That left a big house and just Kristoph and me, and we didn't have much to say to each other any more. The tension was getting to me. I felt knots in my stomach all the time, especially those nights when I knew he was with *her*. I knew if it kept up much longer, I would run screaming from the house, tearing my hair, doing damage to myself and everyone around me. Or worse, I'd become ill. The consuming kind of ill. The *all-consuming* kind of ill.

Yet, every time I thought about taking some kind of action— moving out, kicking him out, putting the house up for sale—it didn't seem right, it didn't seem real.

But I needed to make sure I was alive. I needed to do something for myself that was a little bit risky, a little bit outlandish. And…secretly, I'd always wanted a tattoo.

I'd finished looking at all the anchors and the panthers and the scantily clad women and was on to the second wall, starting with cartoon characters, when the inner door opened and a man looked out.

"Yes?" he said.

I felt suddenly shy. "Hi," I said.

He just stood there and I realized that he thought I was a saleswoman or something.

"I'm thinking about getting a tattoo."

"Oh," he said, and he came out, coffee cup in hand. "See anything you like?"

"They're all really nice," I said, "but..."

"But they're not you."

"Yeah, I guess so." I wanted to leave. I felt so stupid.

"Where were you thinking of putting it? Shoulder? Back? Hip?"

"Thigh," I said, and then I couldn't believe I'd really said that.

"Inside or outside?"

"Outside. Of course." I knew I was blushing, and I hated it. This guy meant nothing to me. He was just a salesman and an artist. I was the customer. I needed to get a hold on myself and get a hold on this situation. "I was thinking of something a little more..."

"Come inside here," he said, and opened the door to a brightly lit room.

I walked in and for a moment, I thought I'd walked into a doctor's office. One wall was curtained; there was a window on the other side into the waiting room. People could watch a tattoo in progress, if it wasn't too personal. There was an adjustable padded brown leather table, white cabinets, white countertops, an autoclave, sterile packaged instruments on a stainless-steel tray—and it was all absolutely spotless. I watched him as he busied himself in the corner filing cabinet.

Sailor Mike was about forty-five, with a nice, full reddish beard just beginning to gray. His hair was cut short around the ears and gray showed there, too. He wore little round glasses, which made him look curiously studious. He carried an extra ten or so pounds on his compact frame, held in by a finely tooled leather belt. When he turned around, I saw that his eyes were green and his T-shirt was clean. He handed me a drawing and I saw that his fingernails were clean, too.

"I'm Mike," he said, and held out his hand. I took it.

"Alice." His hand was warm and soft, and his grip was firm.

"I don't do women after noon," he said, and we both looked up at the clock. It was eleven-fifteen.

"Why?" And we had a moment of each other's eyes.

"Personal policy. I want to make sure they're sober, for one thing, and that they don't get hassled by a bunch of guys in the waiting room. You know." He looked at the floor. Amazingly enough, *he* was shy, and that gave me a little thrill, as if I had found myself to be attractive again. For the first time in years.

I looked at the drawings he handed me, but they weren't right, either. They were too magical, too fairy. I was not a fairy type of person. I looked up to say so, and saw a queer look in his eyes. His hand came up to touch my cheek, and I moved backward.

Startled, he flushed and apologized. "I'm sorry," he said. "But your skin—" Again, he brought his hand up and I let his thumb touch my cheek. "I've never seen skin like this before." My eyes closed involuntarily as he touched me, thrills running down my back, goose bumps coming up on my arms, and I wondered when Kristoph had last touched my cheek. Had Kristoph *ever* touched my face? Then Mike had my fingertips and he was looking at my hands. He pushed the sleeves of my blouse up and looked at my forearms.

Then he reached over and locked the door. "Can I see your shoulders?"

I can't explain my lack of fear. The intensity in his eyes was more than heat, was more than desire, I was not afraid that he would touch me, I was rather afraid that he wouldn't touch me. It never occurred that he might hurt me.

He closed his eyes so as not to see the rejection he expected, his face showed the anticipated pain. Then he just whispered, "Please?" and I began to unbutton my blouse. He opened his eyes again and watched me. I kept telling myself I was being foolish, but I couldn't stop.

"Skin is my business. I've been doing tats for twenty years, and I've seen all kinds of skin, but I've always dreamed of "—my blouse fell off my shoulders—"this. This skin. Oh God, *this* skin." He came away from the wall and touched my shoulder with such reverence. He pulled my blouse down in the back, and ran his fingers lightly over my shoulders, down my spine. Now it was my turn to close my eyes. This was unspeakably erotic, here in the brightly lit room of a tattoo artist's studio. "It's almost translucent. You've hardly ever been in the sun. It's almost like a baby's skin, there are no blemishes, there are no moles, no freckles, no odd colorations." He pinched some skin on my shoulder. I dared not flinch. "It's magnificent," he breathed.

Is there no fool like an old fool? I thought. The skin was forty years old. True, I never went out in the sun, never had, but I always thought I looked too thin, too pale. Kristoph always said I should go out and get some exercise, but I didn't. I didn't. And now this man, this tattoo man, is he taking advantage of my age, my naivete? Is he selling me a perfect con job?

Then he lifted my blouse back up over my shoulders and turned me to face him.

"Listen," he said. "I can give you a tattoo. I can give you the most incredible skin illustration you've ever seen. Know how the painters, the artists, the old masters, know how they created masterpieces that live on forever? That's because oil paints are translucent, and you can put layer after layer of paint on a canvas, and it all works to one advantage. I can do that with your skin. I can do that with *your* skin. I can make your body into the most wonderful work of art you could imagine."

"What would you do?" My mouth was dry.

"Can I see the rest of you?"

Convinced now that I *was* but an old fool, I shrugged off the blouse, unbuckled my belt, kicked off my shoes. Soon I stood in my underwear, hoping that would be enough. It was. He trailed his fingers over my arms, inspecting them as a jeweler might look at a new stone. He had me get up onto his table, where he looked at each leg, each foot, then I had to pull my panties down and expose my tummy. He was working. He wasn't going to harm me. And all the while, I gloried in his touch.

"Okay," he said, and moved to the side, where he poured himself a fresh cup of coffee.

I waited.

"A snake," he said.

I remembered the snaky pictures outside on his waiting-room walls. They were gross.

"No," he said to my frown. "Not like those." He set his coffee cup down and walked over to me, took my little finger in his hand and led me down from the table. "A great snake. I would start here, with the tip of its tail coiled around your little finger. I would wrap it here, around your hand, across your wrist." His fingers trailed his vision on my skin. "It would come across the top of this arm and lay across your chest here, resting on you breasts. It's six, eight inches thick here. Heavy. It comes around the top of your other shoulder, down across your back, under the arm, around your belly, across your right buttock and wraps itself around your right leg. The head is here." He was kneeling on the floor, two fingers about four inches apart on my foot. "I would mix all my own inks."

I felt the weight of the snake. "I don't know."

He stood up and looked me in the face. He took off his glasses and wiped his hands over his eyes. He resettled his glasses and fixed me with a steady, serious gaze. "It would be the project of my lifetime," he said, then turned to his coffee and I began to dress, self-consciously.

He was still facing the cabinets, his hands on the counter when I finished dressing. I didn't know what to say, so I just unlocked the door and left.

I went home to a large, empty house. I walked upstairs to what had been my son's room. I'd redecorated it for something to do and now I wished I could still smell him in this room, but it was now sterile.

I went into the master bedroom and took off my clothes. I tilted the mirror forward so I could look at my entire body. It looked different than it had this morning. It now had possibilities. It was not too skinny, it was not too pale. It could bear the weight of a snake.

Oh my god, what would people think?

That night, as I lay in bed, Kristoph a firm distance next to me, I felt the weight of the snake again on my chest. I felt Sailor Mike's fingers on my skin. I'd forgotten what it meant to be touched. I'd forgotten what it felt like to be aroused. That night, the night that everyone but me had forgotten was my fortieth birthday, I lay awake almost the whole night, and shared my birthday with the remembrance of warm, gentle fingers and the promise of a snake.

I went back to Mike's the next day.

"What would it look like?"

He didn't seem thrilled to see me. He looked intense instead, as if he dared not hope. We went back into his studio and again he rummaged in his filing cabinet. Then he came out with a tissue-covered drawing. He handed it to me.

Under the tissue was a six-inch section of snake, drawn in iridescent colors. Each scale was defined, the shadowing and shading magnificent.

"When did you do this?"

"That, right there, is the reason I opened this shop. I knew that some day I would get to do that." He sat on a little wheeled stool. "I've been waiting. Practicing. Getting better. I can do better than that drawing on you. That's on board. On paper. On your skin, I can make that snake *live.*"

"Will it hurt?"

"Yes."

"How long will it take?"

He shrugged. "Depends on how frequently we work, how long the sessions go, how long it takes you to recover, how thin your skin is." He looked at the floor, shrugged again. "Six months."

Six months!

I stood leaning against his table, while he sat on his stool, and we both looked at the floor in silence. We both knew I would do it.

"Okay," I said, and it came out like a whisper.

"There's just one thing," he said, then he stood up and came over to me. "I am a man of my word, and I believe that you are as good as your word, too."

His eyes were deeper than any I had ever seen. "I am," I said.

"Then you need to promise me that once we start, you will finish. Unless you are dead, you will finish the drawing."

I nodded, my mouth dry.

"Say it," he demanded.

"I will finish it," I said, and I felt as if I'd just sold my soul.

On the first day, I lay naked on his table while he examined me again. He looked at me from all angles, all perspectives. I lay every which way on his table, and he touched me occasionally with the point of a felt-tip pen. The second day he made dotted lines. The third day he changed the lines. The fourth day he said he was ready to begin.

Day after day I meditated to the pain, the relentless buzz of the needle and the firm way he held me as he worked. There was nothing to my life but Mike and the "work" as he called it. The routine—the pain—became normal. He worked according to his own agenda; day by day I didn't know where he would be working next. But every day I went home with a fresh bandage. Somewhere I always had a bandage, a scab, and sore spots in varying degrees of healing, while he created new ones day by day.

The pain of the needle, I found, could be broken down into strings of vibrations. I lay on the table, eyes closed, and divided the pain into chords. The long sweeps of the needle had a different orchestration than the short coloring strokes, and the music went on in my head as the drawing appeared on my body. The inner thigh was the worst. Tears leaked onto the small pillow. Mike kissed my cheek periodically, handed me a fresh tissue and continued.

Sometimes at home, when a bandage came off and I could see whole sections of what Mike had done, it appeared as if the snake was emerging from within me.

Sometimes, in bed, I would feel the weight of it pressing on me, and it grew heavier as time went on.

No one noticed.

Mike and I rarely talked; he and I were not important. There was only the work.

At three months, he was well into the color. The weight of the drawing grew, as if he breathed bulk into it as well as ink.

One night I awoke from a deep sleep with a startling revelation: *it's a male.*

He felt cold.

Mike lost weight. He greedily snatched bandages off every day and relentlessly examined and reexamined the finished portions for flaws. He worked in a rare heat, sometimes climbing right up on the table and straddling me in order to get just exactly the correct angle.

I was curiously unaffected by Mike's frenzies. I had distractions of my own. I lay on the table, day after day, feeling feminine, important, beautiful, and impatient to show my masterpiece.

And a masterpiece it was. It took my breath away. I began to understand why I never wanted to go into the sun. I now saw how the events of my life had led up to this point—I was *supposed* to wear this snake.

I began to identify with it wholeheartedly. It was my claim to fame. I couldn't wait until it was finished, and I could show the world. I could show my friends. I could show Kristoph.

Kristoph! He would die.

At night, when Kristoph came home smelling like her perfume, undressed and got into bed, I watched with slitted eyes. And I felt the snake twitch.

He, too, wanted this project to be finished. He waited not so patiently to be fully drawn.

When the inking was finished, there were still daily bandages to be removed, and then touch-up work when the scabs lifted. Some of the scabs went deep; the needle had a tendency to tear my fragile skin. The daily routine of going back to Mike's became a drain, not only because I was ready for it to be finished, but Mike's appearance had become seedy and unkempt. His fingernails were no longer clean, his studio no longer spotless.

The day he pronounced the drawing finished, he cried. I wanted to put my arms around him, this man who had given me back so much of myself, but I couldn't. I sat with him, but I had nothing to say. He said he was going to go on a little trip, a vacation, and I nodded my agreement that he needed a rest, and then I left. I left with my prize. After six months of meditation, anticipation, pain and fear, all the bandages were gone, there were no more scabs, I was ready to reveal my elegance. But to whom?

I wandered the street for the rest of the afternoon, so very conscious of a snake wrapped around me. I did some window shopping, some people-watching, wondering what to do next. I felt adrift without my daily routine of meditation to the pain and the needle at Mike's.

I passed through the alley next to a Chinese restaurant back toward the parking lot, when I felt the snake stir. I stopped, startled. It moved. My shirt bloused as the snake took its form. I felt its taut muscles as it inched its way around me, its head seeking the pavement. I felt it slide right off me. Its weight had been incredible; without it, I felt as if I could float. I watched it go into the dark behind the restaurant, and I followed on tiptoe.

Four cats waited by the back door. The snake singled out the black and white one, and before the cat understood what was happening, the snake had it. It wound around the poor thing and squeezed. The cat screamed, then meowed with its last breath, then wheezed like a bellows. And then the mighty jaws disjoined and opened and the cat disappeared, inch by inch, heaved down the snake's gullet by intense, superb muscular contractions.

I watched in horrified fascination as the cat disappeared, head first. When the last of the tail had been swallowed, the snake came back to me in esses and nosed at my pant leg. I closed my eyes. The snake came slowly, heavily up my leg—I had to help it where the cat bulged—wrapped around me, climbed into its exact position, fell asleep and melted back into my skin.

I watched the bulge of the cat over the next week as it diminished in size and moved from my thigh up across my butt and around my back.

I weighed myself, too. Or rather, I weighed myself wearing the snake. He weighed sixty-five pounds.

I paid less and less attention to Krisoph as the weeks went by. My life was focused, instead, on the phenomenon in and on my body. The snake left me at regular intervals. I felt him wake, and rise out of my skin at night, and I watched the blanket ripple as he silently left me in search of food.

Toward dawn he returned, sated, bulging and cold, and I shivered as he took his place and soaked up my warmth. I fell in with his rhythms. They became my own.

Daytimes I wondered at the mind of a snake, as I sat by the window and stroked his smoothness, talking to him. Occasionally, I undressed and walked around the house naked, surprised, always, by our reflection in a mirror, a window, a glass.

A year since the inking began, and still Kristoph hadn't noticed. He lived only for his work and his trysts. I wondered why he didn't leave me and go to be with her. He could give two women peace with one stroke. He was a weasel, that's why. I began to hate him. I found it harder and harder to sleep next to him at night. I hugged the edge of the bed, sleepless, staring into the night, thinking empty thoughts.

Then one night, when my snake roused himself and went hunting, I went with him.

I drew on black pants and a black jacket. We went out the kitchen door and through the back yard. We cut across all the neighbors' back yards until he found the spot he'd apparently noticed before. A neighbor's dog was sleeping at his dog house. I waited in the shadows and watched.

The dog barely yipped. And when my friend's jaws distended, I opened mine, and felt them unlock. I opened my throat to the night, and almost felt that dog chunking down my gullet, little hairy head first.

We were both almost too sleepy to make it back home, but just before dawn, we slithered into bed, I felt his aching coldness wrap around me and we fell asleep.

I took to curling up on the coffee table in the living room during the day when the sun shone brightly upon it. I'd fall into a restful nether state, neither sleeping nor awake. I was aware, yet dreaming peaceful scenes of cool caves, moist burrows and hot, flat rocks.

At night, I'd eat eggs; crack their ends and suck the goop right out of the shell. I'd eat a half dozen, and then go out. Or sometimes we'd just curl up in the bedroom easy chair and watch Kristoph sleep. I'd pet my friend's head and watch his beady eyes gleam in the darkness as he stared with a reptile's nonemotion at the man who had robbed me of myself.

One night I dropped by Sailor Mike's. He was there and the shop was empty, but we didn't have much to say to each other. He seemed wrung out, as if he had given me everything he owned, and I suppose he had. We hugged, and he commented on my loss of weight. I had to smile to myself. The scale said I'd gained.

Winter fell abruptly mid-October. I slept round the clock, waking only to eat at night when Kristoph turned on the electric blanket. I knew the signs. I knew what was happening, but while it was happening to my body, it was also happening to my mind, and it seemed the most natural thing in the world. The winter passed in a blur of half-light, half wakefulness, half restlessness.

I dreamed of Kristoph talking to me, I dreamed of concentrating far beyond my energy resources to understand and answer. Those periods of hard work were rare; mostly I dreamed of lounging loosely on tree branches overhanging bird nests, swimming gently in green, scum-lidded rivers, nosing out burrows of small warm rodents.

Spring dawned gently. I woke more frequently, began to wander the house in the sunshine, took regular showers. I would turn the electric blanket on and feel my friend awaken and move about my body. The smoothness of his skin delighted and energized me, and while I looked for signs of affection in his face and found none, I soon discovered that affection was no longer in my range of emotions, either.

I merely wanted him.

We played this erotic scene daily; it seemed to have no beginning and no end. I was never conscious of waking up and beginning, nor was I ever aware of finishing and drifting back to sleep. It seemed as if I merely drifted in and out of sleep, and his shiny skin was constantly moving, restlessly seeking, all over me, all the time.

Then one morning as the camellias were looking in the window at us, he brought my passion to a frenzy, and in the panes of sunlight on the wrecked bed I felt him enter me, fill me, and we thrashed and rolled, tumbled and entwined with the sheets, with each other, with ecstasy and madness.

When it was over, he melted back into my skin, leaving me breathless and alone, tingling still and suspicious of my sanity.

When the eggs came, they were soft and creamy and I could feel life vibrating within them. One after another they slipped from me until the muscle fluttering stopped and I held a nest of seven of them. They were like precious fruit. I nestled them into a pillow and put it under the bed.

Kristoph became more of a presence, more of a mystery. He would stand in front of me and shout, but I could no longer comprehend either his emotion nor his words. He gesticulated wildly, his arms flailing about; he looked cluttered, as if he had far too many appendages and couldn't control them properly. I lay curled up in my chair, trying to discern meaning, and resisted the temptation to taste his air with my tongue.

He packed boxes of things and took them away, but continued to sleep in what had been our bed. I slept in the chair.

One night he came in looking odder than usual. He was disheveled, he smelled of poisons, his hair was messed, and I thought the human species was an ungainly and ugly sort. He stood, weaving, looking down on me in the chair, then threw his coat into the corner and made his way unsteadily to the bed. He pulled off his shoes and lay back, muttering something, then began to snore.

My friend awakened, lifting his head from where it rested on my foot, his tongue tasting the close, comfortable air of our home. He disentangled himself from me and made his way across the carpeting to the nest under the bed, and suddenly I felt the activity as well. I crawled under with him and we watched as the eggs moved gently with the persistence of those within. They seemed to struggle so.

I thought perhaps they would have an easier time of it if they were warmer, so I brought the nest out, put it in the bed and turned on the electric blanket. Then we went back to the chair to watch the window, waiting for morning.

Kristoph began to twitch about dawn, slapping and pawing at himself. We watched with detached amusement.

Midmorning, he finally roused himself and went into the bathroom. I heard his strong stream of urine, the flush, the water in the sink began to run. And then I heard the gasp. The shout, the faint shriek of hysteria present in his squeaky human throat.

He came out naked, and I saw my children, my wondrous children, my seven beautiful and glorious children as they were illustrated at random about his body.

One lay coiled elegantly around his right nipple.

I stroked the head of my mate and stared off into the day.

❋

Purple Shards

With grim determination, Kathryn wrestled the wheel of the Jeep through the muddy ruts of the little-used logging road. Rain sheeted down in the twilight, and the little girlish squeaks of fear that came from the seat next to her didn't help any.

Headlights bounced crazily as the Jeep's tire slammed into a boulder and glanced off. Kathryn gunned it, spit mud from the rear and got back on the road.

"Fuck," she said, her heart hammering, then caught a glimpse of a long-dead, lightning-split tree to the right. She turned the wheel, and the Jeep cut brand new ruts through what might have been a dirt road long ago.

Deep into the woods, on solid ground, Kathryn felt a little more competent at the Jeep's wheel. Once they left the wretched mudslide of a road, her confidence returned.

A small cabin loomed out of the misty rain.

"Thank God," she whispered.

"What?" Tina asked, releasing her death grip on the Jeep's handles. "Are we there?"

"We're here."

Kathryn unlocked the cabin door and shouldered it open, then took a deep breath of musty air. Horribly familiar, that smell. It conjured up memories. Memories of lovemaking. Memories of fighting. Memories of Steve. "C'mon," she said. "Let's unload."

Within moments, bedding, cooler, overnight bags and brown paper sacks of food were all in. Kathryn lit an oil lamp, raised it over her head, and took a quick walk around the inside of the cabin, inspecting the ceiling. Shadows waltzed crazily around her.

"No leaks. That's a relief."

"I love this place. It's so remote. It's so cool." Tina pulled a bottle of wine from a food sack.

"I hate this place," Kathryn said, and began to crumple newspaper for the fireplace.

Soon, a fire warmed the cabin, two oil lamps provided plenty of light, and the two friends sat cross-legged on a sagging couch.

Tina pointed at a set of deer antlers mounted over the door. "Bet Steve used to hang his hat there."

"Hat, shirt, whatever."

A pair of hip waders hung on a hook near the door, along with a couple of heavy wool plaid shirts. A dusty mounted fish hung cockeyed on one wall.

"Did you come here often?" Tina asked, then refilled their wine glasses.

"No, this was Steve's hangout. I used to come with him, but, I don't know. I had other things to do." She opened a package of cheese, sliced off a chunk and handed it to Tina. "I'm glad we're here. We can sweep out the cobwebs and get this place ready to sell."

"Sell? You're kidding. This place is really cool." Tina grabbed a bag of pretzels and began wrestling with it.

"Steve was the one who liked to hunt and fish and stuff, not me. I never want to come here again."

Tina stopped crinkling the pretzel bag and put a hand on Kathryn's arm.

"I'm just here to get his things." Kathryn leaned her head against Tina's shoulder. "I could never have come here without you."

Tina kissed Kathryn's head, then ripped open the pretzels. Pretzels flew from the burst package and they both laughed. "Come on," she said. "We're going to have fun in spite of everything." She stood up, fished around in one of the grocery sacks, then came back. "Junk food feast," she said, and ceremoniously set down a package of gummy bears, two boxes of Cracker Jack and a bag of marshmallows.

"Gummy bears? With wine?"

"It's very chic."

A roaring gust of wind shook the cabin. The two long-time friends looked at each other, eyes wide.

Kathryn thought Tina looked great in the light from the oil lamp. Both thirty-four, Tina had never been married, and she still looked young and blonde and pert and fresh. Kathryn was now a widow, and she was afraid that the stresses of marriage and Steve's death showed on her face.

The rain came down with a vengeance, pounding the roof. A slash of lightning x-rayed the room, followed instantly by a crack of thunder.

Tina grabbed Kathryn's hand, and they held on to each other. The thunder rumbled off into the distance, and then there was only the steady drone of rain again. They relaxed in the relative silence.

Tina gulped her wine. "Where did they find him?"

Kathryn took a deep breath. "About a hundred yards from the cabin door."

"And they never found out who did it?"

Kathryn raised the rifle and trained it first on the horse, then on Steve, hefty, hardy, handsome. The rifle was heavy, and she was unsure. The crosshairs wavered, the rifle trembled, she lowered the rifle to give her plan a little more thought.

"It was an accident. A hunting accident," Kathryn said.

Before she could change her mind, she brought the rifle up abruptly. With grim determination, she focused directly on Steve's head, just as he stopped the horse, just as he turned to look behind him, just as he made a perfect target.

Bam! The gun slammed into Kathryn's shoulder, knocking her back a step. Steve's horse reared and began to run.

"But if you shot at something you thought was a deer," Tina pursued, "wouldn't you go looking for it?"

"They're not sure where he was shot. They think his horse brought him home."

"Yeah, but if you were a hunter, and you heard that somebody had been killed in a hunting accident, shot by somebody by mistake, wouldn't you go to the authorities?"

Kathryn fishtailed the rental car to a stop on the dusty road next to the reservoir. For a moment, she almost lost control of it. For a moment, she wished she had driven it right into the lake. She got out of the car, slammed the door, opened the trunk and pulled out the rifle. With a mighty heave and a yell, she end-over-ended it into the water.

Then anger turned to grief. She leaned against the car, but as the grief rose up through her, her knees gave out. She slumped to the ground, holding her stomach, and sobbed.

"I don't know," Kathryn said. "It wouldn't bring him back. No matter what." She drained her wine glass and filled it again. "It was an accident."

Tina held her glass up to be refilled. "Why Steve?" she asked quietly. "He was such a great guy."

Kathryn set a bag of groceries on the kitchen counter. "Steve?"

No answer.

"Steve, honey, I'm home."

Still no answer, but she heard a noise coming from the back of the house. Senses alert to an intruder, she grabbed a kitchen knife and walked stealthily through the hall.

The bedroom door was ajar. Quietly, she pushed on it, and saw two sets of bare feet. She pushed the door open wider. It was him, she realized with a wrench to her gut. Steve was fucking some woman right there on their bed.

Some sound came out of her mouth, and the knife fell soundlessly to the carpet.

Steve turned his head and looked at her, but her presence broke neither his concentration nor his rhythm.

"He was troubled," Kathryn said.

"His mom?"

Kathryn looked at her girlfriend. "How do you know about his mom?"

"You didn't have to know Steve very well to know he had unresolved issues on that score."

"His mother died when he was sixteen. You know what jerks guys can be when they're that age. He never got over the guilt."

"Guilt. Yeah, guilt." Tina set her wine glass down on the coffee table, stood up and stretched. She turned around and saw a large, sheet-draped object that was mounted on the wall. "Hey, what's this?" She pulled the sheet off, revealing a huge mirror with a big, heavy gilt frame.

"Ugh. Cover it back up. I hate that thing."

"Wow. Look at this. It's so cool. What's it doing here?"

"I don't know," Kathryn squirmed with distaste. "It's always been here."

Tina looked at her reflection, checked her makeup, fluffed her hair. "I've never seen anything like this before." She grabbed a fresh bottle of wine and can of nuts from the dining table and walked back to the couch, back past the mirror.

Vainly unable to pass a mirror without looking, she glanced at it, and jumped, startled.

"What?"

Tina stopped and looked into the mirror a little more closely. "Nothing." She frowned at it, then turned her back on it and sat down on the couch next to Kathryn. "Nothing." She looked back up at it. "It just seemed as though something moved. Maybe—I don't know—inside. Kind of deep down inside the mirror."

"I hate that mirror."

"Why?" Tina opened a can of nuts and helped herself to a big handful.

"It gives me the creeps. For one thing, it's so big. It takes up a whole goddamned wall. And it's kind of purple. Wait until you see it in the daylight. The glass has a purplish tinge to it."

"Yuck," Tina said, crunching nuts. "Who'd want to look at themselves in purple? Who'd make a purple mirror?"

"I don't know." Kathryn picked a cashew out of the can. "Steve used to talk to it."

"Talk to it? You mean talk to himself?"

Kathryn rolled the cashew between her thumb and forefinger as she spoke. "No. . . I don't know. It was weird. Sometimes I'd wake up in the middle of the night and he'd be standing over there talking to it. Then he'd act real guilty, like I'd caught him doing something wrong."

"Weird."

"Too weird. I stopped coming out here with him."

"So he came out here by himself and talked to the mirror?"

Kathryn shrugged and popped the cashew into her mouth. "I guess."

They listened to the steady drone of the rain while Tina spun the top off the fresh bottle of wine and refilled their glasses.

"I'm going to try," she said, then stumbled up off the couch, a little tipsy.

"Try what?"

"Talking," Tina said, and walked over to the mirror. She struck a pose and examined her reflection.

Kathryn watched her.

Tina giggled and waved at Kathryn, who scowled back. Tina struck a stern pose, arms crossed, and cleared her throat. "Hello, mirror."

No response. Tina's eyes flickered back and forth between her reflection and Kathryn's. "I *said*, hello, mirror."

She giggled drunkenly at Kathryn. "Nobody home." She looked back to the darkened image of herself and challenged the mirror, hands on hips. "If you don't answer me, I'll break you."

Kathryn watched Tina gaze into the mirror too long, too long, too long. "Break it," she whispered.

Tina whirled around, her face flushed.

Kathryn woke up and saw Steve standing with both hands up on the mirror. His forehead was pressed against it. "I never meant to hurt you, Mom," he said.

Kathryn sat up in bed. "Steve?"

Steve whirled around, flushed, a strange, guilty expression on his face.

Tina stood protectively in front of the mirror. "No," she said. "Don't break it."

Kathryn crossed her arms over her chest and leaned back into the couch. "I'll break it before we leave here. It's evil."

Tina swept her hand gently over the carved frame, then trailed her fingers lightly across the smooth surface of the glass. "I'm tired," she said. "I think it's time for bed."

This was not turning into the good time Kathryn had planned. Maybe they'd both had a little too much wine. Maybe Kathryn's expectations were a little too high. "Fine," she said testily.

They moved the coffee table, pulled out the hideabed and un-rolled their sleeping bags. Kathryn blew out the last candle and with barely a good night, they settled down, the fireplace coals casting long shadows through the room.

"Tina?"

"Hmm?" Tina moved in her sleep, disturbed, unsettled.

"Tina!"

Tina's eyes cracked open. She looked around, disoriented, still a little bit drunk.

The fire had burned down to red embers. She could hear Kathryn breathing softly and rhythmically next to her.

Then she heard the urgent whisper again. "Tina! Over here."

Tina looked around in suspicion and fear.

"Come over here, babe. To the mirror."

Gently, so as not to wake Kathryn, Tina sat up. Making as little movement or noise as possible, she slipped out of her sleeping bag and walked over to the mirror, wearing only t-shirt and panties.

She saw her own darkened, rumpled reflection.

"Hi, baby," Steve said.

Tina looked into the mirror, down, deep into the mirror.

There was Steve, hands in his pockets, the way he always stood. He looked perfectly well. He looked like he was standing a story below her.

Tina gasped, put her hands up on the mirror, looked down on him. "Steve?"

He smiled up at her.

"Steve, is that you? Is it really you?"

"It's me, dollface."

"Oh, baby, I've missed you. I've missed you so much." She began to cry. "Where are you? What happened?"

"I don't know. I was hunting, and then. . . I was here." He opened his arms, looked around. "I don't exactly know where I am."

Tina wiped her running nose on her t-shirt and wiped her hands over her wet cheeks. "Are you okay?"

"Yeah. Lonely. I miss you."

Leaving one hand on the mirror so she didn't lose him, Tina reached over to the table for a tissue, knocking over a wine glass in the process. She blew her nose.

Kathryn lay quietly listening.

"We should have gone to Alaska like we planned, honey," Tina said. "While we had a chance."

Kathryn's eyes narrowed.

Kathryn rummaged through the glove compartment of Steve's Jeep. "Insurance card, insurance card. Where the hell do you keep the stupid insurance card?" She pulled out napkins, packets of fast food ketchup, pencils, and then maps. Maps of Alaska, with routes marked in red. She climbed up into the seat and sat down, puzzled. Mixed in with the maps was a folded classified section from an Anchorage newspaper. A couple of rental apartments were circled in red.

Understanding stabbed her in the heart. She crumpled the papers in pain, then smoothed them out again in cold fury. "You will not dump me, you fucker," she said, put the papers back into the glove compartment and slammed it shut.

"All I can think about," Tina said to the mirror, "is what a good life we would have had. A place in the woods, a couple of kids. . ." She collapsed against the glass, sobbing. "Oh Steve, baby, I miss you so much. . ."

Kathryn sat up in bed. She picked up the wine bottle and swigged straight from it, her slitted eyes watching Tina, watching Tina confess her betrayal.

"We should have gone. We should have gone. Oh Steve, why did you stay with her?"

"If I'd only known how little time we had. . ."

"*She* should have died, not you."

That was enough for Kathryn. She took the last two gulps from the wine bottle, dropped it on to the bed and slid out of her sleeping bag. Quietly, she grabbed the fireplace poker. "It was you," she said.

Tina didn't hear. She was pawing at the mirror, trying to get inside to Steve.

"You," Kathryn continued. "You were the one. Tina. *You* were the one." She shook her head in disbelief. "You bitch." She walked right up to Tina's back. "If I had known that, I'd have shot *you* instead."

Tina heard that. She turned, bleary-eyed and runny-nosed. "Fuck you," she said.

Kathryn raised the poker and just as she was about to take a mighty swing, she looked down into the mirror and saw Steve.

He stood there, hands in pockets, grinning triumphantly.

Then the poker sliced down with all the force in Kathryn's body. It split Tina's skull and shattered the mirror, which exploded into fire-lit fireworks of sparkling purple glass.

Kathryn, breathing hard, stood amidst the ruins. She dropped the poker onto Tina's lifeless body and looked around.

Dawn was beginning to gray the windows. Morning.

She looked down again at the mess on the floor, and something skittered across it.

With a startled cry, Kathryn jumped back.

But there was nothing there. No mouse, no movement.

She stooped and picked up a jagged shard of purple glass and held it up to see her reflection. It was the face of a grief-stricken, half-drunk mad woman.

Then she looked closer. Deeper. Lower.

Steve stood there, with his arm around Tina. They smiled and waved like newlyweds.

❄

Afterword

Without question, this is an eclectic collection of fiction, pairing dreamy erotica next to the genetic enhancement of an alien life form. And all to what purpose? Do I suspect that the human race has benefited from the admixture alien life plasma? Maybe. Do you? Do I suspect that people harbor vengeful, traitorous secrets within their hearts at least as often as they do loving, altruistic ambitions? Possibly. Do you?

What are we to do with these suspicions?

We could insulate ourselves against those who mean harm, or worse yet, those who harm out of a misguided sense of what is right. To me, this type of insulation means isolation, a drastic cure.

Or instead of isolation, we could choose immersion. With full awareness. Awake. Alive. On guard, yet not guarded.

The observation of those around us in their natural habitat, unaware of being observed, is the stuff of life, and the meat of our richest experiences.

This has been, and will continue to be my choice. Whoever the behind-the-scenes director is, I'm certain s/he does not want us sitting in our dressing rooms, fretting about blowing our lines. We must get on stage and act. Vigorously, sincerely, and with passion. If we blow it, we blow it. The moments for self-recrimination (or self-congratulation) are brief, because the next act swiftly follows.

Live expansively, suspicions notwithstanding. Be awake, be aware, be engaged, and always guard your truth.

About the Author

Elizabeth Engstrom lives in the Pacific Northwest with her husband and dog, where she teaches the fine art of fiction. She is the Director of the Maui Writers Retreat and its Department of Continuing Education. She is always working on the next book.

www.ElizabethEngstrom.com

About the Stories

• Rivering ©1991 – appeared in *Magazine of Fantasy & Science Fiction, Nightmare Flower*, and WestByNorthwest.com
• Renewing the Option ©1998 – appeared in *The UFO Files*, edited by Ed Gorman
• The Pan Man ©1991 – appeared in *Magazine of Fantasy & Science Fiction, Nightmare Flower*, WestByNorthwest.com
• Elixir ©1994 – appeared in *Love in Vein*, edited by Poppy Z. Brite, *Nosferatu*
• Ramona ©2002
• Fogarty & Fogarty ©1988 – appeared in *Magazine of Fantasy & Science Fiction, Nightmare Flower*
• Music Ascending ©1988 – appeared in *American Fantasy Magazine, Nightmare Flower*
• Undercurrents ©1995 – appeared in *Palace Corbie, The Best of Palace Corbie*
• One Fine Day Upon the River Styx ©1998 – appeared in *Imagination Fully Dilated*
• The Cloak ©2002
• Hot Cheeks, Cold Feet ©2001 – appeared in *Strong Currents*
• In a Darkened Compartment ©1999 – appeared on Erotasy.com
• The Goldberg ©2002
• Crosley ©1998 *The Alchemy of Love – Thirteenth Annual Year's Best Fantasy & Horror*
• Fates Entwined ©2002
• One Afternoon in Hana ©2002
• Mothballed ©2000 – appeared in *Dark Whispers, Denali*
• Reggie ©1994 – appeared in *Cemetery Dance*
• Gemphalon ©1998 – appeared in *Imagination Fully Dilated vol. 2, The Alchemy of Love*
• The Shyanne Letters ©1998 *The Alchemy of Love*
• Empty Walls ©1991, appeared in *Cemetery Dance, 100 Fiendish Little Frightmares*
• Harvest Home ©1998 – appeared in *Once Upon A Crime*, edited by Ed Gorman
• Riding the Black Horse ©2000 – appeared in *Horror Garage, Fourteenth Annual Year's Best Fantasy & Horror*
• Genetically Predisposed ©1992 – appeared in *Nightmare Flower, Cemetery Dance*
• Purple Shards ©1997 – appeared in *Wetbones, Dead on Demand*